SCRIBE

BY

BRIAN RUSSELL

For my wife,
who loves me.

Prologue
1966

It was only because Rupert called him a coward that Graham agreed to show him the Keep in the first place. It was a costly mistake.

He and Rupert had ridden out to the ruined fortress where they propped their bikes against the towering walls and lay side by side in the warm grass, gazing up at the sparse summer clouds. As usual, Rupert was doing all the talking, spouting a dissertation about the nature of pain. As he rambled, he calmly pulled the wings from a hapless butterfly that had made the mistake of lighting close enough to be captured. Unable to watch the cruelty, Graham continued to stare at the clouds. His squeamishness made him feel childish. It was something he'd lived with ever since Rupert Marni entered his life. He accepted that Rupert was clever for a boy of thirteen, but he seemed odd. Graham was, in fact, afraid of him.

"If ever anybody caused me pain," Rupert was saying, "I'd eviscerate them. Do you know what that word means, Graham?"

Without waiting for an answer, he tossed the mutilated insect to the ground and watched as it lay convulsing. Then, losing interest, he scrambled to his feet and marched toward the fortress.

"Damn you," Graham muttered. They'd never before entered the ruin. That was the deal.

As he sat staring in disbelief, he listened to the sound of Rupert's voice.

"Don't be afraid, wee man. Come on. Let's see what's so scary about this place."

Graham rose slowly from the grass. His legs felt numb, and his mouth had gone dry. All his life he'd been warned about the Keep and the evil that waited inside. He stepped on the still-squirming insect and reluctantly followed the voice.

Graham had enjoyed a peaceful twelve years in the vale, but with the arrival of the summer boy, his life was changed forever. Long hikes through the hills, searching for old ruins and plover nests, had left him fit and brown, and optimistic. His father had delighted in Graham's hobby but had instructed him to take only one egg from a nest, explaining that the mother wouldn't notice the loss of just one. Never once had Graham disobeyed.

The endless days at the village school, where his mother was headmistress, had provided him with a restless mind and an ability to endure almost anything.

Rupert Marni was pale skinned with reddish hair, slender as a whip, and a complete ass. He'd made it plain to anybody who'd listen that being stuck in the lowly village of Kilbride, miles from the city, with no friends, was a dreadful bore. Not that he had friends at home in Edinburgh, but at least there were things to do there.

Despite his protests, he had been compelled to spend the summer with his mother and her new fiancé at Ainsley House.

According to the village gossips, Lorraine Marni had purchased the place, sight unseen, from an advert in the Edinburgh newspaper, and although the place was in a sad state, she had plans for its complete renovation. The grand old house was well positioned above a private cove and enjoyed a fine view of the Loch Awe.

When Graham's mother heard that her new neighbor was *the* Lorraine Marni, a bona fide celebrity who'd starred in numerous plays and had actually appeared on the BBC, she decided that her son would become Rupert's playmate for the summer.

When Rupert first suggested that they have a look at the ruins, Graham adamantly refused.

"Not a chance," he said. "The Keep's an evil place and nobody ever goes there."

"Well, we'll have to go and have a peek then, won't we?" Rupert spoke in a nasal, affected tone that Graham found irritating. "Don't be such a twerp. Hell, if you're a scaredy-cat, I'll just have to go by myself. You realize, of course, that if anything happens to me, you'll get the blame."

The taunting continued for days until Graham was forced to capitulate. Even though he was afraid, he was too proud to mention that his father had forbidden him to ever go near the place.

After their first visit, Rupert badgered him constantly. The fortress fascinated him. Graham hated the Keep. He would never have returned there if Rupert hadn't threatened to blab.

✡ ✡ ✡

Graham trudged toward the fallen boulders, took a deep breath, and began to climb. When he reached the top, having sustained one or two scrapes in the process, he looked down on a huge quadrangle. He made a careful descent until he reached the floor of the courtyard. To his left, the walls sprouted a variety of mosses and lichen; to his right, the stones were bare. Although it had crumbled in places, Graham could see that in times past, the fortress had provided absolute protection for the Campbells.

Directly across from him, a flight of broken steps traversed the wall, reaching all the way to the creneled battlements. Although he knew Rupert was reckless, Graham couldn't imagine that he'd attempted such a dangerous climb.

"Oh Graham. Where are you?" The voice echoed through the enclosure so that he couldn't get a fix on it. He eventually spotted a small doorway hidden in the shadows of the north wall and assumed that Rupert had found a way in. He crossed the courtyard, wiped his sweaty palms on his shorts, and stepped through the portal into a wide corridor whose roof had collapsed in places, leaving huge stones scattered across the floor. He moved forward, trying to ignore the hammering in his chest.

"Rupert," he called softly, "Where are you?" There was no answer. The only sound was that of water dripping, somewhere far away. The air smelled stale and musty, like the inside of an old trunk. He called out again. Still, no reply. He kept moving, picking his way among the boulders, all the time berating himself for his stupidity.

Darkness gathered around him as he made his way deeper into the ruin. The walls loomed closer, and the roof was intact, allowing almost no light to penetrate the gloom. A moment later, he reached the end of the corridor. His hands were as cold as the stone wall that blocked him. The air was heavy as a shroud.

"Graham!" The cry reached from a place Graham didn't want to go. "There's something very interesting in here. You must see it. You're not scared, are you?"

He wanted to flee, but he couldn't. He knew he would never hear the end of it. He held his breath, listening for the source of the voice.

"Be brave, Graham. Be a man, for once. That's not your sniveling I hear, is it?"

The sound came from somewhere behind him. Carefully, he headed back the way he'd come. If he hadn't been tracing the wall with his hand, he'd never have found it. The fissure was so small, he'd passed it in the dark and hadn't noticed it. He turned sideways, squeezed himself through, and entered a narrow shaft that smelled foul, like rotting moss. The fust was so strong it stung his throat.

Inside the tunnel, the sound of water grew louder. The steady drip, drip, drip, punctuated the silence. To his left, Graham saw nothing but blackness, but to his right, he detected a faint glow. He hunched his shoulders and headed for the light.

As he moved along the slippery floor, he counted his paces, knowing that the crevice he'd entered through would be impossible to find again, unless he knew exactly where it was. With each step he took, the tunnel brightened.

"Rupert!" His echo trembled. There was no reply. As he reached the count of forty, Graham rounded a corner and stepped into a small chamber; the source of the light. The room featured a domed ceiling where fingers of mortar had broken away, allowing shards of sunlight to enter the darkness. At the end of the chamber was a seamless wall, inscribed with a variety of strange carvings. Centered in the wall was the Campbell crest. Graham's heart froze. He knew exactly where he was.

The Crown Room, his father had called it. It was the entrance to the dungeons and Campbell's tomb. Behind the wall lay a maze of tunnels where even a cat could get lost.

Suddenly, from out of the shadows, a dark shape careened toward him, screaming like a pagan. Graham screamed in response, before realizing that it was only Rupert, being a jerk.

"You are such a worm, Rupert," he muttered angrily, "and if you knew as much as you thought you did, you wouldn't be clowning around. We've got to get out of this place. We're not supposed to be in here. No one is. This is the Crown Room. It's the entrance."

Big mistake!

Rupert was on him like a stoat.

"Entrance?" he hissed, "the entrance to what?"

His face sharpened as his eyes darted around the chamber.

"It's nothing. I can't tell you. I promised. I promised my father."

Rupert stepped closer and slapped him, hard. Hot tears flooded Graham's eyes.

"You're so pathetic," Rupert sneered. "You're such a damn coward. Your daddy's precious little secret is nothing but a fairy tale, meant to scare away all you fairies."

"It's no fairy tale," Graham countered. He knew he shouldn't say any more, but he couldn't stop himself. "There's evil in this place."

"You mean ghosts, Graham? Real, live ghosts?"

"It's no joke. You've got to believe me."

"Oh I do, Graham. I do."

Rupert moved to the center of the chamber, spread his arms, and began to chant. "Come out, come out wherever you are. We'll set you free, if you don't go far. Come out, come out of your hiding place. Show your face. Show your face."

"Don't, Rupert. You don't know what you're doing. Please, Rupert. Stop it."

But Rupert was lost in the incantation.

Suddenly, Graham felt the air move, like something had joined them in the chamber.

"They're with us, Graham. Can you hear the voices? Aren't they beautiful?" Rupert began to laugh, softly at first, then building in volume until the room resounded with his wailing.

Graham clapped his hands over his ears and fled. He raced back through the tunnel, praying he could find his way out. In the darkness, he slipped and fell, badly skinning his knee, but he hardly felt it. Mercifully, he found the break in the wall, squeezed through, and ran until he was back outside, safe in the warmth of the sunshine.

Without a backward glance, he hurried home, trying not to think about what Rupert faced in the fortress.

✧ ✧ ✧

Over the next two days, Graham rode his bike to Ainsley House half a dozen times, looking for Rupert. He knocked and knocked, but no one answered the door. The curtains remained drawn. He even tried the back door, but the house was locked up tight. He wondered if the Marnis had packed up and left the village.

He went to the village pub and tried to convince Jock Tavish, the provost, that something was wrong, but Jock dismissed his concerns and returned his attention to the job at hand; the consumption of a tall tumbler of ale.

Graham knew then that he was on his own.

Again that night, sleep was hard to come by. "How could I have been so stupid?" he muttered, as he stood at his bedroom window gazing out at the loch. The water was dead still.

As he once again relived the events of the visit to the Keep, Graham noticed a faint glow coming from the direction of Ainsley House. Although the big house was a good distance away and obscured by dense woods, there was definitely a light.

"Someone's there!" he whispered.

He dressed quickly and crept from his bedroom down the back stairs and stepped into the night. As he did, a sullen moon retreated behind the clouds. As Graham moved along the path, the darkness deepened and the night whispered to him in a hundred voices. He tried not to listen.

Minutes later, the great bulk of Ainsley House loomed in front of him. He crossed the ditch and entered a stand of old beech trees, waiting to catch his breath and his courage. He saw a flicker of light coming from the house, but the garden wall blocked the downstairs windows. He knew he had to get closer.

He emerged from the trees, approached the wall, reached for the iron gate, and pushed gently. Rusted metal groaned in protest. He stopped pushing. Searching the wall, he found a likely spot, clambered over, and dropped silently to the ground. He crouched there, hoping he'd see someone pass by the window. As he watched, his thoughts raced. It had been three days since he'd left Rupert at the Keep. He knew he should have gone to his father right away, but he was had been afraid. He'd been forbidden to go anywhere near the fortress, and never before had he disobeyed his father.

Somewhere nearby, an owl screeched. Graham flinched. He knew he could wait no longer. Creeping low to the ground, he scurried through the moon shadows and reached the house just beneath the lighted window. He took a deep breath, reached for the sill, and hoisted himself up.

The living room was illuminated by three sputtering candles. Although there wasn't much light, Graham saw him immediately. He allowed a deep sigh. Rupert was safe. He lay curled up on the couch near the fireplace with his head on his mother's lap. He was fast asleep.

But something wasn't right. Slowly, the tableau began to crystallize. Although his arms now trembled and his fingers ached, Graham couldn't let go.

Missus Marni was as still as the loch, staring into space. Her face was as pale as parchment, and her eyes never blinked. The bodice of her long white dress was crisscrossed with dark stains.

As Graham's mind processed what his eyes were seeing, Rupert's eyes sprang open. He sat up, stared straight at the window, and smiled, like he'd been expecting the visitor.

Graham let go. He hit the ground hard, scrambled to his feet, and bolted. As he ran, the front door of the house burst open. Rupert was after him, howling like a madman.

Graham raced on until he reached the woods. Only then did he look back. His pursuer was nowhere to be seen.

Hands on his knees and gasping for breath, Graham stared at the house, wondering what had happened to Rupert. Suddenly, one of the large upstairs windows exploded, and heavy curtains billowed from the breach, engulfed in flame. Within seconds, the fire was reaching hungrily for the eaves of the house.

The curse of the Keep had returned, and Graham knew that he was responsible.

CHAPTER 1

1991

The 747 banked almost imperceptibly and began its descent through the patches of cloud. Its shadow swept silently across the myriad islands that lay strewn like puzzle pieces across the Sea of the Hebrides. Valerie MacIntyre yawned and leaned forward to raise her window shade. It was just past sunrise.

Far below, small villages clung like barnacles to the rocky shores. She watched, fascinated, as intrepid fleets of fishing boats departed the safety of their harbors and trudged out to sea on the morning tide. An insistent breeze unraveled the remaining clouds until the hills lay basking in sunshine.

Her husband leaned across her and stared out the window.

"It's somethin', huh?"

"Incredible," Valerie murmured, "I've never seen anything like it."

She sighed deeply, relishing her euphoria and thinking about how nice the holiday was going to be. For a couple of months, she could be Missus John MacIntyre and nothing more. It would be a welcome change from being recognized wherever she went. Not that she resented the fame she'd acquired as a result of twenty years in film and television, but the idea of a holiday in the remote hills of western Scotland was very appealing. During the flight, she'd signed more than a dozen autographs, adhering to her longstanding policy of being gracious about the intrusions, but the thought of being incognito for an entire summer thrilled her.

"We'll be right there this afternoon, if all goes as planned," John said.

His hazel eyes danced with joy as he pointed to a chain of cobalt lakes in the distance.

"I can't wait."

Valerie drew her husband's tanned face toward her, ran her fingers through his cropped salt-and-pepper hair, and kissed him warmly. Although he was nearly ten years older than her, John wore his fifties well. He avoided the gym at all costs, attributing his slim physique to the good genes he'd been blessed with. He was one of those people who could eat whatever he liked in whatever quantity he chose. It was the only thing about him that she resented.

Moments later, the aircraft circled low above the ancient roofs of Edinburgh, readying for final approach. Valerie smiled and pointed as she recognized Arthur's Seat, the rocky steep that had stood guard over the city for more than a thousand years. It was just as John had described. A hundred church spires glinted in the sun, and she imagined she could hear the pealing of the bells. *They're welcoming him home,* she mused.

An hour later, customs behind them, they were safely ensconced in their fancy rental car. The Jaguar XJS was a real indulgence, John had admitted, but he had rationalized that because it was their first trip together to his native land, the expense was justified. She didn't object. She knew that her husband was not a frivolous man. Indeed, he seldom bought anything for himself.

A half hour later, they entered a sedate residential neighborhood, and Valerie began searching for Barrack Place. When she spotted what she was looking for, she directed John into the wide, tree-lined street. The substantial old homes, which stood well back from the pavement, were quite unlike the Beverly Hills monstrosities she was used to. Each house was fashioned from the same dark granite, and their uniformity added to the elegance of the old neighborhood.

When they reached number fourteen, the closed driveway gates blocked their entrance, so John parked at the curb. Unlike the other houses on the street, this one was in need of some care.

"Do you want to come in? I should only be a minute," John asked.

"Oh yes, I certainly do. After all the paces he put us through, I can't wait to meet our landlord."

As they made their way to the front door, Valerie frowned at the state of the gardens. The lawn hadn't been mowed in weeks, and an army of weeds had taken over the flowerbeds. John rang the doorbell while she surveyed her surroundings, surprised that such a beautiful property had been allowed to deteriorate so. Back in California, Valerie's own garden was her pride and joy.

An elderly woman opened the door and eyed them coolly. Without a word, she turned away and led them into a large vestibule devoid of furniture save for one sagging chair, to which she directed Valerie, and signaled for John to follow her.

"Don't you want me to come with you?"

"Actually, I think I can handle this." His curt response made her bristle, but she bit her tongue. She knew that even after twenty-five years of marriage, he resented her inclination to mother him. John shrugged an apology as he was led away.

Valerie perched on the edge of the armchair and watched her husband disappear into the gloom, allowing that he was probably right. Maybe she was too protective, but it was only because she loved him so much.

✻ ✻ ✻

At the end of a long corridor, the old woman stopped before a pair of ornate doors, nodded to John, and hurried away, leaving him alone in the half-light. He felt as if he was back on the set of *The Wicked Ones,* a forgettable horror film he'd directed years before.

He knocked tentatively, and a high-pitched voice bid him enter. He pushed open the door and stepped through into a darkened room. When his eyes adjusted, he discerned the shape of a man sitting behind a large desk, silhouetted by the meager light that seeped through a crack in the curtains.

"Come in, come in, Mister MacIntyre." The lilting brogue was like music. "Forgive the lack of illumination, but you see, I have an ocular condition and can tolerate little light. Please, come closer; there is nothing in the way that might trip you."

He chuckled as John inched carefully toward the desk. He remained seated but reached out his hand. John took it, and nearly flinched. The hand was as soft as a child's and uncommonly cold.

The man's face stayed hidden in shadows. The only distinguishable features were the longish hair and the dark glasses. "I'm Gordon Erskin. I do hope you had a pleasant flight."

"Indeed we did. As a matter of fact, our descent over the coast was amazing. I wish I'd had a chance to get it on film."

"Ah yes. That is your business, is it not?"

"Well, not so much anymore. I'm kinda' retired from the Hollywood thing."

"Glad to hear it. I was never very interested in the cinema. It's all a bit predictable for me." Erskin started to chuckle, but stopped himself. "Please," he continued, "have a seat while I try to put my hands on the keys for the house."

John sat as instructed and watched as the man rummaged through the desk drawers, sending up small clouds of dust.

"Aha." said Erskin. He pulled a large key ring from the top drawer and extended it across the desk. "I'm sure you'll find everything in order at Ainsley. No expense was spared in the refurbishment of the place. It was quite a job. I must say, the directors of the trust are most pleased with the results."

John nodded but said nothing, hoping the man's speech wouldn't take too long. He knew that Valerie would be getting antsy.

"By the way, I've arranged a housekeeper for you. She'll be there tomorrow morning, first thing. And I should tell you, the last room on the upper floor is off limits. One of our directors, the one who supervised the renovations, has some personal things stored in there. But don't worry...I'm sure you'll have plenty of space. It's a fine, big house."

"Thank you, Mister Erskin." John fiddled with the key in his hand, eager to be on his way. "My wife and I are looking forward to our stay. I promise we'll take good care of the place."

"Oh, I know you will. Ainsley is very special. The trust didn't want just anybody to have it, you know. However, you and your wife seemed to possess all the qualities we were looking for. After you've spent some time there, you'll understand why we were so particular. It's a magical place."

"Really? In what way?"

Erskin ignored John's interruption. "When you get to the village, ask at the post office for directions. The house is a bit hidden away."

"Sounds perfect. Just what we were hoping for."

Erskin rose to his feet, and John rose reflexively, wondering how well Erskin could see him.

"I hope you enjoy your sojourn at Ainsley, and I do apologize for not offering you a cup of tea, but as you can see, I'm a bit busy."

"Think nothing of it. We want to get on the road, anyway. We're eager to get to Kilbride. And please, feel free to drop down for a visit. I'm sure we'd be glad to see you."

"Thank you, Mister MacIntyre. That's very kind, but I don't think there's much chance of that. Too much to do around here, and besides, I don't leave the house much anymore."

Erskin moved from behind the desk and walked unfalteringly toward the door.

"Just what line of work are you in, then?" John asked, as he followed along, noting that Erskin was a good couple of inches taller than his own six feet.

"Oh, let me see. I suppose you could say I'm a discoverer. Yes that's it, a discoverer." He laughed softly and extended his hand.

John steeled himself and took it.

"Missus Pearson will show you out." Erskin hurried back to his desk.

The housekeeper appeared from out of nowhere and led John to the front door.

Valerie jumped up to meet him, a relieved smile lighting her face. As they headed back down the overgrown path, John cast a glance toward the house, not knowing quite what to think.

In the car, Valerie turned to him. "Well?"

John tossed the iron key ring into her lap and started the engine.

"What's he like?"

"I don't really know what to tell you. He's pretty eccentric. He didn't want to answer any questions, and I didn't even get a good look at him. Apparently he's got some kind of eye problem. He lives in darkness, so I guess he won't be coming to pay us a visit. It's okay with me. The guy's weird."

✿ ✿ ✿

In the darkened room, Erskin reached behind him and pulled open the curtains enough to admit a little more light. A dusty shaft fell on a framed photograph centered on the huge desk. The faded photo was of a strikingly beautiful woman in her thirties. She'd been professionally posed, like the picture was a publicity shot from a film studio.

"Well what did you think, mother?" he asked. "It's my opinion that he's just what we've been waiting for. Things will be better soon, you'll see."

He felt guilty about the house's state of disrepair and the untended gardens, but he knew his mother would understand. She'd been kind enough to leave him the place in her will, but the funds had been badly depleted during the renovations at Ainsley House, the house where she had died. He reached for the telephone and hit speed-dial.

"They're on their way," he said softly. "Just what we were hoping for, I'd say. Typical American; a bit naive, too friendly for his own good. I know you'll make sure they're properly taken care of."

"Have no fear," said the deep voice in his ear. "I have just the thing."

"Good. I'm looking forward to my return," said Erskin. "It's been too long."

He sighed softly and returned the receiver to its cradle.

CHAPTER 2

———◆◆◆———

The Jaguar slowed and rolled to a stop at the crest of Robbie's Brae, its tires crunching the fine roadside gravel. Beneath the promontory lay the Vale of Kilbride and the dark waters of Loch Awe. It was said that Scotland boasted even more beautiful valleys, but there was a sweet mystery about the vale that had intrigued John since he'd visited as a boy.

Carpets of mist rolled lazily up the hills and dissolved like spun sugar in the deep blue sky. Bands of sheep drifted across the slopes, seeking out the sweetest grass. Safely concealed in the gorse, a meadowlark offered up her best song.

As a boy, John had spent a summer in the vale. His father had exchanged his Edinburgh pulpit with the minister in Kilbride, which was the only sort of vacation a poor clergyman could afford back then. John had been away too long and was thrilled to be back.

He glanced over at his wife. Her eyes were swimming. He reached for her. "What's up?" he asked. "You okay?"

"Yeah, more than okay, actually. I feel wonderful. This is the most perfect place I've ever seen. Why didn't we ever film here?"

"I don't know," John said. "That's actually not a bad idea."

"Too bad you've retired." Valerie wiped her eyes and pulled away.

"Yeah. Too bad."

He leaned back in the plush leather seat and studied his wife as she gazed at the hills. She looked even more beautiful than usual, and John had a thing for beauty. Paintings, architecture, fine automobiles, it didn't matter, beauty stirred his soul. Valerie Todd's beauty had captivated him years ago, and held him still. Although she was in her forties, she looked a good ten years younger. He knew that she was diligent about her appearance. It was a discipline she'd adhered to since her teens, and it had stood her in good stead. Valerie was beyond pretty. She was a true beauty, in the classic sense, with perfect skin and shining blond hair that was actually her natural color. Her sea-green eyes, which sometimes turned blue, sparkled every time she smiled, which was often. Over the years, he'd worked with many attractive women, but he'd never seen anyone like her.

He'd been strangely unsettled by her the first time he saw her. As a novice actress, she'd wandered onto his set and right into middle of the shot. Instead of being angry, he'd been at a loss for words. He'd hired her on the spot, and a year later, they were married. If her beauty was timeless, her nature was nothing less than infectious. Never had he met anyone more ready to laugh or more willing to forgive.

As he watched her, he detected something moving down the hill behind her. He frowned. A creature, unlike anything he'd ever seen, was rapidly descending the slope, alternately revealing itself and then disappearing in the lingering patches of mist. The thing was bright yellow and thirty feet or more in length, undulating like a giant centipede, and heading straight for them.

"Val, do you see that?" He pointed in the direction of the beast.

She followed his finger. "Yes I do. What the hell?"

"I have no idea."

"Does Loch Awe have a monster too? Because that's what it looks like."

John laughed. "And here she comes now."

The serpent continued its advance until it crested a small hill and drew near enough to reveal its true identity. It turned out to be nothing more sinister than a troop of boys wearing bright yellow rain gear, marching in single file.

Leading them was a gigantic man, whose long sallow face was crowned by an unruly mop of nut-brown hair. His wardrobe consisted of military-style boots with his pants stuffed inside, a black shirt, and a clerical collar. He might have looked almost conventional had he not been wearing a long, black academic's gown that billowed behind him like a storm cloud. As he neared the car, he offered a cursory nod and swept past. John and Valerie waved in reply. The boys, about ten in number, scrambled to keep up with their leader's long strides. As they strode by, one or two turned to glare at the visitors. The rest stared angrily at the ground.

Valerie shuddered and reached for John's hand.

"You know," he said, in an effort to distract her, "I'm thinking we should probably drink bottled water while we're here. Looks like the local stuff makes people a bit cranky."

He turned the key in the ignition, unable to suppress a grin as twelve cylinders roared to life. He began the careful descent into the valley, making up stupid stories about the inherent dangers of water until he succeeded in making Valerie laugh.

He drove slowly into the village of Kilbride and stopped to get directions.

"I'll just be a minute," he said and climbed out of the car.

He opened the door of the post office and stepped into a small room with yellowed walls that might have been white at one time. The place smelled of stale smoke, good whisky, and something else he couldn't quite place. He waited patiently for the old man behind the well-worn wooden counter to finish what he was doing. Eventually, the man looked up.

"Och, I'm sorry, my lad. I didn'e realize ye were standin' there. Ye been there all this time? Oh aye, my hearin's no what it used to be, nor the eyes either for that matter."

The thick brogue brought a smile to John's face.

"Jock Tavish is the name. I'm the village postmaster. Some folks have wondered why it's not MacTavish, but I don't know the answer tae that. So what can I do for ye?"

"Well, I'm not exactly lost. My name's John MacIntyre, and my wife and I have rented Ainsley House for a few weeks. Can you tell me how to find it? I'm told it's a bit hidden away."

The smile nearly faded from the old man's face, but he managed to hang on.

"Ainsley House did ye say? Oh aye. Nothin' to it. I'll keep ye straight. And I'm pleased to meet ye, Mister-eh-oh aye." Old Jock reached a gnarled hand across the counter.

"Nice to meet you, too," said John as he took the proffered hand, doing his best to stop staring.

Jock Tavish was a walking caricature; absolutely perfect casting for a village postman, sixty years ago. A tangle of off-white whiskers and a stained mustache framed a set of eroded dentures that whistled as he spoke. His bright red nose shone like a beacon against a backdrop of spider-veined cheeks and faded blue eyes, a glowing testament to the caliber of the local distillery.

"Now let me see, the best thing for ye to do is to follow along this road you're on. Ye did come in from the Callander direction, didn't ye?"

John nodded.

"That's right then. Well, continue on here out of the village itself. Go 'til you're just about two miles this side of the kirk, and turn left."

John stared blankly, wondering how he was going to accomplish that. How was he supposed to know when he was two miles from the church?

"Then, you go on down past Ailes's garden and make a sharp right. Don't make the other right, 'cause that'll take ye back to Callander, see. Then ye continue on past where the antique shop used to be."

The postmaster shook his head.

"Ye know, we all told those folk that an antique shop would never work in this place, but they wouldn'e listen. Not enough tourists ye understand. Oh aye. Anyway, turn left again at old Tom's well, and you're no more than a stone's throw away."

John nodded, doing his best to hold on to the growing list...a right at Ailes's garden, then on past a nonexistent shop.

Jock stopped his gesticulations and peered at his visitor. "Ach, you'll never find it. I'd better just take you myself. I'll not go inside the house, but I'll take you to the gate."

John leaned closer, tempted to question the postman further. All of his creative instincts yearned to know. Was there a local superstition about Ainsley House? He wanted to hear all the details, but it was already after four o'clock and he was eager to get settled. After all, it was to be their first night in a new house, and if past experience was a reliable indicator, the evening ahead would be a romantic one.

"Well, if it's not asking too much, I'd appreciate you showing us the way. I wouldn't want to put you out, though," John said.

"Ach, not at all. I was just goin' out that way, anyway. I've got a parcel here for Graham Nesbit, and he lives not far from Ainsley."

"I'll be right outside when you're ready."

John exited the post office just in time to see his wife wander out of the bakery across the street, clutching a good-sized paper bag. He leaned against the hood of the car and crossed his arms, enjoying the village. Nothing had changed in the forty years since his last visit, except that the cars parked along the street were a new addition. Back when he'd immigrated to Canada with his parents, automobiles were a real luxury in rural Scotland. The tranquility of the village and the sweet smell of lilacs were exactly as he remembered.

He shifted his gaze back to Valerie, enjoying the way her tweed skirt slapped against her long bare legs. When she reached him, she smiled and winked seductively.

"Yes?"

"Nothin'," he muttered and looked away. For some reason, he'd always felt sheepish about openly admiring her. It was as if he didn't want her to know how attractive he found her, in case she might vanish before his eyes. "I was just thinking how great you look—for a woman of your age."

Valerie delivered a smart punch to his arm. "Thanks a lot." She opened the door and folded herself into the car.

John climbed in beside her.

"So, do we have our directions?" she asked, suddenly all business.

"Well, not exactly."

They watched with amusement as Jock performed the ritual of locking and double-checking the door of Her Majesty's Post Office. He nodded politely to Valerie, who politely nodded back.

Old Jock moved quickly around the side of the building and reappeared wheeling a bicycle that was at least as old as him. He bent over, applied a clip to his trouser leg, pushed off with one foot on the pedal, and vaulted aboard like a man half his age. For a moment, the bicycle wobbled precipitously, but somehow managed to remain upright. Beaming with relief, Tavish beckoned to the MacIntyres. John carefully backed the Jaguar into the street and fell into formation behind the bicycle.

Although the postmaster tipped his cap to the people he met on the way, John noticed that not a one paid him the slightest attention. They were all too busy ogling the Jaguar.

Feeling more than a little conspicuous, John and Valerie watched the curious watching them. John waved once or twice, but there was no acknowledgement. Valerie reached for John's hand and gave it a squeeze.

"Not too friendly, are they?"

"Oh, don't worry honey," he replied. "They'll warm up soon enough. The Scots are a bit leery of outsiders at first."

The Jaguar followed solemnly along as the postman pointed out various features of the little village. Since they couldn't hear a word the man was saying, they merely nodded. A few minutes later, the bicycle turned off the main road onto a narrow lane where, in places, the hedges actually brushed the car. The bushes were festooned with blossoms, white and pink, yellow and blue. The drone of bees and the smell of raspberries hung like bliss in the warm air.

After about a mile, they rounded a bend, and John braked to a stop. "Wow," he groaned softly, "it's glorious." They sat on a grassy ridge overlooking a protected cove, behind which stretched the deep blue waters of Loch Awe. Although they had seen pictures, no photograph could ever do it justice. The grand house, built of pale gray stone, sat on a low rise, taking full advantage of the incredible views. The entire north end of the house was blanketed in red roses.

Tavish opened the gates and stepped aside as John pulled into the driveway. As if in a trance, he climbed out of the car and went around to open Valerie's door, but by the time he reached it, she was already out. Taking her hand, he led her toward the house. His heart was filled with awe and anticipation. He knew he'd come to the right place, that he'd be able to write here. He could already feel the stirrings.

Hand in hand, they crossed the driveway and discovered a cobblestone path that led around the house and ended at a flight of steps that meandered down to the water's edge. On the loch side, the house boasted a full-length verandah, which John knew would be perfect for wiling away the endless twilight of Scotland's summer months.

Without a word, he reached for Valerie, enfolded her in his arms, and sighed like a man returned home from a long journey. For a time, they just held each other and gazed out over the shimmering glory of the loch.

By the time they arrived back at the front, eager to see what the inside of the house had to offer, Jock was long gone.

"He didn't give us a chance to thank him," said Valerie. "I hope he didn't think we were being rude."

"Och, hae nay fear o' that lass. The boy'll hae plenty o' time tae find out how rude ye really can be."

"Oh very good, John. Nice accent. Have you been practicing?"

"Na," he replied, grinning happily. "It comes back whenever I'm in Scotland. Strange huh?"

"Oh, there's no doubt about it. You're definitely strange."

"Thank you so very much," John said as he gestured toward the front door and bowed theatrically.

"Missus MacIntyre, my own *Lady of the Loch*, may I present to you your home for the summer. If you would, kindly step inside and I'll show you strange, just the way you like it."

Shaking her head, Valerie took his arm and allowed her self to be led to the front door.

"We can unpack later," John said, winking meaningfully.

CHAPTER 3

The Crown and Thistle had stood its ground since the fourteenth century. Once a coach house and later a hunting lodge for Malcolm Campbell, Earl of Argyll, it had eventually settled comfortably into being the local pub and four-room hotel. Many a yarn had been spun within its timbered walls. The public room was a good size. Its centerpiece was a gleaming mahogany bar that had reputedly been in service since the defeat of the English in 1512. Directly across from the bar stood a great stone hearth where a peat fire sputtered contentedly, filling the air with its musk.

The Thistle sat right on the shore of the loch and, as was typical for every evening but Christmas, the sounds of merriment drifted out across the water. Old Jock sat at a large table surrounded by his cronies, who were bursting with curiosity about the village's visitors. The beer and the whisky flowed freely, and Jock took full advantage of those who knew that plying him with drink would enhance the stories.

On a low stage at one end of the room, trying to be heard above the din, a three-piece band played traditional Scottish country music. A heavyset man perched precariously on a high stool pumping an ancient concertina, while another chap with not a hair on his head played an ebony flute. Between them sat Alistair Frazer, an unkempt young man, fingering an acoustic guitar while glowering at the noisy crowd. Although he played well, nobody paid the slightest attention.

A particularly loud roar of laughter from old Jock's table provided the last straw for Alistair. He set his guitar down on its stand and stormed off the stage. No one noticed. He walked out the door, slammed it behind him as loudly as he could, and strode toward the harbor.

He climbed the stone steps, leaned his elbows on the wall, and glared out at the loch, his mood as dark as the water. He lit up a cigarette and inhaled deeply. As he muttered to himself, a hand reached out from the darkness and stroked his curls. He jumped.

"What's the matter, Alistair? Doesn't anybody love you?" asked a husky voice.

He recognized the lilt immediately and leaned forward for a kiss, but as he did, the girl pulled away.

"See, I knew you were lonely, didn't I?"

"Moira, where have you been? It's hell in there tonight. There's some new folk here in the village, and everybody's gone daft. It's as if there's nothing ever happens here."

"Well it's true, isn't it? Nothing ever does happen in this stupid village, but if you really must know where I've been, well, I've been off to see my lover."

Alistair choked on his cigarette, tossed it onto the ground, and stomped it out.

"That's not funny."

"No, Ali, it's not. But I'm just teasing. I just wanted to see how you'd react. Come on, let's go in."

"You're going to hate it. They're in no mood for music tonight. They're all chatterin' away about the new people."

"We'll see about that." Moira grabbed him by the arm and led him back to the pub.

Inside, the merriment continued. It was Friday night, and with the week's work done, it was time to celebrate. A large, florid man downed yet another pint and turned to face the postmaster.

"So, Jock, is she as bonny as when she was in that mermaid film she made?" His brogue was as thick as his girth.

Jock considered for a moment, watching the man's eager face. "Oh, she's much bonnier now, I'd say, Sandy, oh aye."

"What dae ye mean, Jock? That film was made over fifteen years ago."

"Oh I know that, Sandy. But now she's got two legs."

The crowd screamed with laughter. Jock called for another round.

A few minutes later, the band returned to the stage. The music started, but the noise continued unabated.

Then, a pure clear voice rose through the tumult, and as if a spell was cast, all conversation ceased. The crowd fell silent. They turned toward the stage.

In the smoky beam of a single light stood a breathtakingly beautiful girl. Woven into her black, waist-length hair were clusters of tiny silver bells that sparkled like stars in a winter sky. The bells were Moira's cachet. She'd come to be known throughout the shire as The Bell of Argyll.

Even if she couldn't sing at all, it was easy to see why Moira MacLeod caused conversation to cease. As she sang, she swayed to the music, like a whisper in the wind. Her pure white skin accentuated her dark green eyes, and although she wore no makeup, her lips were red as wild berries. Her beauty was truly remarkable, but it was more than that. The girl was haunting.

Throughout the room, men and women alike dabbed at misty eyes. Even Alistair regained his civility. He played masterfully as Moira sang of ancient pain and suffering, spinning her tale with a weaver's skill.

When the song finished, she was met with thunderous applause. Next, she sang a happy familiar song, encouraging her audience to join her. She stepped down from the stage and moved through the room, touching people as she went.

When the song ended, Moira slipped out the door and ran into the darkness. A moment later, she heard someone running after her, calling her name. She stopped and waited until Alistair appeared out of the mist.

"Where are ye off to then?" he asked. "We're not done with the music."

"I'm sorry, Ali, I can't. I'm feeling a bit restless. I don't know what it is. Maybe you were right. Maybe it's just a bad night."

She took his hand and led him down to the water's edge, where paltry waves lapped at the shore. She perched on a rock and watched as her companion skipped flat stones across the water.

"How can you feel like this, Moira? I don't understand you. Did you see the faces on these folks tonight? They love you." He hurled another stone. "Everybody here loves you."

"I know that, Ali, and I know it should be enough, but it isn't. I need more. I need to find out about myself, and I don't think I can do that in this wee place."

Alistair walked slowly back to where she sat and bent his head to kiss her.

For a moment, she responded, before pulling away. "I can't deal with this, Ali. I'm sorry. It's not you, it's me."

Anger flashed in Ali's eyes. "I don't know who you think you are, Moira MacLeod, and why you think you're so much better than the rest of us. You should be grateful for what you've got, instead of always dreaming about the stars."

"I know. That's what's disturbing to me. And I am grateful. I know God's given me this gift, and I feel I've got to use it. I mean really use it. Not just here in the shire but out there in the world. Please don't be angry with me. I hate it when you're angry."

Alistair relented. He reached for her hand, pulled her to her feet, and gently stroked her cheek. "I could never stay angry with you, Moira, even if I wanted to."

✿ ✿ ✿

Valerie awoke to a glorious morning. She rose quietly, donned her terry-cloth robe, and tiptoed from the room. She skipped down the stairs and made her way to the kitchen. Although the room was filled with sunshine, the stone floor felt cold on her bare feet. She'd forgotten her slippers. Damn!

She didn't want to go back upstairs and take the chance of waking John, but it was her lucky day. She spotted a couple of pairs of Wellington boots standing in the corner by the back door. She selected the larger pair, and they slipped on easily. As a matter of fact, they were huge. She clomped across the room and into the pantry, where she discovered what she was looking for; coffee and the makings of breakfast. As she gathered the items she needed, she hummed cheerfully, pleased that the house had been stocked for their arrival.

As she backed out through the pantry door, her arms fully laden, she was stunned to discover a stranger standing in the middle of the kitchen staring at her. She jumped and dropped everything. The visitor didn't flinch. She just stood there staring at Valerie and the oversized Wellies.

Valerie managed to regain her voice, if not her composure. "What the–? Who are you? What are you doing here?"

"I'm Missus Small, the housekeeper. Didn't they tell you I'd be here?" Valerie guessed the woman to be in her late thirties. She was redheaded and pretty in a round sort of way, with full, rosy cheeks and an even fuller bosom.

Valerie shook her head. "No. No one mentioned that you'd be here. But never mind. I'm Missus MacIntyre. It's very nice to meet you. Oh, you can call me Valerie. What would you like me to call you?"

"Oh, Missus Small will be fine, and maybe we should–um—." She indicated the awful mess on the floor.

"Oh look," said Valerie, "I've broken all the eggs."

"No bother. They were yesterday's anyway. I've brought fresh, and milk too."

Missus Small quickly organized a couple of wet cloths and handed one to Valerie. Together, they got down on their knees and began mopping up the gooey puddle. The floor creaked overhead. John was up. Realizing he'd be down momentarily, Valerie scrambled to get the mess cleaned up before he arrived on the scene. She knew he would never pass up an opportunity to rag her about her clumsiness.

Too late. The wicked chuckle behind her announced his presence.

"Well Missus MacIntyre, and don't you look fetching this fine morning? I swear that's the cutest butt ever built, and a very fine motion it has too."

Valerie cringed, realizing that John hadn't seen Missus Small, who was hidden by the door.

"Oh John," she groaned, flushing with embarrassment. "You haven't met Missus Small, here. She's the housekeeper. We weren't expecting her, were we honey?"

Still on her knees, Valerie glared over her shoulder.

John stepped forward just far enough to see the housekeeper gaping up at him.

"Eh—no, no we haven't met. I'm so sorry. Please I'm—well, I hope you're not offended by my—oh what the hell. Just chalk it up to the fact that I'm a crazy American."

He managed a sheepish grin.

Missus Small struggled up from her position on the floor, raised herself to her full height, thrust out her ample breasts, and extended her hand. Her face was very pink.

"Good morning, Mister MacIntyre. I'm right pleased to meet you. It is a bonny mornin' at that, and might I say, there's never any need to apologize for expressions of, em, affection between married folk."

Still blushing, she retrieved her hand and wiped it on her apron.

"Now Missus MacIntyre," she offered, "why don't you and your husband go and make yourselves comfortable on the verandah? I'll get your breakfast for you. I've brought the paper. I thought yis might like to see what goes on around here. It's not much though, I'll tell ye."

Valerie curled her finger, motioning for John to follow her, and led the way outside.

He selected one of the cushioned chairs, settled himself in, and stretched lazily. "What a morning," he murmured.

"It's glorious," she agreed, lowering her self into the other chair. She sighed softly, feeling a wave of contentment like she hadn't felt in years. As she gazed out across the still water, she was forced to concede that John had made a great choice. Maybe this house and this loch and this village would be just the place for them to reconnect. They hadn't exactly grown apart, but the spark they'd once enjoyed had dwindled a bit over the last year or two. Real physical contact had become a rarity, something reserved for special occasions like wedding anniversaries and last night.

After twenty-two years, it was to be expected, she knew, but that didn't alter the fact that she missed the closeness that had once been part of their relationship. It wasn't the sex she missed so much; it was the nearness that came from the touching, and the holding and the safeness she felt in the arms of the man she loved.

As she sat absorbing the warmth of the sun and the quiet beauty of the loch, she spotted something unusual, although it was too far away to make out. Excitedly, she grabbed a pair of binoculars from the wrought-iron coffee table and raised them to her eyes. When she'd adjusted the field of sight, she identified a large hawk hovering high above the loch. She watched, enthralled, as the bird rose effortlessly through the air currents until it was almost out of sight. The raptor then folded its wings and dropped from the sky like a dart. As it reached the water, it spread them open, dipped its talons beneath the dark surface, and plucked a fat fish.

"Val, do you see that?" John sat bolt upright and pointed out across the loch.

"Yeah. It's fantastic," Val breathed, lowering the binoculars. "I've never seen a hawk fishing before. I wish I could do that."

"No honey, not the bird—and by the way, it's an osprey, not a hawk. I'm talking about that ruin thing, way on the other side, on top of that headland. It's in shadow now. Do you mind?"

Valerie handed him the binoculars. She squinted, but the sun was in her eyes, and she could make out nothing but a rocky cliff in the distance.

"The place is huge. It must be an old fortress. What a film set. Couldn't build that on a sound stage." He gave a low whistle and passed the glasses. "Here, take a look. The place has a view of the entire loch. Talk about location. It's brilliant."

The squeaking wheels of the trolley announced the arrival of Missus Small, and by the time the food reached the table, Valerie was salivating. Never had a breakfast smelled so good. She whiffed the mingled aromas of fresh-baked scones, strong coffee, and good Scottish bacon.

"Hungry?" she asked.

"Ravenous," John said.

She glanced at him just in time to catch his eyes shifting from the food to Missus Small's impressive cleavage as she bent over to pour the coffee, confirming once again that he could never pass up a peek.

"By the way, Missus Small, what's that tower thing I see there in the distance?" he asked, forcing his eyes to behave.

"Oh that? That's Campbell Keep. Been there forever, as far as anybody knows. Been a ruin for hundreds of years. Don't nobody go up there, though, least, not nobody from round here. It's an accursed place. There's some right bad stories. But I'm Catholic ye see. I'm not supposed to pay any heed to that stuff."

"Stories? What kind of stories?" John reached for a hot scone with one hand and the bramble jam with the other.

"I can't tell you just now, Mister MacIntyre," Missus Small shook her head vigorously, and Valerie watched the flush rise from her throat to her freckled cheeks. She certainly wasn't acting.

"Oh come on. I would really like to—"

"John, honey! Maybe some other time," Valerie interrupted, seeing the housekeeper's discomfort. "Missus Small's got things to do. Isn't that right?"

"Yes, yes I do. Plenty." She bowed gratefully and retreated.

Valerie sighed, relieved that an awkward moment had been averted. She was ready to enjoy her breakfast and the undivided attention of her husband.

"Why did you do that?" John asked, as soon as the housekeeper was out of earshot.

"Because she obviously didn't want to talk about it. As a matter of fact, she looked terrified."

"Terrified? You're crazy."

"I don't think so," she replied softly.

As Valerie sipped her coffee, she prayed that the trip to Scotland would turn out to be everything John had hoped for. She understood his need to write, how important it was for him to feel good about himself. And she knew how badly he dealt with disappointment.

She had a need too; a need to feel the closeness they'd once had.

✪ ✪ ✪

At the end of their first week, Valerie answered the door to find a somber young man standing in the driveway beside a small van.

"Mornin'," he muttered. "Missus MacIntyre?"

Valerie nodded.

"I've got a delivery for you."

Then she heard another voice.

"Good mornin' to you, Missus MacIntyre. And isn't it a bonny mornin'?"

She recognized the voice immediately and looked up to see the postmaster waiting at the gate. "Good morning, Mister Tavish. How are you?" She remembered her manners. "Would you like to come in for a cup of tea?"

"Oh, no thanks. Oh no. I'll not be comin' in. I've just brought out this young fella here. He's got something for Mister MacIntyre."

He gestured to the van where the young man was busy unloading boxes.

"A computer and a printer. Fella says it was supposed to have been here last week. Says it's not his fault, though. It seems that this model was hard to come by here in Scotland. Anyway it's here now."

Valerie felt a bit silly. It was odd to be standing on her doorstep having a shouting conversation with the postman.

Jock signaled to the delivery boy, and Valerie headed inside to find her husband.

"Hey John. Good news. Your computer's here. Do you believe it?"

"Finally!" He appeared from the living room carrying a book. "Thank God. I came here to write, not to read every book in the damn house. Tell them to bring it into the study. On the desk facing away from the water. That'll be perfect."

Valerie was surprised. "You really want it facing away from the water?"

"Yeah. Too many distractions the other way."

Valerie shook her head.

"Don't you worry, honey," he said. "I'll get my money's worth. The view will be there when I need it."

When, after a few minutes, the deliveryman hadn't appeared, Valerie went to the front door to see what was keeping him. She was surprised to see the boxes piled up on the front steps and the van pulling away.

The postmaster climbed aboard his bike and offered a feeble wave. "Better be off. Another busy day."

"Bye Mister Tavish. Thanks." She watched as Jock pedaled away, thinking that he seemed terribly eager to leave.

Behind her, John grabbed one of the boxes and headed into the house. "This is great," he said as he re-entered the study. "I can finally get started."

Valerie had known for years that John wanted to try his hand at writing. He'd directed lots of films, some of them quite successful, but he'd never received the respect he sought. He'd been known in the industry as an action director and had come to accept that he'd never get the nod from the Academy. The day he'd overheard himself being referred to as a hack was the day he'd decided to hang up his megaphone. Valerie remembered the night he'd told her about his painful decision, and although she didn't agree with him, she gave no indication. He was at the place in his life where he could do as he wished, and he wished to write. When he'd brought up the subject of a summer in Scotland, he'd explained that a return to his roots could provide the inspiration he sought. As usual, Valerie had been willing to go along.

Although he wasn't sure what he was going to write about, he was more than ready to get started. He was torn between a modern day thriller and a heist idea he'd been tossing around in his head. He knew he couldn't write an entire novel in the few weeks he had, but with Scotland's help, he expected to make serious headway.

As she watched her husband eagerly tearing open the boxes, Valerie felt she was watching a man on the threshold. "I think this place'll be good for you," she said.

"Well, I do feel at home here. Maybe my roots will show."

He laughed at his own feeble joke as he sorted out cords and plugs, completely ignoring the instruction book.

As she watched him go about his task, Valerie smiled to herself. It was good to see John so happy.

She continued to watch as he tried to connect the pieces. When, finally, he reached for the instructions, she decided to leave him to it.

✿ ✿ ✿

Half an hour later, the computer's start-up ditty announced its readiness.

For a full five minutes, John stared at the empty screen. He swallowed, took a long breath, and forced his fingers to move.

The thoughts began.

Two hours later, he came to and pushed back from his desk. He waited for a moment before reaching to scroll back to the beginning.

They'd been killing all night, but as the blood red sun rose through the murk, the battle raged on. The English had the Campbells with their backs to the river, and the fighting was savage. Ambushed and outnumbered, the clan had been ill prepared for this fight, but they were a ferocious lot. The rhythmic toll of claymores cleaving helmets heightened the horror as some men screamed in agony while others begged for death. Horsemen on both sides fell on quick swords as their exhausted mounts were hacked from under them.

Robert Douglas, heir to Perthshire and kinsman to the Campbells, remained in his saddle, killing his share. Riding hard beside him, his brother Hamish fought on bravely. He was canny for such a young lad, but there were few horsemen left, and their swords were heavy. At first light, they'd tried to outflank a detachment of dragoons but were met by a hail of bolts and forced back into the ever-tightening field.

Douglas could see that Hamish was nearly done and pulled the lad's horse close enough to be heard. "I'm proud of ye. Yer father would be, too."

Hamish's frantic eyes begged his brother's for the truth.

"Will we die, Robert?"

"Never," he roared. "Yer a Douglas."

Together, they spun to face a score of charging cavalry. Hamish feinted to the right, then turned sharply back, trusting that his mount still had its legs, and neatly severed an English head.

Robert spun his horse in place, wielding his dripping blade until his heart cramped from exhaustion. By the time he was surrounded, he'd toppled half a dozen English from their saddles and hacked three more into retreat.

At the moment his leaden sword fell from his weary fingers, the sweet, plaintive skirl of the bagpipes reached Robert's ears. Hearing the unearthly wail, the English faltered. They turned to see a terrible, raging horde descending on them from the heather hills, screaming like hellions.

Leading them was Campbell himself, riding like fury. The sight of their chief, girded by his stoutest warriors, was enough to rouse the weary Scots. Their swords became new again, their axes like liquid.

Within an hour, the English were done. Their vaunted cavalry fled from the engagement, leaving the infantry to be decimated. Douglas and Hamish gathered a handful of horsemen and galloped off in pursuit.

By morning's end, the Campbells had slaughtered so many English that the sodden ground steamed crimson. Scores lay dead. The victorious Scots combed the battlefield, searching for signs of life and bearing their wounded from the scene on makeshift stretchers. Others moved grimly among the crippled horses, putting the poor beasts out of their misery.

Malcolm Campbell, the Earl of Argyll, quietly surveyed the devastation. He had lost many good men this day, but they had turned back the English vermin yet again. Although the price had been dear, the taste of victory was sweet; the alternative, unthinkable. To live under English tyranny would be far worse than honorable death. He would gladly shed his own blood rather than bow down to the Saxons.

His men looked to him, murmuring their allegiance and their respect. If not for him, the day would surely have been lost. Blood seeped steadily from the gash in his shoulder, but Campbell's gaunt face belied the pain. He raised his sword and nodded proudly to the men who had fought so well.

It was a weary, straggling band that slowly made its way back toward Campbell Keep. By the time they reached the fortress, the sun was long set, but the torches were lit, and the victory colors soared high atop the castle tower. A swift messenger had been sent ahead with the news. There would be a fine feast of celebration this night.

As Campbell and his men rode across the drawbridge and into the courtyard, a girl watched from the shadows, a girl of such beauty that the darkness seemed to melt away from around her. Her anxious eyes focused intently, hopefully, on the face of each passing warrior. After the last man had crossed, the girl sighed softly and shivered in the damp cold. She drew her shawl closer around her and slipped away into the night.

John pushed back from his desk and took a deep breath. His fingers felt icy cold. The words had come easily, too easily, as though they were not his own. He dismissed the disturbing thought and climbed the stairs to bed.

He slept deeply that night, amid dreams of the Campbells and a dark fortress in the clouds.

CHAPTER 4

A s the days turned into weeks, Valerie watched her husband
become more and more distant. She felt his impatience as
they strolled the banks of the loch. He seemed increasingly
preoccupied, more and more eager to get back to his writing.
Eventually, the day came when he begged off from their outing.
The long walks and picnic lunches became a thing of the past.

He immersed himself in his work, oblivious to the fact that
she missed him. The hours they used to spend together eventually shrank to the few minutes when John emerged from his lair
for a quick bite to eat. Any effort to engage him in conversation
proved futile. He grunted his responses and stared off into space.
Even when he retired to bed, often very late, he slept fitfully.

"This is silly," Valerie chided herself one bright morning as she sat alone in the kitchen, waiting for her tea to brew.

How could she be jealous? She had never been so before. After all, it wasn't like she'd lost his heart to another woman. His faithfulness was one of the things that had attracted her in the first place. She placed a high value on fidelity. Yes, there had been one incident, but it was buried in the past.

Even though, on numerous occasions, she'd been thrust together with some of the world's most attractive men, she had never strayed, not once. Sure, she'd been tempted a couple of times, when she'd been on location in some idyllic romantic place where her leading man had been seducing her all day, even though his words had been scripted for him by some faceless writer. She had allowed Randolph Best to kiss her one night in the lobby outside her room when they were filming *The Sands of Time* in Morocco, but thankfully, she'd refused to let him enter.

Although her reasoned approach to John's behavior sounded good, it did nothing to alleviate her frustration. But every time she considered the dilemma, she felt guilty. He had waited so long to try his hand at writing and had always made her the priority in the past. She resolved to be patient, and not interfere.

Wednesday began as another beautiful day. She slowly sipped her tea on the verandah, enjoying the shimmering loch and the warmth of the morning sun. John remained locked in his study with his back to the world.

By the afternoon, she'd finished yet another novel. Now that she'd finished reading everything of interest in the house, she had to find something to do. She surveyed the room in search of any inspiration and focused on the trophy salmon mounted above the fireplace. She hadn't really paid attention to it before, maybe because she didn't much care for the art of taxidermy.

She sat up, her thoughts chasing each other with newfound excitement.

She'd always loved fishing, ever since the summers spent with her father in the Muskoka Lakes of Ontario. "Finest lake fishing in the world," he'd say to her, "outside of Scotland, that is."

Valerie had never understood why her father had said that. He'd never been to Scotland. As a tenured surgeon at Princess Margaret Hospital in Toronto, Dr. Glen Todd had seldom ventured far from home. He'd assumed he was always on call, and didn't feel right being away from his patients.

She recalled the happy times they'd shared aboard his elegant launch, sitting in silence on the stern bench, watching their little red floats bobbing in the black water, hoping for a bite. The classic craft, a 1947 Century, had been the doctor's pride and joy, but he had never seemed to mind using it for fishing excursions with his daughter. Years later, after her mother died, Valerie had tried time and time again to have her father come to live with them in California, but he had always declined. He would visit for short periods, but had always seemed preoccupied, rather like John now.

✿ ✿ ✿

Valerie knocked softly and pushed open the study door. "Sorry to interrupt, but I'm running into town. Anything you need?"

John sighed irritably and said nothing.

Valerie shrugged her shoulders and tiptoed out. She left the house by the back door, crossed to the garage, backed out the Jaguar, and headed for the village.

In town, she stopped in at the bakery and bought half a dozen fresh scones and a bramble tart from a disinterested shopkeeper. As she gathered up the goodies and paid for the purchase, she mustered her nerve. "I wonder if you could help me. I'm thinking of renting a small boat. Would you have any idea where I could ask?"

The shopkeeper, a sad-looking middle aged woman, had dark circles under her eyes and deep lines running from them to the corners of her thin mouth. They looked like they'd been etched into her cheeks by years of tears. The woman shook her head and frowned.

But Valerie continued on. "You see, I'm thinking of doing some fishing. I bet the fishing's wonderful around here." Her enthusiasm seemed to do the trick.

The cold stare relaxed, and the woman almost smiled. "Och aye, it is that. Our loch's the best. Now let me see. Graham Nesbit–aye, that's it. Graham'd know. He'd also be able to tell you the best places for the good fish. Besides, he's got nothin' else to do."

"Thank you so much. And where would I find this Mister Nesbit?"

The woman glanced behind her at the clock on the wall just as the church bell began to peal. "In about one minute, you'll find him in the pub. Across the street there." She pointed out the window toward the inn.

"But how will I know him? What does he look like?"

"Who?"

"Mister Nesbit. The boat man."

"Oh aye, well ye can't miss 'im. He's a right bonny man, as good lookin' as that Sean Connery, and Graham's still got his hair."

Valerie offered her thanks and crossed the street in the direction of the pub. As she entered the dimness of the Thistle, it took her eyes a moment to adjust. When they did, she found herself peering into a smoky room that was nearly filled with people. Almost immediately, conversations ceased, and she was greeted with stony silence. She saw one or two of the patrons whisper to each other and had little doubt what the whispers were about. Feeling out of place, she spun on her heel, eager to escape, and smacked right into a man who'd come up behind her in the doorway. Reflexively, the man reached for her. Feeling both clumsy and embarrassed, she pulled away and looked up into the face of an incredibly handsome man. It took her a moment to find her voice.

"I'm so sorry. I um—I was just leaving." As she pushed past him, she felt her blood rising and her fists tightening. Over the years, she'd become a woman who was not easily cowed, and decided she'd be damned if she'd let a few bumpkins scare her off. Besides, she was determined to have a go at the fishing. She took a breath, headed back inside, and approached the man she'd collided with.

"Em, excuse me," she began, willing her voice to remain calm, "but I came here looking for someone. Would you be so kind as to point out Mister Graham Nesbit to me?" She breathed deeply, slowly. "You see, I'm looking to rent a fish, eh—I mean a boat. Yes, I'm looking to rent a boat." Valerie realized that she was babbling, but she couldn't help it. She wanted desperately to flee.

At that moment, the man saved the day. He reached out his large hand and smiled warmly, revealing a row of perfect teeth.

She took his hand and noticed how rough and calloused it was. It was the hand of a working man.

"I'm Graham Nesbit." His voice was soft, almost intimate. "How can I be of service?"

She studied his face to see if he was being impertinent, but his expression was entirely guileless.

"Well, the woman at the bakery said that you are the man to talk to about getting a boat—a small boat to rent."

"I see. And she told ye right, she did. Come on over here an' have a seat. Tell me what exactly it is that you're lookin' for."

Valerie allowed herself to be steered toward a corner table, aware that every eye in the place was on her.

"Mister Nesbit, would it be okay with you if we sat outside? Cigarette smoke really bothers me." In truth, she had no problem with cigarette smoke. She was actually an ex-smoker who still had the odd puff in weak moments, but she was not comfortable sitting inside the pub, in the company of an attractive stranger, providing fodder for the village wags.

Graham shrugged his broad shoulders and led the way back out to the safety of the sunlight. She followed him around to the side of the building to a small stone patio. He chose a table under an ancient oak tree, shaded from the sun but with a nice view of the loch. Like a true gentleman, he pulled out her chair before taking his own seat. "So, tell me, Missus MacIntyre," he began, once they were seated, "are ye enjoying yer stay?"

Valerie raised an eyebrow.

"You know who I am?"

"Well, it's right hard not to notice the arrival of a big movie star from America, especially one as lovely as yerself." He shrugged, smiling.

Again, Valerie searched his face for guile. There was none.

"I must say I'm a bit surprised by your request," he continued, "I mean, for the boat. Don't you know that you already have one out at the house?"

"No, I had no idea. There's no boat there. At least, I haven't seen one." She felt a surge of excitement at the idea of having her very own boat. It was too good to be true.

"Oh it's there, all right. It's in that wee shed down by the rocks. The keys are on the mantle piece in the kitchen."

Valerie grinned. "We wondered what was in that shed, but it's all locked up, and there are no windows."

"She's in there. I put her there myself after I spent nearly all last year restoring her. The trust that owns the place wanted everything just so, including the boat." He averted his gaze. His eyes darkened for a moment, as if he'd remembered something disturbing, but by the time he looked back at her, the shadow had vanished. "Actually," he went on, "she's one of the finest boats on the loch. I'll be right pleased to come out and help you get her in the water. By the way, would you like a drink? A beer? Maybe a glass of wine? You know, Scotland's renowned for its wine. Oh aye, we get it directly from France."

Valerie shook her head. She was tempted to stay, but she was already feeling guilty, although it was nice to have someone to talk to. The man's charm was infectious. She'd worked with many heart-throbs over the years who couldn't hold a candle to the man sitting across the table. Late-thirties, she guessed, and from the tan on his face and arms, clearly an outdoorsman. He was tall and ruggedly built, but his eyes were warm and wise, in spite of the impish spark. His longish hair was chestnut brown, but the sun had bleached it in places, rewarding him with a color job that would have cost two hundred bucks in Beverly Hills. His mouth lurked on the verge of a smile and was too damn sexy.

Val decided not to dwell there. Instead, she tried to remember what he'd just asked her.

"A drink?" he repeated.

She was rescued. What a guy.

"Oh, no thank you, Mister Nesbit. I was just thinking of something I have to do. I really have to get going. My husband will be wondering what happened to me."

"Well, I can certainly see why he'd want to keep you close."

Valerie chose to ignore the compliment and offered her hand. "Maybe I'll take you up on that offer to get the boat going, though.

John and I—that's my husband—would really enjoy having the use of it."

Valerie rose from the table and headed across the street to her car. For some reason, she was feeling better about herself.

She had an urge to look back, but there was no need, she could feel his eyes following her.

✿ ✿ ✿

The cottage, not much more than a crofter's hut, was nestled high in the hills above the village. From its vantage point, Moira MacLeod could plainly see the twin peaks of Ben Cruachan, although the mountain was more than twenty-five miles away. For hours on end, Moira would sit by herself in the meadow above the cottage, gazing off toward the great crag. It had become her inspiration. She had been born in this cottage, and during her twenty years, had never ventured far from it—until recently.

It was the subject Moira was contemplating as she tuned her guitar, enjoying the warmth of the summer sun. She'd begun to perform her music in nearby towns and villages, and Ben Cruachan somehow had come to symbolize her dream of escape from the confinement she felt in Kilbride. It was in the high meadow that she wrote her songs; songs about sadness and loneliness, and sometimes about hope. She had no reason to feel lonely. She had her mother Susan, who loved her dearly, and supported her as much as possible. Her brother Ian, at fifteen, had little time for her, but she was convinced he loved her in his own way. She'd heard that Ian was actually quite proud, although he would never admit it, especially to her.

Satisfied with the tuning, she laid the guitar across her lap and stared off to the distant mountain and sighed. The real bane of her existence was her stepfather, Alan Moore. He'd become a bitter man over the years. Her mother sometimes spoke of the happy times when they'd first been married, when Alan had been kind and easy-going, but the accident had changed all that. Late one night on his way home from the pub, Alan's motorcycle had left the road at high speed and tumbled hundreds of feet down the hillside. They didn't find him until the next day, after he'd failed to arrive home, by which time it was too late to save his leg. Actually, he'd been fortunate. The thick gorse had broken his fall and saved his life. Nevertheless, Alan was inclined to blame everyone but himself for his plight. Sometimes, when he'd been hitting the whiskey bottle too hard, Moira had even heard him berate God for the darkness on that fateful night.

For some reason, he loved to take out his bitterness on her, maybe because she represented everything young and vibrant. He took every opportunity to demean her. Her mother tried to come to her defense, but somehow this always led to Susan being branded as the enemy and Alan venting his anger on both of them. Moira couldn't wait to leave the place. She knew his life had become unbearable; that his leg was not the only thing shattered that night. His heart had been broken as well. In his self-imposed martyrdom, Alan had decided to be housebound. He spent his days planted in front of the telly watching anything that it had to offer, although he preferred Kung Fu films and Australian football or wrestling. His appetite for mindless violence was insatiable.

Moira re-cradled her instrument and strummed softly until she was lost in her music. She was crafting a moody ballad about a mystic prince, his quest for righteousness, and the hand of his lady fair. As her imagination transported her to the perfect world of her creation, her voice filled with joy.

The moment was shattered by the loud yelling of her stepfather. "Moira! Moira! Where the hell are you? Moira!"

She opened her eyes to see Alan sitting in his wheelchair, gesticulating wildly from the front step of the cottage. She was tempted to ignore him, but she knew there'd be hell to pay if she did.

"Coming," she called back, and headed for the house. By the time she got there he was fuming.

"I don't know who you think you are, makin' me miss my program, my lass. You should stay in the house if you're expecting somebody to call. It's not my job to come hiving after you, you know."

"I know, Da. I'm right sorry. I wasn't expectin' anybody to call."

Alan had always demanded that she call him Da, although she never really could understand why. It was a sign of respect, he said. Anyway, it wasn't worth fighting about, so she had complied. She didn't hate Alan really. Mostly she felt sorry for him.

Moira squeezed past him into the humble cottage. She crossed the living room, entered the kitchen, and plucked the receiver from where it dangled against the wall. She was aware of Alan lowering the volume on the telly.

"Hello, this is Moira."

"Hi, beautiful, it's Ali. What are ye doin'?"

"Oh, nothin' really. I was doin' a bit of writin', but I got interrupted by the damn phone."

"Very funny. All right then, I won't ask ye to go to Oban and see the Reapers then, will I?"

"Well, I couldn't go anyway. I've got to be here 'til Mum gets home. She's workin' late tonight. It sounds super, Ali, but I just can't. I've got to get supper ready for Da. Otherwise I'd be there. Really I would."

A fat marmalade cat stretched lazily on the windowsill. He jumped down and crossed the floor to rub himself against Moira's legs. She smiled down at him.

"Well, we'll miss you," said Ali, sounding disappointed, "especially me. You take care, okay?"

"All right then, and thanks for asking. Some other time."

She hung up the phone, took a deep breath, and forced herself into the living room where the television volume had miraculously returned to its previous blare. Alan had moved from his chair onto the couch, where he sat glaring at her.

"So who was that, then? One of them laddies that wants to get into yer knickers, I suppose."

As always in this situation, Moira studied the floor, shamed by Alan's vulgarity. She managed to stammer a response. "It was only Alistair, the boy from the band. He wanted me to go into Oban with them tonight to see The Reapers. They're only gonne be there the one night. He thought it would be good for us to see them, that's all."

Alan scoffed. "Oh aye, I'm sure. I'm sure that's all—"

Moira interrupted before he could gather a full head of steam

"What would you like for supper, Da? How about some nice mince and tatties? You always like that."

"Mince and tatties? Is there none of that sirloin steak left we had last night? What did you do, eat it all?"

Moira did her best to manufacture a smile. "No, Da, I didn'e eat it all, but I have a good idea who did."

Alan almost grinned. The ugly moment had been diffused.

Grateful, she left the room to start preparing the meal.

"Oh and lassie, I wouldn't go setting my heart on this music business. There's no future in it."

His voice followed her like an angry swarm, but she kept walking, struggling not to listen.

"And ye know what people think of girls like you, that sing in the taverns, don't you?"

Moira clapped her hands over her ears, trying not to hear him, determined not to respond. It wasn't time.

Mercifully, the yelling subsided, bested by the roar of the telly.

CHAPTER 5

———◆◆◆———

John settled into hermitage. He no longer spent time with his wife. He'd even taken to having his meals in his room and resented being disturbed for any reason. His once healthy pallor had become pale and drawn. Dark circles underscored his eyes. He'd started writing late into the night, heading for bed sometimes just as the sun was beginning to paint the hills.

Valerie was terribly distraught. Her patience was reaching its limit, and dark clouds had begun to invade her disposition. After all, she was supposed to be on vacation with her husband. She resolved to indulge him for just a little longer.

A few days later, early in the morning, not long after John had drifted off to sleep, Valerie was surprised to hear a knock on the door. It occurred to her that during the weeks they'd been there, not one person from the village had come calling. She'd wondered what kept them away.

She opened the door and found herself looking straight into the smiling eyes of Graham Nesbit.

"Well good morning, Missus MacIntyre. And how's everything with you? Ye don't write; ye don't call, so what's a man to do?"

Valerie laughed out loud, in spite of herself. She was actually happy to see this face, any face. It was like fresh air.

"Mister Nesbit. It's nice to see you. Would you like to come in for a cup of tea?"

"Aye, I would that, and the name's Graham. Actually, I was just curious about whether you'd got the boat going yet. If not, I thought I could give you and your husband a hand, seeing that I know everything there is to know about her, if I do say so myself."

"Well, come on in. My husband's aslee–eh, busy, but–."

She started to explain, but realized that she was under no obligation to do so. She blushed and looked away.

She'd forgotten how damned attractive Graham was. John was a good-looking man too, there was no doubt, but there was an earthiness about Graham that was almost overpowering. She recognized that, unlike the actors she was used to working with, he had no idea how attractive he was. She suspected he was the type who only looked in the mirror to shave.

They moved into the sunny kitchen, where Graham took a chair from the pine table, spun it around, and sat astride it. She noted the smile lines at the corner of his eyes that made him look older than she remembered. But still, there was the mischievousness. He had the demeanor of a truant boy.

The kettle began to sing, and Valerie crossed the room, lifted it from the stove, and poured the scalding water into the china teapot. She watched the dancing tealeaves and remembered the turbulence in her own life. Oh how she hoped John's project would bring him the peace that had so far eluded him. She realized that it was sometimes tough for him, a proud man, to live in the shadow of her success. She'd always believed he was the more talented, but she'd been blessed with success. Maybe it was all in the luck of the draw.

Graham's polite cough snapped Valerie out of her reverie. She felt her cheeks flushing again, for no reason.

"Hey, I imagine that tea's well steeped by now. Should we drink it, or just let it stew away 'til it's treacle?"

His laugh filled the room, and she looked up just in time to catch his approving grin. Pretending she didn't notice, she carried the tea tray to the table, feeling strangely self-conscious. As a celebrity, she was used to people looking at her, and she wondered why she was so aware of Graham's attention. In truth, she felt flattered and safe. There was nothing salacious about his manner; rather, he was genuine and respectful.

"So why did ye decide on this place?" he asked, "If ye don't mind my impertinence."

Valerie set down the cups, took a chair, and concentrated on pouring the too-dark tea.

"Well, it was one of several we considered, but this one seemed just right for us. It was on the water, close to a village, and had just been renovated. The pictures were beautiful. Besides, it was in the part of Scotland my husband had visited before. It's where he wanted to be. Why do you ask?"

Graham carefully stirred two heaping spoons of sugar into his cup. "Before we go any further, Missus MacIntyre, I'd like to propose a deal. If you promise to call me Graham, instead of Mister Nesbit, which makes me feel like some relic, I'll be happy to answer."

"Deal," she said, enthusiastically. "And I'm Valerie."

"Fair enough." Graham surveyed the room. "The place's been nicely done up, and they certainly spent some money. I hardly recognize it. Never thought it would be lived in again."

"So we're the first people to live here in a while?"

Graham nodded. "Nobody's lived here for years."

"Well, we certainly had to go through hoops to get it, I'll tell you." Valerie felt expansive, happy to have someone to talk to. "The application was five pages long, which I found a bit strange. It was easier to join our golf club back home in the States. I was ready to pass, but John had a feeling about it. He said he admired the thoroughness of the owners. He figured they cared a lot about the house. He was intrigued."

"Actually, you're the first here in twenty-five years. The place has quite a history, you know."

"Really? Is there something I should know? Is there a reason you're our first caller?" She saw him stiffen and, using all her skills, managed to sound nonchalant. "Is there anything you think you should tell me?"

He looked away. "Oh no. It's not that. I just meant that the house is very, very old. Three-hundred years, at least. I'm sure it's got stories to tell."

With that, he leapt to his feet. "So what about the boat? Have you seen her yet?"

"No. Actually, I haven't. I guess I've been too busy with other things."

"Now, what could possibly be more important than a bit of fishing, may I ask?"

"Nothing, I suppose. Nothing at all."

Graham retrieved the keys from a jar on the mantle and led the way outside. They crossed the verandah and hurried down the flight of stone steps that led to the shore. It was a still, warm morning, and the air smelled of gooseberries and wild roses. Carefully, they navigated the flat rocks below the house until they reached the sandy cove that housed the boat shed. Listless little waves lapped at the shoreline, strewing a rainbow of bubbles across the sand before retreating to the coolness of the loch.

Valerie saw at once that the boathouse had not been a priority during the refurbishment of Ainsley. Its weathered boards were in dire need of paint, and the doors hung from their frame like an ill-fitting suit. Graham inserted the key, undid the padlock, and with some effort, hauled the doors open. He stepped back, and with a flourish, ushered Valerie inside.

Her face flushed with excitement, she stepped into the dimness and right back into the fondest memories of her girlhood. Nothing smelled quite like a boathouse. She closed her eyes and inhaled deeply, remembering the rich smells of fine wood and tung oil and her father's cherry tobacco.

Graham began to unfold the cover from the boat, and Valerie immediately joined in, eager for the unveiling. As the tarp fell away, and the sunlight hit the boat, she gasped, unable to believe what she was looking at. There, resting on a set of steel rollers was an exact replica of her father's boat. She raised her hands to her face in an effort to suppress the burst of joy.

Aside from the fact that the upholstery was dark green instead of maroon, it was a twin to the classic launch she'd grown up with. It was a twenty-two-foot mahogany Century, split windshield and all. Valerie hastily wiped a tear from her cheek, hoping that Graham hadn't noticed, but she was too late.

"What's the matter?" he asked. "Are you all right?"

"Oh yes," she breathed softly, "I'm more than all right."

She reached out to stroke the gleaming hull, remembering the feel of her father's boat and how good it felt to hoist her chilled body from the cold water of Lake Muskoka and stretch out on the warm deck.

She walked around to the stern and smiled. This boat was named *Bridie*. Her Dad's had been called *Lass*.

Valerie's entire being vibrated with excitement as she watched Graham sweep away the sand and pebbles from the rails that would carry the craft down to the water. He oiled the winch, turned the crank, and within moments, *Bridie* was free, floating on the loch, elegant as a swan.

Without hesitation, Valerie waded into the water and clambered aboard. Graham splashed his way out to join her. He turned the key, and the twin inboard engines roared to life. Gently, Graham nudged the throttles and headed the old craft out of the cove. The twin screws churned the black water into cream.

It was a fine, calm morning, and Loch Awe was as flat as slate. Graham opened the throttles full, and *Bridie* flew across the water. Valerie stood in the cockpit with the wind stretching her hair straight out behind her. It had been a long time since she'd experienced such joy.

Graham glanced at the fuel gauge and turned to his companion. "She's a bit low. We'd better run into the village and fill her up." He struggled to be heard above the splendid roar of the engines. Valerie returned a thumbs-up. She was as carefree as a meadowlark and didn't care where they were going.

A few minutes later, Graham pulled into Kilbride harbor and carefully maneuvered the boat close to the petrol pumps. Valerie leapt ashore and made fast, the bowline knots perfectly executed.

Her companion watched, smiling broadly.

"Hey! And where'd you learn to do that?"

"It's a long story." She turned and marched toward the village, heading for the bakery. Again she resisted the temptation to look back. As she strolled through the village, she couldn't help but wonder what John would think. Would he approve of her little excursion? Probably not, but she refused to allow the guilt to sap her euphoria. After all, it wasn't her fault she was spending time with Graham. It could have been John enjoying the beautiful morning with her, if he wasn't totally absorbed with himself and his precious book.

She shoved her nagging misgivings aside, and returned her thoughts to the glory of the day and the promise of the bakery.

By the time she returned to the harbor with the scones, Graham had completed the refueling. She undid the lines and hopped aboard.

"Just a minute," she said, "I didn't pay for the gas, and unfortunately, I forgot to bring any money. The woman at the bakery was very nice. She said I could pay next time."

"Don't worry, you've got a charge account here, but this time, the petrol's my treat, this being our maiden voyage together and all."

He steered *Bridie* toward the open water, and when they were clear of the harbor wall, he offered Valerie the wheel. "Do you think you can handle her?"

Valerie grinned wickedly and moved over to take the controls. "I think so."

She threw the throttles wide open, causing Graham to tumble into the stern bench like a sack of potatoes. She giggled wickedly.

John awakened to a pounding headache. It was well past noon, but he'd worked most of the night. He struggled out of bed and headed immediately for a hot shower. On the way, he downed four Vicodin. They hadn't been able to find Excedrin in Scotland, but the local stuff seemed to work quite well. Single malt whiskey had become his favorite companion during the past weeks, and he was feeling like he'd overdone it just a bit the previous evening.

"*Never mind,*" he muttered to himself, "*the work's going well. It's worth the odd headache.*"

As he stood under the scalding shower, he wondered where Valerie was. He hadn't seen the coffee she usually left for him. Maybe she'd gone into town and simply forgot the coffee, he considered. Still it wasn't like her. He wondered if she was miffed. He allowed that maybe he had been a bit inattentive for the last couple of weeks. He decided that he should do something to make it up to her.

John dried off with a huge towel from the heated rack, wondering why they didn't have one of these things at home. He really loved warm towels. He'd ask Valerie when he saw her.

Black Watch was turning out to be just what he'd hoped for. Although he'd had no second opinion, he felt he was onto something good. The words seemed to fly from his fingers, circumventing the strictures of his mind, as though they'd been written before. Sleep had become an unwelcome necessity, food an inconvenience. John dressed hurriedly, his thoughts still on his work. He hadn't planned to write a historical piece, but that's what was pouring out. The story simply demanded to be written, like it had been sent from another time.

And yet, while it was a compelling story, something about it worried him. There was no doubt the time spent in Kilbride was paying off, but John had an uneasy feeling.

His story was about a beautiful young girl, sold into a marriage not of her choosing. It was a familiar one, he knew, but somehow this was different. The characters were more than alive for him; they were eerily familiar, the situations felt excruciatingly real. This was a story he needed to put on film. He would do it justice, and it just might do the same for him. Sometimes, late at night, he found himself racing through the pages, desperate to find out what would happen, like he was reading someone else's words.

"John, you'll never guess!" He was so absorbed in his thoughts, he hadn't heard her bounding up the stairs. She burst into the room, radiant as a summer storm. Her hair was wind-blown, her cheeks pink as petals. She looked fantastic. She was babbling so fast, he couldn't understand what she was trying to say—something about a boat and her father, and someone called Nesbit. He couldn't glean the half of it, although he felt her excitement.

He could see that she missed him and realized that he missed her too. He knew he should spend some more time with her. He reached for her and as she eagerly entered his arms, he bent to kiss her mouth. She stopped talking.

Together they fell onto the unmade feather bed and started to make love. In a moment, he was lost in her, oblivious to the patter of raindrops against the windows.

✵ ✵ ✵

Down at the boatshed, Graham busied himself reassembling the jetty. He hauled the heavy planks from behind the shed, oblivious to the rain, and began piecing them together. He hauled the completed sections into the loch, searching out the concrete pilings that would secure the structure. He'd built it himself, so he was confident it would withstand any summer squall.

By the time he was finished, he was soaked and exhausted, ready for a hot shower and a pint of ale.

CHAPTER 6

It poured for three days and three nights. A cold northeasterly
whipped the twenty-three miles of Loch Awe into a frenzy. The
normally placid lake was transformed into a cruel sea. Strong
winds rattled the huge windows of Ainsley House, and a hard rain
hammered her thick walls. The MacIntyres made the best of it.
For hours at a time, they sat before the roaring fire, enjoying each
other's company once again. They played Scrabble and checkers,
and sometimes Valerie even let John win. She'd told him all about
finding *Bridie* and her new acquaintance, Graham Nesbit. Well,
almost all. She made no mention of how attractive Graham was.

She was well aware that John had never been supportive of her
having male friends. It was his contention that it was impossible for
members of the opposite sex to be just friends. He'd admitted that

over the years, he'd found it difficult to watch her making love on the screen, even though, as a professional, he knew it was all make believe. His rationale was that although he trusted her, he had little faith in his fellow man.

Ironically, the one serious threat during their twenty-two year marriage hadn't come from her. John had developed a crush on a girl who worked in his office—not one of the many beauties he'd directed on film, but a plain little thing who had become his personal assistant during one of their long separations. Valerie had decided to let the situation run its course, which it eventually did. The incident had happened years ago, and John had seemingly forgotten all about it. Valerie never would.

✿ ✿ ✿

On Saturday afternoon, the rain stopped. If the Vale of Kilbride was beautiful before, it was now absolutely magical. A rainbow spanned the sky above Campbell Keep, framing the fortress in color. The earth had been washed clean, and the birds sang their appreciation.

Valerie, tired of being housebound for days, approached her husband with an idea.

"John, today's Saturday, you know. Why don't we take the boat out for a spin and go to the Crown and Thistle for dinner? I hear the food's really good, and there might be some music."

She crossed to where John sat on the window seat staring out at the beauty of the day. She lifted his arm so she could insert herself, wriggled onto his lap, and hugged him fervently.

"Come on. You'll love the boat. I'll even let you drive."

An hour later, they were out on the loch, and although it was early evening, the sun was still well up in the sky. There were hours of light remaining.

"Hey," said John, "It's so beautiful out here, why don't we head up the loch and take a closer look at that ruin? I'm really curious about the place."

"Why not?" Although she was less than thrilled at the prospect, she was willing to go along, happy to be in her husband's company.

John opened wide the throttles and pointed *Bridie*'s elegant prow toward Campbell Keep. Valerie saw the excitement in his eyes as he glanced at her, smiling roguishly. For a moment, she felt like a woman who had everything. He'd been so preoccupied; she'd almost forgotten how much fun he could be. He'd been her best friend since the day they met, and it was that friendship that had kept their marriage strong.

Within minutes, they'd halved the distance to the Keep; the closer they got, the more impressive the structure became. Soon they were able to distinguish that the crumbling tower was part of a much larger fortification. The place was huge.

A short time later, they floated directly beneath the fortress. From their point of view the monolith was formidable. John stared up at the hulking bastion, his eyes filled with awe. Valerie couldn't understand the fascination. She shivered in spite of the warmth of the evening and pulled her sweater tighter. The Keep was overwhelming. To Valerie, it looked like an ocean liner straining at its moorings, hungry to be free.

She noticed that the water in this part of the loch was thick with weeds and smelled putrid, like a flooded grave. As she stared up at the ruin, it shifted, ever so slightly, like it was a living thing.

She knew her imagination was playing tricks, but she didn't care. "Let's go, John," she whispered. "I don't like it here."

He didn't respond.

She tried again. "John!"

"Huh? What'd you say?"

"I said, let's go. I'm getting hungry."

"Oh, sure," he muttered, still gazing at the Keep. "I'm sorry, honey."

He restarted the engines and pointed *Bridie* back toward Kilbride. Every few minutes, he turned to glance back.

For some reason, his fascination worried her. She slid closer and slipped under his arm, wondering if she'd ever be able to stop trying to protect him.

✳ ✳ ✳

Saturday night at the Thistle was just getting started. It was too early for the pub side to be full, but a few customers sat in the dining room. John and Valerie entered tentatively, but were immediately made welcome by Janet, the hostess, whose name was embroidered across her left breast.

"I'm sorry," John said, "we don't have a reservation, but we'd like to have dinner if that's possible."

"Certainly, Mister MacIntyre. Locals don't need reservations. We've been looking forward to seein' ye both."

"You know who we are?" Valerie asked.

"Oh aye, Missus MacIntyre. It's not often we have somebody as famous as you around here, you know. Right this way, if ye please."

The hostess led them to a table by the window where there was a fine view of the loch.

Over on the tavern side of the Thistle, the regulars began to drift in. Old Jock was already ensconced at his favorite table, where one of his pals was in the middle of a story.

"So my wife takes young Jimmy with her to visit her sister Janet, whose got a baby just a couple of months old. Jimmy's about six at the time, and already ahead of his years. Anyway, Janet, who's a rather substantial woman, takes out one of her tremendous breasts and begins to feed the baby. Jimmy's never in his life seen anything like this."

"Ma," he whispers, "what's she doin?"

"Oh," says Jen, "she's just feedin' the baby."

"Oh," says Jimmy, surveying the huge bosom with the baby firmly attached

"That greedy bairn'll never eat all that."

The men at the table howled with laughter.

John and Valerie grinned at each other, enjoying the merriment from the next room.

"Sounds like it's gonna be a fun night," said Valerie.

By the time they'd finished their dessert and coffee, things in the bar were definitely heating up. The volume of conversation had risen several decibels. Music mingled with the laughter until the lure of the gaiety was irresistible. John settled the bill and headed next door with his wife in tow.

As soon as they walked through the door, the merrymaking stopped. The effect of their entrance was as chilling as a bucket of ice water. The patrons stared openly at the interlopers. Even the music halted.

Valerie and John eyed each other, silently debating whether they shouldn't just leave. John smiled bravely, took Valerie firmly by the hand, and led her through the room in the direction of the bar. The silence was palpable as he stared into the eyes of the barman. The huge fellow gazed right back, expressionless.

"Good evening," John said amiably, "a single malt please, no ice, and a glass of white wine for the lady."

The man didn't respond; rather he shifted his attention to Valerie, quietly appraising her.

"So, will ye have a dance with me?" he asked.

Valerie studied the big man's face. A moment passed. "I'd be delighted," she replied.

The barman signaled to the band, and the music resumed. He wiped his meaty hands on his apron, removed it, folded it carefully, placed it on the counter, and stepped out from behind the bar. He bowed respectfully before taking Valerie in his arms.

The man danced beautifully, elegantly. As he watched the improbable pair circle the floor, John was reminded of a little girl dancing with her father. He smiled.

Satisfied, the patrons returned their attention to their drinking and their conversations. A pretty barmaid placed John's drinks on the bar in front of him, and he reached into his pocket.

"There'll be no paying tonight, Mister MacIntyre. You'll be guests of the house for this evenin', to be sure. You've passed the test with flying colors." The noise had resumed with a vengeance.

When the song ended, the bartender bowed again to Valerie before taking her arm and escorting her back to her husband.

"Thank you for the dance, Missus MacIntyre, and thank you, Mister MacIntyre, for your graciousness. And might I say, you're a right lucky man."

Next thing they knew, they were invited to join a table. Two chairs appeared from nowhere, and drinks were replenished all around.

It was a wonderful, festive evening. John and Valerie danced several times, heady from the alcohol and the stirring rhythms of Scottish country music. An hour or so later, after a band break, Alistair, the guitar player, returned to the stage and stepped up to the microphone.

"Ladies and gentlemen," he announced, "please welcome tae the Crown and Thistle our very own Moira MacLeod, the beautiful Bell of Argyll."

Conversation subsided. Lights dimmed, and a slim figure stepped up into the darkness. She stood with her head bowed as the music began. A single spot gradually intensified until the girl was bathed in rose colored light. Slowly, she raised her head.

When the light hit Moira's face, John gasped. Valerie glanced at her husband, who quickly raised a hand to his mouth and coughed.

"Excuse me," he muttered.

Valerie slowly returned her attention to the stage.

The girl began to sing, and the folk sat entranced. As her show proceeded, people called out requests.

Between songs, Valerie leaned in to John and whispered. "She's incredible, isn't she?"

John's eyes remained fixed on the stage. "What did you say?"

Valerie shook her head. "Nothing."

At the end of her set, Moira removed the microphone from its stand and addressed the crowd. "I understand that this is a very special night at the Thistle." Even her speaking voice was music. "It's been brought to my attention that we have some visitors with us from very far away. I'd like to take this opportunity to make them feel welcome."

The crowd applauded heartily. Valerie smiled and nodded graciously as John felt his face redden. He had never enjoyed being the center of attention.

"Now I understand that the gentleman here is actually returning to his homeland, that he was born and raised in this bonny country. Well sir," she said, gazing into John's eyes, "this song's from my own heart to yours."

John broke the eye contact and stared into his drink as the girl began to sing:

> Oh I'm no awa tae bide awa,
> Oh I'm no awa tae leave ye.
> Oh I'm no awa tae bide awa,
> I'll aye come back an see ye.

During the song, Moira stepped down from the stage and drifted through the audience. Soon other voices joined in with hers, until everyone in the room, except John and Valerie, was singing along.

As the sentimental old favorite came to an end, Moira reached John's chair. She took his hand and sang the last words right to him. When she'd finished, she leaned down and kissed his cheek, smiled impishly, and ran from the room.

Valerie blanched. "I think I want to go home."

She stood up and, without another word, walked from the room. John dropped a twenty-pound note on the table, shrugged to the others, and hurried after her.

✼ ✼ ✼

Minutes later, the speedboat cruised slowly across the water, making its way toward Ainsley House. Although it was past eleven o'clock, the twilight lingered on. As he drove, John was aware of Valerie studying him.

"Well it's certainly an evening I'll never forget." she said.

The air was heavy, like the tension between them. It felt like a squall brewing.

✼ ✼ ✼

"What was all that about?" Alistair's voice trembled as he faced his companion. "You made a bloody fool of yourself."

Moira gazed calmly into his angry eyes.

"I don't know what you're talking about, Alistair. I was only trying to make them welcome. Tavish told me that the man used to live in Scotland, so I thought that it would be nice to make him feel at home."

"Well you certainly accomplished that. Aye, you certainly did. No matter that everybody thought you looked daft, like a cheap tramp."

Moira's eyes flashed as she delivered a resounding slap to Ali's face. She spun on her heel and stomped across the parking lot to where her little motor scooter sat waiting. Rolling the Lambretta off its kickstand, she clambered aboard, shot him a withering look, and roared off into the night.

Despite her mother's fear of motorcycles, Moira had purchased the scooter with the few pounds she'd saved for herself after sharing her earnings with her family. She'd promised to always be careful and treated the little blue scooter like it was a new puppy.

✿ ✿ ✿

Alistair barged through the door of the pub and headed straight for the bar.

"Gimme a large whiskey, George." He raised his hand to touch his still-stinging face.

The barman returned with the drink and set it down. "So what got into Moira tonight, Ali? I've never seen her like that before."

"I've no idea. She's been actin' kinda strange lately, not herself."

"Ah well, don't you mind, they're all a bit unpredictable at times. You might as well get used to it. Anyway, the drink's on me.

Cheers." George nodded sympathetically and switched his attention to the needs of his other customers.

✿ ✿ ✿

Moira muttered to herself as she rode higher into the hills. Heavy clouds began to gather around the quarter moon, and the darkness deepened. The single lamp on the scooter didn't provide much relief, and she was going much too fast for the conditions. Carelessness was quite out of character for her, but she was angry.

As she rounded a tight bend, she ran into a patch of loose gravel and braked too hard. The scooter went into a skid, heading right for the edge of the road and the precipice beyond. She fought to regain control, but overcorrected. The bike went out from under her and skittered away in a shower of sparks. Moira hit the ground hard and lay still, watching helplessly as her precious little machine kept sliding toward the edge. At the last second, it hit a clump of gorse and came to rest hanging over the five hundred foot drop. Moira rose gingerly to her feet and limped to the scooter, relieved that she only had a couple of sore spots. Her knees throbbed, and she felt the sting of the scratches on her face, but most importantly, her prized Lambretta was still in one piece. With shaking hands, she wrestled the bike from the bushes.

As if the darkness had served its purpose, the moon reappeared, and in the distance, Moira glimpsed the Keep. She felt the fortress watching her.

She restarted the scooter and rode off, her mind in an uproar. She'd crashed at exactly the same spot where her stepfather had gone over the edge. She knew it was no coincidence.

Twenty minutes later, Moira arrived home. She hid the badly scraped scooter in the shed and tiptoed to her room. She turned on her light and went to the mirror to survey the damage. Her right eye was beginning to darken and swell, and there were two good-sized welts crisscrossing her cheek. She wondered what she would tell her mother. She knew she'd have to come up with a good story, or it would be the end of the Lambretta.

"This is gonna be trouble," she murmured.

✿ ✿ ✿

John closed the boatshed and walked slowly toward the house. In the living room, he poured himself a large Glenlivett and retired to his study. Valerie heard the computer start up. Slowly, she made her way upstairs and started to undress. She returned the pale blue peignoir to the drawer, put on a long cotton nightshirt, and climbed into bed. She lay staring at the beams in the ceiling until they started closing in on her. She thought back on the conversation she'd had with Graham Nesbit, and wondered if indeed there was something sinister about Ainsley House—something not settled.

Old timbers creaked, as though the house had read her thoughts and was displeased. She buried her head in her pillow and tried to focus on pleasant things, but they remained just out of reach.

CHAPTER 7

John leaned back in his chair and stared at the screen. The words had been pouring out of him for hours. He was breathing heavily, and his hands ached. He stared out at the loch, unsure as to whether the night had ever come. He felt completely spent and a little afraid. Something was happening to him, something he had no control over.

The sun was well up and the scotch had taken its toll. He slowly made his way upstairs, undressed, and climbed into bed. Valerie turned to him and said something apparently important but completely unintelligible. John was about to respond until he realized that she was asleep. He gazed at her for a long moment, then pulled the covers over his head to block out the day. His breathing slowed and deepened until his mind was lost somewhere in another realm.

After having his wounds tended by his physician in his private chambers, the Earl of Argyll donned his finest tartans. The vivid reds and blues were a marked contrast to the colors he wore during battle.

Resplendent in his kilt and plaid, Argyll looked magnificent. His heavy silver brooch, the symbol of his position as chief of the Campbells, gleamed softly in the candlelight, and the jewels on his bearskin sporran sparkled like winter fire.

It was with great pride that Argyll surveyed his splendid reflection. Malcolm was not a large man, but at fifty years of age, he was feared far and wide. He was a ferocious warrior, a formidable adversary, a cruel, humorless man with few friends, a fact that was of no importance to Campbell. He was the chieftain of the most powerful clan in western Scotland. All that was missing from his life was an heir, a son to continue the line that he'd made so powerful.

Three years earlier, his wife Agnes had died during childbirth, and the child, a boy, had been lost as well. She'd been a strong, capable woman, a worthy helpmeet. Campbell had been saddened by her death, but the loss of an heir had angered him deeply and turned him into a bitter man.

After all, there was a kingdom to be held.

Many years before, Campbell's ancestors had built the castle that stood high on the headland overlooking the entire length of Loch Awe. From their vantage point, the lookouts spotted any invaders long before they reached the fortress. The Keep had remained impenetrable for two hundred years. The great wealth of Argyll was safe within its thick walls.

On the night of Campbell's defeat of the English, the great bastion was lit up like a city. Hundreds of torches and candles bathed its vast chambers and wide corridors in the warmth of victory.

Campbell descended the staircase in regal splendor, followed closely by his cadre of lieutenants: Alsh, Falkirk, and Sutherland. He swept into the feasting hall, where the celebration was already under way.

Upon his arrival, the scores of guests rose from their seats and bowed deeply. With a grand gesture, he bade them resume their merrymaking and strode to his place of celebrity at the center of the hall. This was the sign for the feast itself to begin. Five enormous deerhounds skulked into the chamber and took their places under the table at the feet of their master. There was some growling and snarling as the beasts maneuvered for position.

Right on cue, the doors from the kitchens swung open. Through them entered a stream of servants bearing huge silver platters heaped with the kinds of delicacies that only a recent victory could provide. The English army had been well stocked, and the spoils were fit for a king. Peaches and plums, oranges and lemons, exotic figs and pomegranates, and mountains of purple grapes were deposited on the tables.

Argyll was pleased with himself, for the plunder had been substantial, more than his guests would ever know. Malcolm Campbell stood up from his place holding his jeweled goblet.

"Lords, ladies, gentlemen, Scots all," he thundered, "I offer ye yer health on this fine night. The enemy is turned away. We weep for our dead, and we thank our God for delivering us. Eat, drink, be joyful, for tomorrow, we may meet our own death. To the rightful King and to Bonny Scotland, may they live forever."

Campbell raised his cup, and two hundred stood as one. The men unsheathed their broadswords and raised them to their chief before smashing the heavy blades three times on the plank tables.

His warriors roared back in unison. "Tae the King and tae Bonny Scotland."

The noise was deafening.

The feasting began in earnest. The servants presented trays of pheasant and venison, roast wild pig, and silver salmon. The wine and the ale flowed freely, and the sounds of music and laughter filled the great hall. Campbell and his men ate like lions and drank with a thirst that would not be slaked.

Campbell had provided well for the amusement of the crowd. Jugglers and acrobats, minstrels and dancers kept the guests entertained as they gorged themselves.

At dinner's end, a large brown bear was hauled into the room blindfolded and secured to a pillar by a stout chain. The cloth was removed from its eyes, and a dozen baiting dogs raced forward. The bear killed eight of them before succumbing to the relentless ferocity of the onslaught. The enormous beast was then dragged from the room, staining the stone floor with its blood. The body would be fed to the dogs that had survived the battle.

The revelers laughed mightily and howled their approval.

Late in the evening, a young girl dressed in white was led into the chamber. A piper began to play, and the girl danced. It was the traditional sword dance of victory, but no one noticed. Most of the guests were fast asleep, their heads resting on the tables. Campbell felt a bit groggy, but the dancer managed to capture his attention. He tried to focus, but she kept moving. Her long hair was black as death, and her dark eyes flashed in the candlelight, teasing him brazenly.

As he watched her, Campbell felt a strange stirring. He nudged the man on his right. "William," he whispered. There was no reply. William of Alsh was dead to the world. Campbell prodded him with his fist. "That lassie, William. Who is she?"

"What lassie?" William tried his best to rally.

"That one there." Campbell pointed to the dancer.

With some effort, William managed to concentrate. He studied the girl.

"Och, she's the daughter of old Duncan MacLeod. his only one, I believe."

"I'll have her, William, tonight. Have her brought to my chambers. I'm going there now."

"But my Lord Campbell," William of Alsh said, suddenly wide-awake, "she's the daughter of a compatriot, and betrothed to a

Douglas, if I remember right. It wouldn't be wise, sire. Not at this time."

"Bring her," barked Campbell. "Bring her now."

He rose from the table and stumbled out of the great hall.

A half hour later, Campbell was giddy with anticipation and very impatient. He had donned his sleeping robe and sent the servants packing.

There was a knock on the door.

"Come in."

The door opened to admit Alsh and Falkirk, who had the girl firmly in his grasp. She allowed herself to be led into the chamber, where she stood quietly, taking in the surroundings. She bowed to the man who was rising from the curtained bed.

"My Lord." Her voice was soft and trembled slightly.

He almost felt sorry for the girl, but her fear excited him. "My Lady."

With a wave, Campbell dismissed the others. They eagerly took their leave.

The chieftain walked slowly toward the girl, drinking in the beauty and enjoying her attempt at bravery. She looked steadily into his eyes.

"I'll have you to know, m'Lord, that I'm not some wench from your village," she said defiantly." I'm Eileen MacLeod, daughter of Duncan and troth to Robert of Douglas. You'll not have yer way with me as though I'm your own property. Not while I can stand and fight you."

The girl clenched her little fists and glared at him. "I know you're the Lord of Argyll, but to me, that makes no mind. I'm righteously promised tae another."

Campbell would have laughed out loud at the audacity, but the drink was severely paining his head, and he was in no mood. "Woman, you'll not speak to the Earl of Argyll that way. Do ye understand?"

"I' do, m'Lord, but I never thought a man such as you would need to force his way with a helpless girl."

Campbell was torn. Although he was moved by the girl's valiance, his desires were raging. He pushed the nagging doubts aside, and reached for his prize. Eileen struggled to fight him off, but he was too strong by far.

The fabric of her dress gave way, giving her attacker full view of her comeliness. He forced her down on the bed and gazed at her, awed by her beauty. He sighed deeply, and his eyes rolled upward. In slow motion, he collapsed in a heap, sprawled across the girl like a felled tree.

The Earl of Argyll was out cold.

John awoke, feeling like he'd never slept. Instead, he felt like he'd been on a long, difficult journey. He climbed wearily out of bed and headed for the shower, his mind in turmoil.

✠ ✠ ✠

Friday afternoon, Valerie was out on Loch Awe with Graham. It was the fourth day in a row. The loch and her new friend had been welcome diversions since John had ceased being available. Although the two of them had explored the entire length of the loch, Graham never ventured anywhere near the Keep. When she asked him why, she saw the twinkle fade from his eyes. He explained that, as a young boy, he'd lost a friend there, in a terrible accident, but refused to provide the details. He did, however, warn her away from the ruins.

"It's a vile place, Val. There's something there that's not of this earth. I know it sounds far fetched, but what I'm telling you is true."

He steered them to a quiet inlet on the west side of the loch, where a small stream fed into the larger body of water. They laughed and talked like old friends as they cast their lines far from the boat and reeled them slowly back. The whole rhythm of the procedure was easy and relaxing. They'd been in the same spot for over an hour, and the fishing had been good. The soft, flannel grey light allowed no reflection. The conditions were perfect. They'd caught two good-sized trout each. They'd hooked several others but had thrown them back.

Val expertly flicked her rod, watching the line soar out over the dark water, and squealed with joy as she hooked into another fish. Graham grinned back at her, caught up in her enthusiasm.

This time, Valerie was onto something big. The line sang from her reel, and it was several minutes before she made any headway at all. Just as it seemed like she was making some progress, the fish exploded again. She yelped with excitement. Eventually, she managed to turn the fish and began winding feverishly.

Realizing that she'd hooked into something serious, Graham reeled in his own line and watched.

Through tightly clenched teeth, she whispered hoarsely, "Well, don't just stand there. Get the hell over here, and help me."

He laughed, put down his rod, and went to help. As he did, a huge silver salmon leapt from the black water, no more than fifty feet from the boat. The fish hung in the air, staring at them as if sizing up the opposition. After what seemed like forever, the salmon splashed back into the loch, sending a spray of water high into the air. Valerie whooped and reeled just as hard as she could.

Ten minutes later, her arms gave out. She was exhausted from the battle and the exhilaration. She struggled to hand the rod over to Graham, but just as she did, the line snapped, sending her sprawling. She landed unhurt on the rear bench cushion.

Graham laughed like it was the funniest thing he'd ever seen.

Valerie glared up at him.

He managed to wipe the laughter from his face, reached out his hand, and pulled her to her feet. She was suddenly in his arms, very close to him—too close. He bent quickly and kissed her mouth.

Valerie gasped and pulled away, her cheeks flushed crimson.

"Graham Nesbit! What the hell are you doing?" She was shaking with shock and shame.

Graham was nonplussed. He didn't know what to say, so he said nothing. Instead, he quietly gathered up the fishing gear and stowed it away.

Valerie sat in the rear seat, staring at the water. When he was done with the tackle, Graham fired up the engines and headed for home. It was a quiet trip.

When they reached Ainsley cove, Graham slowed and turned to face her.

"Valerie, I don't know what to say to you. I assure you, I've got nothing but the deepest respect fer you, and I wouldn't do anything to ruin the friendship we have, new though it may be. I don't know what happened out there. It's not even as if I got carried away. It was just that I wanted you to know how damned attractive you are, though it seems that the one that matters to you the most has stopped noticing. I can see I was wrong. But for what it's worth, I think you're the most glorious woman I've ever seen, and I'm sorry for what happened. I hope you can find a way to forgive me, but if you can't, I'll miss you something terrible. Thanks for listening."

As Valerie watched him speak his heart, he became the boy she sometimes glimpsed. She stepped toward him, put her arms around him, and hugged him tightly. A moment later, she pushed him away but held his gaze.

"Graham, I do forgive you. Let's not mention it again."

When they reached shore, Valerie saw John standing on the verandah with a drink in his hand, watching them. She waved to him and couldn't understand why he didn't wave back. She and Graham winched the boat back up into the shed, closed the doors, and proceeded toward the house.

Valerie pecked John on the cheek. Graham extended his hand. John ignored it. After an awkward moment, Graham pulled his hand back.

"Honey?" Valerie inquired, "are you all right? What's the matter?"

John stared at them, shifting his glance from one to the other. "So what gives here? What's going on with you two?"

Graham didn't know where to look. He chose the floor. Valerie tried to speak.

"I–I don't know what to say–."

"Say? There is nothin' to say. Let me tell you. A few minutes ago, I was standing here wondering where the hell my wife could possibly be. I look out on the goddamn lake and see you in the arms of some stranger who must be half your age, like there's something going on. Now, would one of you like to try and explain this to me so that I'll like it?"

Valerie could think of nothing. She could see that John was drunk. There was nothing she could offer that was going to help. It had been a long time since she'd seen him this angry.

Graham coughed and seemed to find his voice. "Er, Mister MacIntyre, sir, I understand what you think you saw, but let me assure you, there is nothing at all but friendship going on 'tween me and Missus MacIntyre. The truth of the matter is that eh–I'm eh–ye see–well, I've never had any interest in women, even one as beautiful as your wife here."

John continued to bluster, but the wind was now gone from his sails. Graham again offered his hand and bid goodnight. This time, John took it. He was speechless.

So was Valerie.

"Well, I'll just show Graham to his car. I'll be right back."

Valerie grabbed Graham's arm and led him away.

"What the hell was that all about?"

He stopped and turned to her, looking a bit sheepish.

"You're not gay," she chided.

"I know that," said Graham, "but it was the only thing I could think of at the moment. I must have panicked."

She grinned as she watched him fold his lanky frame into his Mini Cooper, trying to look as effeminate as possible. He offered a jaunty wave and pulled away.

Valerie returned to the house to find a humbled John waiting in the living room. He began to offer an apology, but Valerie put a finger to his lips and shook her head. She leaned in close and kissed his mouth.

"I'm actually pleased and flattered that you can still get jealous. It's adorable. And it's nice to know that you're still paying attention."

For once, John was unable to generate a suitably snide response.

"Hey, I've got a good idea," said Valerie, "let's go back into town tonight and have dinner. I'm in the mood for salmon, and just wait until I tell you my story about the one that got away."

John nodded, and Valerie hurried away to shower, excited about the evening out.

John poured himself another scotch and stared into the amber liquid. Something was happening to him. He'd worked hard over the years to manage his temper, but for some reason, he'd lost control. He had the uneasy feeling that the anger he was dealing with was not entirely his own.

✼ ✼ ✼

It was a quiet night at the Thistle, but the food was every bit as good as before, and the MacIntyres were enjoying each other.

"So how's the writing coming?" Valerie stirred the heavy cream into her coffee. "Is it everything you hoped for? I've tried not to pry, but I am curious."

John thought for a minute before responding. "Yes, I'd have to say it is what I hoped for. It's really strange though. Sometimes the words just fly out without me really thinking about them, as if I'm only a messenger. It's pretty amazing."

Valerie could see his excitement and felt a little pang of guilt for the resentment she'd been feeling. "When do I get to read some? I'd really love to see what you're writing."

"Well, maybe soon. Perhaps I should let you read a few pages, just to make sure this whole idea isn't a waste of time. Maybe it's awful. Maybe I'm totally nuts."

"Oh John, no one thinks you're *totally* nuts."

When they'd paid the check, John suggested they stop in the pub for an after-dinner. Valerie reluctantly agreed.

She saw him cover his disappointment when he discovered that there would be no music that night. After they finished their cognacs, they said goodnight to big George and headed out.

At that very moment, the door burst open, and in rushed Moira MacLeod, in such a hurry that she ran smack into John.

"Oh excuse me, Mister MacIntyre," she said, making no attempt to extricate her self from his arms. "I'm dreadfully sorry."

By the time the girl pulled herself away, John's face burned bright red. He continued out the door and walked slowly to the car. Valerie trudged along beside him, seething.

Inside the pub, Moira approached the bar. "George, have ye seen Alistair tonight?"

The barman shook his head and replied that he had not. Moira ordered a lager and lime and took it with her to a corner table, where she sat by herself, contemplating her fingernails. When she finished her drink, she returned to the bar and ordered another.

George complied, but as he set the drink before her, he said, "That's it fer you, my lass. I'm not supposed to be servin' you at all. Your ma would hae a fit, and you know it."

"I know, George, and I appreciate it, I really do." She offered one of her irresistible smiles.

The door opened, and Alistair entered the room, his chest heaving, and his brow dripping sweat. He spotted Moira and crossed to her.

"What is it? What's the matter? I got your message and came right away."

He didn't even acknowledge George, who stood waiting to take his order.

"Would ye like somethin', Alistair?"

"Oh aye, I'll have a pint of bitter. Thanks George."

The big man poured the umber liquid from the tap, crowned it with a perfect head, and delivered it to the table.

"Cheers."

Ali turned his attention back to Moira and tried to see into her downcast eyes. "So, what's goin' on?"

She didn't look up.

"It's my step-dad again. I can't go back there. I just can't."

Alistair waited patiently for her to continue, but she just stared at the table, sliding her glass back and forth through the puddle of water.

"So, what happened?"

Moira continued to scrutinize the patterns she was creating, completely ignoring the question.

"It's not my fault he's in that stupid wheelchair."

For a few moments, she said nothing more, then looked up, her eyes on fire.

Alistair had seen her like this before. He knew better than to push her. In her own good time, she continued with her story. "Remember when I phoned tae tell you about crashin' my bike?"

He nodded.

"Well, I didn't tell them anything about it. I said the scratches were from you letting a bramble bush go while we were pickin', and it smashed into my face. They believed me until mum saw the dents on the scooter. Actually, I think my stupid brother told on me. He thinks that if I'm in trouble, things will go easier for him. He's probably right, but still."

"Then what happened?"

"Oh aye. So then the old drunk told me I couldn't ride my scooter anymore, said it was too dangerous. I don't know why he cares, really I don't. He said I was causing my mum too much worry."

"So what did you say?"

"Well that's where I made my big mistake. I've never talked back to him before, but this time I did. I don't know what came over me, but I told him to take a flyin' leap, and he nearly did, right out of his chair at my throat. I told him there was nothing he could do to stop me, that I was a grown woman and perfectly capable of making my own decisions. My mum just stood there like a turnip, and Ian was no help at all."

Alistair suppressed the urge to smile, and Moira proceeded with her story.

"I knew the man couldn't catch me, but I also knew I'd have to go to sleep sometime, and I don't trust him. So I went to my room to pack some things. I heard the bastard telling Ian to remove a wheel from my bike so I couldn't ride it. I locked myself in until they'd gone to bed, then I sneaked out. I took the wheels off Alan's chair and tossed them over the crag. Knowing that Ian's as brainless as a toad, it didn't take me long to find my own wheel, hidden behind the shed. I put it back on and rode out as fast as I could. And here I am."

Alistair grinned at her, shaking his head. "So where are ye gonna' stay? What are ye gonna' do?"

"That's the part I don't know. That's why I needed to talk to you."

"Well, I suppose ye could stay at my place, at least until ye find something better. We'll have to sneak you in and out, though. You know how Missus Pratt is about that kind of thing."

"Oh I couldn't, but thanks for the offer. It would just get you thrown out. It's not worth the risk." Her face brightened with a glimmer of an idea.

"Wait a minute—"

She rose from the table and crossed to where George was busy polishing tumblers.

By the next night, The Crown and Thistle had a new waitress. Although Moira was really too young to be working the bar, if she also worked the dining room, serving drinks from the bar was perfectly legal. The arrangement was ideal for everyone concerned. In exchange for working several nights a week, Moira received free room and board. It also left her the flexibility to take the weekends off if the band had an engagement. She had considered explaining her situation at home to George, but decided not to. Instead, she said that the arrangement would be a real convenience. She knew that when her mother had time to think about it, she would agree that her moving out was a good idea.

It was time for her to be on her own. After all, she was nearly twenty years old, a grown woman.

CHAPTER 8

———◆◆◆———

Valerie headed home from the village with the nagging feeling that she'd forgotten something, but she hadn't. Rather, the feeling was one of loss. She'd posted her letters home, picked up some fresh rolls from the bakery, and some chops for dinner. As she slowed for the turn at St. Agnes church, she noticed a tall figure dressed in black standing among the gravestones. The man was studying one of the monuments. It was by far the most elaborate in the cemetery.

As though he felt her presence, the man turned and stared right at her. He raised his hand as if imparting a blessing, but blessed was far from what Valerie felt. It was then that she recognized him. It was the man they'd encountered on the day they arrived in Kilbride, the man leading the somber troop of boys. She felt the same chill she'd felt the first time she'd seen him.

At the house, she was surprised to find her husband out of his lair. Lately, he didn't often appear in the middle of the day. He was sitting on the verandah, staring off into space, as if he was in a trance. She sat down in the chair next to him. He paid no attention.

Valerie coughed discreetly, but he didn't respond. She tried again, this time a bit louder. Still nothing.

"John? Are you okay?"

He nodded but said nothing.

"John, I need to ask you something."

"Sure. Anything."

"Well, I need to know what's going on. Why does that girl have such an effect on you? It's impossible not to notice."

John glanced at his wife.

"I really can't explain it, Val, not even to myself. It's the strangest thing. I don't know if you can believe this, but I feel I know her. She's the image of the girl I've been writing about. They've even got the same last name."

Valerie blinked. "So you made her a character—"

"No, that's the crazy part. I wrote her before I ever saw her. That's why I had such a strong reaction that night at the Thistle. I'd like to think it's just a coincidence, but I'm not so sure. It's pretty damn weird."

Valerie looked away. "Yes it is."

✿ ✿ ✿

Later, in bed, Valerie lay quietly beside her husband. After a few minutes of uneasy silence, she spoke.

"Tell me more, John. Tell me more about her."

"Who?"

"You know who."

She rolled toward him and propped her head on her arm so she could see his face.

"I don't know what to tell you. I admit, it sounds crazy, but she's right there on the page. Sometimes, I feel like my mind is being invaded."

"John?"

"Yes?"

"Are you falling in love with the girl in your story?"

"Come on, Valerie. Of course not. She's fiction, for Pete's sake."

"Okay, John." She sighed and pulled away, leaving her husband to think about his lie.

In the corner of the room, a shadow moved, like someone had been standing there, listening. With her heart pounding, she stared into the darkness, but there was no further motion. She rolled onto her back, deciding that she'd probably just been spooked by John's bizarre revelations.

✡ ✡ ✡

In his richly paneled library, Gordon Erskin sat hunched over his desk, his face buried in a dusty old volume. The telephone purred softly. He reached for the receiver.

"Yes?"

"You were absolutely right. Things are proceeding as planned. I hear the woman is spending a great deal of time with Nesbit.

I think the poor chap's infatuated. It's more than we could have hoped for"

Erskin nodded thoughtfully.

"Yes, well I'm not surprised. You of all people should have a little faith."

CHAPTER 9

The Reverend Kenneth Drummond was not well liked. He'd been the minister at Saint Agnes kirk for almost five years, but he'd never felt totally accepted by his congregation. They had all loved Reverend Menzies up until his untimely death from a stroke. The old man had been a vigorous and happy soul, with a kind word for anybody he met. Drummond, on the other hand, exhibited few of those qualities. Some of the parishioners had actually admitted to being a little afraid of him.

After the death of Reverend Menzies, the church had been without a minister for some years. The village was too small to attract a qualified man. They'd been surprised when Drummond had arrived to take on the work of St. Agnes Kirk. He was a man with excellent credentials, educated at Edinburgh University, and the fact that he'd served four years in the military was viewed as a plus.

Most folks agreed the village boys could use some structure, and Drummond was good at structure. He'd done a stint as a chaplain in the marine guards, and during his deployment in the Falklands, had witnessed things that changed his life. It was during a firefight on a rocky beach where five of his comrades died that the headaches began. They'd never left.

He was a married to a mousy little woman who did little to advance the cause; rather, she kept to herself, participating in the work of the church only when absolutely necessary. Strangely enough, attendance at Sunday services was better than it had been during the tenure of Reverend Menzies. Although Drummond was not well liked, he was respected.

Every Wednesday evening, he conducted the meeting of his boys club, which he'd dubbed the New Covenanters. Although he'd remained an outsider with the adults, he seemed to have a strange affinity for the boys.

When asked about the minister, the Covenanters would invariably reply, "Och, he's all right. It's just that he likes all the military stuff. He's fond of the secrets and all."

Once a month, Drummond took the twenty or so boys on a field trip, hiking for miles across the hills. The boys often returned from the outings sullen and withdrawn, but were always eager to participate the next time. When asked what they did out in the wilds, they never offered any details, and since Drummond was ex-military and a Christian minister, the parents were inclined to just go along.

One or two members of the congregation had whispered that the reverend could make himself a bit more approachable if he would just abandon the black robe. Drummond had no intention of doing any such thing. He understood the power of a uniform and was pleased with the effect the robe had.

Sunday morning was cloudy and cool. John and Valerie were the last to arrive for the service at St. Agnes. The processional had already begun when they slipped quietly through the doors and found a vacant pew near the back of the church.

Valerie had been surprised by John's suggestion. They'd never been regular churchgoers. She'd gone along with the idea only because she was happy to have his companionship.

It was a lovely old sanctuary, simple in typical Scottish fashion, but warm and inviting. The muted colors of a large stained-glass window behind the chancel bathed the church in rose light in which even Rev. Drummond looked beatific. His lanky frame dwarfed the lectern, and his hymnbook almost disappeared within his huge hands. A mass of unruly auburn hair tossed in the light as he sang with great tuneless gusto.

John was moved by the sermon, impressed by the minister's eloquence and conviction. He was somewhat surprised by the appeal to Scottish nationalism that was woven into the address, but Drummond's power was undeniable. Valerie, on the other hand, felt like bolting. She felt uncomfortable in Drummond's presence and couldn't wait for the service to end.

After the closing hymn and the benediction, the congregation filed out. Seeing no way to avoid greeting the minister at the church door, Valerie strolled to the front of the church and made a pretense of studying the memorial windows. She noticed a small door, opened it, and slipped through. She found herself standing in the graveyard on the side where she'd seen Drummond examining one of the monuments. She moved through the headstones, making her way toward the vault that the clergyman had been studying so intently.

John was last in the line of worshippers, and when he reached the minister, he introduced himself.

"Oh, I already know who you are," the reverend exclaimed heartily as he shook John's hand.

John began to introduce his wife and was surprised that Valerie wasn't at his side. He returned his attention to the minister.

"So what brings a man such as you to this wee place?"

"Well if the truth be known, Reverend, I was born not far from here, in Edinburgh, actually, and I've been in your church before, although it was many years ago. I've returned to my roots, hoping that the surroundings will provide some inspiration for my writing."

"So you're a writer, are you? How interesting. You know, I'm from Edinburgh myself, oh aye. I still feel like a bit of an outsider here.

"Tell me, Mister MacIntyre, have you and your wife managed to make any friends since ye've been here? The folks can be a bit stand-offish, you know."

"Not really. I've been so immersed in my work that I've become a bit of a hermit I'm afraid. Valerie, my wife, she's made one or two friends, I think."

"So what kind of writing do you do, may I ask?"

"Well, I've started a Scottish historical novel. I've got a long way to go though. It's a daunting task."

"I'm sure it is. You know, it's a subject that really fascinates me. I pride myself on being the un-official historian around here. There are some very interesting stories that make up the history of this vale. Perhaps we could get together sometime and compare notes. Maybe I could be of some help to you."

John suddenly remembered that he'd left his wife to fend for herself. He excused himself, promising Drummond that their discussion would continue some other time.

He found her in the cemetery, surveying the inscription on a large, elaborately carved monument, by far the grandest one in the graveyard. The monument was ancient, much older than the church.

John walked up behind his wife and spoke her name. She jumped and barely managed to stifle a scream.

"John, dammit, you scared the sh…eh life out of me. Don't do that."

"I'm sorry, darling. I didn't mean to scare you."

He put his arm around her and peered at the plaque she'd been studying. "What's this?" He traced his fingers across the inscription that was barely legible.

"Somebody Campbell," he read aloud, *"'Lord of Argyll, felled by the horns of fate, here to rest 'til the judgment come.* My God!'"

"What's wrong?"

"Well, it's completely nuts. But, I'm writing about this guy, and I thought I made him up. Pretty creepy, huh?" He saw her blanch and quickly changed the subject. "Hey, are you hungry? Why don't we go get some lunch?"

He took her hand, and they walked slowly to the car. He tried to appear calm, although he was anything but. The tomb of a Campbell chieftain from the time he was writing about? He couldn't wait to continue his conversation with Reverend Drummond.

Doris's Tearoom was full, but after waiting for just a few minutes, they were seated at a table right in the middle of the room.

When John's bountiful breakfast arrived, Valerie could only shake her head.

"Well," he shrugged, "someone has to bear the fat burden for this family. If it was left to you, we'd both live to be a hundred and twenty, and you know we could never afford it."

"That's not funny, John. Don't joke about things like that. I'm serious. However, I would like to know why your cholesterol is seventy points below mine."

"Honey, it's in the blood, you know, that good Scottish blood. It's not my fault."

As they enjoyed their meal, they nodded to the other diners, who greeted them. A few minutes later, Jock Tavish entered the place, noticed them, and strode toward them. He doffed his cap to Valerie and addressed John.

"I've got a letter fer you at the post office. Came in late Friday, oh aye, all the way from California. Man's hand I'd say. Do ye want me to send it out with Graham in the mornin', or do you want to get it yerself? Either way's fine with me, but Graham's probably comin' out there. He's there a lot, from what I hear."

John, seeing Valerie's cheeks flush, said calmly, "You can send it out with Graham if you like, Jock. He's been coming out regularly to help me with some things. And the letter, it's probably from our son." He paused, eyeing the postmaster carefully. "Is there anything important in it? Or just the regular news?"

Jock grunted like he'd been punched in the stomach.

"Now Mister MacIntyre, I don't believe that you would think–."

John raised his hand to stop him.

"Just kidding, Jock, just a wee joke. Have a nice day."

Jock pulled himself together and strode out of the place with as much dignity as he could muster.

"John, that was cruel," Valerie whispered when the door closed behind the postman.

"Cruel, but fair, my girl. I just don't think that he should be allowed to meddle free of charge. Serves him right."

They finished their meal and decided to have a wander through the village. They passed a young couple out for a stroll with their children. Valerie stopped to admire the beautiful baby in his brand new pram. When the couple moved on, she took John's arm.

"You know John, everything's so real here. I don't think a psychiatrist could make a living in this valley."

John nodded his assent, although he wasn't entirely in agreement.

CHAPTER 10

John got dressed and descended to the kitchen. It was too early for Missus Small, so he brewed his own coffee, just as strong as he liked it, and sat out on the verandah enjoying the crisp morning air. He thought about his book, the only thing he seemed to think about these days. Although he was pleased with how the work was going, he was troubled by the strange parallels he couldn't explain.

Before leaving the house, he headed back upstairs to leave a thermos of coffee at Valerie's bedside. Mercifully, she'd lapsed back into her dream. He grabbed his camera from the dresser and headed back downstairs. He left the house by the back door and crossed the beach to the boatshed, winched *Bridie* down to the jetty, climbed aboard, and pointed her toward Campbell Keep. He felt excited but apprehensive. Something told him it would be a memorable day.

A half hour later, he was floating in the shadow of the old fortress, searching for a place to beach the craft. He found no landing on the rocky shore and made his way around the outcropping, hoping for something better on the other side. Much to his surprise, he came into a small, protected cove, quite hidden from the loch where the smell of stagnation disappeared and the water was clear of weeds.

Rather than run the boat aground on the pebble beach, John tossed the anchor over the side and found purchase no more than ten feet below. He regarded the shore some fifty feet away and wondered how he was going to get there without getting his clothes wet. He didn't really want to go exploring in wet clothes. He thought about it for a minute, looked around, and remembered Missus Small telling him that the locals avoided the place.

Feeling as carefree as a kid, he peeled off his clothes, wrapped his things in a piece of tarp, and hopped over the side. His heart nearly went into revolt. He couldn't believe how cold the water was. When he eventually regained his breath, he reached for his clothes and started swimming to shore, holding the bundle high above his head.

By the time MacIntyre pulled himself onto the beach, he was shivering violently and slightly blue. He dressed quickly, donned his shoes, and began scouting for a route up to the fortress.

After a half hour of searching, John grew frustrated. Sheer cliffs mocked him at every turn. He formed a real appreciation of just how impregnable Campbell Keep was. After exhausting every conceivable possibility, he returned to the shore, disappointed. Once again, he stripped off his clothes, not at all eager to reenter the icy water.

When he reached the boat, he hung for a minute on the rail, catching his breath before hauling himself over the side. With some effort, he pulled himself aboard and made for the foredeck, intending to stretch out there and warm himself in the sun. As he climbed around the windscreen, a movement caught his eye. He looked up to see Moira MacLeod draped across the stern bench, wearing nothing but damp underwear and a cheeky smile.

As if the situation wasn't embarrassing enough, he noticed that his manhood had been severely diminished by the icy water. Aware that his face was bright red, he sat down with his back to the girl. Dignity was something John cherished.

The girl laughed heartily, and the sound echoed around the cove.

"Good mornin', Mister MacIntyre. So, I gather you weren't expectin' me."

John gathered the presence of mind to reach for his clothes. As he pulled on his trousers, the girl chattered on, totally unfazed.

"Actually I've been watching you since ye got here. You see, I think of this as my own private place and was curious about who might be trespassing."

As John listened to her voice, a warm prickling sensation spread slowly across his scalp. Unable to resist, he glanced over his shoulder, and just like the night he'd first seen her, he couldn't tear his eyes away. His gaze lingered on her long slim legs and her thrusting breasts, and by the time they reached her face, he had trouble finding his voice. She met his eyes with ease, as though he was nothing more than a camera lens. She was in complete control, an uncomfortable scenario for him.

"So what are you lookin' for, then?"

He averted his eyes. "I was eh—trying to find a way up to the Keep. I guess you know I wasn't successful." Now that he was clothed, he felt more comfortable.

"Well, I could show you the way if you've a mind. There aren't many that knows the way up, but I suppose it would be all right. You seem like a man who can be trusted to keep a secret."

"Oh yes, absolutely." John chastened himself for sounding so damned eager.

"Ye'll have to take your clothes off again, though. I left mine on the shore."

Moira stood up, giving John a moment to appraise her before diving into the black water. He peeled off quickly, gathered his clothes in a bundle, and followed her over the side. This time, he left his shorts on.

On the beach, Moira retrieved her things from where she'd left them, and after they'd both dressed, led the way toward the cliff, pointing out a deep fissure in the rock. He followed her through the cleft into a small enclosure. She crossed the sandy floor and pulled aside a thick bush to reveal a set of well-worn steps.

"Are you ready?" she asked, grinning. As she began the climb, he was right behind her.

Thick moss covered the walls of the passage, and the water that dripped from the stone ceiling made the path slippery in places. A couple of times, he lost his footing and was forced to reach out to steady himself. Moira never missed a step. They climbed upward for fifteen minutes or so and emerged from the tunnel high above the cove.

By the time they reached the fortress, John was struggling for breath and trying his best to disguise the fact. Up close, Campbell Keep seemed even more formidable. Thick walls towered high above them, blocking out the sun. John turned back to see the path they'd taken, but it was hidden from view. He felt as if he'd been transported to another world.

Moira led the way around the base of the walls until they reached the fortress gates. Although partially crumbled and obscured by overgrowth, the gate towers still managed to convey their intended menace.

They climbed over a pile of boulders and entered a large courtyard that lay completely in shadow. John shivered as a chill brushed his skin, which was damp again from the exertion of the climb.

Moira scampered across the courtyard to a flight of steps that had been hewn from the interior wall, and started up. John followed, careful not to look down. High above him, a company of ravens sat watching his progress. He looked up just in time to see them rise into the air, cawing in protest. At that moment, the stone on which they'd congregated broke loose from the parapet, fell to the courtyard floor, and shattered into a thousand pieces.

At the sound of the stone smashing, Moira looked down at him and shrugged.

But John had a feeling his presence was not welcome—that the Keep resented the intrusion. He pushed the thoughts aside and kept climbing. A few harrowing minutes later, he stood on the very highest ramparts, looking out over the loch and the purple hills beyond. He leaned on the parapet, breathing deeply.

"Amazing," he whispered.

"It is that. Worth the effort, isn't it?"

"Oh yeah." He nodded, smiling, unable to remember the last time he'd felt so alive.

"Come and see this," said Moira with unabashed excitement.

She ran the length of the battlement and disappeared through a small door.

John followed, bowing his head to get through, and stepped into a tiny chamber where the ceiling was so low it touched his hair. The room felt warm from the sun, with only the slightest breeze coming through the slit windows. Moira slid to the floor and leaned against the wall.

"There's a great treasure hidden in this fortress, you know."

John flopped down beside her.

"But it's sealed away," she continued, "deep under the Keep, in Campbell's tomb. And it's protected by a terrible curse."

At the mention of the word, a strange sound began. Hushed voices whispered from the walls, as if passing a secret. Alarmed, John glanced at Moira. She sat with her eyes closed, completely unperturbed, as if the incantations were meant for his ears only. He listened, trying to understand what was being said, but couldn't.

"It's only the wind," she said softly.

Looking around, he realized that the tiny slit windows were responsible for the strange soughing.

Relieved, he asked, "You come here all by yourself?"

"Oh aye. I'm not afraid. I like it here. I feel safe."

"So, tell me more. Tell me about yourself."

"There's not much to tell, really–at least not yet."

"Well, tell me what there is."

So she did. She described her quiet life in the vale, her life with her family, and her plans for the future. John listened attentively, captivated by the melody of her voice, terribly aware of her nearness and afraid to look at her face. He was feeling things he shouldn't.

✡ ✡ ✡

Too soon for John, they returned to the sunshine and began the hike back down to the beach. He hadn't seen nearly enough, but when he looked at his watch, he was surprised to see how the time had flown. Pangs of guilt prodded him. He knew Valerie would be worried.

As they said their goodbyes, Moira requested that he tell no one about their morning together.

John happily agreed. He bent to kiss her cheek, but she pulled out of reach.

"Mister MacIntyre, can I ask you something before I go?"

"Of course."

She smiled coyly. "Do you find me attractive?"

"Well…you're a very beautiful girl. I'm sure all men find you attractive."

"But I don't care about them. It's your opinion that I care about." She moved closer.

"I, I–"

She put a finger to his lips, raised herself up on her tiptoes, and kissed him on the mouth.

"Well, I think you do. And it's okay. I quite like it."

✿ ✿ ✿

When John arrived back at Ainsley House, Valerie stood waiting on the beach with Graham Nesbit. She ran into her husband's arms.

"Where have you been? I was worried sick. We were just about to come looking for you."

Graham's face showed his concern.

"She can be a right-dangerous old loch, Mister MacIntyre, especially for someone who doesn't know her moods. I'm glad you're all right. I'll be off then, Valerie."

He nodded and headed back toward the house.

Focused on her husband, Valerie offered a cursory wave.

"Where did you go?"

John was excited to tell her all about it, even though he knew she'd be upset with him. He took her by the arm and led her back into the house.

In the living room, when he'd poured himself a whiskey, he began his story.

"Well, as a matter of fact, I went to the Keep."

"You what? You know I asked you not to go there. You deceived me."

"Well, I was going to tell you, but when I left, you were sleeping, and I didn't want to wake you."

John figured that if he just kept talking, he would soften her ire. "Anyway, I got out there and decided to look for a way up to the top."

He suddenly remembered the promise he'd made.

"But, unfortunately, I couldn't find one."

John felt terrible about having to lie to her.

Valerie studied her husband's face. He was acting strange again. She didn't know what to make of it.

"However, I did find a great little cove. I anchored the boat and sat there to just think for a bit. I guess I must have fallen asleep. I'm sorry honey. I didn't mean to worry you."

Valerie was still mad at him, but relieved he was safe. She had no reason not to believe him.

"Well, I bet you're pretty hungry, Captain Cook. Come on, I'll fix you a sandwich."

✡ ✡ ✡

Later that evening, John sat staring into the fire, remembering the events of the day. There were so many things he couldn't explain. He'd felt the power of both the Keep and Moira MacLeod.

Valerie had to repeat her question before he responded.

"So would you like to hear how the kids are doing without us?" John managed to focus.

"I'm sorry, honey. I was somewhere else."

"You certainly were. I was talking about the letter. You remember—the one from your son."

"Oh yeah. Sorry. So, how are they?"

"They're just fine. Annie's still in Aspen, but Johnny seems to be doing fine by himself. He sure doesn't sound lonely. He says they're talking about getting married next summer. He wonders if Scotland would be a good place for their honeymoon."

"Married? That's funny. Hell, he doesn't even know how to pick up his socks."

"That's true." She had a thought. "John, you don't think they stay together at the house when we're away, do you?"

John looked away and rolled his eyes. "No honey, not a chance. They wouldn't dare."

For the second time that day, he decided that what Valerie didn't know wouldn't hurt her.

An hour later, he was back at work. His book was becoming a very demanding consort.

Long after the sun had risen, Campbell stirred in his bed. His body felt like he'd endured a dozen battles. He was in a foul temper. He lay still, trying to will away the searing pain from inside his skull while the events of the night before assembled in his mind. When his thoughts turned to the Lady MacLeod, he winced. He sat straight up and peered around the chamber. He was alone.

He couldn't remember what had transpired after the girl had been deposited in his room, but he knew that it hadn't been totally satisfying. With a burst of inspiration, he leaned over the side of his bed, lifted the linen bed skirt, and looked underneath. It was a big mistake. So overcome was Campbell by the rush of blood and pain, that he tumbled from the bed onto the stone floor.

"Guard!" He tried to shout, but managed only a gurgle. On the second attempt, he made himself heard, and the doors burst open to admit two men, one bearing a battle-axe, the other a drawn sword.

They watched impassively as their chief pulled himself up off the floor.

"Where is she?"

The men looked confused. The larger one addressed his chief. "Who, my lord? Where is who?"

"The girl, damn it. The girl who was here with me last night."

The smaller man found his courage and offered a reply. "Sire, it's late in the morning, and we've been at our post merely these last three hours. No one has entered nor left your lordship's chamber during that time."

Campbell's fury filled the room. "Who then was at post before you?"

Neither of the men wanted to respond, but they knew the futility of obfuscation. The smaller one answered again, eyes on the floor. "It was Jamie, Sire, the youngest son of Frederick. He was posted because he was the only one who could still stand."

"Throw him in the dungeon."

He dismissed the men with a flourish. They scurried gratefully from the chamber.

After Campbell had bathed, dressed, and eaten, he felt better. He summoned his officers to the great hall and issued his instructions.

In three days' time, he announced, he would journey east to pay a visit to Duncan MacLeod. He would require thirty men. The journey would take the better part of four days, so the cooks would have to start readying provisions immediately. The stewards would gather suitable gifts, for the Earl had announced that it was his intention to ask for the hand of Lady Eileen Macleod.

Pleased with his plan, Campbell dismissed his men. Only William of Alsh remained behind.

"Malcolm," said Alsh, treading carefully, "is this really such a good idea? You've just returned from a terrible battle, and you're far from healed. Would it not be more prudent to take some days to rest, so as to make an even finer impression on the Lord MacLeod and his fair daughter?"

Campbell searched the man's face, looking for his real motive.

Alsh looked unwaveringly into the eyes of his chief, all too aware of the political implications of Campbell's plan. The girl's betrothed lacked the might of the Campbells, but he knew that young Douglas could make himself a bloody nuisance. They certainly didn't want him as an enemy. At the same time, Alsh was sure the girl's father could be bought. The advantages of being related by marriage to Campbell would not be lost on an old fox like Duncan MacLeod.

Brothock Castle, seat of the MacLeods, sat high on a wind-swept bluff overlooking the wild North Sea. In the great hall, which was much more modest than Campbell's, Duncan MacLeod sat solemnly listening to Campbell's emissaries. An alliance with the Campbells, one that would be difficult to break because of a marriage, sounded tempting indeed. He would, however, have to weigh the consequences of a breach of agreement with Robert Douglas. There were many things to consider. The feelings of his daughter were the least of them.

When the emissaries had concluded their entreaties, MacLeod turned to the gaunt man seated at his right elbow. The man was impeccably dressed in a fine black robe, black stockings, and elegant French shoes. His skin was as pale as parchment, and his bony fingers were heavy with rings. His glittering eyes betrayed nothing.

"Well Lasker, what dae ye think? What dae ye make of all this?"

Lasker took his time before responding.

"There is certainly a great deal of possibility in the offerings at hand, I grant ye. Being given control of the lands west from here to Perthshire is indeed a boon, but our enemies won't take to it kindly. I recommend that we await the arrival of the Campbell himself and see what assurances he delivers."

Duncan rose imperiously and addressed a waiting attendant.

"See that these men are housed and fed. They have traveled far and are most welcome here. Begin the preparations, for in three days, we will be visited by Lord Campbell. I want him to enjoy the very best we have to offer."

Duncan MacLeod strode from the room, trying to look as important as possible. Three steps behind him trotted Lasker.

Eileen MacLeod sat quietly in the window seat of her chamber lost in thought, reflecting on all that had happened at Campbell Keep. She'd been back home at Brothock for only a few days, but had resolved that never again would she journey so far, unless of course she was with her beloved Robert. She was terribly worried about him. Six days before, he had departed from his home in Kintyre to face the English at Campbell's side. He had leaped at the chance to fight.

Eileen had received Robert's message about meeting him and had traveled to the Keep to await his return from the battle, but he hadn't appeared with the others. She'd questioned anyone who would listen about Robert Douglas, but she got no information. At last, she found a man who'd seen him shortly after the battle. He remembered specifically a red-haired Douglas riding a chestnut horse alongside a young lad on a bay mare. Greatly relieved, Eileen resolved to wait as patiently as possible for Robert's return.

The next afternoon, there was still no sign of him.

When the opportunity to do the sword dance for Lord Campbell had presented itself, Eileen had jumped at the chance, thinking that she might get a word with the chief. She would try to convince him to *help her. She couldn't possibly scour the hills by herself, but a band of Campbells on horseback would be quite another thing. She knew she did the dance very well and resolved to capture Argyll's attention. She'd never dreamed just how well she might succeed.*

A knock on the door snapped Eileen back to the present.

"Come in."

A pretty girl of about seventeen poked her head around the door. "I must speak with you, m'Lady."

"What is it, Meg? Is it news of Robert?" She rose to her feet.

"No, my Lady, it's not about Robert, but I've got some bad news, I'm afraid. I overheard that the Earl of Argyll is on his way here from Campbell Keep. He intends to ask for your hand in marriage. It seems he thought a lot more of you than you did of him, and from the reaction of your father while he was listening to Argyll's messengers, it looks as though he will break his agreement with Douglas."

If Eileen hadn't been standing beside the bed, she would certainly have fallen to the floor.

She groaned and sank onto the coverlet.

"It can't be so. What am I to do? Oh, Robert my love. Where are you when I need you so much?"

Eileen began to cry.

The prospect of living her life with Campbell was unthinkable. She had to find a way out. Eileen understood from experience that it would be no use pleading with her father. Duncan MacLeod was a shrewd man, and the opportunity to form an alliance with Campbell would be irresistible for him.

If only her brother James was home from the wars in Europe. He would never permit such horror. He'd been gone so long this time, and she missed him more than ever.

She murmured his name and the name of her beloved as she began to pray.

John's eyes slowly closed and his head fell onto his chest. He slumped in his chair fast asleep, murmuring the prayer, unaware that the voice was not his own, and the dialect was one he'd never spoken.

✵ ✵ ✵

Alistair didn't know what to think. Moira had just left his flat, and he couldn't for the life of him imagine what had happened. She was happier than she'd been in weeks, and she'd been talking with great enthusiasm about her music and her future. At no time, however, did she include him in her plans. She'd told him about someone she thought might help her career, but she didn't mention any names.

He rose from the sagging couch and began rummaging around the room in search of the capo he knew was there somewhere. Finally, he found it sitting on top of the toaster, of all places. He reached for his guitar, applied the capo, and began to play. He was in the mood for the blues. As he played, Alistair thought of Moira. But then, he always did.

He played until he tired of his mood, slipped on his new running shoes, and headed for the pub, determined to drown his sorrows. It was just past five when he entered the quiet bar. He spotted Moira sitting at a corner table with Reverend Drummond, of all people. Alistair was surprised. He'd never before seen the minister in the pub.

Moira didn't see him enter, so he crossed to a place at the bar where he could watch without being seen. The conversation was animated; Moira repeatedly shook her head. The minister reached for her hand, but she pulled it away.

"It's not right," she said, loudly enough for everyone to hear. "I don't want to have any more to do with it."

Drummond sighed in defeat, pushed back his chair, and rose to leave. "I'm sure you'll change your mind, Moira, when you've had a chance to consider."

As soon as the door banged shut, Alistair rushed over to the table. Moira glowered at him, her eyes flashing.

"Is it him?" he asked. "Is he the one—the one who's going to take you away from all this? And what does he want in return, may I ask?"

"You must be daft. Maybe you're *all* daft, you men. Here's the minister, trying to pressure me into singing for him at some stupid program in his measly wee kirk, and you, you're thinking the most despicable things about me. You're a right plonk, Ali. Do you know that?"

Moira kicked back her chair and stomped out.

CHAPTER 11

———— ◆◆◆ ————

Graham battled the weeds in the front of his modest house. The flower garden had been his mother's obsession, and since her death, it had become his responsibility. Over the years, he'd tried to keep the beds as tidy as his mother would have wanted.

He heard the gate squeak, and looked up to see Valerie MacIntyre walking up the path toward him, looking most beguiling in blue jeans and a simple white tee-shirt. With some effort, he dismissed his prurience.

"Morning, Graham." The flush in her cheeks told him she was shy about being there.

Although the misunderstanding between them had been resolved, he still detected a certain distance. He was angry with himself, knowing how close he'd come to ruining the only real friendship he'd had in years. There had been Moira, of course, but she was only a girl, and he hadn't seen much of her lately. Occasionally, Graham found female companionship on his visits to Oban or Glasgow, but his feelings for Valerie MacIntyre were something quite different.

"Hello, Missus MacIntyre," he said. "And what brings you calling on such a lovely morning?"

"Well, I tried phoning you, but there was no answer. Then I saw you here in the garden when I was driving by."

"Oh I'm sorry," he said, "I keep meaning to get a secretary, but I keep forgetting. Would you like a cup of tea?"

"Oh aye, that would be very nice, if it's nae too much bother," she responded, using a very passable Scottish brogue.

"Och, it's nae bother, nae bother at all," he grinned. "Nice accent, by the way."

Valerie wasn't aware that she'd slipped into the dialect, but it came as no surprise. She was an incorrigible mimic. Any time she visited a new country, she acquired the accent in no time. It had, for years, been a source of amusement for her husband because she never realized she was doing it.

They entered the house, and Graham headed for the kitchen. Valerie made herself at home in the living room, absorbing all she could about Graham Nesbit, past and present. It was a comfortable, homey room, although it felt more like the parlor of an old married couple than that of a young bachelor. There were dozens of framed photographs, some of Graham as a college student and several of him as a boy. One in particular caught Valerie's attention. There was something haunting about it. The picture was of young Nesbit and another boy standing in front of a very unusual church whose roof was in the shape of a crown. Graham looked bored. His companion looked angry.

Nesbit returned to the room carrying a tray and found Valerie intently studying the model sloop that occupied one entire corner of the room. The mast was nearly as tall as she was.

"You like it?"

"Yes. I love boats, but I've got to tell you, I've never seen a model as beautiful as this one."

"Well actually, the Cygnet's more than just a model. She's a fully functional racing ship. She wins the local regatta almost every year. She's actually my most prized possession." He spoke with real reverence. "She was very special to my father."

"I can see why." Valerie crouched down and stroked the gleaming hull.

When they were comfortably settled into the well-worn chairs, sipping tea and nibbling on shortbread biscuits, Valerie eventually got around to the reason for her visit.

"Tell me, Graham: What do you know about this Moira MacLeod?"

He studied her for a moment before responding.

"Well, she is a fine singer. She has a way with her that can captivate an audience. I think she's destined for great things; if she can just get heard by the right people. She's also the best-lookin lassie in the vale…present company excepted, of course."

Valerie became serious. "You see—and I don't know why I'm telling you this—but my husband seems to be totally captivated by her. He says it's because she reminds him of the girl in the book he's writing, but I'm not so sure. Should I be concerned, Graham? What kind of a person is she?"

He took a moment to answer.

"She's a good girl, Valerie. She doesn't run around with men. There is one young fellow in her life, but I think it's more his enchantment than hers. From what I can see, she's very focused on her career. It's the most important thing in her life."

"But I've seen her flirt with my husband, and unfortunately, I've watched him respond. He hasn't actually spent any time with her, but I'm not sure what to think. I certainly don't want to overreact. Maybe I'm being silly."

"Ye know, Valerie, it's hard fer me to tell you what to do. Maybe Moira thinks that your husband could help her with her dream. You two are certainly the most influential people she's ever had a chance to meet. Maybe she's just trying to make the most of it. Having been on the receiving end of some heartbreak myself, though, I do think it's wise to be careful. That was my big mistake."

He stared out the window toward the rose garden.

"Oh Graham, I'm sorry. Here I am, completely caught up in my own problems, as if they were all that mattered. What happened? Do you want to talk about it?"

She leaned forward, ready to commiserate.

"Thanks, but not today; maybe some other time, when it's my turn. In the meantime, all I can say is, don't be paranoid, but don't be blind. If there's nothing there, you shouldn't create something, but if there is something, it's best you know while you can do something about it."

Graham took a sip of tea. "How much longer are you gonne be here in the vale?"

"We were supposed to leave in just over two weeks, but now John's talking about extending our stay. His work's going well, and I just can't deny him. He's waited so long for this."

"Well if there's anything I can do, don't you hesitate to ask."

"Yes, thanks, and thanks for listening. I didn't come here looking for advice. I just needed someone to listen to me. I wondered if my concerns would sound totally nuts if I spoke them out loud."

"Well, they don't, and I feel right complimented that you chose to share them with me."

Valerie took a long breath and found Graham's eyes. "Won't you tell me about what happened to you, if it's not too personal?"

"It's a bit late to be worrying about being too personal, don't you think?" He chuckled, and his eyes smiled back at her.

"Yes, I suppose it is. I'd like to know, though, what keeps you here in this place. I can see that you're an educated man, and I'm curious about why you've chosen this life."

"It was never really a choice, Valerie. I've found that sometimes, life makes the choices for us. You see, some things happened to me years ago that made life in Kilbride a welcome respite."

"Your heartbreak?"

He nodded. "I was at the University of Edinburgh, studying history and archeology. I had dreams then. I was going to explore this country, unearth her hidden treasures and find out all I could about her past.

"But things started going badly for me. First, I received word from home that the girl I was engaged to had run away with another man. Then my father died. I'm afraid I reacted badly. I found myself drinking too much, doing drugs—bad drugs—and failing at school. My supposed friends encouraged all my bad habits until we'd drained my bank account. I was eventually expelled, and returned home to Kilbride, the Prodigal Son. My mother made me suffer for it, I assure you."

Graham's thoughts seemed to drift away.

"I'm sorry, Graham. It was really none of my business."

"That's okay. It's not often I speak of it. It's probably good for me to do so now and then, although I don't much enjoy re-living it."

Valerie rose to leave.

"Ye know," said Nesbit as he stood, "getting back to your own predicament, I understand that you don't want any advice, but here goes anyway."

He placed his big hands on Valerie's shoulders, and gazed into her eyes. "There's an old expression, 'familiarity breeds contempt'. Now, maybe instead of John being allowed to make Moira whatever he wants in his mind, he should see more of her in reality. It's been my experience that the fantasy is vastly more exciting. If he spends any time with her at all, he'll come to realize that she's only a wee girl, and that he already has the very best he could possibly hope for."

He opened the front door, and Valerie squeezed past into the sunshine.

"Thank you Graham, thank you so much."

She stood on her tiptoes and deposited a grateful peck on his cheek.

As she made her way back down the path, enjoying the banquet of flowers, she looked up to see Jock Tavish riding past on his dilapidated bicycle. He doffed his cap and offered a cryptic smile.

CHAPTER 12

———◆◆◆———

By nine o'clock, the Thistle was full, as usual. Jock was firmly ensconced at his regular table with his florid-faced pals, regaling them with his stories, basking in the attention.

"Oh aye, she was so flat-chested, we had to have 'front' stamped on her t-shirts." His companions roared with laughter, as if they'd never heard the story before.

Just then, the door opened to admit the MacIntyres, who were greeted warmly by big George. At Jock's table, the guffaws gave way to quiet whispers, but the MacIntyres didn't notice. Although they didn't spot an empty table, they were invited to join a group sitting beside the fire. John ordered a round of drinks.

"So, how are you enjoying your stay in our wee valley?" asked the pert little woman seated beside Valerie.

"I really can't say enough about how beautiful this place is. You all must be very proud," Valerie replied."

"It's hard to know, really. I've never been anywhere else." The others at the table smiled in agreement.

"Well trust me," said Valerie, "you won't find any place in the world more beautiful than this."

She pretended not to notice her husband searching the room.

A few minutes later, the band took the stage and played a couple of songs. They were greeted with polite applause. Moira didn't appear. As the time went on, John squirmed in his chair, anxiously drumming his fingers on the tabletop. He could barely make conversation. He kept looking over his shoulder, watching the front door. Valerie remained civil.

The band finished the set and left the stage—still no Moira. Valerie excused herself from the table and was immediately joined by three other women.

John smiled to himself, recognizing that the time-honored ritual applied even in rural Argyllshire.

A familiar voice interrupted his musing.

"Good evening, Mister MacIntyre. And how are you this fine evenin'? You look very well, I must say."

John managed not to drop his glass or stammer. It was just as well, because the others at the table were watching him closely. He started to stand, but thought better of it.

"Miss MacLeod. It's nice to see you, you're looking eh...very well yourself."

John felt everyone's eyes focused on him.

"You're not singing tonight then?"

"No. Actually I'm not. I've had it with that stupid band. That Alistair Frazier thinks he owns me, and I assure you, nobody owns Moira MacLeod."

John thought he detected a fleeting wink, but decided that it was only his hopeful imagination.

"I've just come on, and I wanted to deliver a drink, courtesy of George."

John nodded his thanks to the bartender, but the big man offered no response. She placed a large whisky before John and a glass of white wine at Valerie's place, flashed a smile, and made her way back to the bar.

He managed not to watch. Instead, he focused his attention on his drink and carefully raised it to his lips, aware that his hands were shaking. For some reason, the coaster remained stuck to the bottom of the glass. As he was about to remove it, he noticed something written on it. The word *TOMORROW* stared up at him through the amber liquid.

He took a quick swallow, returned the glass to the table, and managed to slip the coaster into his pocket just as Valerie returned to the table. He smiled guiltily, unsure of how much she'd seen.

✿ ✿ ✿

The evening proceeded without incident, and they stayed on until closing time. Valerie enjoyed the company of her new acquaintances and chose to ignore her husband's preoccupation.

She'd had more to drink than usual and hummed happily on the way home. John was relieved. Presumably, she hadn't seen Moira at the table.

As they neared Ainsley, John gazed across the water in the direction of the Keep, thinking about Moira and their plans for the next day. As he watched, he saw what looked like a light, high up in the fortress tower. He blinked and looked again. There was indeed a light, swaying back and forth like a signal. He eased back the throttles.

"Valerie, look—look there." His voice was thick with excitement. As Valerie followed his pointing finger, the light disappeared.

"What is it?" she asked, hearing the urgency in his voice.

"Nothing…I guess. I was probably just seeing things. Maybe too much of the old malt."

He opened the throttles a little and cruised slowly toward the house. He turned back for another look, but there was only darkness.

✵ ✵ ✵

High in the fortress, a slender figure walked toward the tower room with her candle lantern swaying in her hand. She opened the door and stepped inside, placed the lantern on the floor of the chamber, opened the slide, and snuffed out the flame. She stretched her body out on the cold stone and stared up into the darkness.

✵ ✵ ✵

At the house, instead of going to his study to read through his pages, as was his habit, John immediately readied for bed. In the kitchen, he poured himself a glass of water and called to Valerie, asking if she wanted one. She replied in the affirmative and went about turning off the living-room lights before making her way upstairs.

In her dressing room, she wrestled with a too-familiar dilemma. She knew that what she wore to bed sent definite signals. Over the years, they'd developed an understanding based on her choice of attire. If she decided on something provocative, her message was clear. If she went with the floor-length flannel, John knew there would be no cuddling that night.

Valerie didn't make all the boudoir rules, although for the first few years they were married, her husband referred to her as the warden. But these days, she was all too aware of his physical avoidance. She'd tried to rationalize that after twenty-three years of marriage, it was silly not to expect some ebb in his ardor, but this was more than just the sex.

Tonight, she was in a quandary. She needed to be close to her husband, but she didn't want to pressure him. Then she remembered the nightie she'd bought just before leaving home. She opened the bottom drawer of the dresser and pulled the ace from the bottom of the pile. In the safety of the bathroom, she held it against her, and after careful consideration, decided to go for it. She climbed out of her jeans and tee shirt and slipped the nightie on. It was perfect: not too obvious but very flattering. It emphasized her full breasts, and she knew he liked that. She'd always been a little self conscious about them, but John had managed to convince her that they were a wonderful contribution to their marriage. Her dowry, he called them.

Valerie felt pleased with her decision. She would look alluring without making John feel obligated.

She applied just a dab of his favorite nighttime fragrance, and slipped silently into the bedroom, where she found John asleep, snoring like a bulldog. She stood watching him for a moment, sighed softly, and withdrew. She returned the negligee to the drawer and donned the flannel. She covered her eyes, trying to shove the tears away, trying to be brave. It didn't work.

By the time she awakened the next morning, John was gone. Beside the coffee pot on the bedside table, she found his note:

Gone back to the Keep. Know you have no interest.

Back by supper time, J.

Don't be mad. I love you.

Valerie stared at the wallpaper. The floral pattern swam before her through angry tears.

☆ ☆ ☆

John's heart was in his throat as *Bridie* thundered across the loch. Not since he'd been a teenager had he felt this kind of excitement. A twinge of guilt was quickly banished to his subconscious. He focused his thoughts on Moira and began to feel downright giddy. It seemed to take forever to reach the Keep.

At last he rounded the rocky outcropping and entered the cove beyond the fortress. The sound of the engines echoed back to him from the granite slabs. He cut back the throttles, and the exhaust burbled softly. He floated on the black water, searching the shore for any sign of Moira, and his heart sank.

"She isn't here," he said.

He felt like an old fool. He shut off the engines, tossed the anchor over the side, and rummaged through his knapsack for a writing pad. He settled himself comfortably in the stern bench and stared up at the towering walls. From his angle, the fortress floated in the clouds, like a lost world.

As if he'd been summoned, his thoughts began to drift.

Robert Douglas was glad to be finally leaving the cave where they'd been forced to hide for three days. He hadn't seen his young brother take the blow that was the reason for their present predicament.

When it had happened, the battle was already over, and they'd been heading back to the Keep. Hamish's horse had suddenly bolted, taking off across the low hills to the west, heading directly into the path of the retreating English. By the time Robert realized what was happening, Hamish was well gone. He spurred his own mount and took off in pursuit, wondering why his brother was unable to slow his horse.

As he drew closer, Douglas saw that Hamish's head was lolling on his chest. He was slumped in his saddle, unconscious, but somehow he was wedged in place and couldn't fall. By the time Robert reached him, he could hear the sounds of the English army just over the hill. Just then, by the grace of God, Hamish slipped from his saddle and fell to the ground. His horse continued on at a dead run.

Robert knew that when the English encountered the animal, they would come looking, searching for any Scot to torture and kill as some measure of vengeance for an ignominious defeat.

When he reached his brother, Robert saw the blood-soaked shirt, and the ragged gash in Hamish's shoulder. Unfortunately, there was no time to tend to the wound and Robert realized that two of them on one horse would be easy quarry for the English scouts. What he needed was a place to hide until the enemy had passed, and Hamish could be safely moved. He couldn't understand why the boy had said nothing about the wound, or why he himself hadn't seen the blood.

It took all his strength to lift the dead weight of his brother and secure him in the saddle. Robert then led his horse back toward the river they had passed earlier.

Hamish Douglas was hardly more than a boy, a boy who worshipped his older brother and had refused to be left behind when Robert announced he was heading for Argyllshire to join Campbell against the insurgent English.

Robert swore he would save Hamish, or die trying.

When he reached the river, he immediately spotted the cave, high on the hillside among the rocks on the far side. It was perfect. He could swim his horse across, and hopefully his tracks would disappear on the rocky ground.

After a bit of coaxing, Robert's horse stepped into the freezing water. They had to swim a good part of it, and when they emerged on the other side, Robert was shivering so badly that he couldn't hold onto the reins. Thankfully, his horse followed him as he climbed the steep slope. Hamish remained unconscious, totally unaware of the predicament.

The cave was the ideal hiding place, just large enough to hold them all—even the horse. Robert quickly gathered some soft bracken and formed a bed on the floor of the cave. He then lifted his feverish brother down from the saddle and placed him on the bed. He led the horse inside, tied him up, and went to gather some good grass to keep the animal quiet.

He covered the mouth of the cavern with great clumps of gorse that he hacked from the hillside with his broadsword. He then retreated inside, pulling the last of the gorse into place behind him. He prayed they were well hidden.

After tending his brother's wound as best he could, Robert lay down to rest, wearier than he'd ever been. He fell asleep almost immediately and dreamt of the seashore at Kintyre and the face of Eileen MacLeod. He tossed in his sleep, murmuring to himself, dreaming of a fierce battle, a battle in which Campbell had become the enemy. He slept on.

The ringing of steel striking stone brought him wide-awake. Hamish moaned softly, but lay still. Robert crawled to the cave mouth, carefully parted the branches, and peered out. Below his position, on the far bank, he saw a mounted troop of English. There were six of them searching up and down the riverbank for tracks. He watched them discover where the hoof prints entered the river and search in vain for where they emerged. It was the sound of a horseshoe striking stone that had roused him from his sleep.

Robert watched with relief as the English headed upstream. At that moment, Hamish let out a bloodcurdling scream. Robert moved quickly to cover his brother's mouth, but it was too late. The English had heard it. They were heading back, studying the rocky outcropping high on the slope opposite them. By the time Robert returned to the cave entrance and looked down, four men had already crossed the river and were heading right for his hiding place.

Suddenly, another scream erupted. He turned back to Hamish, but the boy hadn't moved—he was sleeping peacefully. As Robert watched the soldiers, tasting the bile in his throat, an enormous golden eagle rose majestically from the rocks above the cave and soared toward the English. It screamed once more and wheeled away into the sky.

The horsemen halted their progress. One of them pointed to the bird. They turned back, re-crossed the river, and rode off. Robert looked to the heavens and nodded his thanks.

Two days later, Hamish was well enough to travel. Although Campbell Keep was closer by far, and Campbell had fine doctors, Robert felt uneasy about going there. He decided instead to head straight home, home to the peaceful valleys of Kintyre, where Hamish could get well. Then and only then, when he knew the boy was on the road to recovery, would he travel east to meet Eileen MacLeod.

He'd send a messenger as soon as he got home. He knew she'd be thinking the worst.

John came to and sat up. He breathed deeply, as if he'd been running. Although his pulse was racing, he felt clammy and cold. He knew the writing was not his own and that now, even his dreams belonged to someone else.

He rubbed his eyes and surveyed his location. He was alone, sitting on the floor of the tower room, but had no idea how he'd gotten there. He remembered that he'd waited in the boat for almost an hour, but Moira hadn't made an appearance. He had decided to make the best of the day anyway, and this time, he was better prepared. In the boatshed at Ainsley, he'd found a small rubber dinghy and had patched the holes with a bicycle tire kit. He'd used the dinghy to get ashore and had made the long climb up to the fortress.

Feeling a pain, John reached to the side of his head and grimaced. Then he remembered slipping in the dark passageway from the beach and reaching out to steady himself. In the process, he'd banged his head.

He couldn't remember climbing to the tower, but he had an uneasy sense that he hadn't been alone. Feeling completely disoriented, he rose stiffly to his feet and leaned against the wall for a moment before stepping back outside. A cold wind blew off the loch as he began the long trek back down to the beach.

When he reached the bottom of the steps, John discovered that he'd dropped his pen somewhere along the route. Although it was one he particularly liked, a gift from Valerie, he realized the futility of going back to search. It could have fallen out of his pocket anywhere, and he'd had quite enough of the Keep for one day.

As John hurried across the rocky beach, he repeatedly glanced back over his shoulder, making sure he wasn't being followed. He shoved the dinghy into the water, hopped aboard, and grabbed the paddle. As he did, something high on the ramparts caught his eye. An arm extended from the parapet, waving a handkerchief.

A second later, he realized what it really was. He saw the flutter of wings as a large bird lifted off from the battlement and soared down toward the loch. The gray-coated raven landed on a nearby boulder and watched him closely, as if it had been sent to supervise his departure.

Only when he reached the safety of the *Bridie*, and started the engines did John turn back for one last look. In the fading light, the fortress appeared more sinister than ever. The walls appeared to be slowly melting as the Keep cloaked itself in darkness.

CHAPTER 13

The town of Oban was one of the most picturesque spots on Scotland's west coast, a Mecca for tourists from all over the world. Few of them, however, knew of the existence of the seedy bar located at the end of a dark alley, not far from the town center. There was a dimly lit sign proclaiming its existence, but it failed to mention that the Skullery was the seediest dive in town, the hangout of choice for the town's dregs.

The Skullery's clientele was, for the most part, comprised of petty drug dealers, young prostitutes, and other remnants. Occasionally, a group of thrill-seeking college students invaded the place bent on an evening of debauchery, but usually, it was the same old local crowd.

Alistair Frazier sat at a corner table obscured by a thick pall of smoke. He'd been there for hours, wondering what to do about Moira. He knew that, without her, the band would be done for.

He was pretty well loaded. Compatriots, in similar condition, shared the table. One meaty young man with a shaved head and an array of cheap tattoos had his arm draped around Alistair's neck, yelling in his ear in an effort to be heard above the din being created by a tuneless rock band. Across the table, a green-haired girl sporting enough body piercing to induce gangrene, tried to focus... on anything.

The girl smiled to herself as if recalling some private joke, and with some effort, lifted her foot from the floor and deposited it in Alistair's lap. He smiled and began to rub her leg, all the time trying to hear the rantings of his ink-stained pal.

Beside the girl, a skinny black man busied himself filling a small pipe with slivers of dark brown material that he carved carefully from a thumb-sized chunk of the stuff. He completed his task, lit the pipe, inhaled deeply, and passed it on. The girl snatched it from his hand and performed the same ritual before passing the pipe to Alistair, who took a long hit. Overestimating his capacity, he choked, spewing smoke from his lungs. This gaff resulted in some derision from the other smokers. Alistair grinned apologetically and took another toke, this time holding fast. On the dance floor, three couples tried gamely to dance, struggling to hold each other upright.

The door opened, and a well-muscled man in a too-tight suit entered the club. He approached Alistair's table and jerked his thumb in the direction of the door. Ali rose unsteadily, the blood draining from his face, and led the way to the door.

Outside, the man grabbed Ali's arm and escorted him down the alley toward a waiting car. The back door of the shiny American sedan opened, and the boy was thrust inside. He turned to face the man, whose bulk occupied most of the seat.

"Alistair, my boy," whispered Marcus Bersky.

He spoke with a thick Eastern-European accent.

"Do you have any news for me?"

His glittering eyes indicated that he was not someone to be trifled with. He gazed steadily at the boy.

"I was gonne come and see you tonight, Marcus—really I was. Eh...I haven't been able to get in the chamber yet, but—"

The man cut him off.

"One more week, my son. One more week, and the price will be more than you want to pay. Do you understand me?"

"Yes, Marcus, I do. Don't worry, I'll get it done. I promise."

"Very good then. I'll be expecting you at my house in one week's time, and Ali...don't make us come looking for you. There's nothing Rudy would enjoy more."

Alistair nodded silently, climbed out, and scurried back to the club. Safely inside, he released the breath he'd been holding and stumbled to his table.

"Where's the damn pipe? I need a hit, man."

This time, the black man handed him a different pipe, one filled with sparkling white crystals. He struck a match and smiled as Ali raised the pipe to his lips.

✿ ✿ ✿

It was getting late. Moira was alone in the dining room of the Thistle, clearing up after the last customers, when he walked in. She was surprised. John MacIntyre was the last person she'd expected to see coming through the door at that time of night.

She gave no indication, however. Instead, she smiled and ambled toward him.

"Mister MacIntyre. What are you doing out so late all by yourself?"

"I have to talk to you."

"Well it's nice to see you, but you shouldn't have come here. If somebody sees us together, the tongues'll wag. It's a right wee village."

John nodded. "Yes I do...I do understand, and I'm sorry, but I didn't know any other way. I waited for you today, you know...at the Keep. Isn't that what you meant by your message last night?"

It took her a second to answer. "Aye, but I had a bit of bother with my mum, you see. She came to see me, and I wasn't expecting her. We've had some problems at home...oh, but never you mind that—that's another story. Anyway, I'm right sorry you went all the way out there for nothing...but I had no way to let you know."

She watched his face relax.

"That's okay," he said. "I understand. These things happen. So eh...can we meet tomorrow?"

Moira contemplated the slate floor, twisting her long fingers into knots. She took a breath and looked up into John's eyes.

"I've been thinking, Mister MacIntyre, maybe this isn't such a good idea. We'll only start rumors, and that wouldn't be good for either one of us. Do you know what I mean?"

"Yes I do, and I understand your concern, really I do, but I'd really like to see you. I just need to talk to you, that's all. It's about the book I'm writing. Nobody needs to know; nobody goes to that place—you said so yourself. It'll be all right. Please...please, meet me tomorrow."

She felt sorry for him. She knew she shouldn't be leading the poor man on, but she had no choice. "Well, I suppose there'd be nothing wrong with us meeting for a wee chat, but I don't want to bring you any trouble with your wife. She seems like a nice woman, and I don't want her to get the wrong idea."

"Tomorrow, then. Will you meet me tomorrow?"

Moira started to nod her head, then stopped.

"Oh no, Mister MacIntyre—I'm sorry I can't tomorrow...but maybe Sunday afternoon. I don't have to work on Sunday, and no one'll miss me."

She saw his eyes light up.

"Great," he whispered, "I'll be there. What time?"

"Oh, let me see. What about one o'clock? And I'll bring a picnic. It'll be super."

"Moira, what the hell are you doing in there?" It was George, calling from the other room.

"Nothing, George. I'm just finished, I'll be right there."

She pointed to a small door under the stairs. "You'd better go out the back way there." She had a thought: "Oh my, were you seen coming in? And your car. Oh my goodness."

"Don't worry," he said, smiling. "We Yanks are smarter than we look. I left it hidden outside the village, and no one saw me come in. And Moira, since we're getting to be friends, could you please call me John?"

She presented a shy smile. "That would be nice," she whispered, and disappeared through the door.

She knew what she was doing was wrong, and to make matters worse, she liked him.

CHAPTER 14

Jock sat alone in his front room reading the paper for the umpteenth time. He was in no mood for the conviviality of the pub. His thoughts kept returning to the MacIntyres. They shouldn't be living in that house. He had considered telling them, but he was afraid.

There was a time when Jock was afraid of no one. He hadn't always been just a humble postmaster. He'd been highly respected in the vale. If it hadn't been for the Ainsley House murder twenty-five years earlier, things would have been different.

It wasn't his fault. No one else had believed young Graham Nesbit either, although as provost, he should have had Constable Jameson check out the lad's story. The oversight had cost him everything, including his job. Even his wife had lost respect for him before she got sick.

It had taken years for the villagers to stop blaming him.

He'd be glad to see the MacIntyres gone, though. The whole situation was becoming a terrible reminder. He reached for his whiskey bottle and upended it into a grimy glass. The bottle was empty. "God damn them all to hell," he said, rising unsteadily from his chair and reaching for his coat.

He stumbled out the door heading for the Thistle and cursed even more colorfully as the pub's sign blinked out. As he stood scowling at the faithless tavern, he saw a man hurry across the back parking lot and disappear into the shadows. Recognizing the man, Jock shook his head, negotiated an about-face, and listed back toward his house.

✿ ✿ ✿

Valerie awakened from a bad dream. The bedroom was in darkness. She reached out for the reassuring presence of her husband. He wasn't there. She remembered the current state of affairs, and fell back into her pillow, willing her heart to calm down. Just then, she heard him coming up the stairs and breathed a sigh of relief. He must have been writing.

John stepped into the room and waited quietly for a moment. Valerie, whose eyes by now were accustomed to the dark, could see that he was dressed for outside. Strange.

John, unaware that his wife was watching him, tiptoed across the room, furtive as a thief, and ran smack into the half-open dressing room door.

"Shit," he muttered, knowing he'd probably wakened Valerie, and he'd definitely stubbed his toe.

"John. Are you all right?"

"Yeah. Fine. Sorry I woke you."

He made his way through the offending door into the safety of the dressing room, where he quickly changed into the sweats he usually wore for working. When he returned to the bedroom, Valerie was sitting up in bed with the light on.

"Where have you been?"

John took a moment before answering. "Oh, I just had a couple of thoughts and felt I should jot them down before I forgot them. You know what I mean?"

"I do." She knew that her husband had just lied to her, again.

"John?"

"Yes?"

"Why do you smell like cigarette smoke?"

He realized that the smell was from the Thistle. The problem with being a generally honest man, he considered with perfect clarity, was the lack of practice at deception. He jumped on in, anyway.

"I eh...found an old pack of smokes downstairs and decided to have one, eh...for old times sake."

Valerie reached to turn off the light. "I see."

John grimaced. What a damn stupid thing to say.

Valerie knew the lies would continue for some time.

✿ ✿ ✿

The next morning, John arrived at St. Agnes Kirk and headed around to the back, where he found the vestry door. He knocked, and a moment later, Drummond appeared.

"So where's Missus MacIntyre?" asked the minister. "I thought she was to join us."

John had invited Valerie to join them on the trek, but she had declined. She'd used the onset of a headache as her excuse to beg off.

"She's feeling a bit under the weather, I'm afraid," said John. "Maybe next time."

Drummond nodded and moved inside.

John followed him into the study and perused the bookshelves as the minister poured the inevitable cup of tea. The men settled comfortably into a pair of oversized chairs beside the coal fire that warmed the cozy room. As John sipped his Earl Grey, he noticed the golden retriever curled under Drummond's desk, sound asleep. Since the dog had not even acknowledged his presence, he figured it must either be unusually laid back, or stone deaf.

"So how's the work going?" asked the minister.

"Fine. It's coming along quite nicely; although sometimes I wish I could actually live in the era I'm writing about. It's frustrating trying to create images without actually having the chance to personally experience them. Research books are all well and good, but being able to taste the atmosphere of the time would be quite another thing."

The minister nodded his shaggy head.

"You know, there are one or two things I could show you that might be of help. Aside from the pagan temple I mentioned, I should maybe let you see something else. I don't know why I'm doing this. It's a closely guarded secret, but I sense you're a man to be trusted."

John leaned forward.

"There are only one or two of us who know of its existence," Drummond continued, "but if I could be assured of your discretion, I'd be inclined to allow you a look."

John pledged his compliance, and Rev. Drummond slowly unfolded his long frame from his chair.

They left the vestry and entered the sanctuary through a side door. The minister crossed quickly to the front doors and slid closed a heavy iron bolt before returning to the chancel. He signaled John to remain where he was, climbed up to the pulpit, and disappeared from view. John heard a dry, grating sound, that of stone sliding against stone.

Drummond reappeared and beckoned for John to join him. He bounded up the steps and saw that a section of the floor had moved aside to reveal a black hole.

John peered into the void and saw a set of steep stone steps leading underground. Drummond produced a small flashlight from his pocket and descended into the beam of light. John followed close behind, and felt his stomach constrict as the stone slab slid closed above him.

His heart in his throat, he followed the minister down into the ground, counting as he went. There were twenty steps. At the bottom, they reached a passageway no wider than his stretched fingertips. After walking bent over for about eighty feet, they entered a small chamber whose ceiling was just high enough for them to stand upright.

Drummond reached for a Coleman lantern that hung on the wall, pumped its pressure valve, and touched a match to the wick. The room was immediately bathed in light. They were standing in what had to be a war room. In the middle of the chamber stood a rough wooden table and, behind it, a large chair draped in animal skins. A couple of old parchments that looked to be primitive area maps lay on the table affixed by daggers and goblets. Leaning against the wall were a dozen rusted swords. At the left end of the table was a small chair and writing materials, including two quill pens and a crystal inkwell. A heavy woolen plaid had been flung

over the back of the chair, and John recognized the pattern immediately. The tartan was "hunting" Campbell.

He gaped as Drummond grinned, looking very pleased with
him.

"Is this the sort of atmosphere you were looking for?"

John nodded slowly. He had so many questions that he didn't
know where to begin. He crossed to the table and stared at the
old papers. The minister moved closer, holding the lantern so John
could see better. As John reached for the maps, Drummond shook
his head. "I'm sorry, but you can't touch these. You can look all you
like, but I'm afraid they're too delicate to withstand any handling."

"Yes, yes of course. But what is this place? How long has it been
here? How the hell? Oh, please, excuse my language, Reverend, I
eh—"

Drummond chuckled again.

"That's okay, it's just the excitement of the moment. I cursed
myself, the first time I saw it."

"So, who showed you this? Who brought you here?"

"I can't tell you that. Sorry."

"Oh, okay." John's voice shook with excitement.

"Hang on…there's more." Drummond moved off.

The minister extinguished the lantern, replaced it on its hook,
and switched on his flashlight. They were again forced to stoop as
they reentered the passageway.

After thirty feet or so, they came to another set of steps, leading
upward. The minister extinguished his light, and John gulped a
breath. The darkness was smothering.

"I'll just be a moment," said Drummond. "Wait here until I tell
you to come."

John counted as he listened to the minister climb the steps.
Confined spaces had never been high on John's list and, as he waited
in the darkness, he fought the mounting anxiety. After what seemed

like forever, and a series of grating sounds, a panel slid open above him, flooding the stairwell with sunlight. He blinked in the sudden glare and watched Drummond squeeze through the opening and disappear. Without waiting for a signal, John scurried up the steps and stumbled through the opening.

He climbed to his feet, not quite believing where he was. He was behind the Campbell monument in the graveyard. He watched, curious, as Drummond twisted one of the carved stone rosettes. The panel slid shut.

John stared up at the monument, feeling totally overwhelmed. As he was about to begin the questions, a squeaky voice called out Drummond's name, and a small, untidy woman rounded the corner of the church.

"Kenneth, there you are. That was the man from Edinburgh on the phone. He needs you to call him right away. I tried you in the vestry, but you didn't answer, so I thought I'd better come looking. He said it was important—very important."

John found the woman's voice terribly irritating. She scowled at him and walked away.

Drummond frowned and began kneading his temples.

"Is everything okay?" John asked.

"Oh, yes, yes. Everything's fine, but I'm afraid we'll have to save our hike for another time. I've got to return this call, and from the looks of you, you've had enough for your first outing. Why don't you phone me tomorrow, and we'll reschedule."

He reached for John's hand.

"Thank you for the tour. It was absolutely fantastic."

"Your word's been given…remember." The minister's dark eyes glowed like embers; his voice was nearly a whisper. "You must tell no one. Best not forget."

John headed for the Jaguar without looking back, aware that Drummond still watched him.

He raced home, whistling happily and drumming on the steering wheel like a carefree teenager.

✿ ✿ ✿

Sunday morning broke overcast and cool. John awakened earlier than usual, but Valerie was already up. As he opened his eyes, his first thoughts were of the secret chamber beneath the church. He got a tingle just thinking about it. It took him a few moments before he remembered the rest. He had arranged to meet Moira that afternoon...another tingle. He felt a twinge of guilt, but quashed it and began planning his deception.

He showered, dressed quickly, and headed downstairs, where he found Valerie sitting in the kitchen, sipping coffee from an oversized mug. She glanced up at him but didn't smile.

He poured himself a cup and joined her at the table.

"Mornin'. How'd you sleep?"

"Not too badly, thank you, considering."

John felt a moment of panic and stared into his coffee, holding his breath.

"I feel like I'm fighting a losing battle—"

He stirred his coffee anxiously, not wanting to hear what was coming.

"—with this damn cold."

He resumed breathing.

"I'm supposed to go fishing with Graham this afternoon."

John's heart lurched. He needed to have the boat.

"But I just don't feel up to it. I think I'll call him and cancel."

He breathed again.

"And, what are *your* plans?" She sounded nonchalant as she regarded his face. "Are you okay? You look odd."

"Oh no, eh...I'm fine...just fine."

"Well, I think I'll just stay in and read this new book I got. It looks like the sun's trying to break through. Wouldn't be a great day for fishing, anyway."

John tried to read his wife's face, but she was inscrutable. Damn her.

"Probably a good idea to take it easy if you're not feeling well. Maybe I should stay with you."

Again, he held his breath.

"John, please. I'll be fine."

He exhaled.

"Okay, if you're sure. I think I'll do a little exploring."

"Not at the ruin, I hope."

"Oh, no. Actually I'm thinking of heading up the other side of the loch. I heard about a Glen Rossen that was the sight of a great battle. Might be a good place to soak up some atmosphere."

"Well, maybe I should fix you a picnic. Then you wouldn't have to rush back; you could stay as long as you want."

He glanced at her sideways.

Nothing.

"Thanks, but that won't be necessary. I'll just grab some fruit and maybe some chips...or should I say crisps?"

John rose to his feet and headed for the bathroom. His bladder was calling at a most opportune moment. He glanced back at his wife and saw her reaching for her book.

"Thank you God," he murmured, as he bounded up the stairs.

☆ ☆ ☆

By early afternoon, the sun was making headway. *Bridie* rocked gently in the cove beneath the Keep.

On shore, John greeted Moira a little awkwardly. She led the way to a sheltered spot among the boulders, where they were completely hidden from all but a pair of ospreys wheeling in the high sky. As Moira spread out the blankets on a patch of soft sand, John could only stare. His mouth was suddenly dry. She'd chosen to wear very short shorts and a halter-top that, for the moment, had his full attention. She was achingly beautiful.

"So what have you brought for lunch?" His voice sounded a bit constricted.

Moira grinned, threw open the basket, and handed him a chilled bottle of California Sauvignon Blanc and a corkscrew.

Smiling, he opened the bottle and poured into plastic cups.

"I've brought gammon sandwiches," she continued brightly, "and hot-house tomatoes, and an apple tart for dessert. I made it myself. I hope it turned out all right."

Moira was completely at ease—much more so than he was. John began to have doubts, to wonder if he'd misread her. Maybe it was all perfectly innocent. Maybe he was flattering himself.

The picnic was delicious, and the careful small talk led to a discussion of why food tasted so good in Scotland. Now that John had dismissed any thought of a physical encounter, he relaxed. He stretched out on the blanket and allowed his thoughts to ramble.

"You know, back in the States, we're a bit obsessed with size over substance. We grow the world's largest strawberries. Unfortunately, they're completely tasteless, kinda like our role models."

He chuckled.

"Oh, but I'd love to go to America," said Moira. "It's awfully frustrating for the likes of me around here, you know. There's not much opportunity. I'll never be famous if I stay here."

"Well maybe that's not all bad. Fame's not all it's cracked up to be, you know. There's a heavy price that goes with it, and you gotta pay up. It can steal your soul. One day, you wake up and look in the mirror, and you see how much you've paid. Stay true to yourself, Moira. That's the best advice I can give you. Never give them anything you're not proud of. That way, you can be in control of your own life."

"So, are you in control, John?"

"Oh no," he said softly. "Not by a long shot."

He sat up, gathered a handful of pebbles, and tossed them one by one into the water.

Moira rocked quietly, hugging her knees, watching the ripples as they fanned out across the cove.

"No one cares about decency any more, or dignity. Hell, the scripts I was getting were nothing but infomercials for violence. That's why I quit. I couldn't take it anymore."

Moira lay back on the blanket and closed her eyes as John enumerated his favorite peeves. It was a full five minutes before he noticed that her eyes were closed.

"I'm so sorry," he chuckled. "I don't know what got into me. I didn't mean to babble. Please forgive me."

Moira reached for his hand.

"On the contrary, Mister M–eh, John, I don't think I've ever gotten to know so much about anybody quite so quickly. Honestly, I found it fascinating, and it's really nice to know that you care about things so much. I think you're very nice."

John was suddenly warm.

"Now, how would you like to hear what I've got to say?" she asked, her eyes twinkling.

"Good idea. I'm tired of listening to myself," John said, laughing.

Moira reached into the hamper, removed a tape player, placed it on a nearby rock, and inserted a tape. "I made this at Alistair's house. It's not professional or anything, but you'll get the idea."

From the moment the song began, John was caught. The music was lyrical, captivating. As he listened, Moira rose from the blanket and began to dance, all the time watching him, watching him watching her.

When the song finished, John looked away before she could see the effect she'd had. She crossed to his blanket and knelt in front of him.

"Well? Did you like it?"

"Oh yeah. I liked it."

Suddenly, he couldn't stop himself. He reached for her, needing to hold something of her. She came easily into his arms, like she'd been there a hundred times before. He kissed her, at first tenderly, but when her lips began to respond, his passion rose quickly. They fell together onto the blanket and undressed in a fury.

When he crested her, her body rose to meet him. Hungrily, she took him in her hand, urging him to her, but it was already too late. He shuddered once, then again, groaned, and rolled away.

✿ ✿ ✿

A few moments later, as they lay staring at the sky, Moira spoke first. He didn't see the coquettish smile on her lips.

"It's fine, John, really it is. It might actually be considered a compliment, if you think about it."

John didn't want to think about it. He felt humiliated; a damn novice.

When the flush of embarrassment subsided, he turned to face her, resting his head on his elbow. Her eyes were closed, so his own were free to feast. As he studied her, it was as if he was looking at Lady Eileen.

"Moira?"

"Yes?"

"Why me?"

She found his eyes.

"I really can't answer that. All I can say is I didn't expect this to happen, really."

She looked away first. "This isn't good, you know. Not for either one of us."

He knew she was right. Already the pangs of guilt were nipping at him. He promised himself that it would not happen again.

The last thing he wanted to do was go home.

✿ ✿ ✿

After a clumsy goodbye scene at the cove, he cruised the dark loch for an hour or more, not caring where he was.

As darkness fell, he headed back to Kilbride. He tied up at the Thistle where he washed up, had a couple of stiff whiskeys, and talked George into letting him buy one of the flower arrangements from the dining room. He hadn't been at all prepared for the guilt he was feeling. Mercifully, Moira hadn't made an appearance.

As he stepped into the house, he heard the sounds of the television coming from the living room. He entered sheepishly and saw his wife dabbing her eyes with a tissue.

"Hi."

Valerie jumped.

"John, damn you! I've told you not to do that. I hate it when you sneak up on me. I've told you, if you're going to skulk about, be loud about it."

John shrugged and produced the flowers from behind his back.

"I'm so sorry, honey. I really wasn't sneaking up on you. Here, I got you these."

He crossed the room and handed her the little bouquet.

"Why, John." She sniffed the blossoms and wondered why they smelled of smoke. "What a nice surprise. It's been a while since you brought me flowers. What's the matter, feeling guilty about something? Where have you been?"

His heart skipped a beat.

"Well…actually, I went to the Keep after all. I know you don't want me going there, but I can't help it. I feel drawn there. The place inspires me. It's part of the story I'm writing. I guess I lost track of time again. I'm really sorry."

He bent down and kissed her cheek. As he straightened back up, Valerie sniffed his hair. He didn't notice.

"So why the sad face?"

"Oh, it's nothing. I was just watching an old movie. I've seen it a dozen times, but it still makes me cry."

"Well, I could use a bite to eat. Can I get you—?"

"No thanks. I don't need anything."

He headed for the kitchen.

By the time he returned, the movie was over, and the news was on. Valerie was caught up in a story about the murder of a young girl in Glasgow. Apparently, there were no leads in the gruesome crime. As John settled in beside her on the couch and began munching on his sandwich, her attention remained focused on the television.

"I can't believe it. Murder…here," she said. "I guess I was naive, but the thought never occurred to me. It's really awful. Even in Scotland, there are monsters. We might as well be in L.A."

John nodded his agreement.

"Well, honey, I think I'm gonna hit the sheets early. It's been a long day, and I'm whipped. Coming?"

He prayed she'd decline.

"Eh no. I think I'll see if there's anything good on. I'm not real tired. I napped most of the afternoon, I think. But it worked, I'm feeling much better."

He'd forgotten to ask.

"I'm glad," he said. "I'm really glad you're feeling better."

As he reached the door, Valerie called his name.

He stopped.

"Happy anniversary," she said. Her eyes never left the television screen.

John walked out the door. There was nothing he could say—not even to himself. He stood in the dimness of the hall, feeling as if he'd bathed in filth.

✵ ✵ ✵

Not long after John's departure from the Thistle, Moira walked through the door, hoping against hope that John wouldn't be there. She really didn't want to see him. She was too ashamed. He'd been so easy.

So why am I having these feelings? she wondered as she climbed the stairs. She entered her room and felt the need for some mind alteration. She reached under her mattress, pulled out a small plastic bag and a pipe, and proceeded to fill the little bowl. Ali had introduced her to pot over a year ago. He'd told her that it would help her get in touch with her feelings.

If ever there was a time. Moira took a couple of good puffs and lay down on her bed, waiting for the drug to take effect. It didn't take long. Soon, she was giggling to herself, thinking about the day John had climbed onto his boat stark naked. She had known then that he was hers for the taking, even if he was a big mucky-muck Hollywood director. He'd been so shy, so cute, and was much more interesting than any of the local boys.

When he'd first arrived in the village, she had considered that maybe he could help her career—even before Drummond recruited her. At first, she'd declared that she'd have no part in it. But Drummond had left her with few options.

She was forced to comply, and considered that maybe it wouldn't be too horrible. After all, John was very good looking, and it would require no more than a little harmless flirtation. She had never meant for it to go so far. She didn't know how she'd lost control. Evidently, John was in possession of some powers himself. She'd never met anyone like him.

She smiled, remembering the excitement she'd felt, and was almost sorry he wasn't downstairs. Moira rose from her bed and reached for her guitar.

It was a happy surprise for the few people who remained in the pub. She sang a brand new song, a song about the kindness of strangers.

CHAPTER 15

⸺ ✦ ⸺

The boys were quiet as they sat together on the smooth stones that formed a circle around the roaring fire. Just beyond the reach of the firelight was a huge granite altar. Behind the altar stood a rude cross that had been carved from a living tree. Its gnarled roots clung to the earth like talons.

Drummond had learned of the ancient temple's existence from the maps in the chamber beneath the church, but had been unable to find it. Had Alistair Frazier not accidentally tumbled into it during a trek, the overgrown hollow would have remained hidden.

After vows of secrecy, the boys had begun the work of clearing the site. By the end of the first day, they'd unearthed the altar, and as they sat celebrating around the fire pit, Drummond described for them the importance of sacrifice.

On their second visit to the site, the minister had noticed a uniquely shaped oak tree and had an inspiration. During the next two outings, the boys fashioned the tree into a living cross. Although the tree had died from the butchery, its presence greatly enhanced the atmosphere.

The temple provided the perfect stage for Drummond's special brand of spiritualism—the blending of Paganism and Christianity. He knew that somewhere in that union lay the solutions he sought.

✡ ✡ ✡

The fire crackled, spitting sparks into the night as Drummond rose to his feet. He began to speak, and for half an hour, railed about the lowliness of their existence as cultural and economic serfs for the hated English. As they listened, the boys stared into the flames, their faces steadily hardening into masks of hate. When the oration was done, two boys rose and left the circle. They returned a moment later, leading a very young lamb on the end of a rope. They dragged the lamb to the altar, hoisted it onto the stone, and tied it down. The little creature lay quietly as the troop circled the altar, humming softly. On cue, one of the boys stepped out from the circle. In his right hand was a long, curved blade. As the lamb watched his approach, it began to writhe in terror, bleating loudly. The poor creature had recognized its butcher. The boy reached forward and calmly sliced the animal's throat. The others drew closer and watched in silence until the lamb lay still.

They then filed past the little body, dipping their fingers into the steaming blood and smearing it on their faces. When the ritual was done, the boys re-formed their circle and sat staring into the flames. The night was quiet except for the sparking of the fire and the moan of the wind. Drummond crossed to the altar, cut the lamb free, and tossed it into the blaze. The new wool flared briefly as the little carcass was engulfed.

Drummond looked to the sky and began to recite the lament:

> We call on the powers of the ancient ones,
> Fill us, yer men, with fires of old.
> Give to us a heart that's bold,
> To fight 'til Scotland's free once more,
> Free from the grasp of the English dogs.
> Drive them back to the stinking bogs
> From whence they came.
>
> Let them who've come tae take the heart
> From this good land, make their depart.
> And let their veins know ice and fear.
> As cowards from our sacred sphere,
> They flee our mountains and our shores
> And leave to those who've spilt their gore
> Guid Scotia's name.
>
> For all the lives laid down in blood
> So freely shed for country's love,
> We'll drive her enemies in fear,
> Return them to Nectanismere,
> Where Edward, Satan's very son
> Will dearly pay for evils done
> And taste the shame.
>
> Where hundreds fall with hated King
> Their venom blood still lingering

In Scotia's soil to feed the thorns,
The thistles that our hills adorn
Give strength to us who journey on
Until our enemies are gone
And we remain.

Give us back Scotland,
Give us back life,
Give us back freedom.

"Freedom!" The boys roared in unison, rocking together like mad men.

✻ ✻ ✻

An hour later, when the fire and the lamb were ashes, the boys rose and shuffled to the stream, where they washed away the evidence. Mutely, they formed a column behind the minister and began the long trek back to the village.

CHAPTER 16

Valerie took a breath, knocked on the door of the inner sanctum, and pushed her way in. "I've been thinking about taking a cruise," she said boldly. "I'm getting a bit bored here, with you working all the time"

John nodded his head but said nothing.

"Graham says there are some terrific day trips out of Oban, so I'm checking them out. I just wanted you to know."

She turned and walked out of the room. By the time the door closed, he was re-immersed in his story.

✿ ✿ ✿

Two days later, John woke to find Valerie packing an overnight bag. When he asked what she was up to, she explained that she was off to Oban, reminding him that they'd previously discussed it.

"Oh yes." He vaguely remembered the conversation.

"I'm going to take the car. You have *Bridie* in case you need anything in town."

John immediately thought of Moira but forced the image from his mind.

"I should be back late tonight, but if I'm too tired to drive, I'll just stay the night in Oban. I'll let you know."

John hoisted her bag, walked with her to the garage, and helped her into the car. Before closing her door, he stooped to kiss her, but she turned her face away, offering only her cheek. He watched her back the car into the driveway and wasn't surprised when she didn't wave as she drove off.

As he walked back into the house, John felt a disquieting sense of loss.

Valerie was feeling a disquieting sense of quite another kind.

She felt torn. Maybe she should have told her husband that Graham Nesbit would be joining her, but she'd decided that it would serve no purpose. Besides, she felt a certain satisfaction in having her own secret.

A few minutes later, she pulled to a stop at Graham's cottage.

"So what did he say?" Graham asked as he buckled up and pointed Valerie in the right direction.

"I didn't tell him. The hell with him." She grinned and punched the gas.

They proceeded at a leisurely pace up the eastern side of Loch Awe, and as they drove, Graham pointed out his favorite spots. About ten miles out from the village, he pointed to a stand of dense bushes that looked no different from all the others they'd passed.

"That once was the road into Campbell Keep," he said, "but it's been out of use for years. The Keep's no place to go snooping around. You do understand that, don't you?"

"Well, you've certainly told me often enough." She didn't mention John's fascination with the fortress.

They arrived in Oban just in time to watch their ship pulling out from the harbor, and at the ticket office, they were informed that all of the day trips had already sailed.

As they strolled back to the car, Valerie was very quiet. Her obvious disappointment demanded that Graham come up with a solution. He instructed her to wait for him and returned to the ticket office. Within minutes, he returned waving a couple of tickets and sporting a satisfied grin.

"So here's the solution. We're going to take the boat to Jurra instead. We'll have to spend the night in Tarbert, but John's not really expecting you back until tomorrow, and it's actually a much more interesting sail."

A half hour later, the *Cavalier* was ready for boarding, and they raced aboard like two kids on a school outing. The next hours were some of the most fascinating Valerie could remember. She listened happily as Graham related the history of each island they passed.

As the ship crossed the Gulf of Corryvrechan, Graham pointed off the port bow.

"Do you see that strait?"

"Yeah."

"Well, it's got some tales to tell. They say it's the most dangerous stretch of water in the world. The Devil's Cauldron, they call it. During the winter storms, the Atlantic currents join with the tides from the Irish Sea. They come together right there, creating an enormous whirlpool. It can reach two miles across, and sometimes, you can hear the roar from as far away as the mainland. Many a boat's been swallowed up by that rascal."

Valerie shivered in spite of the warm sun. Graham placed his arm around her shoulder and hugged her to him.

"Of course, since we're barely into the month of September, there's almost no cause for alarm."

Valerie pushed him away. "What is it about you men that makes you enjoy scaring the bejeebers out of us women? Are you really so insecure?"

"I suppose there's some truth to that," he said. "Insecurity. That's certainly what you bring out in *me*."

As the sun sank steadily into the sea, the sturdy little ship rounded a rocky headland and steamed gratefully toward the twinkling lights of Tarbert.

When the *Cavalier* was safely berthed, Graham led the way into the village. He stopped at a quaint harbor hotel and booked two rooms. A half hour later, they met in the bar and enjoyed a cocktail before heading into the tiny dining room.

They chatted amiably and managed to eat every scrap of the delicious meal. They also finished off a bottle of very good Burgundy, and by the time they headed upstairs, Valerie was heady from the wine and feeling happier than she had in weeks. When they arrived at her room, Graham reached for her key, unlocked the door, and stepped aside.

As she moved past him, she stopped, returned to his arms, and gazed up into his flushed face. "Oh Graham," she whispered, "I know I've had too much wine, and I'm so tempted to invite you in, but I know that afterwards I'd despise us both, and I just can't let that happen. I'd miss you something fierce."

He bent his head and kissed her softly. "I know. That's why I won't press the issue, much as I'd like to."

"Graham, you're really a wonderful man and I promise you, if my heart was available, you'd be its first choice."

Graham nodded resignedly, stroked her upturned face, and headed down the hall. She sighed softly and stepped into the safety of her room.

CHAPTER 17

Although his hands were stiff and sore, John was deep in his story. He tried to stop, but something wouldn't let him. The compulsion was beyond his control.

Aside from the rhythmic clacking of the keys, Ainsley House was still.

> *Campbell of Argyll was in a rare mood. He rode through a vale of such beauty that he was strikingly reminded as to why he would gladly shed his blood for this land. The sight of the rugged hills, cloaked in heather, lifted his soul. Wildflowers filled the air with their perfume.*
>
> *He rode on, humming to himself, lost in thoughts of life long lasting and of Eileen MacLeod. His troop of thirty men seemed to respond*

to his mood, and the sounds of easy laughter, mingling with the steady clomp of hooves and the clink of harness, echoed back from the rocky crags. Campbell could plainly see what the birds had to sing about.

William of Alsh rode by his side as usual, but knew better than to break the mood with idle chatter.

Just before mid-day, when the sun was almost at its zenith, Campbell spotted a red stag gazing down on them from a stone out-cropping. He reined in his horse and watched the deer as it watched them. The beast was huge. He turned to Alsh.

"What about a hunt, William?"

"Just the thing," Alsh agreed. "We would all enjoy the taste of some fresh venison, and it wouldn't hurt the cause to arrive at Arbrothock bearing some good Lanarkshire meat."

Campbell laughed. The prospect of a good hunt amused him. It had been years since he himself had been on a stalk. He had others to do his hunting for him.

They set up a rough camp, and the best huntsmen were brought before their chief to organize the flush. Campbell wanted to make the kill himself, so the arrangements were made accordingly. The deer-hounds were sent off across the hills to the east, with their handlers. It was their job to circle behind the herd and begin moving it in the right direction. It would be more than an hour before they were in position.

Watson of Ayr and Donald Falkirk were instructed to climb up into the crags with the two lurchers, where they'd wait until the quarry was sighted. They would then release the lurchers, whose responsibility it was to drive the deer to Campbell. Argyll was especially proud of his lurchers. Although the dogs had been imported from England, there was no deny-ing their cunning and bravery. They were said to be part wolf, the finest hunting dogs in the world, directly descended from Romulus and Remus.

Knowing that when driven, the deer would seek high ground, Campbell, along with Alsh, stationed himself on a grassy rise among the trees at the end of the small valley. He dismounted and stretched out *comfortably in the soft grass while Alsh walked the horses deeper into the woods. The Earl of Argyll lay quietly, waiting for the baying of the deerhounds, the sound that would signal that the herd was on the move. The lurchers, waiting in the crags, would make no sound whatsoever.*

Forty minutes later, the deep baying reached Campbell's ears. Although they were still miles away, the deer would be far ahead of them. Campbell and Alsh moved into the cover of the trees.

This was always the most exciting time for Campbell. His blood was up, and his eyes glistened with anticipation. From their hiding place, the two men watched, scanning the slopes for the appearance of their prey. Since they were downwind, the deer would not smell them, but their instinct for survival would cause the animals to be extremely cautious as they entered the narrow glen.

William was the first to spot the prize. The stag was first to cross the rise and enter the valley. Behind him, his small herd moved easily through the bracken. Among the does, there were at least three other stags, younger and not so magnificently antlered, but still, fine animals all. The leader stopped before entering the glen and nervously sniffed the air.

At that moment, the first of the lurchers swept silently down on the herd from above. It was the dog that the stag had smelled. He sniffed the air again and continued directly toward the waiting men, the rest of the herd right behind him.

When they were within three hundred yards of the trees, the stag suddenly changed course, heading for the rocky slope on the other side and certain escape. The deerhounds could still be heard in the distance. The lurcher continued his silent pursuit; still the stag showed no panic.

The men watched, fascinated, as the scene unfolded before them. They readied their crossbows, cranking until the strings were taut. Campbell placed a quarrel in the slot and raised the weapon to his shoulder. He sighted down the burnished stock and waited, struggling to control his breath.

As the deer bounded easily up through the rocks, the dog began to lose ground. The terrain was vastly better suited to the strong hoofs of the red deer than the smooth paws of the lurcher. Just as it seemed that the deer would crest the hillside and make good their escape, a shadow appeared above them and raced to cut them off.

The second lurcher was completely fresh and very good at his work. By the time the stag spotted him racing in from downwind, it was too late. The other dog was still in position to block any escape. There was no choice. The herd of deer turned back and raced to the narrow end of the valley, directly toward the stand of silver birch and Campbell.

When they were no more than thirty yards from the copse, the two men stepped out from between the trees. The deer stopped immediately. Campbell sighted on the lead stag and let fly his bolt. The missile flew sure as death, and took the animal through the neck. The stag took five halting steps before pitching forward onto his knees. He slowly collapsed onto his side and lay quivering as death found him.

William fired and hit one of the smaller stags in the shoulder, missing the kill by inches. Although sorely wounded, the animal continued its flight, crashing through the woods, running for daylight, the lurchers hot on his heels. The first dog, reignited by the smell of fresh blood, bore down on his quarry like a hurled dagger. He caught the creature by the rear hock and held on for all he was worth. The second dog launched himself at the deer's throat. It was over in seconds.

The young stag lay gushing its life into the grass as the dogs calmly returned to their master's feet, looking well pleased. There would be some tasty rewards for their work.

As if they knew the hunt was over, the remaining deer nonchalantly returned to grazing, as if nothing had happened. Another of the stags took up the leader's position and led the herd away from the valley of death, his neck visibly engorging with every step.

That night, a grand fire roared under a cloudless sky. Fresh venison roasted over the sputtering flames as men and dogs salivated in anticipation. An hour later, Campbell had consumed all the meat and wine he could hold.

"There's nothin' like the hunt to fill a man's spirit, is there William?" he asked.

"No my Lord," Alsh replied, "although I'm not at all pleased with missing the heart by so much. That could have been an Englishman that I allowed to escape his maker."

Campbell laughed heartily.

"Oh never you mind, William. At least now I've got some good fresh meat to offer MacLeod in exchange for some of his."

Alsh looked away. He offered no response.

The rest of the journey was without incident, and the weather remained good. Mid-Thursday afternoon, Argyll and his men came within sight of the MacLeods' castle, which sat on a rocky promontory being buffeted by the North Sea wind. As he watched the huge waves pounding against the rocky shore, he decided that Eileen MacLeod should be grateful to be removed from this bleak place. The lands of Argyllshire were far more beautiful than this cold and barren coast

As they rode closer, Campbell could see the drawbridge being lowered and a troop of riders leaving the castle to meet the arriving guests. The Earl of Argyll felt the stirring of excitement, just as he had during the final moments of the hunt. He hoped the girl would be a member of the greeting party. It would be an indication that she was willing—a cooperative acquisition. Not that it much mattered.

As the riders drew closer, Campbell could see no woman in the group. Old Duncan MacLeod raised his right hand in salute and rode forward to welcome his very important guest.

"Sire, you're welcome to my humble house. All that we have is yours."

Campbell was visibly displeased. "That remains to be seen. Doesn't it, Duncan?"

He spurred his horse forward.

Duncan galloped to catch up. "Things will go as you desire, my Lord— have no worries. In my house, there's no one that'll not do my bidding, I assure you of that."

The chief grunted and rode on in silence.

The castle at Arbrothock was a far cry from the grandeur of Campbell Keep. The state of disrepair made very clear to Argyll the advantages that an allegiance with him would bring him. The place was small and draughty, and the reception rooms were poorly furnished. The guest chambers though, were comfortable enough

As Campbell sat in a warm bath reflecting on the purpose of his visit, his humor improved.

Campbell arrived in the banquet hall at the appointed hour and was pleased to see the amount of effort that had gone into the preparations. William of Alsh was directed to his place at the table, and Campbell was shown to his seat at the right hand of MacLeod. Upon Campbell's arrival, Duncan MacLeod rose to his feet and bowed deeply. Campbell did not acknowledge him. Instead he glowered at the empty chair on the old man's left.

Seeing Campbell's darkening expression, MacLeod did his best to reassure his guest. "She'll be here presently, m'Lord. Have no fear. She did have an unfortunate encounter with some poison weed while out on the hills earlier, but she will make the required appearance. Trust me."

The chief of the Campbells took his seat and waited. He felt strangely nervous but reminded himself of his importance and pushed aside the churning in his stomach. As he was greedily downing his second goblet of wine, the doors at the end of the great hall swung open, and through them strode a woman wearing a long black dress. As if she'd been readied for a funeral, the woman was devoid of jewels, and her face was covered by a dark veil.

Suddenly, just outside the study door, the floor creaked loudly, and John snapped back to the present. As he listened to the sound of retreating footsteps, fingers of fear inched up his spine. He held his breath, waiting for the footsteps to return. Nothing. After a few long moments of silence, he decided that what he'd heard was nothing more than the groans of an old house. He returned his attention to his computer, and reread the last sentence he'd written. The soft tap on his door caused his heart to lurch.

Then he remembered. Valerie. She must have returned early. He'd completely forgotten she'd been gone for the day.

"Come in." His voice was hoarse.

The door opened slowly. There in the shadows stood Moira wearing a long dress. The dress was as black as her hair. All that was missing was the veil.

John stared and said nothing.

"Hello John," she said, "I've missed you."

"Wha…what are you doing here?"

"Well I came to see you, of course. I thought you might be a bit lonely. You see, earlier today, I saw Missus MacInty—your wife, leaving the village with Graham Nesbit. It looked to me like they were gonne' be gone for a while, so I decided to surprise you. I brought you some supper. I hope you like fish and chips."

Moira raised a brown paper bag and waved it in the air.

John felt so overwhelmed by her presence, it took a moment for him to register what she'd said.

"Graham Nesbit? You saw Valerie with Graham?"

"Oh aye. They were together in your car. I saw them plain as day."

John didn't know what to think, but decided that given Graham's sexual proclivity, there was no cause for alarm. Still, he couldn't help but wonder why Valerie hadn't told him.

He stood up slowly, feeling a little confused, and noticed the look of concern on Moira's face.

"Are you feeling all right, John? You don't look well. You look like you haven't slept for a week. You're not catching something, are you?"

"No. I'm fine. I guess I've just been working too hard. Maybe I need a break."

John stood in front of her, feeling a bit awkward. As she reached out to touch him, the ringing of the telephone shattered the moment. He coughed nervously, ran back to his desk, and lifted the receiver.

"Hello." He felt the blood draining from his face as he stared at Moira with widened eyes. "Hi Val, where are you?"

He listened.

"Oh nothing," he said. "I'm fine, just fine." He coughed. "It's just a frog. I haven't done much talking today. How are you?" He slowly nodded his head.

"Oh I see...yes, well that's too bad. So you're where? Uh huh. And you're sure you'll be alright–all by yourself?"

He waited.

"Okay then."

He listened again.

"All right. I'll see you sometime tomorrow afternoon. Have fun...eh, me too, you. Bye."

John carefully hung up the phone, not knowing what to think. He turned back to face Moira, whose dark eyes were searching his face.

"Everything okay?" she asked.

"Oh yes...fine. Just fine, thanks."

"You didn't know she was going away with Graham, did you?"

"Well come to think of it, maybe she did mention it. Anyway, it's nothing to worry about. You know how he is."

"Oh aye, I certainly do." Moira was surprised by John's lack of concern.

He walked around the room turning on the lamps, trying to avoid any physical contact. "So would you like to eat...or a drink maybe?"

"That would be nice," she replied. "A drink would be very nice. Do you have any wine open?"

"I don't know, but we can soon open some."

John tried to move around her, but she held her ground. As he squeezed past, she slipped into his arms. The dam broke. He covered her face with kisses, holding on to her for dear life. She grabbed his hair, forced him to her mouth, and kissed him with such longing that it took his breath. He lifted her, still clamped to his mouth, and carried her across the room to the couch, where he laid her down and began to undress her. He pulled his lips from hers and bent to take her breast to his mouth. Her body responded to his every touch, and she sighed with pleasure as he explored her and tasted her. When he parted her trembling thighs and touched her with his lips, she moaned softly.

When Moira reached her orgasm, the convulsions of release were so intense that John was forced to let her go. He rolled away and waited for the storm to subside. A moment later, he reached for her again and drew her to him. As he entered her, she whimpered and clasped him to her.

✠ ✠ ✠

Later at the kitchen table they nibbled on Stilton and crusty bread and gazed at each other.

John broke the silence.

"I called a friend of mine in London about you," he said.

She arched her right eyebrow.

"I mean about your music."

She eyed him impishly. "Oh thank God. I didn't know what you were going to say there for a minute."

He shook his head.

"Anyway, he's an executive in the music business, and he's promised to do whatever he can. As a matter of fact, he told me that next weekend, there's going to be a big charity event at Gleneagles Hotel, and he's planning to attend. There'll be lots of music people there, and some movie stars. He said that a couple of the Royals are expected as well."

Moira watched him as he spoke, seemingly more focused on the shape of his mouth than on what he was saying. He became aware of her lack of concentration.

"Are you listening to me, young lady? This is important."

"So are you, John; really, really important. Could we talk about the other stuff tomorrow? I'll get up early and make us a huge breakfast. We can talk about your plans for my success then."

She stood up, gathered his shirt around her body, and came around the table to sit on his lap, making it difficult for him to focus. Then he registered what she'd said.

"Breakfast? Here?...I don't think so. That would surely be the last straw for my poor housekeeper. She already thinks I'm some kind of deviant. I'm afraid, dear girl, that you're going to have to go home, and unfortunately, I can't offer to drive you. Valerie took the car."

"Oh never you mind. I've got the scooter, and I never really wanted to stay with you, anyway. I've had all I need from you."

As she rose from his lap, John delivered a resounding smack to her rump.

She spun back.

"Deviant," she scolded and skipped happily from the room.

He sat staring after her, trying to ignore the word she'd chosen.

CHAPTER 18

———•••———

Miles away from the moodiness of Ainsley House, Valerie
rose refreshed and relieved that the evening had ended as
it had. She sang to herself as she did the mirror work and
smiled, remembering that John had always discouraged the use of
her voice for anything other than speaking. He'd told her that she
sang like an ailing bagpipe.

By the time she headed downstairs to meet Graham for breakfast, she felt almost euphoric. She was pleased with herself and
grateful for her newfound freedom.

Graham rose to meet her as she entered the dining room.

"My, my, Missus MacIntyre, and don't we look ravishing this
morning. Sleep well?"

"Yes, thank you. And as a matter of fact, you do look ravishing."

The man's attractiveness was undeniable, and she knew she could have justified the indiscretion. Thank God, she'd resisted the temptation.

✧ ✧ ✧

The sail back to Oban was almost as wonderful as the outward leg, until she began to think about returning home to John and his moods.

When Graham suggested they take the long way home so that he could show her Loch Lomond, she was thrilled.

As they drove slowly along the loch, they joined together in song. Their voices together created the perfect discord. Completely oblivious, they sang their hearts out.

Oh you take the high road
And I'll take the low road
And I'll be in Scotland afore ye,
But me and my true love will
Never meet again,
On the bonny, bonny banks
Of Loch Lomond.

Valerie returned home feeling better about things, but the feeling didn't last long. Although John said he was pleased to see her, he seemed distracted as she described her trip. It was only when she saw the unfamiliar silver bracelet lying under the table next to the couch that her suspicions were confirmed.

Her husband had been neither alone nor lonely.

✪ ✪ ✪

A few days before Moira was due to sing for the rich and power-ful at Gleneagles, John faced a dilemma. He had not yet come up with a plausible reason for leaving town. He'd considered a dozen excuses, but he knew they'd never pass muster.

Just when he'd about given up, providence, or something else, offered a helping hand. He received a call from the proprietor of a book-shop in Edinburgh that he'd contacted on Drummond's recommenda-tion. The bookseller said that, per John's inquiry, he'd come across a rare book on the Campbells. He explained that the book was not for sale but suggested that John drive into the city to have a look at it.

It was almost too perfect.

That night over dinner, John spun his lie. He wasn't sure how he was going to dissuade Valerie from joining him on the trip, but incredibly, she herself provided the solution.

"I hope you don't mind if I beg off," she said. "I'm feeling a bit punk again. Maybe too much of that brisk sea air."

Valerie felt bad about her little fib, but she simply didn't want to be with him.

He explained that the book would probably take hours to peruse, so he'd likely be away overnight.

Although her heart felt cold, her expression gave nothing away.

✪ ✪ ✪

Friday arrived overcast and blustery. It felt like autumn was upon them. Rain threatened. John didn't care. He was caught up in the excitement of the road trip. As he drove, he chatted away about any subject that entered his mind.

"I remember reading somewhere that the name Gleneagles has nothing to do with birds. It was named by the French. It was actually the Glen D'Eglise, the glen of the church. Interesting huh?"

Moira listened in silence as he rambled on.

"Did you know that hundreds of years ago, there was a vigorous trade between the French and the Scots? The French wanted the Scottish woolens and their whiskey. In exchange, they brought things like glass and spices, from as far away as Egypt."

Moira gazed at the speeding scenery, only half listening.

"They say that the Scots can actually trace their ancestry all the way back to Egypt; to Scota, the daughter of the pharaoh. That's how we became such accomplished stonemasons. We're actually part Egyptian. How about that? Drummond was telling me about it."

When there was no response, John glanced over. She was asleep.

✵ ✵ ✵

Their suite on the third floor of the grand old hotel was large and luxurious with creaky floors. Moira strolled through the beautifully appointed rooms, fascinated by everything she saw. The fact that there were two bedrooms surprised her. She wondered which one they'd end up in.

John tipped the bellman, closed the door behind him, and went to join Moira in the living room. He removed the chilled champagne from the silver ice bucket, and with great flourish, popped the cork. He poured two glasses, handed one over, and smiled.

"To the bonniest girl in all of Scotland. May your evening be a very special one." He raised his glass to his lips and took a sip.

Moira didn't drink.

"What's the matter? You don't like champagne?"

"I don't know. I've never had it before. But I do know that it's bad luck to toast yerself."

"In that case, here's to me, John MacIntyre, the luckiest man in all the land."

Moira took a tentative sip and curled her pretty nose.

"Oh," she said, "I do like it. It tickles, but I like it fine."

"Well, drink up, and I'll take you on a tour of the gardens. They're incredible. We're meeting Ronnie here at four so he can go over the program with you. That gives us just enough time."

"Thank you, John, but I shouldn't drink anymore. I never do before a performance, and this is a really important one."

John stepped toward her and took her in his arms.

"Now my girl, don't you worry about a thing. I told you that when Ronnie called me after hearing your stuff, he said you were fantastic. You're gonna knock their silk socks off. I know it."

She offered a hesitant smile and kissed him softly on the mouth.

"Thank you, John. Thanks for everything."

A few minutes later, they wandered through the formal gardens enjoying the beauty of the late-season roses, when a squall sprang up out of nowhere. They dashed for the front door and managed to get there before getting completely soaked.

As they crossed through the hotel lobby, Moira stopped dead in her tracks and raised her hands to her mouth. John followed the direction of her stare. At the desk, a terminally skinny young man in an expensive Italian suit was signing the guest register, unaware of the reaction he was causing.

"Oh my God. It's Alec Zander. Do you see? It's Alec Zander. He's right there."

John had no idea what she was talking about.

"Who? Who the hell is Alexander?"

"Ye don't know? Why, he's the lead singer for the Disappearing Dream. He used to be with Lilly White and the Bleachers, but he left to form his own band."

"Oh I see," said John, feeling completely out of touch. He took her by the arm and steered her toward the elevator in an effort to stop her from staring.

"He'll be there tonight, I'm sure. As a matter of fact, he'll be asking for *your* autograph before the night's over."

Moira punched his arm and giggled. She was excited. John sighed and shook his head.

The elevator doors opened, and they stepped inside. He pushed the button for the third floor and the doors began to close. At the very last moment, an arm thrust its way through the crack, and the doors sprang back. Moira almost fainted dead away when Alec Zander sauntered into the lift. As John reached to push the open button, the girl grabbed his arm in an effort to keep from falling. The good-looking young man glanced at them.

"Thanks, man," he mumbled. "Two please."

As the old lift limped its way upward, Zander stood with his back in the corner and openly ogled Moira, completely ignoring John's presence. The possibility that the old gent might be the girl's companion apparently never occurred to him. "Are you going to the banquet tonight?"

She nodded.

"Well then, I'll look forward to seeing you there. Maybe we can have a drink afterward or something."

As John opened his mouth to respond, the doors opened and Zander stepped off. He waved to the speechless girl and breezed away whistling to him self.

John didn't know how to react. Never before had he been insulted quite so casually. He knew his cheeks were flushed. Moira glanced at him.

"I didn't think he was nearly as attractive up close, did you?"

Her effort made him feel even worse.

"No, not nearly," he said.

As he wrestled with his tie in the bedroom mirror, he listened to Moira vocalizing in the bathroom. He was feeling pretty good, due in part to the three scotches he'd had during the visit from Ronnie Harper. Harper had been so bowled over by Moira, he'd made a complete fool of himself. If Moira noticed, she'd made no mention.

John turned from the window as she entered the room. She wore a long ivory dress that clung fiercely to her body. A fine tartan shawl draped her bare shoulders, and her raven hair sparkled with tiny bells. He felt a powerful urge to steal her away, to keep her for him self. Instead, he crossed the room, placed his hands on her shoulders, and looked deep into her eyes.

"You're incredible," he said softly. "Everything you want will be yours."

He placed a kiss on her forehead and reached to pick up her guitar case.

They entered the banquet room, and all four hundred guests turned to stare. John saw his friend Ronnie Harper beckoning furiously from a table close to the stage. As John and Moira approached the table, the men rose eagerly to their feet, falling over each other to get noticed. The women remained firmly planted.

Ronnie disappeared backstage with the guitar, and, after a minute or two, returned to join them.

He'd arranged to be seated next to Moira.

"So, are you nervous, my dear?"

"No, Mister Harper. I'm not exactly nervous. More excited, I'd say. John's been so kind. He's arranged this wonderful opportunity for me, so I'm determined to do my best."

As she spoke, Ronnie gazed at her face, seemingly mesmerized.

At that moment, the lights went out, leaving a thousand candles to illuminate the room as the sound of bagpipes drew closer and closer. At the back of the room, a pair of huge doors swung open to admit a young piper who was followed by a distinguished-looking man, also dressed in kilts.

"Would ye rise one and all, and lift yer glasses," said the man. He waited as the guests rose to their feet and raised their water glasses.

"Tae the Queen," the man thundered.

"To the Queen," responded the four hundred.

The crowd remained on its feet as a quartet of liveried men entered the banquet hall carrying a great silver tray on which rested something that looked like a headless carcass. The master of ceremonies raised a second glass, this one filled with whiskey. The people followed suit.

"Tae the haggis," the man roared.

"To the haggis," they roared back.

The master of ceremonies poured the whiskey over the object of everyone's solemn attention, and set it alight. The sudden burst of blue flame was greeted with a resounding cheer. The evening's festivities were officially underway.

From that moment on, the noise was deafening. Lively conversation mingled with laughter as scores of waiters and waitresses scurried about, presenting the evening's delights. The mood was joyful; the food divine. As the guests feasted, a five-piece band played traditional Scottish country music. The happy lilt of jigs and reels was the perfect accompaniment. Under the table, Moira's foot tapped continuously.

Even though the food was the best she'd ever tasted, she could only pick at it. As she skewered one last coconut shrimp, she had the uneasy feeling that someone was staring at her. Glancing around, she spotted Alec Zander about three tables away, raising his glass in her direction. She nodded in reply and turned back to Ronnie, who was chatting away, oblivious.

After the dessert has been served and coffee poured, the master of ceremonies crossed to the microphone and attempted to get the crowd's attention. This was easier said than done. The endless flow of whisky and fine wine had created a rather rambunctious crowd. It took some severe banging on the cymbal to penetrate the merriment. The noise gradually subsided as the throng turned to face the stage. Stagehands in black tee shirts moved a high stool and guitar stand into place.

"Ladies and gentlemen," he announced, "this evening ye're all in fer a rare treat, Gleneagles Hotel is pleased tae present fer yer pleasure, all the way from the land of the Campbells, the bonnie and gifted Miss Moira Macleod, the Bell of Argyll."

The stage went dark. The applause faded to silence as a single spotlight discovered Moira.

She began to softly strum her guitar, and by the time her glorious voice reached for the people, she already had them captivated. She sang an old song, a very beautiful one.

> Speed, bonnie boat like a bird on the wing,
> Over the sea to Skye.
> Carry the lad that was born to be King
> Over the sea to Skye.

As she sang about the escape of Bonnie Prince Charlie from the hands of his enemies, the effect on the crowd was amazing. People who were not even Scottish found themselves dabbing at their eyes. Captains of industry found themselves strangely moved. When the song ended, there was silence. Then, as if it had been on a delayed fuse, a tidal wave of applause descended on the room. Moira stood, smiling shyly.

From then on the evening was hers. John was bursting with pride as Ronnie pumped his hand offering his congratulations.

As Moira continued with her performance, the band joined in on the songs they knew. The effect was sublime.

When her set came to a close, the crowd leapt to its feet, yelling for more. Moira smiled gratefully and obliged. She sang one of her new songs, one about reaching for the stars. When the song ended to thunderous applause, she thanked the members of the band and hurried from the stage.

John was immediately surrounded by raving fans. He answered as many questions as he could. "No there's no record on the market yet, but pretty soon." He must have repeated himself a dozen times.

After a few minutes, he realized that Moira hadn't returned to the table, so he excused himself and went to look for her. He headed backstage, where he found her chatting and laughing with Alec Zander as if he was an old friend. The arrogant bastard had wasted no time.

"Oh John," Moira looked vaguely disappointed as she watched him approach, but not as disappointed as Zander.

"Ah yes, Mister eh—?

"MacIntyre," said John. The younger man reached out his hand. Begrudgingly, John took it.

"So, what are we going to do with this talented young lady?" Zander asked.

John forced his voice to remain calm. "Well I don't know. Just what exactly did you have in mind?"

Zander sized up his adversary. John gazed right back.

Moira broke the awkward silence.

"Oh John...Mister Zander here–Alec–has invited me to come to London. He says he can get me a recording contract in no time at all. Isn't that wonderful?"

"Well did he, now?" John smirked. He'd dealt with pups like this before. Zander was first to drop his eyes.

"Of course, if you're representing her, your input would certainly be more than welcome."

"Well thank you, Alec," said John. "May I call you Alec? That's a most generous gesture. How kind. Do you have a business card? We'll consider your offer and let you know."

"I don't carry cards, I'm afraid. People usually know me."

John took Moira's arm and began to lead her away.

Zander watched them carefully.

"See you soon, Bell of Argyll."

In the corner of his eye, John saw her turn back and flash Zander a quick smile.

By the time they returned to the banquet hall, the place had pretty well emptied out. The few stragglers who remained waved to Moira, extending enthusiastic thumbs up. She was on Cloud Nine.

John was on Cloud One.

Moira made for the table to gather her things, while John arranged to have the guitar delivered back to the suite. The after-party would be just heating up in the bar, and John was eager to mingle, to show off his prize.

As they strolled toward the cocktail lounge, Moira was pensive.

"You don't like him, do you? He was just being friendly. I think he really wanted to help."

John stopped and turned her toward him. He cupped her perfect chin in his hand.

"Listen to me, young lady. There's no such thing as a man just being friendly—not when it comes to a girl that looks like you... unless of course he's gay, like your friend Graham."

So intent was John on making his point, he didn't notice the blank expression on Moira's face.

"There's only one thing they're after. Trust me. I know."

Moira started to say something mean, but changed her mind.

"Why, John MacIntyre, I do believe you were just a wee bit jealous…and I must say, I'm flattered."

"Oh don't be ridiculous."

Already, he could feel her slipping away.

When they entered the lounge, the party was in full swing, and Moira was quickly surrounded by well-wishers. Everybody wanted to buy drinks. By this time, Moira was ready to indulge, and ordered a Rum and Coke. John decided to stick with the whisky. After a few minutes, he excused himself to find the restroom, determined not to leave Moira alone too long.

No sooner had John left the room than Alec Zander slid off his barstool and sidled up beside her.

"I meant what I said, you know." He noted the slight intake of breath as she turned to his voice. "I'd be happy to do anything, anything I can to help. I realize that your friend thinks I'm insincere, but I assure you, your music is really very special."

"Thank you. That's very nice, but I'm kind of leaving things up to John. He's very smart, and he knows a lot about show business. He's a very famous director, you know, from Hollywood."

"Well okay, but if ever you change your mind or find yourself in London, here's my number."

He handed her a small piece of paper, which she folded, without looking, and put in her purse.

"Tell me," Zander said, "How long has he been your manager?"

"Who? John?"

Alec nodded his head.

"Oh John's not my manager. He's my lover."

As Moira sauntered away, Alec Zander nearly choked on his ice cube.

✿ ✿ ✿

By the time they returned to their suite, Moira was tipsy. She'd had the most wonderful evening of her life. She'd met a couple of movie stars and famous athletes and discovered that she quite enjoyed hobnobbing with the rich and famous. And they'd all treated her so well...especially the men. She was feeling awfully good about herself as she undressed for bed.

They made love hurriedly, but with great intensity. When it was over, Moira collapsed on her pillow, exhausted from all the excitement, not to mention the five Rum and Cokes. As she was drifting off into sleep, she began to murmur to herself, whispering barely intelligible words.

"I'll show ye; I'll show ye all. She's there still. It's her light ye see."

She murmured something else that John couldn't make out, then whispered perfectly clearly. "Can't let it. Mustn't ever let it."

She moaned, rolled away, and began to snore. John studied her for a moment, before pulling the covers over her. It took him a long time to go to sleep.

✿ ✿ ✿

On the drive home, John asked about her sleep talking, but Moira denied any knowledge of it. The rest of the drive was quiet. They didn't have much to say to each other, and they both had a lot to think about. By the time John dropped her off in Kilmartin, where she'd left her scooter, she seemed distant.

They didn't kiss goodbye.

✡ ✡ ✡

At Ainsley, John volunteered little information about his trip, and Valerie didn't ask. He retreated to his study, went to his computer, and tried to write, but there was nothing flowing. As he sat at his desk daydreaming, John thought about Drummond and their plan to hike out to the pagan temple. He picked up the telephone and dialed.

The minister sounded pleased at the prospect, and they made arrangements to meet the next day.

John sat staring at his monitor until the words were out of focus, and slowly, mercifully, his mind was transported to the distant past.

The remarkable entry of a veiled Eileen MacLeod was greeted with stunned silence. Her father struggled to his feet and tried to speak, but his voice failed him. Campbell could not help but read the implications of the girl's attire. As if there was nothing amiss, she strode regally to her place and bowed to her father before offering a curtsy to their guest. Campbell rose to his feet and bowed, stiff with anger.

When they were once again seated, MacLeod leaned in close to his daughter's ear.

"What in God's name is the meaning of this effrontery, my lass? What the hell's in your mind? Are you trying to offend the most powerful man in the land?"

"No father, it's nothing like that at all, I assure you. My face is so badly marked from the stinging nettles that I couldn't be seen by anybody this night, especially by Lord Campbell. I knew you'd be right angry if I didn't come to greet him, so I had no choice. Would you please explain the situation, and offer my apology?"

MacLeod seemed relieved. He took a deep breath and turned to impart the information to Campbell.

When the explanation was completed, Argyll leaned forward to stare at the girl, not sure if he should believe her. Eileen turned in his direction and offered an apologetic shrug. He turned to Duncan and glared.

"Tomorrow! I'll see her face tomorrow, or this evening's choice of wardrobe will prove appropriate. Do you understand me?"

MacLeod glowered in the direction of his daughter. "Oh aye, my Lord, I certainly do. I understand you plainly."

The evening proceeded awkwardly. Campbell seemed bored, and as soon as the meal was over, he rose, shook a warning finger at the old man, and charged from the room. William of Alsh offered apologies and hurried after his chieftain.

The next day, Campbell was escorted to the chamber of Eileen MacLeod. Although he was aware that such a visit was highly improper, his patience had run out. He was in a dark mood.

Campbell strode on with old Duncan running alongside him trying to keep up. They passed through a succession of draughty corridors before climbing the worn steps to Eileen's rooms. Campbell himself pounded his fist on the heavy door and winced in pain, hoping that no one had noticed. The door opened slowly to reveal Eileen. She was sitting in the window seat, with her back to the door, gazing out at the sea. Meg, her attendant, announced the visitors. Eileen did not respond.

"Turn ye around," thundered MacLeod. "Turn around this instant, or it'll be your darkest day, I promise you."

She slowly turned to face the intruders. Campbell was dumbstruck. Gone was the girl he'd had been dreaming of. The face before him was unrecognizable and hideous. The skin was covered with oozing pustules. Her lips were cracked and bleeding, her eyes swollen nearly shut. The affliction was very real. Campbell experienced an unfamiliar pang of remorse.

"My sincere apologies, my lady," he said. "I can see you're in great misery, and I can but wish you a quick recovery. At the risk of appearing crude in your company, but having seen this before, I suggest the liberal application of cow's urine, preferably from one that's in calf. With that I'll leave you, and I'm right sorry for your condition. I was perhaps hasty. I hope you'll forgive me."

As Campbell left the room with the others, a ghost of a smile crossed Eileen's disfigured face. She'd endured great pain applying the nettle leaves, but it had been worth it.

Striding down the dank corridor, Argyll halted in his tracks and spun to face MacLeod. The older man barely managed to avoid a crash.

"The wedding will take place on the first of the month at Campbell Keep. You'd be advised to inform your clever daughter that it'll be yourself that suffers the consequences should she not arrive at the fortress properly prepared. Do you understand me?"

"Aye, my Lord, I understand you."

The return to Argyllshire was much more somber than the journey out. The men left their chief to his surly thoughts and were relieved that they didn't encounter a detachment of English. With the mood Campbell was in, he would have attacked an entire army.

As soon as the visitors had left Brothock Castle, MacLeod's chancellor approached his chief. "So, did he give the promises we hoped for, about the lands to the west?" asked the pale man.

"Oh aye, Lasker...I got his promise all right. He promised that if Eileen arrived at his castle two weeks from today, ready and willing to be his wife, he won't butcher us all."

Lasker's eyebrows rose in unison.

The sun was sinking as Eileen sat alone in her chamber studying her reflection in the looking glass. The face that gazed back at her was *one she didn't recognize. Beyond the immediate grotesqueness, she saw something very different about her eyes. Gone was the light that had once shone there. In its place, she saw a pall of resignation. She rose to her feet, crossed to her wardrobe, and began to select her garments.*

She dressed slowly, methodically, donning the snow-white marriage gown that had been her mother's. The fabric had been sent all the way from Egypt and was the finest that anyone had ever seen. It had always been Eileen's intention to wear it at her wedding. Carefully, she arranged the lace veil over her tresses and let it fall over her face, masking the horror. She gathered a garland of wild flowers from her bed and slipped from the room.

She glided silently through the passageways, accompanied only by the moaning of the wind. She reached a narrow stairway and began her ascent. As she climbed the stone steps, she looked down, surprised at just how cold they were, and realized that she'd forgotten to wear her slippers. She shrugged and continued on.

As she climbed, she thought of her mother. It had been so long since she'd seen her mother.

As she stood on the castle's highest battlement, gazing out over the sea, she felt strangely sleepy. The sea had always been her friend. It had whispered her to sleep from the time she was a little baby. She could hear it calling to her now.

She climbed up onto the wall and felt the wind. It steadily grew in intensity until it filled the fabric of her gown. She closed her eyes and offered up a prayer to her beloved Robert and to God, asking them both to forgive her for the path she'd chosen.

Her tears stung the sores on her face as she stared at the jagged rocks far below. The wind howled its anger.

She spread her arms and pitched slowly forward.

John pushed back from his computer, aware of the cold ache in his fingers. He studied his swollen knuckles, wondering what was happening to them. He was shocked. The hands he was looking at were not his. Instead, they were the weathered, scarred hands of an outdoorsman. As he watched in amazement, the hands slowly mutated until they were once again his own. He rubbed his dry eyes, trying to dismiss the transformation as an hallucination, the result of too many hours staring at the computer screen. And in truth, he didn't care what was happening to him. The words were coursing through him again. His guide had returned.

He climbed the stairs to bed and slept soundly. It was a dreamless night.

CHAPTER 19

The next day, bright and early, John arrived at the manse to pick up the minister as arranged. Drummond emerged from the house followed by a big yellow dog, the one that had slept through John's last visit. "Do you mind if Diogee tags along?" asked the minister. "He loves the hills."

"Not at all," said John, releasing the seat catch so that the retriever could get into the small back seat. The minister contorted his long frame and descended into the car. He reached over to shake John's hand.

"This is going to be fun. You'll enjoy this. Take the Callander Road. I'll show you the turnoff when we get there. I'm glad you wore hiking boots. It's quite a trek from where we leave the car."

John pulled onto the road and headed toward the rugged hills. For a few minutes, they drove in silence, enjoying the beauty of the day.

John broke the spell. "Aha," he said, wagging his finger at his passenger.

"What?" asked the clergyman.

"Diogee…Your dog's name. Very clever."

"What do you mean?"

"Well," said John, reaching back to pet the retriever, Di—o—gee spells dog. That's very good."

Drummond nodded and grinned. "I'm glad you approve."

Twenty minutes later, they parked the car in the shade of an ancient chestnut tree and climbed out. They hopped over a drystone wall and began the trek across the moor toward the hills.

John had to struggle to keep up, but managed to hide the fact until he tripped over a clump of gorse and fell. Muttering to himself, he climbed to his feet and trudged on.

During the entire hike, Diogee entertained himself flushing rabbits and birds from their hiding places, chasing every one with tireless glee.

It took almost an hour of brisk walking before Drummond slowed to a stop. Grateful, John fell to his knees and stuck his face into the icy stream that meandered through the glen. When he'd drunk his fill, he looked up, expecting to see the temple. He saw nothing but heather-covered hills and a few sheep, which Diogee eyed longingly, but seemingly managed to resist the temptation to give chase.

Drummond pointed to a rocky crag that looked just like all the others.

"There it is."

John looked but saw nothing.

Drummond smiled.

"You could walk past this place every day and never know that it was here. These ancient Celts were a pretty crafty lot, oh aye, indeed."

John followed the minister as he clambered across the rocks to the far side of the crag. Beneath them lay a small clearing. In the middle of the clearing was a fire pit surrounded by a circle of stones.

Drummond led the way down into the clearing past a thick stone slab the size of a double bed.

"Is this what I think it is?" asked John.

"Yes indeed. This is where the ancients made their sacrifices, sometimes animals, sometimes humans, I'm sad to say."

The surface of the slab was soiled with dark stains that looked a bit too fresh for John's liking. He decided he didn't want to think about it.

He turned away and noticed, for the first time, a towering cross that had taken root in the earth. As he surveyed the macabre symbol, he began to feel a strange sensation. It was as though the thing was reaching for him. The atmosphere of the pagan temple was powerful indeed. The place was almost as creepy as the Keep.

"So tell me about the props."

"Well, the blending of the symbols was my own idea," said Drummond. "It's an effort to combine the best of two worlds—two schools of mysticism. It's a way to try to save what's slipping away from us. The rood, or cross, is the symbol of hope, of life everlasting. The boys carved it themselves, from a tree that had stood in this spot for hundreds of years. It was an inspiration, I must say. Imagine, a living cross. Unfortunately, the tree died from its wounds; still, it does lend a certain moodiness to the scene. Wouldn't you agree?"

John nodded. "Oh, yeah."

"The altar is quite another matter. It stands for truth, absolute reality. It represents something more vital to this moment in time.

The stone has been here forever. In fact, its power is much older than that of the cross."

The minister's eyes flashed as his fervor increased.

"And we Scots do love our stones, John. They're an important part of our history. I'm convinced that the recent return of our most precious stone, the 'Stone of Destiny' from the godless Abbey of Westminster was a sign. It remains a tangible symbol of our great past…and our glorious future.

"The cross, of course, is the symbol of resurrection. Although, it does require death before it can manifest its power."

Drummond crossed to the fire pit and sat on one of the circle stones.

John followed and sat down next to him. "Quite a place," he offered.

"Yes it is," the minister agreed. "You'll have to come back sometime…maybe witness one of our ceremonies."

Drummond was on a roll. His monologue continued throughout the trek back to the car.

"Aye, there was a time when this was the land of iron fists and steel blades, when people were not afraid to spill a little blood for what they held dear."

John pictured the altar, wondering when it had last been spilled on.

After dropping the minister off at the manse, he headed home. He hated not being able to share any of the things that had happened over recent days. It felt strange being exiled from his wife. They'd always shared everything, relying on each other to deal with the stuff life brought, but that night, John had mountains of stuff and nobody to share it with.

He wearily climbed the stairs and entered the bathroom to pour a bath, figuring that a hot tub might make him feel better. He turned on the tap and stood before the mirror, studying his face. It was not something he was in the habit of doing. If he spent three minutes a day at the mirror, that was a lot.

As the steam began to obscure his reflection, John felt a wave of sadness descending over him. He watched himself fade away into the vapor clouds. The image was disturbing.

Although he'd always maintained that life was long and that there would be time for everything, it seemed now that time was disappearing right before his eyes. "What's happened to me?" he asked. "What am I doing?" He'd always been proud of his restraint, his moral courage, his intellectual honesty. In the mirror, he'd seen the truth.

"You damned hypocrite," he whispered.

It was his father's face that he'd glimpsed—a person he'd sworn to never be.

Suddenly, hot water splashed onto his feet.

"Ouch," he howled.

He first turned off the tap, then reached to remove the stopper from the drain. Scalding water stung him well past his elbow. He figured it was what he deserved.

CHAPTER 20

listair Frazier rang the bell at the elegant townhouse and
waited nervously until Rudy appeared at the glass door.
The muscle-bound man opened it and silently escorted
him through the richly appointed vestibule and up the carpeted
staircase. He stopped at a large wooden door and tapped softly.

"Come in."

Rudy pushed open the door, allowing the lad to enter, and
stepped into the room behind him. Sitting behind a huge partner's
desk was Marcus Bersky. He looked up from the assortment of rare
stones he'd been studying.

"Well, well, my boy...let us see what you've brought me."

Alistair extended a package wrapped in newspaper. Marcus
snatched it from his hand and tore off the wrapping. His fleshy

face reflected his delight as a silver dagger, its hilt encrusted with gems, clattered onto his desk. "Aha. You've done well, my dear— very well. One more just like this, and we'll be able to mark your account closed."

"But Marcus, you said that this would be the end of it."

"Ah yes, but you see, it's taken far too long for you to comply with our agreement. There is the matter of accumulated interest, you understand. And yours, I'm afraid, is considerable."

Bersky had a special relationship with the young people of Oban, particularly with the ones who frequented the Skullery. As the town Fagin, he was happy to supply all manner of drugs in exchange for anything of value filched from unsuspecting tourists.

Although he dabbled in a number of businesses, Bersky's true passion was rare artifacts. It was illegal to remove such items from Scottish soil, but Marcus had never concerned himself about such trivialities. The setup was simple; his antique business provided the perfect cover. It allowed him to ship product in and out of the country, satisfying demand in two markets. He was, at the same time, a collector of information. He had the goods on enough important people to ensure that his business would continue to run smoothly. He was a careful man.

Alistair thought back to the night at the Skullery when, feeling no pain and desperate to get his hands on more drugs, he'd bragged to his friends about Drummond's secret chamber and the loot it held. A vial of cocaine had appeared out of nowhere, and by the end of the evening, Alistair had made promises he shouldn't have.

The next day, he'd been taken to meet Marcus Bersky, where he had admitted that he could get his hands on some very old objects. Marcus had supplied the boy with the drugs he wanted, and soon, the first relic appeared.

From that moment, Alistair Frazier was trapped. He knew Bersky's reputation. He also knew Drummond's.

Marcus' face remained expressionless.

"As I said, one more, of roughly the same quality, and we'll be even."

"Drummond'll notice they're missing. He'll kill me. He'll know it was me. He knows everything."

"Well I don't know what to recommend, but I suppose that the manner of your doom should be your own choice. I may not go so far as to kill you, but I assure you, you'll experience some severe discomfort. We don't like people who don't pay their debts. Do we Rudy?"

Marcus's tiny eyes darted to Alistair's face, then back to the dagger. With an impatient wave, he dismissed the boy.

The audience was over. Rudy led Alistair from the room.

✿ ✿ ✿

Moira felt depressed. She hadn't seen John for days. She knew he was avoiding her. The time together at Gleneagles had been very exciting, far beyond her mission, but somehow things had changed, just when it had been going so well. She could feel John distancing himself. She looked at the telephone, wondering if she should try calling him at the house, but thought better of it.

Maybe I should let him miss me for a while, she thought. *Maybe I'll go away and let him wonder where I've gone.*

She thought about Drummond and his stupid scheme and how it hadn't worked at all. She was the one waiting by the phone, and she hated it.

The hell with Drummond, she decided. *And the hell with John MacIntyre.*

She crossed to her dressing table and removed a piece of paper from the drawer. She unfolded it and studied it for a moment before lifting the receiver to place the long-distance call.

✿ ✿ ✿

John was suffering. He'd been totally unprepared for the waves of guilt that now churned in his guts. At the same time, he couldn't stop thinking about Moira. She'd become integral to his work, the living model for Lady Eileen, and he was captivated by both of them.

But he'd let things go far too far. He was losing his wife. Although Valerie hadn't mentioned Moira for quite some time, John had known her long enough to be able to read her. Her unplanned trip and the chilly atmosphere in the house were not entirely lost on him. His work was suffering too. He hadn't written a decent word in days. He missed the writing, and he missed Valerie. He resolved to get back to the job at hand and to his wife, before it was too late.

He found her on the verandah. The day was cool, and she sat bundled up in a blanket writing in a small, hardcover notebook

"What are you up to?" He pulled up a chair and sat down.

"Oh, nothing much. I um…started to write a letter home and found that there was so much news, I should probably just call instead."

"So…what are you writing now?"

"Well, I thought that maybe writing down some of the things that are on my mind might help. I'm not exactly sure what's going on…with you, or with us, and I'm trying to be rational about it all." Valerie didn't look at him.

He pulled his chair closer and reached for her hand.

She allowed him to take it.

"Listen, I...I know I've been acting strangely, I don't really understand what it is, myself. I haven't been paying nearly enough attention to you, or to us. We came here to be together and for me to get some work done. Well, neither is happening at the moment. I want you to know, I'm really sorry. I've been acting like an old fool, and I'm asking you to give me a chance to make it up to you. I think that we should head home soon. Maybe things will be easier there...fewer distractions. What do you think?"

She exhaled slowly. "You're right, John. You have been acting like a fool, and in your defense, it's not something I've had a lot of practice with. Actually, I've been thinking about going home and leaving you to sort out what's important. I don't know what else to do."

"Don't go, honey. It's finished, whatever foolishness I've been caught up in. Please don't leave yet. At least wait a few more days. Give me a chance to show you. It'll be different, I promise."

He leaned in, but she turned her mouth away. He kissed her on the cheek.

"How about that cruise we talked about? Would you like that?" he asked.

"John, I'd love to do that with you—at least the you I arrived here with, but I don't think that it's a good idea at the moment. Why don't you get back into your work for a few days? Maybe it'll help focus you. I won't make any decisions. Let's see what happens."

"Deal," said John. "Thank you. Thanks very much."

"So why don't you start now? Go write. It's what you need to do."

"That's probably a good idea. I think I will."

At the door, he turned back to look at his wife. He felt grateful to have her, but still, he felt miserable.

She was busy writing in her journal.

Alistair arrived at the Thistle and was surprised to see a taxi waiting at the front door. He'd come to have a word with Moira, to try to make her change her mind about leaving the band. Without her, the bookings had been much harder to get, and he really needed the money. Begging was not beneath him. As he stepped inside, he was surprised to see her coming down the stairs with a brand-new suitcase clutched in her hand.

"Where you off to, then?" He assumed the posture of a penitent.

She surveyed him coolly and marched right past him out the door. The taxi driver, a gaunt young man with a bad complexion, leapt from the car, clearly thrilled with his good fortune. He took her bag, deposited it into the trunk, and moved to open the front door. She glanced at him with total disdain, hauled open the rear door, and climbed in.

Alistair followed right behind her, opened the door, and leaned inside the car. "Please talk to me, Moira. I'll do anything. It can be just the way you want it. Come on, we need you...I need you. I'm in trouble, Moira—terrible trouble."

"Listen, Ali." She was determined to remain strong. "While it was good, it was good, but things changed. Things are different for me now, far different, and if you must know, I'm off to London."

She attempted to reclose the door.

"I've got a friend there who's promised to get me a recording deal, and I don't know when I'll be back. I don't know if I'll ever be back. I won't be part of what's going on around here...not anymore."

Realizing that she'd given too much information, she grabbed Ali's hand. "You can't tell anyone, Ali. Drummond can't know where I am. I shouldn't have told you, damn it."

"I won't tell, Moira. I promise."

"Listen, it's just something I've got to do. I've been telling you for years that I was going to leave this place. Well, now's the perfect time, that's all."

"But London? It's so far away. And what friend? How the hell did you make a friend in London? And what about your damn boyfriend? What's he going to say? What's John MacIntyre going to say?"

She glared up at him. "What did you say? What do you know about me and him, then?"

"You were being watched, Moira. Drummond's always had you watched." He let go of the door.

Moira slammed the door.

As the taxi pulled away, Ali stood watching, biting his lip, holding in the tears. She didn't look back.

✡ ✡ ✡

Graham tired of CNN news and rose to switch off the set. For the life of him, he couldn't understand why yet another thug was on television touting his latest book and claiming that society bore the responsibility for his indiscretions.

"Oh well, it's no wonder their country's in such a condition," he muttered.

Graham had never much liked Americans. The times he'd encountered them, whether at university in Edinburgh or more recently on the streets of Oban, they'd always seemed a bit crude, unfinished. He chuckled to himself. "I suppose I'm a terrible snob."

His thoughts turned to Valerie. She was the exception. She was smart and refined, with a keen sense of humor and an opinion about everything. He was well aware that he'd fallen for her. If only she wasn't completely in love with her idiot of a husband, who didn't have any appreciation for her at all.

Oh well, a man can always dream. For some reason, he thought of his ex–fiancée, Marion, something he didn't often do. He wondered about her life in the States with Bob Bleeker, the woolens salesman she'd run off with.

"Serves her right," he muttered.

Graham choked back the old anger, grabbed his jacket, and headed for the door. As he stepped into the street, an unfamiliar car came hurtling around the bend, heading right for him. He leapt back as the taxi braked hard and skidded around him. As Graham shook his fist and cursed at the fast-moving vehicle, the person in the back seat turned and waved. He was surprised to recognize Moira, her pretty face clouded with sadness. As he continued across the road, wondering where she might be off to, he pulled his jacket closer around him. There was a too familiar chill in the air.

He entered the Thistle, and as he crossed the threshold, George began pouring a pint of bitter. He set it down on the bar at Graham's regular spot.

"George."

"Graham."

"So where's Moira off to in that taxi that just about ran me down?"

The barman picked up an already spotless glass and began to polish it. "They say she's on her way to London. Gone to get famous."

"She's what?" Graham sputtered. "What did you say?"

"Gone to the big city, Graham. Aye, she's gone willingly into the tent of the enemy. She's turned her back on us."

"I don't believe it," Graham growled, trying to get control of his anger. "She wouldn't. Something must have happened."

"What's the matter, Graham?" The voice came from the far end of the bar. "Did she not get your permission?"

Nesbit turned to see a drunken Alistair leering at him.

"Watch your mouth, my lad, or you'll be wearing it backward."

Alistair returned his attention to his glass and upended it into his mouth, spilling most of the contents down the front of his shirt.

"Who's she seeing in London, George?"

"Nobody knows," replied the barman. "She didn't tell anybody she was going. Alistair there just happened to catch her as she left."

Graham handed his glass across the counter. George poured him another.

✿ ✿ ✿

Hours later, a thoroughly inebriated Graham Nesbit knocked loudly on the door of Ainsley House. The door opened, and John ushered him inside. They entered the living room, where Valerie sat cross-legged at a Scrabble board set out on the coffee table before the fire. She seemed a bit taken aback when Graham plopped himself onto the couch and sat staring at her.

"Drink?" asked John.

Valerie shot her husband a withering frown.

"How about a nice cup of coffee?" She began to rise from her pillow.

"I thank you, John. A whiskey, if you don't mind. Aye, a wee whiskey'd be just the thing. On second thought, make that a large whiskey. This could take a minute."

John crossed to the liquor cabinet.

Valerie studied her drunken guest. With no idea what was coming, she settled back onto her pillow.

John handed Graham his drink, then returned to the cabinet and poured a stiff one for him self. "Can I get you anything, Val?" he asked.

"No thanks. I'm fine." Feeling uneasy, she watched Graham out of the corner of her eye.

When everyone was settled in, Graham began. He raised his glass in John's direction.

"Mister MacIntyre, you're indeed one of the luckiest men in this world, and undoubtedly one of the stupidest. That's what I came here to tell you, so I thought that I might as well get it said right off."

John took a breath and started to respond, but Graham raised his palm, indicating that he required silence. He looked squarely at Valerie.

"This is unquestionably the finest woman I've ever had the pleasure to meet." He continued on, even though he was having a bit of trouble forming the words. "And you, you blind fool, are doing everything in your power to force her out of your life. There isn't a man alive who wouldn't give his right crocus to be married to the likes of her. To have her for a partner through this life must truly be a blessing—one that you, John, don't seem to appreciate. She could get the flippin' fairies to fly right-side up."

Graham chuckled at his little joke and continued on.

"So, my advice to you is to remove your head from up your arse and smell the flowers before they're all withered. Do you get my gist?

Valerie gazed at him, her eyes shining with tears.

John was speechless.

Nesbit rose from the couch, crossed unsteadily to the bar, and poured himself another whiskey.

"How about you John? Do you need another?"

"No...no thanks. I'm fine, thank you."

Graham downed his drink in one gulp and started for the door but apparently changed his mind and teetered back to John for one last volley.

"Be warned, John MacIntyre: I'll not say it again. Strange things have been happening since you arrived here, and there's probably more to come. I hope you haven't gotten yourself into more than you bargained for. People aren't always what they seem in this vale, and you shouldn't be staying in this house any longer than you must. I've a feeling you've outstayed your welcome as it is."

Nesbit turned away again, and reached the door. He paused, swayed for a beat, and offered a final thought.

"I don't know what you know about this, John, or if you had anything to do with her decision, but Moira's left for London. She went today. For you, John, that might be a good thing. For some of us, it's a terrible thing. She's just a girl. She's not ready. I thought that maybe you'd like to say a wee prayer for her well-being."

He lurched out of the room.

A moment later, they heard his little car roar to life and the crunch of gravel as it accelerated away. John eyed his wife, but his thoughts were somewhere else. His brain was bombarded with images of Moira...and Alec Zander.

A resounding crash snapped him back. There was no doubt; it was the sound of small automobile meeting an immovable object. The MacIntyres leapt to their feet and raced outside, fearing the worst.

"We should never have let him drive," said Valerie as she ran.

Fifty yards down the road, the car had smashed into an electrical pole. Clouds of steam, or smoke, or both, billowed from its engine compartment. Somehow, the little vehicle had managed to partially climb the broken pole, and Graham sat unconscious, steering for the sky, his head lolling back at a peculiar angle.

It looked bad.

John grabbed Valerie from behind.

"An ambulance! I'll get him out. Call for help."

He urged her back in the direction of the house.

"Quick!"

She relented, and John raced on toward the smoldering vehicle. He grabbed the car door, lifted it open, reached inside, and began to pull Graham from the seat.

Why the hell did I send her away? he wondered. *Just when I need her most?*

The perfect irony did not escape him.

Eventually, he managed to pull Graham out. He dragged him away from the smoking car and laid him flat on the road. He placed his ear to the man's chest and listened.

✿ ✿ ✿

"London? What the hell do you mean, London?" Alan Moore sat seething in his wheelchair.

The news was so astounding that he'd actually turned down the volume on his telly.

Ian stood quaking in his sneakers as he delivered the information to his stepfather and his mother. Susan sagged into the nearest chair and covered her face with her hands.

"Oh no," she wailed, "my poor baby. What's to happen to her all the way down in London by herself?"

Ian nervously shuffled in place.

"She told Ali that she's got a friend there who's to get her a recording deal. He made me promise not to tell, but I had to tell you, Mum. I couldn't let you worry."

Moore snorted loudly, but the sudden exertion caused him to embark on a coughing fit. He choked up a great wad of phlegm and spat it in the direction of the fireplace, missing his mark by a foot. His wife glared at him in disgust but said nothing. She returned her attention to her son. Ian shuffled his feet and assured his mother that he'd told her all he knew.

"How dare she, the little bitch," Alan snarled. "Without even the decency to say goodbye to her poor mother. She's got obligations here, and she knows that. How are we supposed to get on, with her taking off to London? She'll end up a filthy whore, just like them girls on the telly—you can mark my words."

The absolute certainty of her husband's prediction reduced poor Susan to sobs.

"Oh shut up," said Alan, "that's not helping anything. I'll show her when she comes crawling back here for our forgiveness. Aye, I'll show the stupid brat."

CHAPTER 21

Moira stepped down from the train at King's Cross station in London and excitedly searched the waiting faces, but Alec Zander was nowhere to be seen. As she trudged slowly toward the exit gate, she was approached by a distinguished-looking older man in a smart gray suit. He removed a uniform cap from his head.

"Miss MacLeod?"

"Yes," she replied, cautiously.

"Good afternoon, Miss. I'm Roberts, Mister Zander's driver. Unfortunately, he's been detained and sends his apologies. I've been instructed to take you to your hotel, help you to get checked in, and make sure everything is to your liking."

Before she could protest, Roberts reached for her bag and guitar case and led her out from the grime of the old station into a brilliant London afternoon. Immediately, she started to feel better. The excitement returned, her disappointment at not being met by Alec momentarily forgotten.

Roberts escorted her toward a dark blue Bentley sedan, popped open the locks by remote control, and as Moira watched, intrigued, the windows slid down, allowing the heat from the sun to escape.

Feeling terribly chic, she giggled to herself as she was helped into the back seat.

The discreet Cuduggan Hotel was hidden away on a tiny square bearing the same name. Roberts bypassed the desk and led Moira directly to the stairs. They climbed to the second floor and stopped at number eight, which turned out to be a delightful bed-sitting room with huge French windows that overlooked a private, walled park.

"Beautiful," she whispered. As she gazed out the window, Roberts watched her impassively.

"Now, you understand, Miss MacLeod, that all your hotel expenses will be taken care of during your stay here, so please make yourself comfortable. Mister Zander will be calling you later this evening."

"Oh yes...yes of course." She suddenly remembered why she was there.

The chauffeur removed an envelope from his inside jacket pocket.

"This is to cover any additional costs you may incur during your visit." He sounded a bit embarrassed. "If you need more, don't be afraid to ask."

Moira tore open the envelope to discover five new one hundred-pound notes. It didn't feel at all right.

"Thanks all the same, sir, but I'll not be needing your money. I've brought my own. I couldn't possibly accept this."

She placed the envelope back in Roberts's hand. Surprised by the girl's pluck, the chauffeur nodded and returned it to his pocket.

"If there's anything you need while you're here, Miss MacLeod, anything at all, please call on me. I'd be happy to be of service."

Roberts let himself out.

After she'd unpacked her few things and put them away, Moira poured herself a bath. She soaked for almost an hour in the endless hot water. This was a level of luxury she'd experienced only once before, but she knew how to appreciate it. It was something she could learn to live with.

Three hours later, she was still waiting for the phone to ring, and famished. She decided to be brave and order room service. She'd seen John do it at Gleneagles and was confident she could handle it.

"Oh, dear John." She hadn't thought about him for hours. The excitement of the day had kept her mind on other things. "I do miss you."

Dinner was delicious. She'd ordered the fillet of sole from the menu, because it was something she recognized, and discovered that the chips were the best she'd ever tasted. Moira wished she'd thought to order dessert. *"Who knew the food was going to be this good?"*

She decided not to bother the kitchen any more and, instead, opened up the minibar to find a bounty of delights. She decided on the cashew nuts in the pretty glass jar, and a bottle of champagne. "Why the hell not?" she asked the little jar of cashews.

✿ ✿ ✿

At midnight, the phone rang, by which time Moira was stretched out on the couch, dead to the world. It rang eight times before she could rise through her stupor to answer it.

"I'll be there in twenty minutes," said a vaguely familiar voice before the line went dead. It took a moment for reality to penetrate her swirling brain. She rose carefully and wandered to the bathroom, where she applied a dab of lipstick, nothing more.

The bell rang, and she opened the door to find Zander leaning against it. He almost fell as he entered, but he managed somehow to right himself. Obviously, he'd already been to the party. He pushed his way past her, lurched across the room, and collapsed on the bed where he lay breathing heavily, ogling the delicacy.

"Well, Moira my dear, don't you look ravishing? Even better than I remembered. It does my old heart good. C'mere and give us a kiss. There's a good girl."

Quickly, she decided on a course of action.

"Alec," she purred, heading the minibar, "it's great to see you, too. How about something to drink while I'm over here?"

She poured herself a Perrier.

"Yeah, sounds great. I'll have a scotch if you don't mind."

Moira kept her back to Zander and managed to pour two of the little bottles into a glass. She sauntered back to the bed and handed over the drink. He reached for her, but she managed to evade his clutches and moved a safe distance away.

"Why don't we make this really special, Alec? I'd like to do something nice for you."

Zander was intrigued. He sat up and took a great swig of his whiskey. Moira turned on the radio, found some appropriate music, and began to dance. Soon, the man was completely enraptured.

As she danced, discarding her clothes as slowly as possible, Alec continued to slurp greedily from his glass. When he'd emptied it, Moira took it from his hand and made pouring him another drink part of her show. Totally transfixed, he didn't even notice when she handed the glass back to him.

A few minutes later, Moira was down to her panties, dancing with her back to Zander and becoming increasingly nervous. She heard a strange snorting sound and turned to look. Alec was sound asleep, the tumbler of scotch balanced carefully on his scrawny chest. Moira sighed with relief and allowed a rueful smile. So much for the effectiveness of her show.

She donned a nightie, curled up on the couch, and covered herself with a blanket. She lay awake for a long time. *What have you gotten yourself into now?* she wondered.

The morning found Zander with a pounding headache and Moira with a very stiff back. Alec looked around the room, bleary eyed, unsure as to the culmination of the previous evening. He was cheered by the presence of Moira, who, noticing he was awake, poured a cup of coffee and delivered it to him in bed.

"Do us a favor, love," he croaked, as the first sip of strong brew reached his churning belly. "Bring us that bag there on the table."

Moira handed him the black leather bag and watched, fascinated, as he downed a handful of pills, some yellow, some white. He chased them down with a healthy slug of pink liquid and two snorts of white powder from a tiny glass bottle.

She'd seen coke before, at the clubs in Oban but she politely declined the proffered vial. After finishing his coffee, Alec rose painfully and listed toward the bathroom.

Moira heard the shower being turned on. She knew that she wouldn't be able to postpone the inevitable much longer and tried to remind herself that what she was doing was only to help her career. After all, Alec Zander wasn't just anybody. There were thousands of girls who'd gladly trade places with her.

She became aware of the sounds of laughter coming from the park. She opened the French doors and stepped onto the balcony, where she watched a group of little girls, all dressed in identical straw hats and pale gray uniforms, playing Ring around the Rosy. She smiled sadly.

Alec returned from the bathroom hitching up his towel and feeling like a new man. He sat down on the bed and patted the spot beside him.

"Come Moira...come sit here. Let me tell you about all the things I've arranged for you."

He had her attention. She made her way slowly to the bed and sat down.

All the time he was talking, Alec was stroking her hair, drawing her closer as he reclined onto the pillows. She knew there was no getting out of it this time.

"Alec, let me pull the curtains, please."

He grunted his consent.

She crossed to the French doors and pulled them closed, shutting out the squeals of laughter from below. She then pulled the curtains and turned back to Zander, who lay eyeing her like a hungry cat. She loosened her robe, shrugged it to the floor, and stood motionless, giving him a moment to stare, before climbing into the bed and pulling the sheet over her body.

With a groan of pleasure, Zander slid across the bed and rolled on top of her. She stared at the ceiling as he had his way.

Thankfully, it was all over in a matter of minutes. He cursed loudly and pulled out of her, striving to hold himself back, but he was too late.

"Damn it." He muttered angrily as he rolled off and reached for a cigarette.

"That was wonderful, Alec." She slid from the bed and sauntered toward the bathroom. "Thank you."

That afternoon, Zander took Moira to her first real recording session. While his band laid down a driving rock track, she sat in the darkened control room right beside the engineer, completely enthralled as layers of sound were applied to the mix. Her heart soared with the possibilities. The recording studio was absolutely fantastic. It was everything she'd dreamed of. She allowed that the compromise might be worth it after all.

✿ ✿ ✿

That evening, Alec introduced his newest protégé to the night-life of London. They drove through Hyde Park and arrived at San Lorenzo, which he assured her was a very "in" spot—a favorite of the Royals. On the way there, Moira noticed Roberts stealing glances in the rearview mirror, as if to satisfy himself that she was okay.

The meal was delicious. Alec ordered a bottle of Tattinger Rose champagne and began to point out the various luminaries. Three times during the meal, he excused himself from the table and headed for the men's room, leading Moira to worry about the condition of his bladder.

Alec drank most of the champagne by himself, ordered another bottle, and drank most of that one, too. By the time they left the restaurant, it was past midnight, and Alec, having by now toasted her imminent success at least a dozen times, was feeling no pain. Moira couldn't understand how he was still walking, but smiled to herself in anticipation of another undemanding night. It wasn't so terrible really, she rationalized.

Alec directed Roberts to give them a tour of London's most famous landmarks and leaned back into the sumptuous leather. As the car slipped silently past Buckingham Palace, Alec reached for his companion and dragged her toward him. She struggled, plead-ing with him to let her enjoy the sights, but he merely sniggered and pulled her closer. Moira felt very uncomfortable. To be plundered in the privacy of the hotel room was one thing; it was quite another in the presence of another man.

Mercifully, the car phone purred, and Roberts lifted the receiver.

"Mister Zander's car," he said. "Eh...yes he is, madam. Just a moment, please."

"I don't want to talk to anyone," said Alec. He continued to grapple, thoroughly enjoying the skirmish.

"But Mister Zander, sir, it's your wife, and she knows you're here."

Zander froze. Muttering to himself, he ran his fingers through his hair and reached for the backseat receiver.

"Hello?...Hello?" There was no response.

He glowered at Roberts, who stared straight ahead, concentrating on the road. Zander slammed down the phone.

By now, Moira was curled up in the corner of the seat as far away from him as possible. He shrugged his skinny shoulders and reached for her hand.

"Don't. Don't you dare touch me. Your wife, Alec? That was your wife? Don't even speak to me." She sat bristling, staring straight ahead.

When she seemed a little calmer, he tried again.

"Um...we're not together anymore, Linda and I. We've been separated for months. That's why I was by myself at Gleneagles. You remember?"

Moira saw Roberts watching in the mirror.

"Let's not spoil a wonderful day with this nonsense," said Zander. "Trust me. I'm telling you the truth. What do you think I am?"

Moira was far from convinced, but by the time the Bentley pulled up in front of Annabel's, she'd begun to relent.

Inside the club, the noise was deafening. They were shown to a table that had been reserved for them at the back of the room, far away from the teeming dance floor. Moira had never heard music so loud, but she was pleased that there wouldn't be much conversation. Without even asking what she'd like, Zander ordered another bottle of champagne.

As the overly flirty waitress left the table, they were joined by a swarthy, heavily perspiring bald man who badly needed a shave.

"This is my pal, Bobby Lee," Zander yelled. "He's agreed to help us. He's an important record executive, so I want you to be nice to him."

Several times, the men disappeared together into the bathroom, returning to the table reenergized and clamoring for more to drink. An hour or so later, Zander announced that he was bored. He dropped a handful of notes on the table, lurched from his chair, and headed for the door with the other two close behind.

As they stepped outside, the Bentley rolled silently to a stop. Roberts leapt out to open the doors and somehow managed to insert Zander into the front seat. Moira flashed him her gratitude.

After a short ride to Mayfair, the Bentley pulled up in front of an elegant townhouse, and they all piled out. The door was eventually opened by an aging Asian man who looked less than pleased to have been roused from his sleep. Without a word, he closed the heavy door behind them and disappeared.

Moira followed the men into an elegantly appointed living room, where their host headed for the bar and began fixing yet another round of drinks. Although she'd managed to minimize her consumption, several glasses of champagne had already passed Moira's lips, and she was feeling lightheaded. She collapsed on the nearest couch, leaned back into the deep cushions, and closed her eyes. As the room started to spin, she felt someone sit down beside her. She opened her eyes and was surprised to find Bobby Lee leering into her face.

"You sure are one beautiful thing." Close up, his breath stank of whiskey and cigarettes. "If you can sing at all, you can't miss, and I could be a great help."

As he talked, he began to stroke her neck. She flinched, but didn't immediately pull away. Soon, he was sliding his hairy fingers ever closer to her breasts, but when finally he reached his objective, she leapt from the couch and ran to Zander.

"Alec, what's going on here? I don't like this."

Alec didn't answer her. Instead, he crossed to the stereo and turned up the volume. It was then that Moira became afraid. She knew she couldn't fight them both.

Suddenly Bobby grabbed her from behind and ripped her dress wide open. Zander chortled and began to advance. When he reached for her, she kicked out at him, but she missed. He punched her hard, and she dropped to the floor. Bobby Lee was first. He tore her panties off, pried her legs open, and forced his way in. She gasped with pain.

When he was finished, he rolled her onto her stomach and grinned at his companion.

"She's all yours, Alec my boy—just the way you like it."

The agony and humiliation of the penetration was something Moira had never imagined. That was all she remembered.

✱ ✱ ✱

When she came to, she found both men stretched out on the couches, sleeping like innocents, and her humiliation evaporated. It was replaced with cold fury. She tried to gather her torn dress around her, without much success, and noticed Zander's jacket lying on a chair. She decided it would have to do, and as she slipped it on, she felt a weight in the pocket. She removed the wallet, took out a few pounds, and tossed it on the floor.

As she searched the room for something to smash, she remembered a story Graham Nesbit had told her years before. She picked up a crystal cigarette lighter from the coffee table and walked to the windows.

She flicked the lighter, touched the flame to the silk curtains, and watched impassively as the fire took hold.

As she limped from the house, she heard a man's voice, but paid no attention until his face appeared out of the shadows.

"Oh, Roberts. You wouldn't believe what they did to me." She moaned as he helped her into the car. As they drove away, she turned to stare back at the house, where the flames were steadily engulfing the drapes.

"Oh I could believe anything," said the driver. "You've no idea." If he noticed the fire, he said nothing. "Now listen, my girl—here's what we're going to do."

☆ ☆ ☆

It was still early in the morning when Roberts shook the girl's hand in front of King's Cross station. They'd already been to the hotel to collect her things.

They'd agreed that there was nothing to be gained by reporting the incident. It would only serve to delay her escape from London.

"Have a safe trip home, and try not to think too badly of us Englishmen. We're not all like them."

"What will he do to you when he finds out you helped me?"

"Absolutely nothing," Roberts replied. "I know far too much."

With a wry smile, he touched his cap. "Godspeed, Miss Macleod. You deserve only good things."

Moira kissed his cheek.

As she entered the station, she thought about the girl who'd stepped off the train just days before, and wondered if anyone passing by would recognize her as the same person.

CHAPTER 22

Miraculously, Graham Nesbit had escaped the crash with only minor injuries. At the clinic in Inverarry, the doctor explained that he was an extremely lucky man, probably due in part to the degree of his intoxication. Aside from a few lacerations, he'd sustained only a mild concussion and a very sore shoulder. Although he would be laid up for a while, he would, with proper care, recover completely.

John was relieved, at least until Valerie announced that since she felt partially responsible for the crash, Graham would be staying with them at Ainsley House until he was well.

"If that's not acceptable," she said, "I'll have to move into his house until he's up and around."

John weighed the equally odious options. "But what will people say?"

"*Say?* Listen, if we haven't given them enough to talk about by now, they're in sore need of some fresh gossip."

John didn't ask her to elaborate.

✠ ✠ ✠

Two days later, Graham moved into the small room off the kitchen at Ainsley House. The room had a wonderful view of the loch and was close to all he'd need.

After Valerie had her patient comfortably propped up in bed with enough books and magazines to get him through a life sentence, she proceeded to fix him some lunch. It was nice having someone to look after. It had been a long time.

John made the mistake of disturbing his wife while she was making Graham's sandwich. She grumbled impatiently, and he retreated.

That evening, he found himself at a bit of a loss, totally unwelcome in his own house. He'd found it impossible to concentrate on his work all day. His mind was being constantly invaded with disturbing thoughts of his wife and Graham Nesbit.

After eating supper alone in the kitchen, John decided he had to do something. Valerie was again busy tending to Graham. He walked down the hall and knocked on the closed door. "I'm going out, Val. I won't be long."

He waited.

There was no response.

He walked away, feeling terrible.

✧ ✧ ✧

Valerie sat in a small armchair by the window and glanced at Graham, who was propped up in the bed. She paid no attention to her husband's voice. She was busy trying to formulate an answer.

"I think it's better not knowing for sure," she said, after careful consideration. "If he's involved with her, there's nothing I can say or do."

Graham remained silent.

"And if we can just make it through the next few days, we'll be all right. We'll be on our way home, and the spell of this place will be broken."

✧ ✧ ✧

John pulled the Jaguar out of the garage and drove slowly toward the village. He wasn't sure he wanted to deal with the pub, but he needed to get out of the house. There were so many things going on in his head that it felt like he was on spin cycle. He didn't know what to make of the relationship between Valerie and Graham, but he knew he didn't like it. He tried thinking about something else.

As he passed the church, he saw a light on in the small meeting room behind the sanctuary. Thinking that he'd rather see Drummond than the townsfolk, he parked the Jag and made his way around to the back of the church, hoping to find the minister alone. He could hear the sound of Drummond's voice through the open door and moved closer. Inside the room, a group of about twenty boys sat in a circle on the floor with their eyes closed, listening intently as the minister chanted a poem in a dialect John couldn't understand. Feeling out of place, he decided to go, but as he started out the door, a young man barged past him and took a seat on the floor with the others. John recognized him as Moira's friend, the guitar player.

"Join us if you like." It was Drummond's voice, and he was addressing John. "Have a seat. I won't be long here, and there is something I wanted to speak with you about."

John nodded and settled onto the floor with his back against the wall.

"It's happened again," the minister announced to the assembled. "Another item has gone missing, and it's something very precious to us all. Campbell's own dagger has disappeared this time. It's apparent someone else has learned how to enter the chamber, and that person's a damn traitor. We must find him, and he must be severely punished."

When the meeting was over, the boys rose in unison and filed from the room. Drummond sank into a chair.

"I need to get my hands on this thief, John. You're one of the very few who have ever been inside, and I assume you're no thief. Apart from us, there are only two others who know how to access the chamber; or so I thought. I'm sure you'll be happy to help with the investigation."

✵ ✵ ✵

Back at the house, John found Valerie and Graham ensconced in the living room, deep in conversation. Graham was bundled up beside the fire sipping a whiskey, apparently feeling better. As usual, the conversation stopped when John appeared. He got the distinct impression that they'd been talking about him.

"I'm just going to fix a snack. Can I get anyone anything?" he asked.

"We've just had something, but thanks for asking," replied Valerie, not unkindly.

John switched his attention to Graham. "What do you know about Reverend Drummond?" he asked. "Is he a friend of yours?"

"Oh I don't think Kenneth Drummond's got many friends, John. I'd be careful of him, if I were you."

John retired to the kitchen and made himself a sandwich. He felt uneasy, as if things were closing in around him.

✿ ✿ ✿

Moira knew that she couldn't go back to Kilbride, at least not yet. She needed some time to heal, safe from the inquisitive stares of the villagers. The humiliation of the London debacle was still too fresh. Besides, she had no desire whatsoever to see Drummond. She knew he'd be furious with her—she hadn't done her job. She reminisced about the hours she'd spent with John MacIntyre and how safe she'd felt in his presence. He was the only thing she missed about the village.

She took the two-o'clock train from Glasgow to Oban, where she knew one or two people and could maybe find a job, although she realized that the tourist season was winding down. Fortunately, she still had a little money left, enough to give her some time to try to get past the shame she felt. She wondered how she could have been so stupid?

She arrived in Oban late afternoon and managed to find a small room close to the harbor. It was quite affordable now that the summer visitors were leaving. The large window that faced out to the sea made it not too depressing, and by the time she'd unpacked her few belongings and washed up, she was hungry. It occurred to her that she hadn't eaten anything all day. She hadn't been interested until now.

By the time Moira left the rooming house, the sun had set. In the afterglow, the town was bathed in bronze, but Moira didn't notice. She trudged on toward the harbor with her head down, praying that the coldness in her heart wouldn't last forever. If only she had someone to turn to, but there was no one.

She spotted a fish-and-chip shop across the square and made her way over. As she arrived, a young turbaned man was locking the door, but seeing the disappointment on the girl's face, he let her in.

He threw two pieces of fish and a handful of chips into the deep fryers and watched as the hot fat rose up in noisy protest. A couple of minutes later, he removed the food from the fryers, doused it with salt and vinegar, wrapped it in newspaper, and handed it to her.

As she reached for her money, he shook his head.

"That's really not necessary, miss. The cash register's already closed up, you see, and I would only be throwing the fish out, anyway."

Moira was not totally convinced, but accepted the kindness.

She tramped back to her drab little room and spread open her meal.

Never had she felt so completely alone.

Moira hadn't touched her guitar since London. Sometimes she would sit and stare at the case, but she couldn't bring herself to open it. Her guitar had come to represent the lurid, sinful ambition that had destroyed her.

She loathed her music, and she loathed herself.

✪ ✪ ✪

Graham sat in the kitchen at Ainsley House across the table from Valerie. He was concerned. It had been ten days since Moira's departure from the village, and no one had heard a word.

"People are worried," he said. "Although we're not always the best of friends, we do look out for our own in this village. The bonds run deep. It's very strange that nobody's heard from her."

He took a breath and forged ahead. "Do you think that there's any chance your husband might know something?"

Valerie dropped her eyes.

"One night, I answered the phone here," he continued. "It was late, after you and John were in bed. When I said hello, nobody spoke, although I could hear someone breathing on the other end. I had a feeling it was Moira."

Valerie offered no response.

"I have to ask him about it," Graham said. "I hope you understand."

"Oh I understand," she replied solemnly. "As a matter of fact, I'd like to be there when you do."

✪ ✪ ✪

"John," Graham said as they were finishing dinner that evening, "There's something I've got to ask you about. Now, it may be a sore subject around here, but I've got to ask it anyway."

John braced himself.

"It's about Moira MacLeod," Graham announced. "You know that ten days ago, she left the village, apparently bound for London. Something about a recording deal and someone there who was going to help her."

Graham leaned forward in his chair so he could see John's face more clearly. "Now, as far as I know, the lassie's got no friends in London, so I'm wondering, how did she make contact with a record company? You see what I'm getting at?"

John shifted uneasily and nodded his head. He could feel the noose tightening. "Yes I do, but what's this got to do with me?"

Valerie watched her husband carefully.

"I'm not sure," said Graham. "I don't know the extent of your relationship with her, but I'm given to believe there's been some discussion of her career and your desire to help. Am I wrong?"

"No, you're not wrong, but if you think that I'm responsible for her leaving, you're mistaken."

He sounded convincing. Valerie believed him.

Graham pressed on.

"Well John, I don't know what to think. I really don't. Young Alistair Frazier told me that you and the girl might have been together at a fancy hotel recently, where she sang at some big event."

"He's crazy. He doesn't know what he's talking about."

Valerie knew then that her husband was lying.

"Believe me, Graham, if I knew, I'd tell you. And whatever relationship we had, innocent though it was, it's over."

He stole a glance at his wife. Her face was a mask.

"At the same time, I wish Moira well." His words sounded hollow. "Although I'm sure she's fine. She's off pursuing her dream, and somebody will hear from her soon. She'll be calling with good news. She's very talented, you know."

"Oh yes, I know," Graham said. "Well John, if you do hear anything, be sure to let me know, will you?"

"I sure will. You can count on it."

Valerie remembered the way John used to behave in business meetings. She recognized the fake sincerity.

"Well, if you'll both excuse me, I've got some work to do," John said. He rose and left the room.

Alone at his desk, John dropped his head into his hands and closed his eyes. He didn't want to deal with it, but he couldn't stop. He'd lied to them. Even though he'd had no choice, the lies had come too easily. What had he done? His thoughts turned to Moira and the loathsome Alec Zander. He prayed that the girl was unharmed. First thing in the morning, he would call London. Maybe Ronnie Harper had heard something. He wondered how long it would be before the truth came out.

John tried to focus on the computer screen. He needed desperately to escape. His fingers began to type, but his brain refused to join in. It was useless.

He rose from his desk and crossed the room to the couch by the fireplace. He stretched out and stared at the ceiling, accompanied by the steady drumming of raindrops on the windows.

He closed his eyes and listened to the sounds of the rain and the wind. Before he knew it, he was summoned again. His mind took flight as the scribe took command of his thoughts.

Ninian Lasker, Chancellor of Arbrothock and chief advisor to Duncan MacLeod, sat at his ornate writing desk, reviewing the state of the treasury and listening to the wind that whined through the ill-fitting window sashes. The papers littering the desktop didn't offer much promise. Lasker understood better than anyone the need for an alliance with Campbell. He knew that the wedding must take place.

As he reached for a fresh quill, a movement high on the battlements caught his eye. He turned to the window and looked closer. When his mind grasped what was happening, his entire, conniving life flashed before him.

He watched, horrified, as Lady Eileen spread her gown and leapt from the parapet. Lasker considered screaming but realized the impracticality and decided to save his breath. As he watched the girl plunge toward the rocks and certain death, something miraculous happened.

A great gust of wind seemed to gather the girl in its strength. He watched as it carried her past the shoreline and settled her onto the crest of a surging wave. For a moment, she floated, like a crippled swan, before the sea saturated her gown and began to drag her under. Lasker ran as fast as his spindly legs could carry him.

By the time he arrived at the water's edge, he had shed his heavy robes. He waded into the tide, but unfortunately, the girl had slipped beneath the surface by then, leaving only her garland of flowers to mark the spot. Lasker pushed on against the power of the sea and plunged beneath the waves, reaching out for any piece of her gown. Nothing. He rose to the surface, gulped the air, and dived again.

After many moments, he felt fabric, grabbed a handful, and held on for dear life. Somehow, he managed to pull the flaccid body to the surface and began to drag it ashore. A helping surge lifted them over the rocks and deposited them safely onto a small patch of sand. Lasker lay gasping for breath.

As soon as he was able, he crawled to the motionless girl, rolled her onto her stomach, and applied all the strength he had left. For a long time, there was no response, but then she coughed, spewing a great gush of seawater onto the sand.

A moment later she came to, not understanding what had happened. She looked up into Lasker's face and began to comprehend. She moaned softly and closed her eyes.

A *half hour later, the door to Eileen's bedchamber burst open to admit a furious Duncan MacLeod. He scowled at his daughter, shaking with anger. Behind him stood her hated rescuer, still dripping wet. The chief of the MacLeods gathered himself.*

"Ye would have killed us all," he snarled. "Do ye know the horror that Campbell would have brought upon us? Yer own father butchered, and the castle razed to the very ground.

"I, Duncan of MacLeod, gave the man my solemn word. Do ye not know what that means? I promise ye, my lassie, if ye don't marry the good Lord Campbell with a smile on your wretched face, I'll fetch your young Douglas and burn him alive. Do I make myself clear enough, ye stupid, selfish bitch?"

He spun on his heel and stormed from the room. Lasker remained behind. He sidled to the bed, peered into the blemished face, offered a self-satisfied shrug, and scurried after his master.

Robert Douglas tended to his sorely wounded brother for seven days, and only then did he feel right about traveling to Arbrothock to meet his Lady Eileen. Hamish had been slipping in and out of consciousness for days. He'd lost so much blood, Robert had had to physically remove the doctors who had wanted to bleed the boy, and in spite of all the dire warnings to the contrary, the lad had begun to show signs of recovery.

One morning when Robert entered the darkened room, Hamish was sitting up in bed drinking warm milk. He offered his older brother a wan smile and asked that the curtains be opened. It was only then that Douglas felt right about his journey.

It was with a happy, eager heart that Robert, accompanied by a handful of men, rode out from his small castle, crossed the river, and broke into an easy canter heading east. It was time to arrange his wedding.

Eileen had allowed Meg to nurse her back to health from the terrible fever that had invaded her body. Her bout with the icy sea, and the knowledge of what was to come, had left her in a deep depression. She knew that the chill would never leave her bones.

She made her last-minute preparations for the journey, going about her tasks like a sleepwalker. The time had come. They were to leave at the next day's dawn. She'd been barely civil to her father during the past days and refused to speak even a word to Lasker. She was busy plotting her revenge.

It took Robert and his men two days of hard riding to reach the MacLeod castle at Arbrothock. He noticed immediately the strange quietness hanging over the place and was surprised that Eileen did not appear to greet him. He soon discovered that were no more than a dozen armed men and a handful of servants left in the entire castle. It took some time to find out why.

Those who had remained behind seemed very nervous. No one wanted to give him the news until eventually he pried the story from an old livery who was apparently more afraid not to tell him.

Robert listened carefully, but it took a moment for the terrible reality to sink in. When it did, his wail of anguish resounded from the courtyard walls.

He flung the old man to the ground, leapt into his saddle, and galloped off into the falling darkness, his men close behind.

John awoke feeling stiff and still tired, as weary as Ninian Lasker. Since his wife no longer delivered it, he made his way to the kitchen for a much-needed cup of coffee. He heard Valerie and Graham talking together and decided he was in no mood to face them. Instead, he returned to the study and picked up the phone. Moira was very much on his mind, and despite his earlier protestations, he did feel responsible for her disappearance.

He got no information from Ronnie, but was delighted to hear that Alec Zander had ended up in the hospital after being dragged from a burning house. John dismissed any thought of Moira's possible involvement.

Circumventing the kitchen, he made his way to the boatshed and winched *Bridie* into the water. He climbed aboard and steered for Kilbride.

The village was quiet. Doris's Tearoom was completely empty. It was after the morning rush, and John was the only customer. He sat at the counter and ordered coffee and a treacle scone. He wasn't sure if Doris was a bit less friendly than usual, or if it was just his imagination. As he pondered, the door opened, and Jock Tavish entered, saw him at the counter, and took a seat as far away as possible. There was definitely a chill in the air. John stared across the room, trying to catch the man's eye, but there was no acknowledgement.

A few minutes later, the door opened again, and in walked a boy of about fifteen. John didn't know the lad's name, but remembered having seen him at the Covenanters meeting. The boy walked right over. "Mister MacIntyre?"

"Yes, I'm MacIntyre, and who are you?"

"I'm Ian MacLeod, Moira's brother. I heard you were in here. I'm told that you were one of the last people to speak to my sister before she left. Well, we haven't heard a word from her, and folks are saying that you might know something. I've come to ask if there's anything you can tell us that might help."

John became aware that Tavish was now paying rapt attention.

"Believe me, son, if I knew anything, I'd tell you. As a matter of fact, I didn't speak to your sister for several days before she left."

"Well, we wouldn't want to think that you were responsible for her leaving the village, would we, Mister MacIntyre?"

John recognized the threat.

"I assure you, I had nothing to do with it, but I will do all I can to help. If there's anything you need, money or whatever, you can count on me."

"We'll not be needing your money, but thanks all the same." Ian about-faced and stalked out.

MacIntyre glanced in the direction of the postmaster, but Jock was once again engrossed in his morning paper.

John dropped a few coins on the counter and approached the postmaster. "Morning, Mister Tavish, and how are you this morning?"

"Oh, about the same, I'd say. About the same, aye."

"So let me ask you: What the hell's going on around here? Why am I getting the cold shoulder? And why are people saying I'm responsible for young Moira's disappearance?"

The old man kept his eyes glued to the paper. "Oh, I imagine you can probably answer that better than me, Mister MacIntyre. Some folks think you know more than you're sayin', and they don't like to be misled. I'd advise you to tell what you know before it's too late."

"This is crazy." John spun away and strode out of the tearoom.

"Maybe it's time to be heading back to the States," he muttered to himself as he strode angrily toward the harbor. "It looks like we've overstayed our welcome in Kilbride."

He decided he had to call Alec Zander. He had a feeling the creep knew something.

✡ ✡ ✡

Alec Zander lay in his hospital bed in London, full of as many pain pills as he could coax from the young nurses. They were all eager to please their famous patient, especially because the pills seemed to help him deal with his ghastly appearance.

The phone rang, and he reached gingerly to answer it.

"Yes," he croaked. "This is Zander."

"So where is she?"

He recognized the American accent immediately. "I've got no friggin' idea where she is, asshole. But I'd love to know, in case you do find her. There's something I'd like to discuss with her. Unfinished business, you might say."

"So, she was there?"

"Oh yeah, she was here all right. Treated like a bloody princess she was—until she burned down the damn house!"

John smiled to himself. *So it was her after all*. "Well, if she committed a crime, I'm sure you reported it to the police. Maybe they know her whereabouts."

"No," he said. "The police don't know shit. They have no idea she was even there. They think it was an accident. But I know different, don't I? Tell you what, why don't you give me your number there, I'll get in touch if I hear anything."

"Not a chance, you stupid little prick."

"Okay, fine, Grandpa...don't give it to me, but let me tell you, I hope the crazy bitch gets what's coming to her, and if you do find her, tell her that her old friend Alec is looking for her. And by the way, before I let you go, I really should thank you. The girl was a lot of fun. You really taught her well."

Zander slammed down the receiver and yelled for the day nurse. A moment later, a pretty young Asian appeared at the door.

"I need a goddamn pill," he snarled.

CHAPTER 23

———◆◆◆———

It was Saturday night again, and Moira was terribly depressed. The reality of her new life had set in, and she'd come to accept that she had nothing to look forward to. She was so tired of thinking.

She dressed quickly and left her room, determined to escape from the darkness that was encircling her. When she walked into the Skullery, the place was rocking, as usual. The doorman checked her out and allowed her to enter without paying the cover charge.

Moira elbowed her way to the bar and ordered a Rum and Coke. The skinny bartender smiled hopefully as he placed the drink in front of her. She ignored him, drank quickly, and ordered another, remembering the Rum and Cokes she'd had at Gleneagles with John. What fun that night had been.

After three drinks, the liquor began working its magic. She felt like dancing, even though the band was dreadful. She rose from her stool and made her way unsteadily toward the crowded dance floor, inserted herself into the throng, and allowed her body to get lost in the furious music. A few minutes later, she opened her eyes to find a small black man gyrating in front of her. The man looked vaguely familiar, but she couldn't quite place him. He gazed at her without smiling until the music stopped, and the band hurried from the stage. It was time for them to get reloaded.

Moira's new friend took her by the arm and steered her toward a table in a back corner, far away from the stage. She didn't feel like arguing with anyone, so she didn't.

"We've met before," he said. "You were here with my friend, Ali. My name's Travis, but they call me Tray."

Moira nodded her head numbly. "I haven't seen Ali for a bit," she mumbled.

They took their seats and Travis beckoned to a bored-looking waitress and ordered for both of them. Moira didn't protest.

After two more drinks and some meaningless chat, the black man pulled a small vial from the pocket of his leather jacket and proceeded to snort a spoonful of white powder up each of his nostrils. He smiled broadly as the coke hit home. He refilled the little gold spoon and extended it to Moira. Without thinking, she held one nostril closed and sniffed tentatively. Nothing happened.

The man laughed.

She made a face and tried again. This time, she emptied the spoon, and the drug hit her like a train. If she hadn't been sitting down, she would have been on the floor.

When she recovered from the initial shock, she felt fantastic. Golden light emanated from everyone and everything around her.

By the time the band returned from their break, they had acquired a new member. Moira danced onto the stage, grabbed a microphone, and joined into the noise. Within a few minutes, the din had become music. The Bell of Argyll hadn't lost her magic. The band had never sounded this good, ever. The head-bangers stopped dancing and began drifting toward the stage. The new girl invented melodies and lyrics as she went, better than anything Krank had ever thought of, and they knew it. They played even harder.

At the end of the set, Moira staggered from the stage, completely wrung out. The lead guitar player ran after her and took her by the arm. "Will you come back tomorrow night? We were friggin' awesome."

Moira smiled and assured him that she would. Never in her life had she felt so good. She returned to the table where Tray sat smiling broadly, clapping his hands. "Ali told us you were something special, but I had no idea. You're incredible."

He reached into his pocket and extended the little vial and the gold spoon.

Moira took two mighty snorts and sat back in her chair giggling, absorbing the rush. "This is more like it," she decided.

At closing time, Moira stumbled from the Skullery, firmly in the grasp of her new friend, who was grinning like a henhouse fox.

✿ ✿ ✿

Graham and Valerie finished watching the movie, and she rose to shut off the set. It occurred to her that having no remote control was probably good for her—she got so much more exercise. It was a corny old movie, and although Valerie had seen it many times, she enjoyed sharing it.

"Ah well," he said, "it's nice to know that some people find happy endings."

She sighed as she settled back into the couch beside him. "It was only a movie, unfortunately. Real life tends to serve up a little more reality."

"Oh I don't know. It seems to me you were fairly happy when you arrived here."

"Maybe so, but I've come to realize that things aren't always what they seem, and I was afraid to face the facts. I used to think that what I didn't know couldn't hurt me, but now I'm not so sure. Now I wonder how faithful John's really been over the years."

Graham reached for her and held her close. "Now you listen, my girl...you have no evidence that John's been unfaithful, so don't go manufacturing things. I actually think your husband's a good man who's gotten caught up in something he knows nothing about. It could happen to anybody—well maybe not to you, Saint Valerie, but to any of us lesser mortals."

He chuckled wickedly as she pulled away from him and delivered his arm a resounding slap.

"By the way," he announced, "I'll be heading home tomorrow, and not only because of the physical abuse you just inflicted. Really, I'm feeling pretty good, and I've stayed long enough."

Valerie's didn't even try to hide her disappointment. "Well, if you feel you must."

"You see, there's always a right time. The trick is to recognize it when it appears," he said. "Now, I know it'll be a sad day for me when it comes, but I think it's time you and John were leaving this place, too."

She eyed him, curious. "What do you mean?"

"Well, there's some strangeness going on at the moment, what with Moira's disappearance and all. I don't like the mood of the village. I've seen it before. When anything bad happens around here, the folk are inclined to close ranks. I don't want anything to happen to you…or to John."

Valerie could see that he was deadly serious.

"Thanks Graham. I really appreciate your concern. You're a good friend."

"And I'll content myself with that, I suppose. Of course, you know I love you, but you're a person who takes her commitments seriously. It's one of the reasons I do love you."

"Graham, I…I—"

"It's okay; you don't have to say anything, but I wish you'd make your plans to leave–the sooner the better."

She put her arms around his neck and gave him a big kiss.

"You're my best friend, Graham Nesbit."

✡ ✡ ✡

As he left his study, John could hear them talking in the living room. He went through the kitchen and slipped quietly out of the house.

It was a dark night as he drove slowly toward St. Agnes Kirk. He'd hit a stumbling block with the writing and needed a bit of inspiration. He'd flashed to the graveyard and its ancient secrets and was heading there to soak up some atmosphere.

As he approached the church, he switched off his lights and rolled to a stop behind a huge sycamore tree. He climbed out of the car and was immediately aware of a glow coming from the direction of the Campbell monument. Silently, he crept through the gravestones, curious about what was happening.

When he was halfway to the monument, the light went out. A second later, he heard a low grating noise, and recognized it immediately. He ducked down behind a gravestone and watched as two dark figures appeared, whispering a heated conversation. He couldn't hear all that was being said, but he caught the word "Moira" and something that sounded like "Marcus." Holding his breath, he raised his head above the stone and immediately ducked down again. The dark shapes were no more than twenty feet away, heading right toward him.

As they passed his hiding place, close enough for him to touch, he heard them plainly.

"So is this the end of it, Ali?"

"It might be the end of me, Ian." The voice sounded grim.

Then there was silence. They'd gone.

Oh shit, John thought, *the car.*

Thankfully, the silence continued. The car had gone undetected.

John considered going right to Drummond with what he'd witnessed, but dismissed the idea. He wasn't sure exactly what the minister was capable of, but he didn't want to find out.

By the time he arrived home, Valerie was asleep.

✿ ✿ ✿

The next morning, he woke alone and went to find her, eager to tell her his plans for heading home. He found her on the front steps waving goodbye to Graham. The little car, which had been delivered just two days before, looked as good as new.

Good timing, John thought.

When she spotted her husband, Valerie dropped her eyes. "John, I need to tell you something."

His heart lurched. He had no idea what she was about to say, but he didn't want to hear it.

"I've been on the phone, trying to arrange a flight home. I don't know if you're planning to come with me or not. Anyway, I can't get anything until the seventh. It seems that this is a busy time."

He was relieved. "It's okay, Val—I already have us booked for the second."

She smiled warmly, stepped into his arms, and squeezed him hard. He yelped, feigning pain, but when she pulled away, he reached out and drew her back. When he released her again, they headed into the house hand in hand and climbed the stairs to the bedroom.

✡ ✡ ✡

An hour later, John awoke to someone pounding on the front door. He grabbed a robe and headed downstairs.

"You were there." Drummond stood seething on the doorstep. "And I have a feeling you witnessed some larceny. Another artifact has been removed from the chamber. You see, your car was spotted at the cemetery."

"What the hell—"

"I know you were there last night, but I'm sure you're no thief. I suspect you don't need the money, and you seem to have respect for your heritage. Actually, I have an idea who the villain is. Now, tell me please, what did you see?"

"Okay. Okay, I did see something." John was amazed by the minister's certainty. "There were two of them. They came out of the Campbell monument. One of them was carrying something. It was too dark to see them clearly, but I might be able to recognize them if I see them again."

MacIntyre was quite sure of the identity of one of the boys, but he had no intention of divulging the information.

"Very well then…as you wish. Oh, by the way, you're invited to join our little outing this weekend. And I recommend you make your presence felt. Maybe we'll have an opportunity to discuss what the future holds. We may even find time to share stories about mutual friends, like Moira MacLeod, for instance."

John winced, but managed to cover as Valerie arrived at the door.

She saw that John was angry. His cheeks were flushed, and his fists were tightly clenched. She looked past him to see whom he was talking to, and visibly recoiled.

Drummond took her reaction as his cue to leave.

"I'll see you Saturday then, John. I'll be looking forward to it."

He nodded curtly and walked away.

The MacIntyres stood together on the front step, watching his departure.

"What was all that about?" she asked.

"Oh nothing. He wants my help with his boys club on Saturday. For some reason, he wants to pick my brain about special effects."

His answer didn't erase the look of concern on Valerie's face, but she didn't press the matter. Instead, she nodded wordlessly and headed back into the house.

As Val crossed to the stairs, a door slammed. It was somewhere on the upper floor.

"John!" she screamed, "Hurry! There's somebody in the house."

Having heard the noise, John was already on his way. He rushed past her and raced up the stairs.

To his left, their bedroom door stood wide open, and he could see that the bathroom door was open as well. He turned right and made his way down the hall, checking the guest rooms they didn't ever use. *Nothing.* There was no sign of an intruder.

Mystified, he made his way back down the corridor and paused at the top of the stairs. Just then, at the far end of the hall, a door slammed again. John raced back the way he'd come, and when he reached the end of the hall, could only gape at the damage. The door of the very last room, the one that hadn't been opened since their arrival, had been slammed so hard that the upper panel was split right down the middle, and the lock was smashed to pieces.

He searched around for something that might serve as a weapon, but there was nothing. He shrugged and gingerly nudged the door open with his foot.

As he stepped warily across the threshold, he suddenly felt a hand on his back. He spun around, his fists raised, ready for battle. Standing there was Valerie, pale as a ghost.

"What is it?" she whispered, her voice trembling. "Is there somebody in there?"

"I don't know. Dammit, Val—you scared the shit out of me."

"I'm sorry. I was frightened. I thought something happened to you."

With his wife right behind him, John pushed on through the door. Inside the room, the air was stale, and it held the faint smell of smoke. An unmade child's bed stood in the very center of the room, and the sheets were daubed with dark stains. The walls were adorned with peeling wallpaper, which featured old racing cars. The corners of the room were black with soot, and the window frame was badly charred. Much more disturbing, however, was the fact that the window stood wide open.

"Someone's been in here," Valerie said.

"Now, let's not jump to conclusions. There may be another explanation. I've seen it happen before. In old houses with large windows like these, they often used rope pulleys to lift the weight. Sometimes, if they've been left unlatched, the windows can rise of their own accord."

John wasn't convinced that they hadn't had a visitor, but he saw no reason to frighten his wife.

He crossed to the window, pulled it firmly closed, and made sure the latch was secured. "There," he said. "It won't happen again."

"But John, this room was locked. How in God's name did the door open?"

"Actually, I just assumed the door was locked. I never tried to get in this room. Did you?"

"No," she said. "I guess I never did."

Noticing that the closet door was ajar, he tiptoed across the room and yanked the door open. The closet was empty.

Relieved, he closed the door and offered his wife a lopsided smile. "How about a drink? I know I could use one."

"Good idea."

✡ ✡ ✡

Moira was the toast of the Skullery. Stoned out of her mind, having now added heroin to her repertoire, she swayed numbly on the stage, trying to remember why she was there.

By her third night as Krank's lead singer, she was completely useless. People laughed and jeered when she collapsed to the floor, exposing all her secrets and having no care.

The Bell of Argyle was in pieces.

✡ ✡ ✡

The next day, Travis rang the doorbell at the elegant home of Marcus Bersky. He maintained a firm grip on his companion, making sure she remained upright. The door was opened by a surly looking Rudy.

"Is Mister Bersky home? I've got a present for him."

Rudy said nothing. Instead, he stepped back inside, allowing the visitors to enter the house, and followed along as Travis climbed the stairs to Bersky's office, dragging the girl along with him.

"She might be just the thing for Glasgow," ventured Travis as he watched the fat man appraise the girl. "No good for much else, I'm afraid."

"Difficult to say," said Bersky. "It's hard to predict what the customers will respond to. I suppose if she was cleaned up, she might be worth a few quid. What do you want for her?"

"Oh I don't know, Mister Bersky. How does six grams sound?"

"I'll give you two. That's it. If you want to know the truth, I think you're lucky to get rid of her."

"Okay," replied the black man. "It's a rip-off, and you know it, but I haven't got much choice, have I?"

"Come, come my boy. You're always free to take your business elsewhere."

Bersky jiggled with laughter.

"Rudy, my dear, would you be so kind as to show the young lady to her room? We'll arrange for her transportation to Glasgow in the morning."

Rudy crossed to the girl, who was by now slumped on a leather sofa, reached his arm around her waist, hoisted her effortlessly over his shoulder, and headed for the door. No one realized that, through the haze, Moira had heard every word.

The coolness of the night air signaled the onset of autumn as the MacIntyres bundled up for their ride across the loch into Kilbride. They'd decided to have dinner at the Thistle, knowing that it was probably for the last time.

The reception they got in the dining room was much like their first night at the pub. This time, though, there was to be no abatement in the chill. Their meal was served by a huffy woman, who made no attempt to be cordial.

"Do you think it's safe to eat this?" John asked when the food was placed in front of them.

"That's not funny," said Valerie. She eyed her own plate with suspicion.

They ate quickly, decided to forego coffee and the pub, and made their way back to the harbor.

Even in the dark, John's ire was plain. "I'll be glad to get out of here," he muttered.

As she watched John untie the boat, Valerie had a thought.

"Hey, how about stopping in to see Graham before we head home? I haven't seen him since he left the house, and I'd really like to see how he's doing."

John was in no mood to be making social calls, but he reluctantly agreed and they headed for Graham's.

Graham seemed pleased to see the MacItyres at the door and invited them in. They sat together in the little parlor, sipping Armagnac and chatting about the good times they'd shared over the past weeks. John didn't have a lot to contribute.

When Valerie excused herself to freshen up, leaving the men alone, the result was awkward silence. Each of them smiled with relief when she reappeared at the foot of the stairs.

"Where are you off to, Graham?" she asked. "I noticed you've been packing."

"Well, I wasn't going to say anything, but I think it would be good for me to get away from this place for a few days. I thought I'd take a run over to Oban and see if I can get a lead on Moira. There's still no word from her, but I hear she's got a couple of friends there. Maybe they've heard something."

"Oh, that reminds me," said John, "I did call my friend in London."

A second too late, he realized his folly. The subject of Ronnie Harper, and where John had last seen him, was not one he wanted to get into.

"A...a guy I know in the music scene. I just thought maybe she might have...you know. But he was of no help, I'm afraid. He didn't know anything."

An hour later, the MacIntyres stood up to leave, and Valerie gave Graham a warm kiss on the cheek.

John shook his hand. "I hope you have some luck in Oban," he said.

John and Valerie strolled back to the harbor without much to say, but when they reached the water, *Bridie* was nowhere to be seen. They scoured the entire pier, trying to be sure about where they'd tied up, and finally they spotted her, sitting on the bottom, water to the gunwales.

"What the hell?" John grumbled.

Valerie shuddered as the reality struck her. "John, do you realize what could have happened if we hadn't gone to see Graham? We'd be at the bottom of the loch."

"Holy shit. You're absolutely right. You don't suppose —" He swallowed the thought, not wanting to frighten her any further.

Hand in hand, they raced back to Graham's house and pounded on the door.

A second later, Graham ushered them inside. He sat them down, listened to their breathless story, and reached immediately for the telephone. "Smiley, get your arse over here. *Now.*"

He hung up the receiver and studied the MacIntyres, deciding what to say. "Well, let's not leap to any conclusions. There could be a logical reason for this. I'll take a look tomorrow. You can stay the night here; there's plenty of room. It's a good thing you weren't halfway across the loch when she let go."

Valerie stared at the floor, fighting the tears and trying to be brave.

John was in pain. He realized that if anything happened to his wife, he'd never forgive himself.

The knock on the door interrupted his thoughts. Graham rose to answer it, and ushered a chubby young constable into the room. The policeman listened impassively as the MacIntyres repeated their story. When they were done, he took a notepad from his jacket and began to write.

"Smiley," said Nesbit, "forget that. Get yourself over to the pub and find out who left there in the last hour or so, to visit the harbor."

"Yes Graham, of course. That's the thing to do."

He grabbed his hat, placed it squarely on his head, and walked out.

✿ ✿ ✿

Early the next morning, Smiley joined the MacIntyres at the harbor as they tried to determine what could have happened. He informed them that he'd gotten nowhere at the pub. He explained that the only person who had gone outside was Jock Tavish, simply because he preferred urinating in the open air.

Graham arrived on the scene with a winch, and a half hour later, *Bridie* was raised from the bottom. He donned a pair of hip waders and climbed into the water to survey the damage. It took only a minute for him to find the leak.

"It's hard to understand how a seam could just separate like this," he said. "It's never happened to her before."

The MacIntyres bailed out the vessel as Graham went about caulking the seam. When the task was completed, he winched the craft back down into the water, assuring the MacIntyres that she was once again watertight. After three tries, the engine coughed to life.

After the goodbyes, the MacIntyres climbed aboard. Understandably, they were both a bit nervous.

Smiley promised to continue his investigation, assuring them that he'd do his best and that he'd report his findings, although he was not hopeful. "After all," he shrugged, "there's no proof that it was foul play."

Gallantly, he pushed them off, nearly falling into the water in the process.

Bridie pulled slowly out of the harbor, and Graham stood watching until she'd rounded the point.

On the way home, John stayed as close as possible to the shore. The trip took twice as long as usual.

CHAPTER 24

Moira awakened from her stupor not knowing where she was. She peered around the dark space recognizing and remembering nothing. Finding a light, she switched it on and discovered she was in a tiny, Spartan room with a severely sloping ceiling. She assumed it was an attic.

She rose from the narrow cot and crossed to the door, but it was locked. Barely managing to control the rising panic, she went to the window to discover she was on the top floor of a large house, a long way from the ground. Moira tried the window, and it opened easily. She stuck her head out, trying to get her bearings while her stomach churned. She felt like she was going to be sick. The height made her dizzy, but aside from that, her body was screaming for something, but she didn't know what the craving was.

Shaking uncontrollably, she returned to the bed and wrapped herself in the blanket. After a few minutes, the tremors subsided, and she began to focus on her predicament. She crossed again to the door and bent down to look through the keyhole, but the light from the other side shone through, unobstructed. Her captor had been too smart to leave the key in the door.

As she straightened back up, she nearly passed out as the blood rushed from her brain. She slumped to the floor and waited for her head to clear. When she felt better, she went to the window again, searching for any means of escape. She had no idea who was holding her captive, but she'd heard enough to know that they meant her no good.

Not far from the window was a large tree, but its branches were just out of reach. Moira searched the room for an implement to try to pull the closest limb toward her, but there was nothing. Disappointed, she returned to the window, and this time she looked up. The room was located just under the eaves of the house, and she saw that if she could climb up onto the roof, she could cross to a spot where the tree was close enough to reach.

It took her a while to gather her courage. She had no alternative, although she knew the slightest slip would kill her.

What the hell, she thought. *I'm half dead anyway.*

She climbed onto the sill and sat for a moment with her legs still inside the room like a window washer. She figured that if she stood up, she might just be able to reach the edge of the dormer, and maybe hoist herself up.

She thought back on the hours spent with her brother, climbing the rocky crags of the vale. Over the years, they'd had many narrow escapes, but this was the most harrowing situation yet. She pulled off her shoes and stuck them inside her blouse

Knowing she had to resist the temptation to look down, she took a deep breath and pulled herself erect. She had to stand on her tiptoes to reach the eave but managed to secure a pretty good hand-hold. Slowly, she pulled herself up from the safety of the windowsill until she was hanging by her fingers, forty feet above the ground. Holding her breath, she searched with her feet until she found a small toehold, and pulled herself up over the edge.

She lay on the roof, panting from the exertion and the fear. It was several minutes before she could go on.

It was a damp night, and the steep slate roof was slippery. Halfway across, she lost her footing and began to slide toward the edge. When, by some miracle, her feet lodged in the rain gutter, halting her progress, she whispered her thanks to God.

By the time she reached the tree branch, her fingers and feet were rubbed raw. She sat for a moment wondering why she was making this great effort when she had absolutely nothing to live for. There was no answer.

She slid on her bottom to the very edge of the roof, and climbed out onto the limb. She didn't once look down. She made her way to the trunk and began her careful descent. When, finally, she was safely on the ground, she removed her shoes from inside her blouse, placed them on her torn feet, and limped away beneath the glare of the streetlamps. There was only one place left to go. It was the only place she'd be safe–a place where no one would find her.

✿ ✿ ✿

Aware that their time was drawing to a close, Valerie began getting things organized. Missus Small had stopped coming to the house, so she was on her own.

John remained locked to his computer, eager to get as much accomplished as possible before he had to leave the vale, knowing that at home, he'd be forced to rely on memory and imagination.

Late Saturday afternoon, Drummond arrived at Ainsley to collect John for their outing. Valerie was not happy about her husband's decision to join the trek, but she knew she couldn't convince him not to go. He was determined.

The men climbed into Drummond's stately old Armstrong Siddeley and drove away. Valerie watched until they were out of sight.

It was a chilly day as the men headed out across the moors, but John quickly warmed up as they tramped along. For a change, Drummond didn't have much to say. When they arrived at the site an hour later, the boys were already there.

"They've been here quite some time," said Drummond, "snaring rabbits for supper and making preparations for the ceremony."

The men perched on a couple of the circle stones and watched the activity.

"This is the eve of Michaelmas, a very special observance," said the clergyman "so, tonight we'll honor the archangel Michael, the protector of the ancient Israelites during their wanderings in the desert."

John glanced at the minister. "Kenneth, for what it's worth, I'm actually quite familiar with the testaments. Believe it or not, I'm a minister's son. Presbyterian, in fact— same as you."

The minister spun slowly toward him. "Actually, John, I'm familiar with your upbringing. As a matter of fact, I know quite a lot about you."

John began to ask but stopped himself. He already knew. There could be only one source for Drummond's information. He felt completely betrayed. Moira was the only one he'd told.

Four or five small carcasses were already roasting on rough spits as the two men moved closer to the fire. The gnarled cross loomed over the flames, casting its sinister shadow across the clearing.

The boys silently acknowledged Drummond, but completely ignored John. He didn't care. His concentration was focused somewhere else. The long trek in the fresh air and the sweet smell of roasting meat had combined to make his juices flow. When, finally, a plate of food was passed to him, he launched in with gusto. The sweet, salty flesh of the rabbit was delicious, causing him to wonder why food always tasted better around a campfire.

His thoughts were interrupted by Drummond rising to address his troop.

"So, where's Alistair Frazier, then? Ian MacLeod, I'm talking to you. Where's your accomplice, then?"

Ian visibly shrank. He stared at the ground and began mumbling to himself, as if praying for the earth to open and swallow him up.

"I know you both visited the chamber, a place you've been forbidden to enter. The fact that you pillaged it is abominable. Mister Frazier's absence tonight would serve to suggest his guilt. But I'll deal with him later. Your own atonement will begin now."

Hearing Drummond's words, the boy began to snivel. John glanced around at the other boys, who squirmed nervously as they focused their attention on the accused.

"You did steal the relic, Ian—didn't you? I want an answer. Now!"

The boy rose slowly to his feet. "Y...yes sir, I was party to the theft. Ali told me that if I didn't go with him to help, something terrible would happen to my sister. He said he knew where she was, and that she'd be in big trouble if I didn't go." Ian dropped his eyes and stared again at the ground. "I didn't even know there was a room down there. I was really scared, but I was more scared not to go."

"So, you placed your own needs before the needs of your tribe. Are you not ashamed, boy?"

"I am, sir. I haven't slept since. I knew you would find us out; you always do. I told Ali we'd get caught, but he said he'd done it before, and you hadn't noticed anything missing."

The minister glowered at the lad before turning slowly to meet the eyes of each boy in turn. "You all know what this means, don't you? You know what must happen."

The boys nodded their heads.

"But what about him?" asked one of the older boys, indicating John.

"Oh, have no fears about him, Jeremy. Mister MacIntyre has his own failings to worry about. You see, we've uncovered some of his secrets. As a result, he appreciates the need to keep ours."

He focused his gaze on John, and pointed his long finger. "Seize him," he thundered.

Immediately, the boys were on him. Although John put up a pretty good fight, knocking one or two of them to the ground, their sheer numbers soon subdued him.

He was tied with a length of rope and led toward the altar, where he was gagged and forced to kneel down. Two of the larger boys stood guard.

"Now him." Drummond indicated Ian.

The boys descended on Ian, who offered no resistance. He was too petrified to struggle. They bound his wrists and ankles, gagged him tightly, and carried him to the altar, where they laid him out. Drummond removed his scimitar from beneath his robe and began to sharpen it with a whetstone.

As he stroked the blade, he began the incantation, repeating the same macabre verses John had heard at the meeting. He saw fear in the eyes of the boys, but none of them attempted to interfere with the ritual. They all joined into the chant as they sat in the circle, rocking to and fro. Some of the younger ones had tears in their eyes. As he watched, helpless, John's legs began to tremble, then his arms, then his face. The strange sensation continued until it seemed every part of him was shaking uncontrollably. His brow dripped perspiration, but his lips felt deathly cold.

Ian's bladder let go. A steaming puddle spread out across the slab and dripped steadily onto the ground.

Drummond moved slowly toward him.

As he watched through tears of anger and frustration, John's brain simply refused to believe what he was seeing. Horrified, he told himself that what he was witnessing couldn't possibly be real. He bit hard on the insides of his cheeks in an effort to banish the nightmare, and although he could taste the blood, for some reason, he didn't waken. He heard someone moaning, and it took a moment for him to realize the sounds of anguish were his own.

Drummond's robe flapped gently in the chill wind as he stood before the altar, all the while continuing to sharpen the blade. John tried to scream, but his gag was too tight. As if he'd been hypnotized, he watched as the minister cut a sleeve from the boy's shirt. Drummond tore the sleeve into two strips and blindfolded the boy before turning back to John. The two boys held John as his eyes were also covered. He screamed again, but no sound escaped.

They dragged him to his feet and hauled him over to the slab. Someone loosened the ropes on his wrists just enough to place the hilt of the sword into his grip. They retightened the knots so as to hold the blade in position as Drummond continued to chant in the language John didn't understand.

Unearthly sensations bombarded John's brain. A pair of strong hands grasped his wrists, and before he could react, they plunged his arms straight downward. He felt the steel tearing through flesh and bone until it reached stone. The screams that escaped from the boy were like nothing John had ever imagined. He felt the gush of warm blood on his hands and smelled the stench of feces and death.

That was it. His brain short-circuited, and he crumbled to the ground.

✿ ✿ ✿

Valerie sat alone in the dark on the verandah of Ainsley House, the house she'd soon be leaving. The beauty of the valley had become lost to her, overshadowed by all that had happened. As she looked out across the loch, she saw a light, far off in the distance. It was coming from Campbell Keep. She remembered the night John thought he saw a light as they were crossing the loch from Kilbride.

She rose from her chair and went into the house to fetch the binoculars from John's study. When she returned, she focused them on the fortress and strained her eyes to see. Sure enough, there was a light, high in the castle, swaying to and fro, as if signaling to someone. She shivered and pulled the glasses from her eyes, feeling suddenly queasy. She thought about John.

When she raised the binoculars again, the light had vanished.

✿ ✿ ✿

Alistair Frazier was afraid. By now, Drummond knew he was the thief, and he had no doubt his punishment would be severe. Besides, now that Moira was gone, he saw no reason to stay in

Kilbride. He'd decided to try getting lost in Glasgow, knowing that Drummond would find him too easily in Oban. Besides, there were people in Oban he needed to avoid.

As he went about gathering his things, Alistair thought back on the night he'd seen Moira appear from out of the Campbell monument and forced her to show him the chamber. Now he wished he'd never known of its existence.

"Don't you ever think about taking anything from this place, Alistair Frazier," she'd warned him at the time. "You'll pay forever if you do."

How right she'd been.

The banging of his front door snapped Alistair back to the present. He'd left the door open to facilitate the loading, and an angry gust of wind had slammed it shut.

He finished packing his wreck of a car and climbed in, grateful to be making his escape. He knew that it was the night of the Covenanters meeting, so Drummond's spies wouldn't be around to see him leave. He'd been ordered to attend the meeting, but he knew that if he did, it would be his last. He had no delusions about Drummond's wrath.

He stashed a hastily wrapped package inside the torn passenger seat and headed west out of the village.

Darkness had descended quickly.

As he slowed for a bend, his faint headlights picked out a tall figure dressed all in black standing in the road, directly in his path. For an instant, Ali considered putting his foot down and driving on, but instead, he slammed on the brakes and screeched to a stop with just inches to spare. The figure never flinched. Instead, he stood completely still, gazing at the boy, dark eyes glittering.

The tall form walked around to the passenger side of the car, opened the door, and reached into the torn seat.

"And where do you think you're going, Mister Frazier?" the man asked softly.

"I was going to the kirk. I...I have something I need to return."

"And would it be this item?" The man hefted the heavy package.

The boy stared straight ahead and started to weep.

"Follow me, Alistair," said the man. "I'll help you to return it. And don't even think about trying to run. We both know it would be futile."

The man strode toward his own vehicle, which had been parked well off the road, out of sight. A moment later, Ali Frazier was following him into the night.

✿ ✿ ✿

As Graham Nesbit sped through the darkness on his way to Oban, the light from the tiny dashboard cast a pale green glow throughout the cramped interior. After the MacIntyres had headed back to Ainsley, he'd spent the day going through his mother's journals, rereading the terrible details of what had happened in the vale, years before. It was not something he liked being reminded of, but strange things were beginning to occur once again. Not only was Graham concerned about the disappearance of Moira MacLeod, but he was very disturbed by the parted seam in *Bridie*'s hull—more so than he'd wanted to let on.

He arrived in Oban too late to find a room, so he parked his car at a secluded cove he knew and spread a blanket on the sand to catch a little sleep before the sun rose. He was suddenly very tired.

As he lay staring at the stars, waiting for sleep to come, he thought about Moira and the closeness they'd once enjoyed. There had been a real connection between them, which was how he knew she was in trouble. It was up to him to find her.

She remained special to him, even though they'd grown apart over the last few years. She'd been a wonderful, happy girl, full of life and imagination until she'd become involved with Drummond and the Covenanters. When she pulled away from him, she'd refused to discuss it, and Graham had no choice but to grant her her space.

His thoughts turned to John MacIntyre. He remained convinced that the man was not telling all he knew.

Graham watched as a meteor streaked across the heavens, and thought about Valerie. His mind kept racing from place to place, and sleep continued to elude him, so he sat up and stared at the sea. He decided to walk for a bit, to get his mind off the strange thoughts he was having. The moon was high in the sky, bright enough to create long shadows. After he'd strolled for nearly half a mile, he breathed a deep sigh as his mind finally quieted.

A moment or two later, he heard something—voices—coming from the direction of the caves. He'd explored the Oban caves many times before, and wondered who would be in such a dangerous place in the middle of the night. He decided to check it out, to make sure that no one had gotten hurt or was trapped in the maze of tunnels. Some people had entered these caves, never to be seen again.

He reached the mouth of the grotto and listened carefully but heard nothing. Then, out of the darkness, he heard a low sigh, like the voice of a woman in distress. He entered the cave mouth and discovered that he was listening to the moaning of the wind coursing through the labyrinth. He turned to leave, but as he did, a woman's voice floated to him through the still air. He wasn't sure what was said, but he'd definitely heard someone call out.

He reentered the cave and was surprised at how well he could see. The moonlight penetrated into the deepest recesses through the many fissures in the cavern's roof. It reminded him of another forbidden place.

Again he heard the voice. This time it was pleading with someone. He moved deeper into the passage following the sound, rounded a corner, and froze, stunned by what lay before him. A man and a woman were in the throes of passion, lying together on a bed of silver sand. Nesbit tried to turn away. He knew he shouldn't be watching, but he couldn't make his feet move.

A moment later, the woman pulled away, rose to her feet, and began to run directly toward Graham. The man scrambled up, pulled on his trousers, and began to follow.

"Don't," the man called. "Please don't leave me."

The woman continued in Graham's direction, and he could see that she was crying. He stepped back into the shadows, unsure what to do, wondering whether or not to get involved.

A second later, Graham gasped, amazed that the woman running toward him was none other than Moira MacLeod, naked as a baby. He opened his mouth to call to her, but she veered into a side tunnel and disappeared. His shock was compounded when he recognized the person following her. It was Alistair Frazier.

What the hell's he doing here? Graham was dumbstruck. *Ali and Moira? It doesn't make sense. Something isn't right.*

He decided to follow them.

By the time he reached the narrow passage, the pair had disappeared, but he could still hear the girl crying and the young man calling after her. He followed the voices and soon came upon a set of crude stone steps leading up into the moonlight. He scrambled upward and found himself standing atop a high bluff overlooking the churning sea. For a moment, he couldn't see anyone, but then he heard the voices again. He peered through the darkness in the direction of the sound, and finally he saw her, silhouetted in a fast falling moon. She was backing slowly toward the edge of the cliff as Alistair pled with her, his hand extended, trying to convince her to take it.

Graham's heart battered his chest wall. He tried to call out, but his mouth was bone dry. He managed nothing but a strangled moan.

Moira continued to inch backward until she stood on the very brink of the precipice. Far beneath her, the relentless crashing of the waves on the rocks added a dreadful fierceness to the scene.

As Graham watched, trying to find his voice, the girl stumbled and disappeared over the edge. Again, he tried to scream, and this time he was successful, but too late. He watched helplessly as Ali ran to the edge and leapt after her.

The screams awakened Graham from his nightmare. He sat bolt upright, soaked with sweat, his heart bursting. He dropped his head into his hands, breathing deeply and trying to gather his wits. After a minute, he climbed to his feet, peeled off his clothes, and ran into the frigid sea.

The sun was barely rising over the hills as Graham swam into the onrushing waves. His powerful strokes soon carried him past the surf to the stillness beyond. He rolled over onto his back, surrendering himself to the swells, and stared at the slowly lightening sky.

CHAPTER 25

———◆◆◆———

When John came to, his blindfold was gone, and he'd been untied. He watched the sky turning pink with the approach of sunrise. Slowly, the terror of the night before flooded back. The surge of adrenaline cleared his mind. He looked at the altar. Drummond was deep in conversation with one of the boys.

John knew he must have lost his mind, because the boy the minister was talking to was Ian MacLeod, looking very much alive. He staggered stiffly to his feet and approached the altar. Lying on the slab was the bloody body of a young lamb. Overcome with both outrage and relief, he turned to Drummond, but he couldn't find words. The minister's face broke into a cryptic smile.

"Well, well, John. Back in the land of the living, I see."

John glanced around the clearing. The other boys were all gone. "What the hell—?"

Drummond interrupted. "It's a wonderful thing, the respite the soul enjoys when convicted of a lesser sin than the one imagined. I would wager that the reaction you are having to murdering this innocent little creature is one of great relief rather than disgust. Is that not so?"

"You're a sick bastard," John said. "*You* should be stretched out on the slab. Now *that* might be worthwhile."

"Thank you. How evolved you are."

Drummond stepped closer until he was inches from John's face.

"I think you've succeeded in making my point. Any man can reach the place where violence seems justified, even preferred. And, heartiest congratulations, you've passed initiation."

Drummond took a step back and chuckled. "The boys and I have plans for you, John…big plans. Whether you like it or not, you're going to help give us a voice, and your involvement in our holy cause will guarantee my silence about…other matters."

"What are you–?"

"Matters that need not concern your lovely wife. Do I make myself plain, John?"

"Listen, you maniac…I don't care what you tell my wife. We're out of here in a few days, and there's nothing you can do about it."

"Don't be so sure, John," said the minister. "A lot can happen in a few days."

John strode out of the circle. He headed back across the moor, hoping he would find his way to the road.

An hour later, he was relieved to see the ribbon of tarmac far below him and made his way down the steep slope. The first lorry that came by stopped and gave him a lift.

He arrived home exhausted and was pleased that Valerie was not yet awake. He retired to his study, curled up on the couch, and fell fast asleep.

✿ ✿ ✿

Valerie had slept fitfully. When she finally heard John come into the house an hour past dawn, she was surprised she hadn't heard the car. She waited for him to come upstairs, but when he hadn't arrived after a few minutes, she rose and went downstairs to find him. She discovered him asleep in the study, moaning to himself. She resisted the temptation to wake him and headed for the kitchen to make coffee.

John tossed on the couch, trying to flee, but held fast by a strong, sinewy hand. Powerful images, frighteningly real, steadily overtook him.

> *Campbell Keep had never looked more glorious. The vivid colors of the banners and the flowers helped to soften the cold austerity of the place. An atmosphere of gaiety filled the fortress as half a hundred servants went about their work with unaccustomed enthusiasm. There was laughter and singing, and the master did nothing to curtail it. Never before had they seen him in such good spirits, and they were determined to make the best of it while it lasted. Some of the younger servants were heard to suggest that the arrival of a new young wife might soften Campbell's disposition. The older ones knew better.*
>
> *The day before the great event, the clan MacLeod arrived at the Keep in all the splendor they could muster. Eileen was quiet, almost*

serene. She expressed her appreciation for all the lavish preparations and offered a wistful smile to all she passed.

She did not meet with Campbell. Thankfully, there was an ancient superstition that saved her. It was said that those who chose to disregard it could expect only girl children. And the Earl of Argyll believed all the myths.

The wedding day brought with it a terrible storm. It was not a good omen. High winds whipped Loch Awe into foam, and a cold rain pelted the stout castle walls. The vast courtyard that had been specially prepared for the ceremony had to be abandoned, and scores of frantic servants scurried about amid the tempest, moving everything indoors. It was hours before the great hall was ready.

When everything had been reset, the Lord Bishop Ramsey, imported from Edinburgh for the occasion, entered the chamber and took his place between the two local priests who would assist him during the ceremony. He watched intently as the Earl of Argyll and his retinue entered the hall and strutted toward the altar, resplendent in their Royal tartans.

To Bishop Ramsay, the groom appeared nervous as he stood fidgeting, awaiting the entrance of the bride. He'd never seen Campbell ill at ease in any circumstance. His curiosity was piqued.

Six pipers droned on as the guests waited for the bride to make her appearance. One or two of the invited began to glance toward the doors. The groom continued to stare straight ahead.

As the darkness descended over Campbell Keep, the howling gale continued its bitter assault. A cold wind moaned through the corridors, reaching to even the great hall. The candles and torches sputtered and flickered in the draughts, casting eerie shadows on the walls. Those in attendance became increasingly uncomfortable. They could feel Campbell's patience running out.

Finally, the doors swung open, framing Eileen MacLeod between them. For a long moment, she stood there and quietly surveyed the room. Then, slowly and deliberately, she walked the hundred feet to the altar, murmuring to herself, counting every step, like a condemned prisoner advancing toward her executioner.

When she reached the altar and took her place beside Campbell, he turned to her and lifted her veil. The Bishop of Edinburgh gazed upon a face of such beauty that he felt a little quiver in his loins, something he hadn't enjoyed in years. He could see that the Earl had much to be thankful for.

The high mass lasted for over an hour. After receiving Holy Communion, the couple was bidden to rise from their knees for the wedding vows.

Campbell seemed unsure of him self and barely managed to mumble his responses, but when it came to her turn, Lady Eileen spoke in a firm, clear voice. Duncan McLeod sat back in his chair and mopped his brow. He was greatly relieved.

Ninian Lasker stood in the shadows, content as a sated viper. He, too, was pleased.

As Campbell began to place the ring on Eileen's finger, a hush fell over the room. But not a moment passed before the silence was shattered. At the back of the great hall, people started screaming. Campbell spun away from the Bishop, tossing the wedding ring to the floor.

A dozen men with swords dripping blood were engaged in cleaving a steady swath between themselves and the altar. Campbell drew his weapon and began barking orders. At the sound of their chief's voice, his men recovered from their momentary paralysis and rushed to his side. Together, they turned to face the fray.

A young, red-haired man led the attackers, storming his way through the crowd like a man possessed.

"Robert!" Eileen screamed, unable to believe her eyes.

He'd come for her. Oh, thank God.

But the joy didn't last for long. Eileen's hopes faltered as she watched the tide turn. Robert's courage was not enough to overcome the sheer numbers. Within minutes, all of his men lay dead, or dying, and Robert, his face spattered with blood, was dragged toward Campbell. William of Alsh pulled a dirk from his belt and stepped forward, eager to remove young Douglas's throat.

As he raised his dagger, he was suddenly struck from behind, and his knees buckled. A lesser man would surely have dropped. Affixed to his back was a screaming fury, ripping at his face, attempting to claw his eyes out. Somehow, Alsh managed to reach back and get a hold of his attacker, and with great effort threw the enraged girl to the floor. Wiping the blood from his eyes, he returned his attention to Robert.

"No William. Not yet. Bring the lady here." Campbell's dark eyes smoldered.

Alsh dragged Eileen to her feet and held her by the neck. As she looked up into the battered face of her beloved Robert, her eyes shone with pride.

The Bishop of Edinburgh remained well hidden, crouched down behind the altar, quaking in his embroidered slippers. He'd had a bad feeling about this wedding from the very beginning.

The heat was now gone from Campbell, but the cold rage that replaced it was far more dangerous. "We'll not kill the pup just yet, I think. Allowing him to depart this earth so painlessly would never do…oh no."

He glanced around the hall, assessing the damage. He'd lost more than twenty good men. He returned his attention to his prisoner. "I have a much better idea. You, my lad, are going to be allowed to rot away slowly so that Lady Campbell can be thinking of you every time I possess her. It'll give you the time to rue your damn treason."

Campbell turned to the girl.

"So this was the hand ye wanted in marriage, was it? Well I think we can oblige you, after all. He turned to Alsh. "Bring him here."

Robert was shoved so hard that he stumbled and fell onto the prayer stool. He remained kneeling as Campbell took his arm and laid it across the white satin altar cloth. As if in slow motion, Campbell raised his sword above his head, and with a great roar, smashed it to the altar, severing Robert's hand.

Without a sound, the young man slumped forward, spurting blood all over the pristine vestments of the horrified Bishop of Edinburgh. Then, before the Bishop's gaping eyes, Campbell reached for the gory hand, turned, and flung it scornfully at the girl. It struck her on the breast and dropped to the floor, where it lay slowly closing into a fist. Without a second thought, Eileen bent down, picked up the hand, and held it to her heart.

"Remove him to the dungeon," barked Campbell.

Three men lifted the unconscious Robert and carried him from the room streaming a trail of Douglas blood across the stones.

Campbell moved back to his place at the altar, his countenance eerily calm. "Let the ceremony resume."

Clutching Robert's hand to her breast, Eileen MacLeod stood quietly beside the monster that was about to become her husband. The Bishop watched in horror as rivulets of blood seeped steadily through Eileen's fingers and streamed down the bodice of her gown.

MacIntyre awoke trembling in fear. He knew his mind was being controlled by a will much stronger than his own, and the visions were becoming more and more graphic, more and more brutal. The terrifying wedding scene had not been the product of his imagination. Instead, he had been a witness.

He rose to his feet and started up the stairs, in desperate need of some Vicadin and a long, hot shower. He had to put a stop to the takeover, even if it meant he had to abandon his writing, knowing that if he didn't, something terrible was going to happen.

As the son of a fundamentalist minister, his young mind had been filled with fearful images of hell and its demons. Night after night, he'd been assailed by terrible nightmares. John had always believed in the netherworld, and now he'd found it.

✳ ✳ ✳

After his swim, Graham Nesbit felt much better, although he didn't know what to make of the disquieting dream. He dressed quickly and drove into town in search of a good breakfast. He was ravenous. He found a small café open and went inside, ordered eggs and bacon and kippers, and ate every scrap. He followed the meal with a tall glass of ice-cold milk and two cups of strong coffee. By the time he left the place, he felt like a new man, eager to get on with his search.

Thankfully, he'd remembered to bring a photo of Moira with him. Actually, it was one of the flyers from the Thistle. It wasn't the best of pictures, but it would serve its purpose. She was not, after all, the kind of girl to go unnoticed.

For the first couple of hours, he had absolutely no luck. One or two people remembered seeing her, but none of them had any idea where she might be. Around lunchtime, Nesbit followed the crowd into a fish-and-chip shop that seemed to be a very popular spot. When he got a chance, he showed Moira's picture to the turbaned man behind the counter, who reacted with pleasant surprise.

"Yes I do remember her. She was in here about a week ago. She arrived just as I was closing up. For some reason, I felt concern for her. She seemed much too sad for someone so young. She's carrying a very heavy burden, I think."

"Yes, I know," Graham agreed. "I have a feeling she's in trouble."

They stepped outside, and the Indian man pointed to the rooming house where Moira had gone after leaving the shop. Nesbit headed off up the hill.

He got little additional information from the landlady, but was pleased to hear that the girl had been a model boarder. The woman did volunteer that she was worried about the girl, expressing that Moira had been very quiet—too quiet for someone her age.

As he took his leave, the woman suddenly remembered something. She disappeared into the house and returned carrying a guitar case. Wordlessly, he reached for the case as his heart sank. He knew Moira would never leave her guitar behind.

He made his way slowly down the hill toward the harbor. He'd followed every lead but had gotten nowhere. He entered a little pub by the water's edge, ordered a pint of bitter, and sat outside contemplating the sea and his next move. That's when the idea struck him.

✴ ✴ ✴

John awakened to find his wife peering into his face, looking less than pleased. She handed him a cup of steaming coffee.

"So what the hell happened to you? Where were you all night?"

"Valerie, I'm so sorry. I knew you'd be worried, but there was nothing I could do. I was with Drummond, but let me tell you, that's the last damn time. I don't care what he does. He's a sick bastard. He took me out to the moors, and before I knew what was happening, I was attacked by his stupid gang of thugs. They tied me up and forced me to—"

"John," she interrupted, "I want to hear this. Really I do, but I promised I'd tell you as soon as you woke up."

"Tell me? Tell me what?"

"Graham called from Oban. He's found out something about Moira and says he needs your help."

John took a swallow of the hot coffee and shook his head, trying to clear the cobwebs.

"I told him you were sleeping. I explained that you'd been out all night, but he said he absolutely needed to talk to you. He said he'd call back in fifteen minutes, that should be right about now."

"What time is it?"

"It's just after two. So, you had quite a night?"

"Oh yeah. I'll tell you all about it after I talk to Graham. But I have to admit, you were absolutely right about Drummond. The man's completely mad, and something's got to be done about him. He's dangerous."

The phone rang, and Valerie crossed to the desk to answer it. As expected, it was Graham. John rose from the couch and went to his desk. He picked up the receiver.

"Hello Graham. What's up?"

He listened carefully as Graham explained the situation.

"Yes…yes as a matter of fact I do," John replied. "It's a bar called, um…the Cellar, something like that. She was there a few times with Frazier. I don't think she'd go there, though. She said she detested the place."

John listened again.

"Of course I will," he said, "if you think it'll help. I can be there within two hours. Where do you want me to meet you?"

He wrote down the instructions. "Okay, I'll be there." He hung up the phone and looked at Valerie. "What I have to tell you about

Drummond will have to wait. Graham needs my help. He's looking for Moira, and he thinks he's found something. She's been in Oban recently, and Graham thinks she's in trouble. I don't exactly know what he has in mind, but he thinks I can help. I've got to go, right now."

"But I want to know what happened to you. Damn it, John, tell me what happened."

"I'm going to tell you, Val, I promise, but I need to tell you everything. It's a long story, and I want you to hear it from the beginning. I'm sick and tired of all the crap."

John reached for his wife, wanting to kiss her, but he felt awkward. Instead, he pulled her to him and hugged her fiercely. "Please understand, Val. Just once more."

"But why can't I go with you?" she asked.

"Graham said I should come alone, and I have to go with what he says. I'm sorry."

Valerie sighed deeply as she watched him leave the room.

✿ ✿ ✿

Twenty minutes later, he was on the road, trying to think clearly about all that had transpired, and wondering what lay in store for him in Oban. He was driving too fast, as usual, when he rounded a blind curve and careened headlong into a rockslide that covered half the road. He hit the brakes and wrestled with the steering wheel, doing his best to swerve around the worst of it. Somehow, he managed to miss all the big rocks and made it through, unscathed. That's when his right front tire blew. He lost control, and a second later, the Jaguar was doing pirouettes down the middle of the road.

Miraculously, he managed to just miss an oncoming lorry before depositing the car into a deep ditch, a hundred feet away. When the four-thousand-pound projectile finally came to rest, John was shaking. He couldn't help thinking that the rockslide had been just a little too timely, and wondered if someone or something had tried to sabotage him.

The two men from the truck he barely missed arrived on the scene, relieved to see that he was not only okay, he was actually trying to drive the car out of the gully. The men climbed down the slope and saw immediately that the Jag was pretty well stuck. John demanded, rather forcefully, that they pull him out, but they had no chain. He had no choice but to accept their offer to send a tow truck from the next town they reached.

It was after six when John arrived in Oban, relieved to find Nesbit still waiting for him at the pub, even though the man appeared half crocked. After listening patiently to John's reason for being late, Graham shared what he'd been able to find out, and what he would require from John.

"I have a feeling she's been at the club. It's the Skullery, by the way, not the Cellar. Unfortunately, from what I've been told, it's not a place for the likes of us to go looking for information. They'll assume we're coppers."

John listened carefully as Graham laid out his plan. It seemed to him that the idea was a bit sketchy, but he agreed to go along. They had a quick drink to toast the success of their mission, and headed for the tourist shops where they purchased a couple of strands of cheap gold chain and a pair of outrageous sunglasses.

☆ ☆ ☆

Valerie opened the front door to find Drummond scowling at her. She could have kicked herself for answering.

"Good afternoon to you, Missus MacIntyre, and did your husband get home safely?"

She knew he was mocking her. "Actually he did, thank you. But he's not home at the moment. I'll be sure to tell him you stopped by."

"Very well then. I'd eh...appreciate that," said Drummond. "By the way, did he tell you anything about his...experience on the moors?"

"As a matter of fact, he didn't. He had more important matters to attend to, but I'm sure he'll tell me all about it when he has time."

"I wouldn't be too sure, Missus MacIntyre. After all, your husband is very good at keeping secrets."

Valerie stared back unblinking, refusing to give him any satisfaction.

"Tell me, Missus MacIntyre—I'm just curious. Why do you exhibit such distaste for me? Do you really disapprove of me so much?"

Valerie responded carefully. "I don't know exactly what it is you want from my husband, Reverend Drummond, but my instincts tell me to beware. And, in case you're wondering, I'm not afraid of you."

Drummond scowled, spun on his heel, and stalked away. Half way to his car he stopped, turned his shaggy head, and started to say something, but seemingly changed his mind. He continued on his way, muttering to himself.

Trembling, Valerie stumbled back into the house and leaned against the wall gulping deep breaths. She knew he hadn't believed her.

Still shaken, she stumbled toward the living room, pushed open the door, and screamed. Framed in each of the three huge windows was a boy dressed in black. The boys stood still as palace guards, unblinking, staring at her through the glass, their eyes glittering with hatred. Valerie gasped and fled.

She raced to the kitchen, ran into the pantry, and locked the door behind her. She crouched in the furthest corner and forced herself to breathe. A moment later, she heard voices just outside the locked door. She strained her ears to hear what was being said, but the visitors were whispering. Valerie made out nothing over the pounding pulse in her ears.

✲ ✲ ✲

Drummond had a lot on his mind. He parked the car in the driveway of the rectory, but instead of going to the house, he crossed the lawn and slipped into his vestry. As he entered the room, the telephone rang. He picked up the receiver.

"Yes."

"Have you got the girl?"

"No," Drummond replied, feeling the onset of a headache. "Eh, not exactly, but we think we know where she is."

"You'd better know," said the faraway voice, "because we must proceed at once. We can't afford to waste anymore time."

"Well, MacIntyre's ready to cooperate," said Drummond. "I'll tell you that. He's been well primed. I own him."

"Come, come, Kenneth. You own no one, and there's a whole lot more to this than your stupid political cause. I've waited years, for

Christ's sake. I need MacIntyre, and I don't want you complicating things."

"But he could be so good for us. And it's such a righteous cause. You know that. The future of our country hangs in the balance." Drummond heard himself pleading. His head was now pounding.

"If MacIntyre was seen as a supporter, people would listen. He'd bring national attention. He could provide the voice we need. Couldn't we wait just a little longer? We've waited this long."

"There's no time, you idiot. You'll find a voice for your stupid cause after we've found the damn tomb. We will not deviate, Kenneth. MacIntyre first, then the pretty wife, just like before. Graham has to believe that history is repeating itself. His own history...and mine."

In the darkened library at the rear of the big house in Edinburgh, Erskin replaced the telephone receiver and returned his attention to the sketch in front of him. The rendering of the Keep, drawn from memory, was almost complete.

"Soon," he murmured, "very, very soon. I'm coming to claim what's rightfully mine. Will you remember me, Graham Nesbit? Will you remember me fondly?"

As he stared at the drawing, his face gradually hardened into a mask. Nail-bitten fingers reached for a lock of auburn hair. He twisted and twisted until the pain finally registered.

CHAPTER 26

————◆◆◆————

John and Graham arrived at the Skullery about half past eight and took a look inside. The place was dead. They approached the doorman, preparing to pay the cover charge. He regarded them sullenly, immediately suspicious. "This isn't the place for the likes of you gents, I don't think. You'd probably be happier at Angie's, down by the pier."

"Oh no, my man," said Graham, smiling cordially, "we're here to check out your band. We heard they're really something. You see, my friend here is visiting from America. He's a famous record producer. He's interested in hearing the lads."

"I see." He quietly studied John, trying not to smirk. Adorned in gold chains and dark glasses, John looked like a throwback to the Seventies.

"Come in then," the bouncer decided. "Krank doesn't go on until later, but you can have a drink at the bar while you're waiting."

John reached into his pocket for some cash in order to pay the entry fee, but the man waved it off. "That'll not be necessary. It looks like a quiet night."

"Well thank you, my good man," said John, as he slipped a ten-pound note into the big fellow's hand. "That's for your trouble."

The man pocketed the money without looking at it. "Thank you, sir. Why don't you take that nice table there close to the stage?"

"Oh, thanks a lot, man, but we'll be just as happy at the bar." John assumed the music would be excruciating.

"Wherever you like." The man moved aside to afford them entry.

By ten o'clock, the place was packed. The interlopers had been scrutinized by each and every person, but the word had quickly passed as to who they were. They moved to a back table in the hopes of being less conspicuous

Eventually, Krank staggered onto the stage and began to play. It was without a doubt the worst music John had ever heard. Graham leaned in to say something but quickly realized the futility. Forty minutes later, the aural assault took a break and the leader of the band made a beeline for their table.

"I heard yous wanted to see me."

"Yes indeed," said Graham. "Why don't you sit down, Spike? That is your name, isn't it? We've already ordered you a drink. I asked the waitress what you liked, and she said you'd drink anything."

The foul-smelling boy took a seat and cautiously eyed the visitors. He extended a bony hand, and John reached unenthusiastically to take it.

"Spike Jones," said the lad.

"John MacIntyre. This here's my pal, Graham Nesbit."

The boy sat slack-mouthed, waiting for what was next. As Graham started to speak, the surly waitress arrived at their table and deposited three drinks.

The boy reached into his pocket, but John waved him off and tossed a tenner onto the girl's dirty tray. She grunted her thanks and sauntered away.

"Well," said John, when they were once again alone, "I think you guys are definitely onto something. The music's certainly original...just the sort of sound Revv Records is looking for."

The boy grinned and turned to send a thumbs-up to the other band members, who were watching intently from across the room.

"But," John continued, "there is one element that I think would make it a slam dunk."

The boy appeared confused.

"In other words, a sure thing."

The boy leaned closer. John leaned back and continued with his monologue. "You see, what we're selling in the States these days, aside from good music, of course, is sex. It's what everybody wants."

The boy snorted and nonchalantly wiped his nose with his sleeve.

Graham sat quietly, marveling as watched his cohort reel the young man in.

"If you had a girl in the band, particularly a good-looking one, doesn't even matter if she can play, it would make it a lot easier for me to sell you. Do you get my drift...eh, do you understand?"

The excitement flooding Spike's face said it all. The lad could barely contain himself.

"We have one. At least we had one until the other night. She's awesome, and smashin' lookin' too. She can sing and everything."

John and Graham leaned forward in anticipation.

"So?" said Nesbit.

"But I don't know what happened to her. I don't know where she went."

Graham let out his breath. John shook his head, looking terribly disappointed. They started to rise.

"Well that's too bad. It really is," said John. "It would have made all the difference."

"All right then. Hold on just a sec. Maybe we can find her." The boy spoke with a bit less enthusiasm. "She's got to be around somewhere."

John settled back down and tried not to sound too interested. "What's her name?"

"Um—"

Spike was straining to think.

Graham watched impatiently, trying to keep from reaching across the table to choke it out of the young punk.

"Moira! Yes that's it, Moira something. She's an absolute cork; body that won't quit."

"So how do we find her?" asked Graham.

Spike considered carefully and made his decision. "Tray. She was with Tray. His name's really Travis, but everyone calls him Tray."

He searched around the room before spotting who he was looking for. He pointed over his shoulder to a table in the corner where a skinny black man in a scruffy leather jacket was deep in conversation with a very young girl.

"It's that black guy, over there in the corner. Let me warn you, though, he's pretty rough. He's not somebody you want to screw with. He's got some nasty friends, and they'd just as soon kick your arse as look at you. But, he might know where Moira is. The last time I saw her, she was leaving here with him."

Graham pulled his chair around the table so he could see the black man without being too obvious. He had the beginnings of an idea.

"Well Spike," he said, "maybe you should have a word with the man for us. You could ask him where the girl is."

A look of panic appeared on the lad's face. "No, mister. No way. He'll kick the crap out of me. He's done it before, just because I was two days late with a payment."

"Payment?" asked Graham. "What kind of payment?"

"He's a dealer." Spike whispered conspiratorially. "He always has the best stuff."

"I see," said Graham. "Very interesting."

"Well, I think it's important that we find the girl singer," said John. "Maybe we should have a little chat with the fella."

"Oh I don't know, mister," said Spike, "I don't think that's a good idea. He's a right-mean bastard."

"Oh, don't you worry, my boy," said Nesbit. "I'm sure it's all in the way you approach him. I'll tell you what; this is important for all of us, and if you're willing to help, without being directly involved, of course, I bet we could make some headway with the chap. He's probably more reasonable than you think."

The boy looked completely dismayed.

John said, "It could mean the difference between a record deal and a career here at the Skullery."

Spike nodded slowly, his mind made up.

"So he's into the drugs, is he?" Graham spoke to no one in particular.

"Aye, he's a big dealer. I told you that."

"Excellent," said Graham "then we have the makings of a deal."

He smiled and leaned closer to the young man. "First of all, I need you to get your hands on an empty liquor bottle and fill it with a mixture of cola and water. I'll also need a large cup, plastic if possible. Do you think you can do that?"

The lad nodded his head.

"Good. Now when you've got them, bring them back to me as inconspicuously as possible. Then I'll tell you what else."

As soon as the boy left the table to attend to his mission, Graham laid out his plan. John nodded as he listened. He'd always loved a good drama, and this one promised to be outstanding.

Within minutes, Spike returned and passed Graham the bottle and a plastic cup from under his shirt. Graham slipped the bottle into his jacket.

"Excellent," he said. "Now after you see us leave, I want you to convince old Travis there that he has a ready customer waiting for him in the parking lot—someone he can rip off. Can you do that? It might just be the most important performance of your life."

The lad nodded. "Yes, I can do that."

"Excellent. Then all you have to do is go back on stage and play...really loud, if you can manage it."

The boy eyed Graham dubiously.

Graham summoned the waitress and ordered three double cognacs. When the drinks arrived, he poured them into the plastic cup. John paid the tab, leaving a generous tip, and they stood to leave.

At the door, John slipped the doorman another tenner and asked if it was okay to take his drink with him. The bouncer was happy to oblige, and the two men crossed the parking lot to the Jaguar.

Within moments the band resumed its terrible clamor, and Graham crouched down behind the car out of sight. A minute later, John raised his hand and waved to the black man as he exited the club searching for his client.

Tray appeared a little reticent when he saw the middle-aged man waiting beside the expensive car, but crossed anyway. After all, business was business.

"You waitin' fer me, man?" He spoke with a lilting West Indies accent.

"As a matter of fact, I am," replied John. He laid on the American accent as thickly as possible.

"You wouldn't be a cop, would you bro?" asked Tray. His mouth smiled broadly, but his eyes were like flint.

"Oh yeah." John laughed, "I was sent all the way from California to bust a two-bit dealer in the teeming metropolis of Oban."

Tray moved a few steps closer. His shoulders slumped as he relaxed.

"So, let's see what you got."

"I got some very fine blow, man, hardly stepped on at all. Good for what ails you."

John reached into his pocket and pulled out his wallet. The Jamaican took another step closer. He was now in perfect position.

Silently, Nesbit rose up behind the man and grabbed him around the chest, pinning his arms to his side. Tray put up a pretty good struggle for a little guy, but Graham was just too strong. He released his grip, spun Tray around, and punched him hard.

When Tray came to, he was sitting on the ground in the dark alley behind the club. He'd been tied to a drainpipe and tightly gagged. His legs were spread apart, held open by a piece of lumber wedged between his ankles.

"Tray, my boy, welcome back." Graham had to yell to be heard over the racket from the club. "I'm going to remove the gag, but should you be tempted to scream out, don't do it. I'd be obliged to put you right back to sleep. Do you understand me?"

Tray, who actually looked a bit pale, slowly nodded his head.

"Very good," said Nesbit as he yanked the strip of cloth from between the man's teeth.

"Well, we have just one or two questions for you, and I hope for your sake the answers are to our liking. Now, first of all, does the name Moira MacLeod mean anything to you?"

The dark eyes flashed with recognition, but Travis shook his head.

"Are you quite sure? Because this'll be your last chance."

"I'm sure, asshole. I'm tellin' you nothing."

He spat angrily, but missed his target

"As you wish," said Nesbit.

The band finished a number, and for a few precious moments, there was beautiful silence.

"All right, John," said Graham, signaling to his companion.

As Tray watched in disbelief, the other man, the American, moved into the picture and proceeded to pour a trail of liquid from a plastic cup all the way to Tray's crotch. The acrid smell of strong brandy was overpowering. The American then turned to his friend, who handed him the bottle from his jacket pocket. Without a word, he unscrewed the cap from the bottle and splashed the remaining liquid all over Tray's lap.

The dealer's eyes opened very wide as Graham took a box of matches from his pocket, struck one and bent to touch the fire to the river of brandy. A bright blue flame sprang up immediately and began inching toward the writhing man. As the flame crept closer and closer, Tray began to whimper.

Graham grinned. The standoff was almost over.

"Okay, okay," Tray said hoarsely, "I'll tell you."

Graham took his time stamping out the fire while Travis spilled everything.

When he'd finished talking, John shook his head in disgust and turned to leave. Nesbit struck another match and lit what was left of the brandy trail. He watched the flame take hold and casually strolled away.

Travis screamed, watching helplessly as the dancing blue fire drew nearer.

His shrieks were lost in the din pounding through the walls.

✡ ✡ ✡

It was after midnight when Rudy opened the door of the Bersky townhouse to find a trio of men wearing trench coats. One of the men brandished a search warrant as he pushed his way into the vestibule. Rudy watched, horrified, as the cops spread out and began their search.

✡ ✡ ✡

John and Graham sat at a corner table in an otherwise deserted Angie's bar. They downed their whiskeys and ordered two more. By the time they were on their third, they were both pensive.

"I was sure the coppers would find her at that house," said Graham. "Or at least those lowlifes would know where she is. Do you really think she could possibly have escaped from that room?"

"I don't know what to say, Graham, but don't you be blaming yourself. If it hadn't been for you, we'd never have found out where she was taken. You know, I really underestimated you. You're a real man after all. That little bait and switch with the brandy was really very clever. I think I'll use it in a movie some time. It was very convincing."

He took a deep breath. "Graham, I gotta tell you, I didn't think that we could ever be friends, but I was wrong. You're really quite a guy for a fa–" He decided not to complete his thought. He was pretty loaded, but not yet completely insensitive.

"A what?" Graham was grinning at him. "Were you going to say *fag?*"

"Well, yeah." John suddenly felt uncomfortably warm. "I mean, you must admit, you damn well don't act gay, do you?" He stopped talking and took a long swig of his drink.

"Well John, since we're being honest with each other, having a male-bonding moment, you might say, I feel it's my duty to tell you about myself." He glanced sideways at his companion. "Since we've fought a battle together, I feel the need to tell you the truth." He cleared his throat. "Well, you see…I'm not gay, John—not by a long shot. I never have been. I'm sorry I deceived you, but it seemed like the best approach at the time."

Without warning, John leaned across the table and delivered a solid punch to Graham's chin. He almost toppled, but somehow managed to remain upright. He rubbed his jaw, and raised his hands in defeat.

"All right, John. Now you've got to listen. You must believe me: Valerie and I nev—"

That's as far as he got. John leapt from his chair and swung again. This time, however, he missed. Graham shrugged his shoulders, stood up, grabbed John by the sleeve, spun him around, and drove a hard fist into his belly.

"That's for your sheer stupidity, and for Valerie," he said, as John bent double from the blow. "The woman loves you. Why don't you ever listen?"

As John lowered his head and charged, the bartender rushed into the fray and managed to steer the men outside.

The harbor was completely deserted. A light drizzle fell as the brawl continued. Each man got in a couple of good licks, but most of the shots missed by a mile. The alcohol was working its magic, which resulted in a lot of flailing and not much damage.

They battled on down the pier, with Graham getting the better of his smaller, drunker, but very determined opponent. John managed to get off a mighty roundhouse right, which missed badly, causing him to lose his balance. Graham stepped around the punch and delivered a good crack to his adversary's jaw. John stumbled and almost went down, but, by sheer force of will, managed to right himself. Dazed, he staggered backward for a few steps until he unceremoniously disappeared over the edge of the pier. Three long seconds later, there was a great splash.

Graham rushed to the side and looked down at the water. John was nowhere to be seen. A spreading patch of bubbles was all that was left of him. Without a second thought, Graham dived over. He hit the water hard and was immediately stone cold sober. By the time he surfaced, John was flailing away beside him, about to go down again, but Graham grabbed him around the chest and kicked out for the shore.

A few minutes later, Graham pulled John onto the beach, where they lay side by side, gasping for air. He became aware of a strange gurgling sound and looked over to see John laughing and choking at the same time. Graham struggled to his feet, joining in the merriment, and helped John up from the sand.

They stumbled along the street, dripping wet, arms around each other.

"What I was trying to tell you, John, is that your wife and I have never been intimate," said Graham. "Not that I didn't try, you understand. But she wouldn't have it. She takes her pledges seriously, that woman. And, for some reason, she loves you to death. You're a lucky bastard, you know."

"I know," said John.

"So, I think I might have an idea where Moira is," said Graham when they were back at John's car. "And from what the police said about her condition, I think we'd better hurry."

✿ ✿ ✿

An hour later, two automobiles raced in tandem toward Kilbride. Graham was tired but determined.

John was lost in thought. He pondered where he'd lost his way, and wondered how he'd turned away from his wonderful wife and allowed another woman to possess him. Actually, two women had invaded him together: Moira and Eileen McLeod, although sometimes he felt like they were one girl, creating a force powerful enough for him to risk everything. He was a fool, and he knew it. He had a lot to make up for.

Suddenly, his rearview mirror flooded with the glare of high beams, and the unmistakable braying of a klaxon shattered his reverie.

"Damn," he said.

Both cars pulled off the road as a blue and white police car screamed past before hitting its brakes and sliding to a stop just in front of them. A red-faced, agitated policeman emerged from the patrol car, placed his cap firmly on his head, and crossed to John.

"What's this then, some kind of damn chase, or are you intent on committing suicide?"

John didn't know what to say. He had no idea how fast they'd been going.

By the time the cop sent them on their way, with a strict admonition about the stupidity of their behavior, John and Graham were each in possession of very healthy speeding tickets. The policeman had questioned why they were dressed in nothing but undershorts and had accepted their explanation, although he seemed a bit dubious.

At the turn-off for Ainsley House, Graham signaled John to pull over. "Why don't you go home and get some rest? I'm going to take a look for Moira."

John reluctantly agreed, knowing that it was probably best if Graham found the girl by himself. He realized that his own presence would only complicate things. Besides, he knew that Valerie would be frantic by now.

In the darkness of the pantry, Valerie awoke to the sound of footsteps creeping across the kitchen floor. She had no idea how long she'd slept, or how she could have under the circumstances, but she was stiff and cold. She cowered even deeper into the corner as the terror flooded back, convinced that the devil boys had returned for her under cover of night, if indeed it was night.

She listened, breathless, as the footsteps stopped outside the pantry door. She heard the squeak of the doorknob turning and prayed the lock would hold. The door creaked as someone applied some weight, but mercifully, the old planks held.

"Valerie? Are you in there?"

"John! Oh God." She scrambled to her feet, spilling tears of relief, ignoring the protests from her cramped limbs. She turned the key, threw open the door, and fell into her husband's arms.

After a long minute, safe in his embrace, she found her voice. "Oh John, it was horrible. They wanted to kill me. I could see it in their eyes. It was Drummond's boys. They hate us, but...why are your clothes all wet?"

"I'll tell you. I need to tell you everything. Thank heaven you're okay. We have to go to the police. Somebody needs to put a stop to this crap."

"Oh, John," she sighed, "What have you done? What are you involved in?"

"Let me go change clothes. Then I'll tell you the whole story."

John returned to the kitchen, wearing a robe and slippers, and Valerie handed him a mug of hot tea. They sat across from each other at the table sipping their tea as John told his story. He described all the bizarre events of his trip to Oban, but when he got to the part about Graham's confession, the ensuing fistfight, and his half gainer into the harbor, Val actually smiled.

He went on to tell what they'd learned about Moira.

"I pray the poor girl's alright," she sighed.

"Well, Graham's trying to find her. He thinks he knows where she is. Actually, I think I know too."

John slowly climbed the stairs and barely managed to reach the bed before passing out. An hour later, he was tossing and turning, his mind flooded with gruesome images. He moaned in his sleep as he tried to escape the long, rotting fingers of his pursuers.

"Stop," he groaned, "please, oh please, let her go. Oh no... don't."

Across the room, the curtains moved slightly, and suddenly, John was wide-awake. He sensed the presence moving closer and closer until its face was peering down at him, inches from his own.

As he watched, terrified, the mouth slowly opened, and the specter spoke to him. "John? Are you okay? You were having a nightmare. You were talking so loud, you woke me up."

Gradually, his agitation subsided as his mind regained control. "Oh my God," he murmured. "I'm sorry, Val."

Valerie lay back down and stared at the ceiling until sleep recaptured her.

John lay awake until the sunrise chased away the darkness.

CHAPTER 27

It was almost noon when John made an appearance in the kitchen. He looked like he'd aged ten years. The skin on his face had slackened overnight, and his bloodshot eyes darted anxiously around the room. He picked halfheartedly at his breakfast, then pushed his plate away and went to the telephone to call Graham. He got no answer. He returned to the kitchen and poured himself a fresh cup of coffee. It was time to tell Val about Drummond.

He told her almost everything, although he was careful to avoid any mention of Moira. He described in detail the secret room beneath the graveyard and the pagan sacrifice that had almost cost him his sanity. She listened attentively as he explained the terrible mission that Drummond was on, and by the time John finished his story, he'd broken into a sweat.

Valerie crossed to her husband, put her arms around him, and hugged him tightly, wondering how Drummond had managed to gain such a hold on him. It wasn't like John to be so easily manipulated.

"Thank you for telling me."

When, finally, his body began to relax, she released him.

"John," she said, "I think I'll take a run into the village and see if Graham's okay. Maybe he's found out something by now. I have to get some groceries anyway."

"Hang on a minute, let me grab a quick shower, and I'll go with you."

"No, honey, that won't be necessary. By the time you're finished showering, I'll be back, and maybe he'll call in the meantime."

"Okay, but don't be long. I'll miss you."

"I'll be back before you know it, and I'll bring you something nice for lunch."

As John was finishing his shower, he heard the phone ringing. Thinking that it might be Graham with some news, he stepped out of the tub, grabbed a towel, and hurried to answer it. He stood dripping onto the wool carpet and lifted the receiver to his ear.

"Hello."

There was no response.

"Hello," he said again. *Still nothing.*

As he was about to hang up, he became aware of someone breathing on the other end of the line.

"Hello. Who's there?"

This time, there was a faint response.

"John? John, is that you?"

He knew immediately who it was.

"Yes, this is John. Where are you? Are you okay?"

"John, I need you. I need you to help me. You're the only one that can. I feel so lost. Come tonight. You'll be safe at night. I'll be waiting in the tower room. But you've got to come alone and tell no one, or I'll perish for certain. You don't know the half, John. The voices came and they said you're the one that can save me."

Once again, all he could hear was her breathing.

"But Moira, listen—"

The line went dead, and the silence screamed at him. He tore the receiver from his ear and slammed it into its cradle. His hand shaking, he dialed Graham's number, but there was still no answer.

What a mess. He'd promised himself there would be no more lies, no more deception, but the girl sounded terrified. *Who on earth would want to kill her?* He knew the answer before he'd finished the question.

When she returned home, Valerie was immediately aware of the change in John. Once again, he was preoccupied. He barely responded when she entered the study to announce that Graham was nowhere to be found.

"Did anyone call while I was out?" she asked, knowing that something must have happened.

"Eh no. . .I, the phone did ring while I was in the shower, but I missed it."

Valerie nodded, knowing full well that he'd lied to her. She retired to the living room to be by herself. She didn't like this John MacIntyre. She wondered who he'd spoken to while she was gone. Curled up in one of the fireside chairs, she stared at the empty grate. The room felt cold, but she knew a fire wouldn't help.

"Just one more day," she told herself. "If we can get through one more day, we'll be on an airplane and far away from all this."

✡ ✡ ✡

Graham had been scouring Campbell Keep for hours. He'd borrowed a boat from his friend George, so as to approach the fortress from the water. He'd anchored in the cove and swum to shore. Although he was familiar with the ruin, it had been years since he'd ventured there. Once or twice, after the fateful incident with Rupert, Graham's father had taken him back inside to acquaint him with the secret passages and the tomb, and to instruct him in his duties as the future gatekeeper.

He'd searched everywhere, from the dungeons to the tower room. He'd found nothing. *No sign.* If Moira had been there, she'd left no trace. He'd been convinced that she was hiding in the Keep. He'd actually considered opening the treasure chamber, but dismissed the thought. Although Moira knew of the tomb's existence, she didn't know how to get in. Since the death of his father, only he knew, and he'd never shared the secret with anyone.

By mid-afternoon, having found no evidence of the girl, he returned to the boat and chugged into the next town. The bakery shop looked tempting, so he entered and ordered a meat pie. As he waited, he caught a glimpse of himself in the mirror behind the counter and cringed. A two-day growth and a mass of tangled hair framed his sunken eyes. His clothes were stained and badly wrinkled. As he turned away, something caught his eye. It was a little blue motor scooter zooming past on the street. Graham raced from the shop and looked down the street, but there was no scooter. He looked the other way just in time to see the bike turn a corner and disappear. He'd first looked the wrong way, disoriented by the mirror.

"Moira!" he yelled, but he was too late.

He trudged back to the shop, collected his pie, and went outside to sit on the wall. He munched thoughtfully, no longer hungry.

He returned to the harbor, untied the boat, and headed back toward the fortress. All his instincts told him she was there somewhere. It was worth one last look. If it was Moira's scooter he'd seen, then surely she was heading for the Keep.

Darkness was falling as he pulled into the cove, and the heavy air smelled of rain. The fortress glared down at him, letting him know that his presence was unwelcome. A score of ravens gathered beneath the walls—wary sentinels, watching him closely.

✖ ✖ ✖

John looked in on Valerie to make sure that she was asleep before he slipped from the house and scurried through the shadows toward the boatshed. He'd made sure he was sitting at his computer when she retired, so she wouldn't lie awake expecting him to join her. It was close to midnight when he inched open the boatshed doors and slid *Bridie* into the water.

He realized that he couldn't immediately start the engines; the sound would awaken his wife for sure. He felt terrible about the subterfuge, but had assured himself it was for the last time and that he had no other choice. He reached for the paddle and dipped it into the black water, making almost no sound—and very little headway, as the current was running strong against him.

Twenty minutes later, he determined that he was far enough away from Ainsley House to start the engines. Besides, he couldn't paddle anymore; he was exhausted. He turned the key, and the twin engines roared to life. He grimaced and pointed *Bridie* toward Campbell Keep, unaware that his wife was watching from the bedroom window.

As the boat scudded across the dark water, John felt more than a little apprehensive. He knew that Moira was there, but he had no idea what else awaited him.

Bridie's hull slapped against the waves as a bank of clouds obscured the moon, and the darkness deepened, descending over the loch like a pall. A cold wind sprang up out of nowhere, and the surface chop intensified.

Within minutes, John was in the middle of a steadily mounting storm, but he was more than halfway to the fortress and decided against turning back. Soon, icy rain pelted him, and angry waves tossed the boat about. He pulled back the throttles and steered directly into the wind.

A great fork of lightning tore open the sky, turning the night to daylight, and almost immediately, the thunder cracked above him and rolled grumbling into the distance. Once again, a bolt of white fire ripped through the clouds, the thunder hard on its heels. John smelled the electricity as it crackled all around him, and he knew he was in terrible danger.

Just then, the engines coughed once and died. Now the only sound John could hear was the wrath of the storm as it closed around him. He turned the key. He heard the grinding of the starter, but the engines wouldn't catch. Quickly, he undid the screws in the floor of the wildly tossing boat and lifted the hatch to determine the problem. As he peered down into the engine bay, the sheer blackness seemed to mock him. It was useless. There was nothing he could do. Grimly, he replaced the hatch cover, preventing the biting rain from inflicting any more damage.

He stared up at the angry heavens. *They'll never find me out here*, he thought bitterly, *I didn't tell anyone I was going. And it damn well serves me right.*

John knelt in the bottom of the boat, the cold rain beating on his bare head, and for the first time in many years, prayed to God.

✵ ✵ ✵

Valerie stared out at the roiling loch and the awesome electrical display. From the security of her room, the great forks of power lighting up the sky were actually quite beautiful, but at the moment, the aesthetics were completely lost on her. Her only thought was for her husband, caught out there in the grip of the storm.

She crossed from the window and phoned Graham. Still no answer. She was about to call Constable Smiley when the phone went dead in her hand. At the same moment, the bedside light gave up the ghost, pitching the room into complete blackness. She made her way carefully to the bathroom, fished around in a drawer, and emerged with a candle. She struck a match and touched it to the candlewick, eager for any assurance. She placed it on her bedside table, but the darkness seemed to smother the candle's efforts

As she had done many times before in her life, she fell to her knees and prayed.

CHAPTER 28

In the treasure chamber, deep inside the fortress, Moira prepared herself. She knew what she must do. She stood naked in the flickering candlelight and brushed her raven hair until it shone. Then, carefully, she hung a half a dozen little silver bells in her tresses. Smiling wistfully, she reached for the simple white gown she'd purchased for the occasion, slipped it over her head, and moved silently through the vault, carefully selecting the appropriate jewels. Every detail must be just right. She considered a ruby necklace and matching bracelet but eventually discarded them. She lifted the lid from another jewel chest, reached inside, and slowly withdrew a strand of pale blue stones. The rosary beads were all precisely matched, each one a perfect star sapphire, and the fine rope of gems was anchored by a heavy gold crucifix.

Moira liked crucifixes. Actually, she was fascinated by all things Catholic. She loved the grandeur and ceremony and the unselfconscious display of riches. There was something vulgar about it, conspicuous, just like her treasure room. Over the years, the secret chamber had become Moira's safe haven, a place where no one could find her. Even Graham was unaware that she knew. She'd long admired the beautiful things the chamber held safe: the magnificent necklaces and bracelets and jewel-encrusted rings. She understood very well why people had died trying to possess them.

The huge casket that dominated the center of the room had made her uneasy at first, but she'd learned to just ignore it, choosing not to dwell on the fact that the chamber was actually a tomb.

Moira held the rosary at arm's length, watching the stones sparkle like tears. Pleased, she placed the strand around her neck. She crossed to the wall and removed one of the tallow candles from its niche, turned, walked slowly to center of the chamber, and placed it on the sarcophagus. She carefully positioned a piece of broken mirror beneath the light and began to paint her face.

Moira had always resisted the temptation to wear makeup, but this was, after all, a special occasion.

When she was finally satisfied, she stood up and reached for the ring she'd selected. She slipped the blood-red stone onto her wedding finger and kissed it tenderly. Removing one of the pitch torches from its bracket, she crossed the room and stopped in front of a solid wall. She reached out, placed her palm against one of the cornerstones, and pushed. The stone gave way. She reached inside, grasped an iron lever, and pulled it toward her. Immediately, a portion of the wall swung open, and she stepped through into a little chapel. She knelt before the altar and whispered her prayer.

A few minutes later, she stepped into the courtyard of the Keep. A howling wind and pelting rain engulfed her, seeking to rip the dress from her body. She stepped carefully across the wet stones, reached the stairway, and, entranced, began the long climb up to the highest battlement and the full fury of the storm. It took five long minutes for her to reach the top, and by the time she did, she was soaked through but completely unconcerned. She reached the tower chamber, opened the little door, and stepped inside.

Miraculously, her pitch torch had remained lit and cast a soft glow around the tower room. Moira sat down on the floor and closed her eyes, gathering her strength.

✿ ✿ ✿

John was bailing for his life. He'd used the paddle to keep the bow turned into the waves, but still the water continued to slosh over the gunwales. Luckily he'd found a bucket in one of the storage compartments. He now used it like a mad man, trying to save his life. The storm continued to batter him with all its might, showing no signs of mercy. He knew Moira was waiting for him, but there was nothing he could do.

He continued to bail.

✿ ✿ ✿

Valerie donned her rain gear and struggled to make headway against the howling wind as she crossed to the garage. She climbed into the car and backed it out into the storm. She soon discovered that even the Jaguar's windshield wipers were woefully inadequate in the ferocity of the downpour. She could hardly see ten feet in front of her. Frustrated, she had no choice but to crawl toward Kilbride.

She had to find someone who could help, but in reality, she couldn't imagine what anyone could do. Sending another boat out would be lunacy. She knew it. But she had to do something.

"And where the hell is Graham Nesbit when I need him? Damn him anyway."

✫ ✫ ✫

The Crown and Thistle was in the throes of a gale party. Although it was well past closing time, the regulars had insisted that George keep serving until the storm subsided. He was more than happy to oblige. If Constable Smiley raised a fuss, the patrons, as always, would be more than happy to pay the fine.

The pub was exceptionally raucous by the time Valerie made her entrance, but, as if scripted, the room immediately fell silent. It was *Déjà vu.*

She stood dripping in the doorway, not knowing where to turn. Every familiar face turned away from her. No one seemed the slightest bit curious about her reasons for being out on this terrible night.

"My husband's out on the loch," she cried, trying to be heard above the wind.

One or two people turned to stare at her.

"I need somebody to help me. He's been gone for hours."

"Serves him right," someone muttered, "just what's comin' tae 'im."

"Aye, the loch'll do 'im the justice," said another.

Valerie couldn't believe what she was hearing. She strode into the middle of the room, her eyes flashing. "What's the matter with you people?" she heard herself say. "Are you willing to just let him die? Are you going to just to sit here and do nothing?"

She looked around the room, frantically searching the faces, but each one turned away from her.

"It's a man's life, and he's done nothing to you. Was everything so damn perfect around here before we arrived? Why are you blaming my husband? It's not his fault that Moira couldn't wait to get away from this place."

She took a breath and continued on. "It's time you people confronted what's really going on. Don't any of you see what's happening, what Drummond's up to? You're going to lose more than Moira MacLeod if you're not careful."

Valerie paused. The room was silent.

"Oh, I know all about your superstitions," she said, "but if my husband dies out there because not one of you would help me, ther will forever be a curse on this place."

As she turned to leave the room, she felt a hand on her arm. "We'll help you, Missus MacIntyre,"

She turned to see Missus Small. Standing beside her was a strapping young man of about eighteen.

"You've been nothin' but kind and generous to me, you and your husband as well. Archie, my boy here, he's a fine boatman, and he knows this loch like he knows our own cottage. As soon as the wind drops a wee bit, we'll be glad to give you a hand. And Missus MacIntyre, I'm sure your husband'll be all right. It's a fair loch is Awe. It only takes the ones that deserve to be taken. We'll find him."

Missus Small scanned the room. "And I for one am sick and tired of bein' told what to do and who to talk to by those that think they've got the God-given right."

Valerie wiped away the tears.

"Now, now," said Missus Small. She placed her stout arm around Valerie's shoulder and led her toward a table. "Come you over here and have a drink with us. We'll go on a search as soon as the wind's down. He's not a stupid man, your husband. He'd know to find refuge as soon as the storm hit."

✲ ✲ ✲

Graham awoke shivering from the cold. He was in the narrow passage that led from the beach to the secret stairway. He'd managed to hold his clothes out of the water as he swam to shore, but the driving rain had soaked them. He wondered how long he'd slept.

He felt Moira was somewhere in the Keep, but couldn't imagine where she could be hiding.

The wind dropped for a moment, and in the brief silence, he thought he heard the sound of a boat out on the loch, but dismissed the possibility. No one would be crazy enough to be out on the water on such a night.

Graham's teeth chattered so badly he could hear them. Eager to head home, he got stiffly to his feet, but when he saw that the loch was still churning, he decided to wait. He looked up the fortress, wondering if he should make one last climb. *Anything to get warm.*

His heart leapt. There was a flicker of light high above him in the tower.

It took several minutes for Graham to make the long ascent from the cove, but as he hurried around the castle walls to the entrance, the storm slackened. He crossed the courtyard and started up the steps to the battlements, carefully picking his way between the broken stones. He was angry that he'd forgotten to bring a flashlight from the boat.

After a seemingly endless climb, he reached the top and leaned against the parapet wall, fighting for breath. Then, above the moaning of the wind, he heard a voice. It was unmistakable. It was the voice of a woman...a woman weeping. He peered into the darkness and caught a movement out of the corner of his eye. He looked up and saw her. She was no more than thirty feet away, standing on the parapet wall with her back to him, staring down at the rocks below. It took him a minute before he realized it was her. Her white dress clung to her body like skin. She was so painfully thin that she seemed almost transparent. He started to call out but stopped himself, thinking that he might startle her and send her over the edge.

The wind subsided a little more. The storm was nearly spent.

Graham crept along the wall, figuring that if he could get to her before being seen, he might be able to grab her. It was risky, but it was his only chance. He inched closer and closer, staying in the shadows, hidden from view. He was almost half way there when his foot found a loose stone, sending it skittering along the pathway. He held his breath, prepared to make a leap as Moira turned slowly and peered into the darkness. She was looking right at him, but apparently couldn't quite make him out.

"John. Is it you?"

Right on cue, the moon broke through the clouds and lit her face. Graham shivered though he was no longer cold.

"I was afraid you'd come," she whispered hoarsely. "I tried to stop you, but it was too late. You see, there's really no choice now. I know this is the only way to put a stop to them."

He had to take the chance. Hoping that in the darkness, she wouldn't realize who he was, he crept closer, using his arms to obscure his face.

She cocked her head like a curious puppy and studied his approach as though she felt something wasn't right. Everything seemed to unfold in slow motion as Graham inched his way closer, staying in the shadows for as long as possible. At the last minute, he stepped into the open and reached out his hand. She hesitated for a moment, then started to move toward him, but then stopped and frowned, suddenly comprehending the deception.

"You're not John," she said. She backed slowly away, and turned to face the loch. Graham saw her gather herself, and he knew it was now or never.

He leapt forward, clambered up the wall, and made a desperate lunge for Moira's ankle.

Before he could reach her, he was tackled violently from behind and thrust across the top of the wall, heading for the edge. He fought desperately, reducing his fingers to bloody stumps on the slippery stones, and managed to twist his body just enough to glimpse his assailant.

It was to be the final surprise of his life.

As Graham tumbled slowly through the fine curtain of rain, he wept for the ones left behind. Who would protect them now?

CHAPTER 29

As the sun rose through the murky veil of morning, it was as though the storm had never happened. The birds soared through the sky, clamorous and carefree, the tempest long forgotten. The leaves on the trees glistened in the early light, washed clean by the deluge. The air smelled crisp and fresh as Valerie scanned the waters of the loch through her binoculars.

She'd met Archie Small on the jetty at just after five. Already, they'd been searching for over an hour. She'd wanted to go out at four, but she had been persuaded to wait for enough light to make the search efficient.

She had taken the young man's advice and allowed him to first comb the many little coves in the direction the current had been running. She'd wanted to head straight for the Keep, calculating that that was where John had been heading when the storm hit, but she'd reluctantly deferred to Archie's judgment, since he knew the loch like nobody else. They explored every inlet on the northwest side.

At just after eight o'clock, they chugged around a rocky headland almost directly across from the fortress, which remained obscured by the morning mist still hanging in the hills. Valerie anxiously searched the rocky shoreline. *Nothing.* She pulled the glasses from her eyes and shook her head at the young man.

"There she is," whooped the lad, pointing toward a small outcropping. Behind it was the stern of a boat.

Archie steered into the little bay, being careful to avoid the submerged rocks.

Sure enough, there sat *Bridie*, firmly wedged between two large boulders. Unfortunately, John was nowhere to be seen.

"John," Valerie cried, "John? Oh please…John!"

There was no response.

Archie managed to navigate the shoals and brought his boat close enough to the shore for Valerie to leap off.

It was tough going on the slippery rocks, and it took several minutes for her to reach the launch. She took a deep breath and forced herself to look inside. He was there, lying in the bottom, half submerged and very still. She quickly climbed in and dropped to her knees. She stroked his ashen face, and as she did, he stirred. A low moan escaped his lips.

"You're alive," she breathed. "Oh thank you, God."

Using her teeth, Valerie tore a piece of cloth from her skirt and began to clean the ugly gash on the side of John's head. She wrapped the wound tightly and stood up to wave to Archie, having almost forgotten that he was still out in the bay waiting for a sign. She signaled that everything was all right, and watched as the boy headed for a suitable place to come ashore.

It took all of her strength to pull her husband's limp body up onto the stern bench. He was blue from the cold. She stripped the wet clothes from his body, then removed her rain jacket and wrapped it around him. She sat on the bench and laid his head in her lap, stroking his face and rocking him gently, waiting for Archie to reach them.

✳ ✳ ✳

By eleven o'clock, John was lying quietly on the couch in the living room of Ainsley House. Valerie sat in a nearby chair studying his pale face, reluctant to let him out of her sight. The ringing of the doorbell demanded her attention, and she hurried to answer it. She opened the door to find a trim young woman smiling up at her.

"Mornin' Missus MacIntyre. I'm Doctor Ashby. I understand there's been an accident. May I come in?"

"Oh. Oh yes, please," said Valerie.

She shook the doctor's hand and led her into the living room.

Doctor Ashby examined John carefully, checking for any sign of broken bones or internal injuries, and when she was satisfied, crossed to the other side of the room and sat down, inviting Valerie to join her.

Valerie sat on the arm of the nearby couch and gazed anxiously at the doctor.

"Well as far as I can tell, there are no other injuries, but he must have taken quite a wallop on his head."

Valerie nodded.

"Has he regained consciousness at all since you found him?"

"No. No he hasn't. He was moaning a bit when I first reached him, but since then, not a peep."

"I see," said the doctor. She glanced in John's direction as if expecting him to say something. He didn't.

"Frankly, Missus MacIntyre, "I'm loathe to move him. There's no facility close by that has the equipment necessary for monitoring his condition. The closest would be Glasgow, and that's over two hours by ambulance. I think that the best thing we can do for the moment is to just let him rest comfortably. This thing might take care of itself within a couple of hours.

I'll stop in again later on, and please, call me on my pager if there's any change."

She handed her card to Valerie.

"Oh my God."

"What is it?"

"I just remembered. We're supposed to be on our way to the airport. We're booked to fly back to the States this afternoon."

"Well, I'm sorry Missus MacIntyre, but there's no possible chance of that. You'd better call and cancel your reservations, because from what I can determine, your husband won't be flying anywhere for a while."

After showing the doctor out, Valerie returned to John's side. She placed a cool cloth on his forehead and studied the too-peaceful face.

"Oh John, what are we going to do? We should have been on our way home. Maybe Graham was right. Maybe the house won't let us leave."

She rose and went to the telephone. By the time she replaced the receiver, their escape had been aborted.

✿ ✿ ✿

Rivulets of blood trickled from the rocks and dissolved in the dark water. A tiny silver bell escaped from among the stones and drifted slowly toward the loch. It tumbled for a moment in the waves before being drawn beneath the dark surface.

A crimson stain formed the canvas for the body that lay broken on the rocks, staring skyward. The hollow eyes of the Keep stared back, unmoved.

As the sun climbed higher, the gray-coated ravens descended from the fortress. They assembled on the surrounding boulders, somber as mourners. After a minute of respectful silence, the largest of them lifted from its perch, flew to the body, and landed on the bloody chest. For a moment, the raven studied the man's face, then bent forward and calmly pecked the eyes from their sockets.

As if this was the sign the others had been waiting for, they fluttered to the corpse, cawing with excitement. Within a few minutes, the ravens were being challenged by a flock of herring gulls who'd arrived on the scene, more than willing to fight for their share of the bounty. After a half-hearted skirmish, the pecking order was established. There was, after all, plenty for everyone.

By the time the birds had finished with their feast, the corpse was completely shredded, and the once-handsome face had been reduced to a mask of pink bone. After the birds had withdrawn from the body, a legion of crabs sidled from the water's edge and skittered across the wet stones, eager for their share.

✡ ✡ ✡

As the afternoon wore on, Valerie remained at her husband's side, praying fervently. By four o'clock, the rumbles from her stomach signaled that she had to eat something. She headed to the kitchen, making sure the doors remained open in case he moaned again. She opened a can of tomato soup, John's favorite, and waited impatiently for it to heat. When it was barely steaming, she poured it into a mug, grabbed a spoon and a handful of crackers from the cupboard, and hurried back into the living room. She sat in a chair by the fire and sipped the lukewarm liquid, enjoying the sensation as it reached her belly. She glanced across the room.

John was staring back at her.

"What's happened?" he asked.

Valerie hurried to her husband and kissed him tenderly. "Hello darling. I'm glad you're back."

She helped him to sit up and fed him her soup as she told him what little she knew.

He had no memory of anything past leaving the house and heading for the boatshed. He remembered nothing about the storm that had almost killed him.

"John," she asked, "do you know where you were going?

Valerie knew the answer. John apparently did not.

✤ ✤ ✤

The doctor was pleased with John's condition when she stopped by Ainsley later in the day. He appeared quite lucid, and Doctor Ashby explained that the memory loss was probably just temporary, the result of the trauma. She predicted that with the proper rest and care, he'd soon be able to remember what had happened to him, although she strongly advised against flying until John was completely fit.

✡ ✡ ✡

Early the next morning, Valerie answered the door to find Constable Smiley standing there with a grim look on his face. With him were two men wearing suits and trench coats. Valerie knew at once that they were police.

"Mornin' Missus MacIntyre," said Smiley, "this is Inspector Wadsworth." He indicated the heavyset black man, "and Sergeant Bailey," pointing to the fidgety little man on his left. "They're from Scotland Yard. We'd like to speak to your husband, if we may."

Valerie looked back and forth among the men.

"What's this about? My husband's sick. He's not up to having visitors."

"Well, we're not exactly visitors, madam." The large black policeman sounded like James Earl Jones doing an English accent. "We do need to see Mister MacIntyre. There are one or two very important questions we must ask him, and we'd appreciate the opportunity to interview him this morning. We won't bother him any more than necessary, but it's essential that we see him."

Valerie reluctantly stepped back into the house and allowed the men to enter. She led them upstairs to where John was propped up in bed, writing in a spiral notebook.

"John, these men are here to speak with you. They're from Scotland Yard, and eh...you already know Constable Smiley." Valerie couldn't understand why she sounded so obsequious, but she had a bad feeling about the visitors. "They say it's important."

The black man stepped forward and stuck out his hand. "Good morning, Mister MacIntyre. My name is Wadsworth...Chief Inspector William Wadsworth. That's Wadsworth not Wordsworth. Believe me, I'm no poet." He produced a laconic grin. "This is Sergeant Bailey, my associate."

The thin man regarded John suspiciously. "We're here to ask you one or two questions," he chirped.

John nodded.

"I understand you've had an accident," said Wadsworth, "and I do apologize for interrupting your convalescence. I hope that you're on your road to recovery. We'll make this as brief as possible."

"So what's the problem, Inspector?" Valerie asked.

"May we sit down, Missus MacIntyre?" asked the inspector. "It makes us seem a bit less intimidating...more comfortable for everyone."

He offered a half-hearted chuckle as Valerie grudgingly gestured for them to be seated.

Wadsworth took the chair beside the bed, while Bailey sat nervously on the edge of the couch, prepared to take notes. Smiley remained standing by the door. Valerie sat on the bed next to her husband and took his hand in hers.

"Now, Mister MacIntyre," said Wadsworth, after everyone was settled, "can you account for your whereabouts on the evening of the twenty-ninth?" He consulted his notebook. "That would be the night before last."

"What's going on here?" John asked. "What's this about?"

"In a moment, sir. First, we'd like you to tell us where you were that night, up until oh...four o'clock a.m. Eh...that would be the morning of the thirtieth, of course."

John sought Valerie's eyes and reassurance.

"Inspector Wadsworth," she said, "the truth is, we don't know. We really don't. My husband got caught in the storm that night, and we didn't find him until the next day. He hit his head and can't remember anything."

"Oh yes, the terrible storm," said Wadsworth.

Valerie wasn't sure if she detected a note of sarcasm in the man's voice and stole a quick glance at John to gauge his reaction.

John's pale face remained expressionless.

"Thank you, Missus MacIntyre, for your response, but I'd really prefer to have your husband answer my questions, if you don't mind," said the inspector.

Valerie was about to apologize, not knowing why she felt so cowed by this man, but her initial reaction gave way to irritation. He was being condescending, and she didn't like it.

"Inspector," she replied, "as you can see, my husband's not well, and you're acting like he's under suspicion for something. Now I realize that this is not America, but in the States, he would not be required to answer your questions. I'm sure we'd be happy to cooperate, but we have to know what this is about."

Wadsworth snapped shut his notepad and took a slow breath.

"I do apologize, Missus MacIntyre. If you were under the impression that your husband is a suspect in a crime, you're mistaken. We are simply seeking information, and have reason to believe that Mister MacIntyre can be of help. We're reasonably sure there's been a homicide, but we're still in the very early stages of our investigation."

"Homicide?" The MacIntyres blurted the word in unison.

"What homicide?" asked Valerie.

"One more question, Missus MacIntyre, if I might…then we'll tell you what we can."

John nodded his head.

"Just how well did you know Mister Graham Nesbit? Did you see him on the evening of the twenty-ninth?"

Valerie gasped. "Graham? Something's happened to Graham? Oh my God. No! Is he…is he–?"

She couldn't finish the question.

"How well did you know him, Mister MacIntyre?" It appeared the inspector's patience was wearing thin.

"Oh…pretty well, I'd say," said John. "We haven't known him long, but we spent some time together over the last few weeks. Actually, Valerie knew…knows him better than I do."

"Really?" said the inspector, as Bailey scribbled furiously. "Spent a lot of time in his company, eh?"

He peered at Valerie.

"Please tell me what happened." she said firmly.

"Well, I suppose you have a right to know. Mister Nesbit's body was discovered yesterday, dashed to pieces on the rocks beneath Campbell Keep."

John winced visibly. Valerie groaned and turned her face into his shoulder.

Wadsworth studied the MacIntyres carefully as he continued. "It's surprising we found him so soon, actually. It's a very remote spot, you know, and if it hadn't been for an unusual confluence of birds, it might have been weeks before the body was discovered. One of the local fishermen got curious and went to have a look."

Valerie lifted her head and glared at the policeman.

Wadsworth kept right on talking.

"Mister Nesbit was never reported missing, so there was no search in progress, and I must tell you, it took us quite a while to identify the body. The crows made a real mess of it."

His dark eyes watched the reactions. "His face was shred to ribbons."

Valerie tore herself from John's arms and ran from the room.

The men sat quietly, listening to the unmistakable sounds of retching coming from the bathroom.

"I think you should leave now," John whispered angrily.

As Valerie returned to the room, gray as the sky, the policeman rose to their feet.

"Please get in touch with us, Mister MacIntyre, should you remember anything, no matter how trivial it seems," said

Wadsworth. "We'll be rooming at the Crown and Thistle during the investigation."

He sighed softly and lumbered from the room with Bailey and Smiley hot on his heels.

Valerie stumbled blindly toward the bed, reached for her husband, and fell weeping into his arms.

✿ ✿ ✿

Drummond took a swallow of whiskey and reached for the phone. It was a call he'd avoided as long as possible. His hand trembled, and his brow was moist, but he realized he had no choice but to report the debacle. He could only guess what was in store for him. *If only I'd gone along,* he thought. He should never have sent the boy to the fortress by himself. It had turned out to be a colossal blunder. But he was terrified of Campbell Keep. He could never have gone there in the dead of night. The place was evil.

"Hello. Is that you, Drummond?"

"Yes. Yes, it's me."

"Well?"

"I've got bad news, I'm afraid. Very bad news–very bad indeed."

"Tell me."

The voice was like shards of ice.

There was a long pause as Drummond gathered himself. He kneaded his forehead trying to blunt the pain. "Well you see, we... eh...we killed the wrong man."

"You what? You did what?"

Drummond swallowed. "We uh...we killed Graham Nesbit by mistake. Well not me. I eh...I wasn't actually there. I sent Alistair

Frazier to do it. I was sure he could handle the job, but there was a terrible storm that night and MacIntyre never made it to the fortress. Alistair didn't know that. How could he? He didn't see that it was Graham. He never expected him to be there. So you see, it was an accident really, a terrible accident. It was nobody's fault."

Drummond used the sleeve of his robe to mop his brow and kept talking as long as he could. "I know how angry you must be, but I never thought the boy would make such a mess of it. He was perfect for the task—willing to do anything to avoid the punishment he had coming. Now he's ruined everything, all our hard work. But you know, maybe the fates have intervened. Have you thought of that? Maybe something even more powerful than you is trying to prevent us. Maybe we're being barred from the tomb."

He heard the click and the dial tone. Carefully, he placed the receiver in its cradle and dropped his throbbing head into his hands.

CHAPTER 30

The MacIntyres sat holding hands. There had been no words yet. The gentle ticking of the mantle clock was the only intrusion.

John was first to speak. "You know, I may have been the last person to see him alive. I was with him in Oban, remember?"

She brushed a tear from her cheek. "You're sure you didn't see him after that? Is there any chance you were at the Keep that night, before you got caught in the storm?"

John's face turned ashen. He looked away. "No. It's not possible. I couldn't...you don't think–?"

"No John, of course not. That's not what I meant. But maybe you saw something, something you don't want to remember. The doctor said that a shock could be the reason for your amnesia."

"God, I hope it comes back to me."

"It will, John." Valerie tried to sound confident. "But the fact that you can't remember anything about that night leaves us awfully vulnerable. If indeed it was a homicide, that inspector will have a field day. We're going to need some help. They're going to be back to question you. We need a lawyer—a good one."

"Come on honey. I don't need a lawyer. I didn't do anything wrong. I couldn't have. You know me. It's just that I can't remember."

"Exactly. And these policemen will find that pretty damn convenient. It's their job to find a suspect, and if a better one doesn't turn up soon, you'll be top of the list."

"That's ridiculous. What possible motive could they find for me wanting to kill Graham Nesbit?"

"I don't know, but they *are* cops. I wouldn't assume they're any different just because they're British." Valerie rose from the bed. "I'll put the kettle on. I think we need a cup of tea."

"It's a terrible thing, this," John said softly. "He was a good man."

"Oh, he was more than that John. Truth is, I did love him. I loved him for his heart and his smile and his wisdom. He was never my lover but for a time there, he was my love. He was my anchor when you and I were adrift. I'll miss him forever."

She walked out of the room, leaving John to his thoughts and headed downstairs to the kitchen. It was a cool cloudy day, and the room seemed somber as she prepared the tea. She crossed to the telephone, picked up the receiver, and dialed a number she knew by heart.

Twenty minutes passed before Valerie returned to the bedroom, where she set the tray on the coffee table and began to pour.

"Well that took long enough." He sounded a bit cross, but Valerie simply chalked it up to the frustration he was feeling.

"I'm sorry. I called Max. He was in Tahoe, so it took me a while to reach him."

"You *what?*" John's eyes flashed with anger.

"He agreed with me, John. He's our lawyer, for Pete's sake, and he says we have to have counsel as soon as possible. He's making a call to a friend in London."

"This is crazy. I don't need a damn lawyer."

Valerie sat quietly sipping her tea, staring out the window at the grayness of the day. She knew her husband was angry, but no matter...as usual, she would be the practical one.

"I think I'll run into the village," she said. "It looks like rain's on its way, and there are one or two things we need from the store."

The truth of the matter was that she had to get out of the house. She needed to think clearly and was convinced that Ainsley was clouding her thoughts. She glanced at her husband. He was dozing.

Valerie arrived in the village and entered the greengrocer shop to purchase the things she needed. If the reception was chilly before, it was now completely frozen over. She paid for her items and turned to leave. The shopkeeper hadn't even looked at Valerie.

She left the shop and walked across the street, heading for the Thistle. When she opened the door, twenty heads turned in her direction, and all conversation ceased. She felt like she was watching a rerun.

"Good afternoon, Missus MacIntyre," said a very deep voice from the corner of the room.

Valerie knew the voice; Wadsworth sat with Bailey at one of the tables. Several of the locals were clustered around them. It was apparent that the policemen had been questioning them, and Valerie got the distinct impression that they'd been talking about her.

"How is your husband feeling?" asked Wadsworth. "Has he been able to remember anything yet?"

The expression on his face told Valerie all she needed to know. Her worst fears were confirmed.

"No, not yet." Without another word, she walked out.

At home, she found John still asleep, moaning to himself, so she tiptoed back out of the room and pulled the door closed behind her. She went into the study, sat down at the desk, and reached for her journal. She read from the beginning, trying to determine when exactly the strange occurrences began.

✵ ✵ ✵

The next afternoon, John was up and around. He was still a bit wobbly, but the pain in his head was bearable.

He emerged from the bathroom toweling his wet hair and found his wife packing her overnight bag.

"I'm off to Edinburgh," she announced. "I have an appointment first thing in the morning with a lawyer. Max called while you were in the shower. It's all been arranged. He said we need someone right here, someone familiar with Scottish law. Apparently, this guy's really good, and well connected. I'll be back by tomorrow night."

John began to protest, but she held up her hand and continued talking. "We're in more trouble than you know, John, and we need all the help we can get. You're a very convenient suspect, and there's more to this story than meets the eye. Some very strange things have happened since we've been here. These folks need a scapegoat and we're it bucko."

John shrugged. After twenty-three years, he knew the futility of arguing.

Valerie helped him move downstairs and spent the next hour preparing meals to leave for him in the refrigerator. She wouldn't hear of him coming with her, so she called Missus Small and the doctor. Both agreed to check on John while she was gone.

It was early evening by the time Valerie was finally ready to leave the house, but she wanted to be in the city when the offices opened in the morning.

John held her tightly as they said their goodbyes.

"Thank you, Valerie. Thank you for everything you do for me. I really don't deserve you, you know."

"Whatever you may be, John MacIntyre, you're no killer, but we're going to need help finding the truth here, especially from a town full of people who don't want to hear it."

She kissed him warmly.

✿ ✿ ✿

In the village, she made a stop at the petrol station, where she was once again greeted with animosity. After paying for the gas, she started up the engine and was about to pull out when she heard a sharp tap on her window. She looked up to see Wadsworth frowning down at her. Valerie pushed a button, and the window slid open.

"So, Missus MacIntyre, and where are you off to at this time of night, and in such a hurry?"

"I really don't think that's any of your business," she replied, and the window started to rise.

"Oh, everything's my business, Missus MacIntyre." He thrust his arm inside the car and the window stopped. "You'll come to realize that, and if you don't want to spend the night in Smiley's jail, you'll answer my question. I feel a bit conflicted about you leaving the village, things being as they are. You are a material witness, you realize."

Valerie could see that she had no option.

"Well, if you must know, I'm off to Edinburgh. I have an appointment... with a lawyer—*barristers,* I think you call them. The way things are going here, I feel we need one. I'm not convinced our rights are a priority with you, Inspector Wadsworth, so I feel the need to find out what these rights are."

He said nothing.

"We're strangers here, Inspector, and that makes us targets. So unless you have any objection, I'd like to be on my way. I have a long drive ahead of me."

"I have no objection, but first, we'll be returning to your house. It would be shortsighted of me to let you leave here with your passport. As a matter of fact, I'll require both yours and Mister MacIntyre's. You understand, I'm sure."

Valerie glared up into the fleshy face and reached for her purse. She removed two passports and handed them over. "I thought the lawyer might need them."

"And who is this barrister you're off to see? I'll need his name and the address."

Valerie returned to her bag, removed a slip of paper, and handed it to the policeman.

"Todd Lyons," he read aloud. "Eighty-five Charlotte Square. Very fashionable...very fashionable, indeed. But I wonder, why would an innocent man have need of such expensive representation?"

Valerie snatched the paper back, floored the gas pedal, and sped away into the darkness.

✡ ✡ ✡

Back inside the police station, Wadsworth tore a page from his notebook and handed it to Bailey.

"Check out this Lyons character, will you, Sergeant? Let's see what we're dealing with."

Wadsworth paid no attention to Constable Smiley, who sat at his desk, feigning interest in the sports section of the *Herald.*

✡ ✡ ✡

The telephone rang loudly, and Drummond struggled awake. He reached for the receiver and glanced over at his wife, who remained asleep. He'd always been amazed by his wife's ability to sleep through absolutely anything. Sometimes she acted like she was deaf.

"Yes," he whispered. "Oh yes. I phoned you earlier because I got word that she's off to Edinburgh to meet with a barrister. His name's Lyons. Todd Lyons. He's on Charlotte Square."

Drummond listened to the chuckling on the other end of the line, but he knew better than to ask. He listened, his eyes casting about in the darkness.

"Yes of course. Right away, anything you say. Yes, I'm relieved. Maybe it's not entirely hopeless. I knew you'd think of something, and I won't fail you again. You have my word on it."

Drummond climbed out of bed, gathered a few things, and slipped from the room. His wife rolled over, closed her eyes, and went back to sleep.

CHAPTER 31

The desk clerk at the Caledonia Hotel recognized Valerie and was most solicitous as he checked her in. He complimented her work, particularly her most recent film, *The Ruiners*. The irony did not escape her. The real-life drama she was currently caught up in was a far different thing than the perfect world of make believe.

She slept fitfully and awakened un-refreshed to a cold, cloudy morning. A biting wind from the North Sea brought tears to her eyes as she hurried along Princes Street and turned into Charlotte Square. In the gloom of the morning, Edinburgh Castle looked more menacing than she remembered. It reminded her immediately of Campbell Keep. With the tourists gone, the old city felt depressing.

At the offices of Todd Lyons Esq., Valerie waited for just a couple of minutes before being ushered into his richly appointed chamber. The mahogany paneled walls displayed several pieces of good art and a half dozen gilt-framed certificates of accomplishment. Leather-bound volumes filled the bookshelves. As she crossed the carpeted floor, she had to suppress the urge to whisper.

Lyons was a silver-haired man in his late sixties, professionally groomed and completely self-assured.

"Missus MacIntyre," he said, "please do have a seat." He sat down across from her and rested his elbows on the desk. "I have some rather awkward news, I'm afraid," he began, without preamble, "I've been suddenly called away to London. I'm on the afternoon train, as a matter of fact. It's a very old client, you see, so unfortunately, I'll be unable to take your case. I do hope you understand."

She didn't understand. "What do you mean you can't? You were recommended very highly, by a friend."

"I'm aware of that, Missus MacIntyre, but there is simply nothing I can do." He watched her anger flare. "I have taken the liberty, however, of arranging an appointment for you with an associate of mine. He's a very capable barrister. You'll be in very good hands, I assure you."

He handed her a piece of paper. "Now if you'll excuse me, I have a lot to do before I leave."

The day was still dreary and cold as Valerie trudged back toward her hotel. The chill penetrated to her bones.

✿ ✿ ✿

The next morning was even colder. Dark clouds were steadily building in the sky, threatening the icy rain that only the North Sea could deliver. Valerie climbed into a taxi, having decided against driving herself, and handed her paper to the driver. He looked at it strangely.

"Are you sure this is what you want?" he asked.

"Yes I'm sure. Why do you ask?"

"Oh no reason," he replied and pulled quickly away from the curb.

They passed the North British Hotel and the driver made a right turn, headed across The Bridges and turned left into the Royal Mile. The ancient street was barely wide enough for the taxi. When they arrived at an even narrower one, the driver was forced to let his passenger out. He pointed up a dark lane toward a decaying building and assured her that it was the one she'd asked for.

Valerie paid the fare and watched as the taxi drove away. As she turned back, she saw Drummond heading straight toward her. Although his face was partially obscured, the long strides and black robe were unmistakable. She shuddered and slipped into the shadows, praying he hadn't seen her. She stood with her back pressed to the wall, holding her breath, and let it out only after he'd passed. He never even glanced in her direction.

Valerie could find no sign, nor could she find a bell. The door, however, was slightly ajar, and she gave it a tentative push. Old hinges groaned in protest as the door swung slowly open. Before her was a well-worn set of stone steps leading upward into near darkness.

Cautiously, she began to climb, grateful for the iron railing bolted into the crumbling wall. At the top of the stairs, she found herself standing in a narrow, airless passageway with almost no light. It took her a few moments to make out the small wooden door at the end of the hall. She reflected on the opulence of Lyons's offices and wondered why in God's name she was in this place. She quickly dismissed her misgivings. After all, John's wellbeing was much more important than any discomfort she felt.

She summoned her courage and knocked on the door. There was no response, so she knocked again. Had it not been for the direness of her straits, she would have fled. Thinking that she may have reached the outer door of the office, she turned the handle. The door opened easily. She crossed the threshold and found herself in a small, dingy space that had not seen a duster in years. She felt like she'd stepped back in time. It was a scene right out of Charles Dickens.

The threadbare rug did its best to trip her as she crossed the room, but wasn't entirely successful. Daylight struggled to penetrate the grimy windows, and through the dimness, Valerie saw that every available surface was piled with books and papers, each one coated with a fine layer of dust.

Apart from a huge black-and-white cat, fast asleep on the cluttered antique desk, she found no one in the room. The air was so stale, she could taste it. The smell reminded her of the front parlor in her Aunt Ida's house in Toronto.

"Hello? Is anybody here?"

No response.

As she turned to leave, an entire section of the ceiling suddenly gave way, and a set of rickety wooden steps descended from above as if by magic. Valerie watched, enthralled, as a pair of dark brown loafers appeared, followed by a set of long legs dressed in corduroy slacks. Next came a baggy tweed sweater, and eventually, an unruly head of auburn hair. As the man turned to greet his visitor, his eyes lit up with unabashed admiration. He was tall and thin and appeared to be in his late thirties. His pallor was as pale as milk, and although they looked nothing alike, the man reminded her of Graham.

He smiled and reached to shake her hand.

"Missus MacIntyre I presume? Nice to meet you. Come in, come in. Grab a seat anywhere. I'm Andrew St. Giles."

He calmly brushed the cat from his desk. It landed on a pile of books, stirred momentarily, and went right back to sleep. The man thrust his hands into his pockets and quietly appraised his visitor.

She glanced uneasily around the room.

"Bit of a mess, isn't it?" he chuckled. "Don't worry, it's no reflection on the state of my mind. Actually, it's not even my mess. This was in fact my uncle's office. Unfortunately, he died a few days ago, and it's my job to sort out his affairs. You see, on top of being his nephew, I'm also his solicitor. Since I was going to be working here anyway, I thought you wouldn't mind. Besides, my own office is much worse." He smiled.

Valerie found a corner of a chair and sat. "I'm sorry for your loss, Mister St. Giles."

"You've no idea," he sighed. "It's a great, bloody disaster. The old boy's certainly left me a job to do, and if you think this is bad, you should see the archives upstairs. I'll be as old as him by the time I'm done."

St. Giles smiled again. It was a pleasant smile.

"Now, Missus MacIntyre, if you'd care to tell me the trouble you're in, I'd be glad to have a listen. If I can help you, I'd be pleased to, and if not, I can probably find you someone who can."

Feeling a bit more at ease, Valerie took a deep breath and began her story.

When she was finished, St. Giles gazed at her, slowly shaking his head.

"You need my help," he said gently.

"Thank you Mister St. Giles. I'm afraid I do."

"I want you to go home. I'll come to you. And don't worry, Missus MacIntyre. Everything will work out."

She rose to her feet, reached to shake the barrister's hand, and headed for the door. Halfway there, she spun back. "By the way, I think I may have been followed here. As I was looking for your office, I spotted the man I suspect is behind this mess. He's easy to recognize because he always wears a long black robe."

Valerie was surprised to see the lawyer's face break into an impish grin.

"Well, to ease your mind, Missus MacIntyre, it probably wasn't the same man. The streets around here are full of men in black robes. You see, we're right in the middle of the University district, and tradition is everything here. Academic gowns remain the uniform of choice among professors and even some of the upperclassmen. So, in all likelihood, you were mistaken."

Relieved, Valerie nodded her head, smiled in reply, and left the room.

"Amazing," St. Giles whispered, shaking his head. "Simply, amazing."

Valerie checked out of the hotel and headed back to Kilbride, anxious to see her husband. She'd called him from the room, but had received no answer. She'd figured he was probably napping.

Mid-afternoon, St. Giles followed her out of the city. He had explained to Valerie that it was his intention to take a room at the local inn and pass himself off as an old friend of Graham's, in town to pay his respects. He wanted to see what information he could glean before revealing his true identity to the community.

Exactly six hours after Valerie's arrival home, St. Giles appeared at Ainsley House. As he entered the living room, John rose from the couch to meet his new lawyer.

"What a wonderful house," said St. Giles, surveying the room. "I can imagine it's been host to many glamorous affairs."

For an hour or so, they chatted over cups of tea. St. Giles listened carefully to John's version of the story, asking questions here and there. By the end of the conversation, John was impressed by the insightfulness of the barrister's questions and was satisfied with his wife's choice.

"So why are you so interested in our case?" John asked as the conversation wound down.

"Well, in truth, there are myriad reasons, some of them personal, which is why your dilemma holds such appeal, but at the end of the day, I feel sure I can prove your innocence. You are innocent, aren't you Mister MacIntyre?"

"Actually, I don't know, Mister St. Giles. As you now know, I remember very little."

"As my client, you are hereby forbidden to ever answer that way again. Do I make myself plain?"

John nodded meekly.

CHAPTER 32

That evening at the Crown and Thistle, Andrew mingled freely with the locals. When he'd registered, he'd let it be known that he was an old college friend of Graham's. This enabled him to be included in conversations where he learned some interesting things. He paid particular attention when the discussion turned to John MacIntyre and his relationship with a local girl who'd recently gone missing. He heard talk about the closeness of Missus MacIntyre and the now-deceased Graham Nesbit, something that her husband had been less than thrilled about. He watched Inspector Wadsworth chatting amiably with the patrons and had the feeling that the verdict was already in.

✿ ✿ ✿

The day of the funeral, the sun made a welcome appearance. John and Valerie arrived at the church and were ignored by everyone else in attendance. The body had been in such a terrible state that arrangements had been made for a sealed casket, and since there was no immediate family, the decisions had been easy.

Reverend Drummond seemed to enjoy the ceremony more than anyone. He was in his glory, more fervent than ever, as he spoke of the quiet dignity of death and the security of the grave. He did manage to weave in one or two references to Scottish nationalism.

Later, standing at the gravesite for the final disposition, John found his mind wandering. He stared across the rows of stones to the Campbell monument thinking of another place and another time. He missed the refuge of his work.

When the ceremony came to a close, Valerie lingered alone at the graveside. She knelt down on the damp grass and wept for Graham and for herself. She would miss him always. She didn't see her husband being approached by Inspector Wadsworth, and by the time she rose from her knees, John had been handcuffed and was being led off toward the police van. She ran, dashing the tears from her eyes, and broke through the ring of onlookers just in time to hear Wadsworth announce for all to hear that John MacIntyre was under arrest for the willful murder of Graham Nesbit.

John was thrust into the vehicle, and Wadsworth directed Constable Smiley to drive him away. As the doors closed, John's eyes searched anxiously for his wife, but he couldn't find her.

Valerie raced to her car and followed along behind the police van. When they arrived at the station, Smiley dragged John from the vehicle, hauled him inside, and deposited him into the single cell. Moments later, Valerie burst through the station door, bristling, ready to erupt, but the sight of Andrew St. Giles, already engaged with the inspector, calmed her a little.

"Just who are you? And what the hell do you want?" Wadsworth was snarling like a lion over an interrupted meal.

"Actually, Inspector," said Andrew calmly, handing over his business card, "I'm a barrister from Edinburgh. I've been retained by the MacIntyres."

Wadsworth took a breath and managed to gather himself.

"Didn't I see you last night in the pub, eavesdropping on privileged information?"

"Oh yes, indeed," St. Giles replied evenly. "I was indeed in the *public* house last night. Any information I got was apparently the privilege of all in attendance, and I must say, I was less than pleased to hear you discussing my client's guilt. Very bad form, I'd say—very bad indeed. It's the kind of thing that can prejudice a person's right to a fair and impartial hearing."

Wadsworth glowered, but said nothing. He was busy sizing up the tall, pale man who stood facing him.

"My client's rights have already been compromised, I'd say." Andrew watched impassively as the large policeman struggled to maintain control.

"Now if you don't mind," he continued, "I'd like to have a look at the arrest report, and then I must ask you all to vacate the premises so that I can consult with my client in private. That is the law, as you well know."

Valerie thoroughly enjoyed Wadsworth's agitation. The policeman gazed at St. Giles for a long moment before reaching for a sheaf of papers and handing them over.

"All right, everybody out," he bellowed.

"Missus MacIntyre," said Andrew, "go on home and wait for me there. This shouldn't take too long. Don't worry, everything's going to be fine."

The small group trooped out of the police station to find that by now, half the village had congregated in the street. This was the most excitement they'd had in Kilbride for a very long time. As Valerie parted the sullen crowd and crossed the street to her car, the policemen headed for the Thistle, followed closely by the clamorous throng.

Inside the police station, Andrew St. Giles pulled a chair close to the bars of the cell and sat down. He studied his client's face before speaking.

"Very well, John," he began, "I now need to know everything there is to know, and I will require all the details of your relationship with the deceased. Wadsworth may be a pompous ass, but I've a feeling he's a wily investigator. Now, there's a report here that says you and Nesbit were caught speeding, apparently involved in some kind of car chase on the night before the murder, and there's an eyewitness account of a brawl in the streets of Oban, also the night before the murder."

John began to protest, but St. Giles waved him silent.

"There's more," he said, "much more. I see they've already recovered physical evidence from the murder scene that proves you were there. Also, there are rumors of your wife having an intimate relationship with Nesbit, as well as reports of your own involvement with a young woman who's recently gone missing."

As he spoke, he carefully studied his client's reactions. "This is not good. These items, coupled with your inability to account for your whereabouts on the night of the killing, pose a real dilemma. All in all, it doesn't look good. I can understand why Wadsworth looks like he ate the canary. So, I suggest you start telling me all you know. The truth and nothing but, if you please."

It took a minute for John to find his voice. "I can explain these things. Really, I can. It's not the way it sounds. I can answer all your questions."

"Well, may I suggest that this would be a good time to start?"

✫ ✫ ✫

It was after dark when St. Giles arrived back at Ainsley House. Valerie was nearly frantic. "What's going on?" she asked.

"Quite a lot, actually. This will take some time. Could I trouble you for a nice, stiff whiskey? And might I suggest you join me? It'll do you good."

"Why, yes. Yes, of course," said Valerie. She was annoyed at her thoughtlessness. "Please come in, sit down. Would you like something to eat? I'm sure you must be famished."

St. Giles nodded his grateful acceptance, realizing that a little distraction would ease the impending unpleasantness.

Valerie poured two drinks and handed a glass to the barrister. St. Giles took a chair and leaned back.

"Now," he said, "I'd like to get as much work done tonight as possible, if you're up for it. Your husband's arraignment is on Friday at the district court in Oban. I'm afraid he'll have to remain in custody until then."

Valerie nodded.

"By the way, where are your passports?"

"Wadsworth has them—both of them."

"Bastard," muttered the lawyer. "He has no right to take your passport. You're not a suspect. I'll get it back for you. It'll give me something with which to irritate him."

Valerie led the way into the kitchen and began to rummage around, looking for something to make for dinner, happy to have something to do. St. Giles perched on a high stool and offered no help. Valerie went about grating cheese and cracking eggs into a glass bowl, unaware that his deep-set eyes were studying her intently. She removed some sausages from the fridge and put them on to fry. Soon, the kitchen smelled wonderful, and things didn't seem quite so bleak.

"Missus MacIntyre," he began.

"Valerie. Please call me Valerie."

"Okay, Valerie. I have to return to Edinburgh sometime tomorrow. My uncle's funeral is on Thursday, and I have some last-minute arrangements I simply must attend to."

Valerie regarded him anxiously.

"Don't worry, I'll be back here Thursday night ready for court on Friday. In the meantime, there isn't much I can do here. I can actually prepare better at home."

Valerie lifted the sputtering sausages from the flame and removed them from the pan to drain on a piece of paper towel. She poured the egg mixture into a shallow skillet and began the omelet. She stared into the bubbling mixture, listening as the man talked.

"I won't give you false hope. Your husband will almost certainly be held over for trial. There's a stack of evidence, circumstantial though it may be, but enough to require the judge to indict. In the meantime, I suggest you call home, arrange for some funds. You'll need something like fifty thousand dollars, maybe more. It is a murder case."

"Of course," she replied, "and I need to let the boys know what's going on. When I spoke to them last, I just said we were staying on a few more days. I didn't want to concern them. Or maybe I should wait until after the hearing." She concentrated on stirring the eggs, determined not to cry.

"You need to tell them as soon as possible. This kind of news will be in all the British papers, so it won't take long to reach the States. Hell, it'll probably be on Sky News and CNN by tonight. It's the price of celebrity, I'm afraid."

A tear splashed into the pan, sputtered, and disappeared.

"Your husband is going to require a strong show of support from your family and friends," Andrew continued. "You're about to find out who your real friends are. And on another topic, although this is a little awkward, I need to ask the question: Do you think there's any truth to the rumors about your husband and the girl from the village?"

Valerie took her time before answering. Without looking up, she whispered, "I don't know, Mister St. Giles. Honestly, I don't."

They sat at the table and ate their eggs in silence. Valerie tasted nothing.

St. Giles, on the other hand, appeared to relish every morsel.

✿ ✿ ✿

Early Friday morning, Valerie and her attorney made the drive into Oban and arrived at the courthouse in plenty of time. Valerie was very subdued. St. Giles did everything he could to lift her spirits, talking about a time when all of this would be behind them, and they could return home to their comfortable life in the States.

Valerie had never felt further away from home.

As they sat waiting for the hearing to begin, a young woman with a severe haircut entered the room, flanked by Wadsworth and Bailey.

Andrew excused himself and rose from his seat. He crossed to the woman, shook her hand, and chatted amiably for a few minutes. When he returned to Valerie, he sat down beside her and sighed.

"That's Irene Cummings," he whispered, "counsel for the Crown, and one of the best in Scotland. It looks like they're out for blood."

Valerie glared across the room at the enemy, realizing that she would happily scratch Irene Cummings's eyes out.

When John was led into the courtroom in shackles, she lost it. She hadn't been prepared. He looked so old, as if he hadn't slept for a week, and worse, he looked like a criminal.

St. Giles reached for Valerie's cold hand, gave it a reassuring squeeze, and smiled into her eyes. He rose and took his place before the bench beside his client.

The hush was interrupted by the entry of the bailiff, who announced the arrival of the magistrate. The Right Honorable Norman Forbes swept into the courtroom and ascended to his chair. He took his seat with and scowled down at the combatants, his eyes like flint beneath the immaculate powdered wig.

Valerie shuddered. Deep inside she felt afraid. As she sat back down, she glanced around and was surprised to discover that there were no spectators except for herself and the two men from Scotland Yard.

The proceedings moved like a blur. The Crown stated its case, calling Wadsworth to the stand to confirm the prosecution's position. By the time they were finished, Valerie knew that her husband had no chance.

St. Giles rose and spoke eloquently about John's character and his status within the film industry. He argued that no real motive had been uncovered to warrant a trial, and that the paltry evidence the prosecution had gathered was purely circumstantial. By the time he sat down, Valerie was feeling a little better.

John sat motionless.

The judge ignored all of the defense's arguments with a sweep of his hand. There was, he said, more than enough evidence to hold John over for trial.

Valerie groaned audibly and leaned back in her seat. John showed no reaction.

The judge continued. The seriousness of the allegations, he said, required him to set bail at one hundred thousand pounds. He set a trial date for the first week of November and ordered John held in the county jail in Oban until bail had been arranged.

As he was led from the room, John managed a quick glance at his wife before being shoved through the door.

St. Giles sat down beside Valerie and took her hand.

"Well it was as expected," he said. "Now don't you worry; that was only round one. We're in for a very long fight, but I wouldn't be here if I didn't expect to win it."

"Oh, Andrew," she sighed, "he looks so pitiful, I can't stand it."

"Oh yes you can, and you will, because you're a strong woman. If you weren't, you wouldn't have become who you are. Now, I want you to wait for me while I have a word with John, and don't go outside by yourself. There may be reporters waiting."

As she watched St. Giles cross the empty courtroom, Valerie sagged. She felt drained already, and she knew that the nightmare had just begun.

✡ ✡ ✡

By the time St. Giles returned, Valerie was eager to leave Oban.

"Well there's no point in driving back tonight," he suggested. "Why don't we find rooms here, and you can visit John in the morning?"

She nodded, glad not to be making a decision.

They ate quietly in the café of the Drake. Their attempts at conversation were awkward. Valerie left the table before she finished her sandwich.

She needed to be alone so she could let the pain come.

✡ ✡ ✡

John knew that the evidence was daunting. He'd forgotten all about the fight on the streets of Oban, but understood that it didn't help his case any. The fact that they'd found his pen at the Keep didn't surprise him, but it was going to be awkward explaining what he'd been doing there.

"Oh Valerie," he sighed.

He knew that she was going to find out about his visits to the fortress with Moira and the trip to Glen Eagles as well. Part of him would just as soon hang now rather than have to see Valerie's face after she'd been given all the damning information. Somewhere in him, he knew he was getting just what he deserved, that his life was turning out to be the mess his father had predicted. John had been well warned that the sinful path he'd chosen would lead inevitably to his downfall. The fact that his father had been right was particularly galling.

He lay back on the cot and stared at the ceiling, willing sleep to come, knowing it would be his only respite, but his mind refused to cooperate.

He'd contemplated telling Valerie about his relationship with Moira, before she heard it from someone else, but she had been devastated, first by his disappearance during the storm and then by the loss of Graham. And to have her husband accused of murder. He couldn't tell her the rest. Not yet.

Mercifully, sleep found him and his thoughts were no longer his own. For the first time in a long time, the scribe reached out for him.

The days passed slowly for Lady Eileen, a prisoner inside her husband's fortress. The thought of Robert, locked away in the dungeons, was the only thing that kept her from doing what she wanted to do. Campbell's cruelty was boundless, and he enjoyed causing her pain. As a matter of fact, it seemed to be a prerequisite for his fulfillment.

Night after night, he mocked her with taunts about Robert before taking his pleasure. Throughout the torture, she refused to cry, no matter how great the pain; she would be damned to hell before giving him the satisfaction.

One morning, Campbell announced that he expected her to direct the preparations for the gathering of the clans, the annual celebration featuring contests of strength and bravery, interspersed with bouts of feasting and revelry. Eileen was actually pleased with the prospect. Not only would it be a welcome break in the monotony, but the gathering might afford her the chance she'd been looking for.

They arrived by the hundreds; the Stewarts and the MacLeans, the Gordons, the Muirs, the Selkirks and Stevensons, the Sinclairs, and the Forsyths—even the MacDonalds. Most of the Western clans were represented. They had traveled for miles to participate and were determined to make the most of the celebration. It was a time of truce. Old feuds were laid aside until the gathering reached its end.

The clans set up their camps outside the castle walls. Campbell was too cautious a man to let anyone, even his staunchest allies, remain within the fortress after the sun had set. Within a day, tents and bulrush huts were scattered over the hillsides for as far as the eye could see. The landscape became a tapestry of tartans, and the air was filled with music and laughter.

An arena had been carved from the hillside. Feats of skill and courage were performed by the champions of each clan. Gigantic men tossed the caber, as if the twenty-foot log was nothing more than a barge pole. Strongmen wrestled each other into submission. The victors were applauded, the vanquished jeered by the unruly throng.

Falconers amazed the crowd with the spectacular aerobatics of their birds as they snatched their prey from out of the sky. Mad dogs and fighting cocks gave their lives for the crowd's amusement.

After nightfall, huge bonfires lit up the night sky, and people gathered together to listen to the legends of old and the songs of lament. The soft skirl of bagpipes lent a sweet haunting to the atmosphere.

Whiskey and ale flowed like water, creating the need for a bit of aggression. A few small skirmishes broke out before being put down by Campbell's warriors. Two men died. A great time was had by all.

Eileen had been allowed to enjoy the festivities. Campbell was unconcerned, secure in the knowledge that his hostage, rotting in the dungeon, would prevent her from trying to escape.

She stared into the fire as she sat beside Meg, watching the flames licking the darkness. She listened as, across the circle, a young girl sang a ballad of betrayal and death. Suddenly, a man rudely pushed his way in beside Eileen and sat down. As she turned to him to protest, she was astonished to recognize Robert's young brother, Hamish Douglas.

"What are you doing here?" she gasped. "If the Campbells discover there's a Douglas in their midst, you'll be killed on the spot."

"I know that, m'Lady," whispered the lad, "but I had to take the chance of seein' you."

Eileen nodded.

"What happened tae my brother?" he asked. "Not a one returned home after he went to find you."

Eileen looked around, and seeing that no one was watching them, recounted what had happened. By the time she finished, the lad was trembling. "Well, what are we goin' to do?" he said. "This evil will not abide. Where's Campbell? I'll kill him myself."

Eileen clutched the boy's arm and held him down. "Don't be foolish, Hamish. You'd never get to him, and if you tried, he'd surely kill us all."

"There must be something we can do. We can't just let Robert die without trying."

"Listen Hamish, I've thought of nothing else for weeks. And I do have the beginnings of a plan. Do you know where my father's camp is?"

"It's in the next vale, close by the river."

"Is Lasker there?"

"Yes he is. I watched as they arrived".

"Go there," she said. "Find Lasker. Tell him I need to see him.
Tell him I have a proposition, one that'll make him a very rich man,
richer by far than his own chief. He'll never resist, I promise you.
Bring him to the shore o' the loch underneath the Keep. I'll have some-
one waiting to bring him to me."

Without another word, young Douglas stole away into the dark.

Eileen waited for several more minutes before rising from the
warmth of the fire to make her way back to the Keep. The dark
fortress looked like a giant bird of prey as it sat silent in the
moonlight, watching her approach. She shivered in the cold air
and remembered that it was the night of Michaelmas. She prayed
that the archangel would protect her this night, as he'd protected
the children of the desert so many years ago.

Two hours later, she smiled coyly at the sleepy guard stationed at
her husband's door and slipped quietly inside. She stood for a moment
listening for Campbell's breathing. As she crossed the cold floor to his
bedside, she prayed that he'd had plenty to drink. She knew his key
ring would be close by his side. Just then, a cloud moved past the moon,
allowing a single shaft of light. It was just enough for her to see by.

It took ages for her to lift the ring from the table and remove the
key she needed. She clasped it tightly in her hand and tiptoed toward
the door.

Suddenly, Campbell sat bolt upright, his eyes wide open. He was
staring right at her.

"Who's there?" he growled.

John's eyes snapped open. He sat up and peered around the
small dark space, feeling as if he was imprisoned in Campbell's own
dungeon. He'd always been a bit claustrophobic, and found himself
smothering, desperate for breath. Then he knew where he was. It
was no dream. He lay back down, closed his eyes, and suddenly,
he began to remember. He remembered everything. Slowly, the

events of that terrible night came back into focus. First there was the phone call–.

"Of course," he whispered. He'd been heading to the Keep. He was going to meet Moira, to help her, but he never got there! *Bridie's* engines had died at the height of the storm. She'd nearly foundered, and he'd had to bail for his life. Then he fell…hard. He could see the corner of the instrument panel rushing up to meet him, and although he couldn't recall what happened after that, he knew he'd never reached Campbell Keep. So, he couldn't possibly have killed Graham.

"Oh God, thank you," he murmured. "I knew I couldn't have."

His whole body flooded with relief, and he thought of Valerie and her faith in him. He couldn't wait to see her face. Then there was Moira. Maybe she was still at the Keep. It was Moira that Graham was looking for the night he was killed.

An hour later, he heard the sound of a key. The door of his cell was thrown open, flooding the box with harsh fluorescent light.

"You've been bonded," said a voice, heavy with disappointment. "You're free to go, for the time being."

John leapt for the door, allowing the guard no chance to change his mind. Waiting in the corridor was a beaming Andrew St. Giles.

They passed through two security stations before reaching the glorious light of day.

"How did you pull this off?" John asked, as they made their way across the parking lot.

"Well I managed to arrange something at the bank, so I'm advancing the funds until things are sorted out in the States. I'm sure you're good for it."

He grinned and patted John's back. As they approached the car, the door opened, and Valerie stepped out. She waited for John to reach her and opened her arms.

"I've got good news," he said. "I remember. I remember everything."

CHAPTER 33

In the living room at Ainsley House, Andrew and Valerie listened intently as John recounted everything he could remember. Andrew made notes, nodding his head as MacIntyre told his story.

"So we have several leads to follow up on," he said when John was finished. "But undoubtedly, the most important task is the unearthing of Miss MacLeod. Now John, I realize that what I'm about to discuss may be uncomfortable for you, but if I'm to properly represent you, there must be no surprises—none whatsoever. We must assume that the prosecutors know everything, even if they don't. If they manage to catch us in one lie, one misrepresentation, we're done. You understand?"

He looked from John to Valerie, and continued. "So, if there are some revelations that might be troubling, I must insist that you tell me."

St. Giles sat back in his chair, placed his computer on the table beside him, and clasped his hands together.

John offered no response

"John, I need to ask you: Did you have a sexual relationship with Moira MacLeod?"

The only sound was Valerie's sharp intake of breath. She looked away and stared out the window, afraid to hear the answer.

John glanced at her. "Um…well yes. I eh…I'm afraid we did."

Valerie moaned. Although she'd suspected for some time, it was quite another thing to hear the words from John's own lips.

"But it's over. I haven't seen her in weeks, but yes, we were eh… intimate a few times." He stared at the planks in the floor.

"How many people have knowledge of this?" asked Andrew.

"I don't know. Really I don't."

Valerie rose from her chair and left the room. John watched her leave and dropped his head into his hands.

"And the rest?" urged the attorney.

John looked up at St. Giles and began to describe in detail the extent of his relationship with the girl.

The barrister returned to making notes as the confession continued, and from just outside the open door, Valerie listened breathlessly. She couldn't bear to be in the same room as her husband, to have to look at him, but she needed to hear the hurtful words.

"So, how many people saw you together?" asked Andrew, when John finished his story. "You know they'll be coming out of the woodwork before this is over."

"I know," John murmured.

If he'd looked up, he'd have seen the amusement on the barrister's slim face.

That night he slept alone. Valerie never did climb the stairs. Andrew had decided to return to his room at the Thistle, refusing the guestroom, proclaiming that he was totally unconcerned about the attitude that awaited him in the village.

"As a matter of fact, a certain amount of animosity can sometimes be useful," he'd said. "It can help loosen the most reluctant tongue."

Alone in his car, St. Giles laughed aloud. Things were going even better than he'd dared dream.

✼ ✼ ✼

The next morning, St. Giles arrived back at the house with an idea. "Tell me, John," he asked as he sipped carefully from a mug of hot coffee, "does the girl have any family in Kilbride? Is there any chance they might know something?"

"Yes, as a matter of fact, she does. Why didn't I think of that? Her folks live outside the village, somewhere in the hills."

Five minutes later, the men were in the car. "I just hope she's not at the bottom of the loch," said John.

"If somebody threw her into the loch," Andrew replied, "or if she jumped in on her own, she would have been found by now. Bodies invariably surface in thirty-six hours. No John, my instinct tells me that Miss MacLeod is somewhere nearby, but she's chosen to stay out of sight."

"I pray to God you're right, counselor."

They pulled up in front of the post office in Kilbride, and St. Giles climbed out.

"Why don't you wait here while I have a word with the postman," he suggested.

John sat in the car, ignoring the scowls from the passersby. He stared straight ahead, going over things in his mind, searching for any detail that he might have missed, knowing that there had to be something he was forgetting.

His thoughts were interrupted by Andrew's return.

"Success," he said. "I got the information."

They drove slowly into the hills without saying much, and several miles later, turned off the main road into a narrow track and eventually arrived at a tiny, whitewashed cottage. They climbed out of the car and approached the front door. St. Giles rang the sheep's bell attached to the wall. They waited for several minutes before the door was opened by a sullen character in a wheelchair.

"Aye what is it, then?" he said.

John and Andrew glanced grimly at each other.

"Mister MacLeod?" asked the barrister, tentatively.

"No, I'm not Mister MacLeod," the man spat. "Who the hell are you, and what do ye want?"

"Well sir, I'm Andrew St. Giles, a barrister from Edinburgh. This is Mister John MacIntyre, my client. We were hoping that you might be able to shed some light on one Moira MacLeod. We were led to believe that she lives here or at least did at one time."

The scowl on the man's face darkened perceptibly. He glared up at John.

"So you're that damned Yank, are ye? Well ye can count yer lucky stars I'm not able to stand. I'd give ye the hidin' o' yer life, I would. What have ye done with my daughter?"

John and Andrew were confused, but decided that clarifications about relationships could wait until later.

St. Giles continued. "Are we to assume, then, that you haven't heard from your daughter? We're desperate to find her. It's a matter of life and death."

"She's not my daughter," said the man. "I'm married to her mother, if ye must know. Name's Moore. And we haven't heard a word from Moira since you there, Mister Bigshot, started fillin' her head with nonsense. Filched the poor bairn away from her family, ye did."

The man tried to impart some emotion, but was not convincing. "Now I suggest ye take yerselves away from here, before I lose my temper. Get outta my sight."

He pointed a stubby finger at John. "And you, Mister MacIntyre," he said, "be very, very careful. I'm warnin' ye. There's a curse in this valley, and it's got ye in its sights. Ye'll not escape it."

Moore began to chuckle, but the chuckle quickly turned into a fit of coughing. He cleared his throat and disgorged a great wad of phlegm, which landed thickly at John's feet. Without another word, Moore wheeled back into the cottage and slammed the door.

The men headed back to the car, less than pleased with the results of their visit, but as they passed the shed, they heard an urgent whisper.

"Pssst, don't look around," said the voice. "Pretend you're talkin' to yourselves. I'm Ian, Moira's brother. I don't know where she is, I swear, but I'd be right pleased if ye could find her."

The two men pantomimed a conversation as they listened.

"We haven't heard a word from her," continued the boy, "but George at the pub told me that her scooter's gone missing from his garage. She'd left it there when she went to London. I don't know what it means, but it might help in some way. Also, you might want a word with Alistair Frazier. I don't know where you'd find him, though. I haven't seen him for a day or two."

The men climbed into the car and drove slowly back toward Ainsley.

✿ ✿ ✿

Mid-morning, Valerie answered the door to find a sullen Jock Tavish looking up at her. He seemed very nervous.

"I'll need you to help me," he said. "I've got a delivery for you, something left to you from Graham Nesbit, and I can't manage it myself. One night at the pub, when he'd had a few too many, he told Big George that if anything happened to him, he wanted you tae have it. George thought he was jestin'."

Valerie looked past the man to where his bicycle leaned against a tree. A large, ungainly brown paper parcel was tied onto the back, making the old bike look like it had sprouted wings. She followed the man across the driveway and balanced the package as Tavish went about unraveling the tangle of ropes that held it in place. Together, they managed to lug the thing to the front door, where Tavish placed his end on the step, turned on his heel, and trotted away.

Although the strange-looking package was nearly six feet long, it wasn't really heavy. Valerie managed to wrestle it into the kitchen, propped it against the wall, and began to tear the paper away. A moment later, a wistful smile touched her face. She was looking at the *Cygnet.* The mast had been removed and laid along her deck. Her sails were all neatly furled and the little ropes wound perfectly. Valerie sighed and lifted the boat onto its wooden stand and carefully screwed in the mast. She sat cross-legged on the floor, gazing at the lovely craft, tears in her eyes.

✿ ✿ ✿

When they arrived back at Ainsley, John stood for a moment in the driveway, studying the house, wondering if it really might be cursed. The place was actually starting to look different to him, more threatening than before. He shrugged off the notion and followed St. Giles inside. Valerie was waiting in the living room.

As Andrew related the events of the day to Valerie, John said nothing. He couldn't look at her. He was very grateful that she'd chosen to remain in Kilbride with him. She had every right to fly home and leave him to it. He wondered what he would do if the situation were reversed.

He noticed the *Cygnet* standing in the corner of the room and glanced at his wife. She caught his glance but didn't look back.

✼ ✼ ✼

The next morning, there was a call from the boat builder in Kilmartin to inform the MacIntyres that *Bridie* was ready. The hull hadn't been too badly damaged on the rocks, and young Archie Small had been able to tow her in to the nearest town for repairs. Kilmartin was on the far side of the loch, so John commissioned the barrister to drive him over. St. Giles was happy to oblige.

At the last minute, much to everyone's surprise, Valerie announced that she'd decided to join them. She said something about feeling cooped up in the house and needing a change of scenery.

They drove for several miles in uneasy silence, each of them busy concentrating on the scenery.

Valerie broke the silence "Stop the car," she ordered. "Stop right here."

St. Giles pulled over to the side of the road, and before the car was completely stopped, Valerie leapt out. She began running back the way they'd come, and disappeared into the roadside bushes. John shrugged, concluding that she must have been very uncomfortable. Just then, Andrew saw Valerie in his rearview mirror, beckoning wildly. He put the car into reverse and backed up. The men got out and hurried to join her.

"It's here! This is it. I can't believe I found it. I'd forgotten all about it."

"What's here?" asked her husband. "What are you talking about?"

"The old road. It's the old road into the Keep. Graham showed it to me one day. He said it hadn't been used for years, but it looks to me like a car's been on it very recently. Take a look."

Valerie pulled the broken branches aside and stepped back through with the men right behind her.

Beyond the bushes was a narrow overgrown lane leading off into the woods. Valerie pointed to the ground where several sets of tire tracks were imprinted in the grass.

"See," she said, "there's been a car here, and not too long ago, from the looks of things."

St. Giles bent down to study the tire marks more closely. After a minute he stood up, nodding his head. "You're quite right, Valerie. Someone's driven down this road very recently, but I don't think it was a car. The tracks don't measure up. I think it was a two-wheeled vehicle."

"A motor scooter!" said the McIntyres in unison.

"Should we go look?" Valerie asked.

"Not right now, I'd say," replied Andrew. "I think we might have more success after dark, when we're not so easy to spot—just in case someone's watching."

"Should we tell Wadsworth?" asked Valerie. "Shouldn't the police know about this?"

"Normally I'd say yes, but in this case, I don't think so. If she's here, we have a chance to talk to her before they do. What do you say, John? Why don't you and I come back tonight and do a little snooping?"

"Fine with me," John said.

They returned to the car and drove on toward Kilmartin, and although there wasn't much conversation between the MacIntyres, St. Giles could feel the atmosphere changing. There was the slightest beginning of a thaw.

"Kilmartin," said John thoughtfully, as they entered the village. "It just struck me. The name of every other town around here begins with the word *Kil*. A bit ominous, don't you think? I wonder if they're trying to tell us something."

"There is a certain irony," St. Giles agreed, "but it's not really as ominous as you might think. The word *kil* simply means 'church'."

At the harbor, they found *Bridie*, all varnished and ready to go. John was so pleased with the work that he attempted to pay the man more than he'd asked for.

"Oh I couldn't," smiled the boat builder. "She's such a lovely old thing, I felt privileged to be able to put her right." He gazed fondly at the boat. "Aye, she's really something. They don't make 'em like this anymore. Oh, by the way, I discovered a crimp in your fuel line. That's why you got stuck out on the loch."

John glanced quickly at St. Giles. There was no reaction.

"And I'll tell you, it's right dangerous out on the loch without your engines, och aye."

John opened his mouth to respond, but the man started up again.

"That old woman was here again this mornin', Mister MacIntyre. She came to watch me workin' on your boat. She was right glad to see her all fixed."

"Old woman?" asked John. "What old woman?"

"Well I don't really know. She was a bit of an odd one, oh aye. Kinda dirty like, you know, long gray hair, old-fashioned frock.

She'd just sit on the dyke there and watch me workin'. Never said much, but she did tell me she knew the *Bridie* well. Said she'd been out in her, oh aye. She claimed she was a friend o' yours, Mister MacIntyre."

"So where could we find this woman?" asked St. Giles. "Do you know where she lives?"

"I've got no idea, but she's not from around here, I'm sure o' that."

John again thanked the man for his work and climbed aboard. He started the engines, undid the stern line, and prepared to cast off. At the last moment, Valerie ran across the dock and hopped in beside him.

Andrew St. Giles smiled to himself as he walked toward his car. The pieces were coming together perfectly.

✡ ✡ ✡

John gave Campbell Keep a wide berth on the way home, although he couldn't help stealing one quick glance as he passed it. Even from two miles away, the castle looked menacing. He cruised slowly, caught up in his thoughts.

He pondered what he had to do later that night. The place was dangerous, but he understood that he had no choice. The answers he needed lay somewhere inside the ruin.

He turned from the wheel to look at Valerie, and she looked back at him. Slowly, she rose from her seat in the stern and moved to join him. *Bridie* skimmed across the flat water, and for a while, neither of them spoke.

"I decided to stop loving you, you know," she said, breaking the silence. "Unfortunately, I couldn't get my heart to go along with my head. Although I hated you, I couldn't stop caring about you. You've been everything to me, for over half of my life, and you were my closest friend."

"Valerie…"

She held up her hand and stopped him. "I'm not done yet, John. Please, let me finish." She took a breath. "I don't know what my decision will be when we're done with this nightmare, but I know that right now I can't abandon you. I realize you've got Andrew, and I'm grateful for that, but right now, maybe more than ever before, you need someone to love you." She faced her husband, and her eyes became misty. "Many years ago, I vowed to be that person, and I intend to keep my vow for as long as I can. I'll stay with you at least until this has passed."

John nodded his head.

"You've made me question everything, everything about us. I discovered that I don't know you at all. I've lost respect for you, John, and I blame you for that. However, I'm still your wife and I'll stand by you. Now please…I don't want you to say anything. Let's just go home."

She slipped her hand into his and stood beside him, staring out over the prow. Tears streamed down John's face, and he made no effort to wipe them away.

✿ ✿ ✿

Andrew was waiting at the house when they got back. He watched as they closed the boatshed doors and walked slowly toward him. He'd already mixed a pitcher of martinis.

When they were comfortably seated on the verandah, watching the sun disappear behind the hills, Andrew poured with a steady hand and passed the chilled glasses to the MacIntyres.

"To us, the wee three," he said. "I've a feeling we've begun to crack the veil. Don't worry, we'll get to the truth, no matter how well it's been hidden." He raised his glass. "It is indeed a pleasure and an honor to be working with both of you, and we've had a very good day."

From the looks of the color in his cheeks, Andrew had already toasted a few times before the MacIntyres' arrival home.

"I think it may have been Stalin," he continued, "who proclaimed that God is always on the side of those with the biggest guns, but I think that old Stalin might be proven wrong. Here's to us."

Valerie rose from her chair, crossed to Andrew, and hugged him tightly. "You're wonderful, Andrew," she whispered.

He recoiled, spilling the remains of his drink all over his favorite cardigan, but was completely unperturbed. Val ran for the kitchen.

"Well John," Andrew whispered as they watched the sky fade to black, "are you ready to have a wee poke around the fortress? See what the goblins are up to? What do you think? It's been a lucky day so far."

"Oh I'm ready. The answer is there somewhere; I'm sure of it."

"So, who do you suppose the old lady is—the one who's been watching *Bridie?*" asked Valerie, as she returned carrying a damp towel and began mopping the vodka from Andrew's sweater.

"It must be somebody who knew the boat before we ever arrived here," John replied. "It could have been anybody."

The night grew cool quickly, so they moved inside, and Andrew lit the fire. They spent the next few hours rehashing all the information they had until the mantle clock struck eleven. It was time.

John left the room, explaining that he needed to use the bathroom and change his shoes.

"Now, don't you worry, Valerie," Andrew assured her, reading her thoughts. "We'll be all right. I'll look after him."

A few minutes later, it occurred to Valerie that her husband was taking an inordinate amount of time to change his footwear. She left the room and headed upstairs to see what was keeping him.

At that moment, she heard a car starting in the driveway and ran to the window just in time to see the Jaguar pulling away.

She raced back down the stairs and into the living room, where Andrew was crouched in the corner admiring the *Cygnet*.

"He's gone. He's gone to the Keep, alone. Didn't you hear the car leave?"

"No I didn't," the barrister snapped. "What the—? He can't do this, damn it. I've got to be with him. I *must be* there."

He reached for the sweater that was drying beside the fire and rushed from the room.

Valerie was startled by Andrew's reaction. He was more incensed than concerned, much angrier than the situation warranted.

She pushed the troubling feeling aside and raced after him. "I'm coming too," she yelled. "I can't stay here. I just can't." She grabbed a jacket from the kitchen and ran into the driveway.

She found Andrew standing beside his car, hands on his hips and scowling. "He took the keys. I left them in the car."

"Oh, no," groaned Valerie, "now what?"

"No problem…we'll take *Bridie*. We'll be there by the time he gets there. He has to walk in from the road, and it's a long way. It's just as fast by boat. I'm sure of it."

Valerie hurried back to the house with Andrew right behind her, ran into the kitchen, and reached up to the mantle piece. She searched around frantically.

"Damn it."

The boat keys were gone, too. Valerie collapsed into a nearby chair. Andrew stomped around the room and said nothing.

"We're stuck," she sighed, staring into the fire. "And why the hell would he go there alone? Oh God, please keep him safe."

✧ ✧ ✧

John pulled the Jaguar off the road as far as he could, slipped through the bushes, and turned on the flashlight. It didn't help much on the moonless night, but the meager beam was comforting, if nothing else. As he stood listened to the smothering silence, he regretted not bringing St. Giles with him, but realized it was a bit late to reconsider.

He made his way carefully along the dark path, doing his best to control the creeping fingers of his imagination. A chill wind whined through the trees. He drew his jacket tighter and continued on.

Off to his right, a twig snapped loudly, and he swung his light in the direction of the sound. Something large was moving through the trees. John switched off his light and stood dead still until the silence returned. When he'd regained his breath, he crept on.

It took him almost forty minutes of hiking before he stepped out of the woods into the clearing. He switched off the flashlight again and waited for his eyes to adjust. The darkness was alive with the sounds of creatures scurrying across the forest floor.

Before him, partially obscured by mist, stood the Keep. John moved cautiously forward until he was standing at the gates. He ordered his body to stop shivering. His body refused.

Although he'd worked up a sweat from the hike, he felt cold. The atmosphere was heavy, and the night was still. It was as if the fortress was expecting him.

John forced himself to enter. Slowly, he made his way across the courtyard to the stone stairs, took two deep breaths to calm himself, and began the ascent. Halfway up, he had to force him self not to think about the consequences of slipping on the damp steps and tumbling over the side.

After a long, slow climb, he reached the top, and stood leaning on the wall, gasping for breath, and trying to muster what little courage he had left. As he stared into the darkness, he saw a shadow sweeping silently toward him, growing larger and larger. At the last second, he ducked out of the way as a huge owl flapped its wings once and disappeared into the ruin, where it began hooting its displeasure.

By now, John was completely unnerved, but he steeled himself and continued on. He moved cautiously across the fortress's highest battlement until he reached the little door. He grasped the iron ring and slowly turned it. The old lock complained, but gave way, and the door swung open. John stepped over the threshold.

✡ ✡ ✡

Valerie and Andrew were at a loss. They'd passed an hour or so with nervous chat, but had run out of conversation.

The time crept by slowly. Two or three times, Valerie rose to freshen the drinks as Andrew replenished the fire.

"So why don't you tell me more about your relationship with Nesbit," he prompted. "Maybe it holds a clue to what we're missing. Did he ever reveal any private thoughts? Did he share any secrets that you're not remembering, no matter how unrelated they may seem?"

"Graham and I were good friends, Andrew," she said firmly, "nothing more."

"Did he ever give you any gifts, or something to keep for him?"

"No," she replied, "I don't remember him ever giving me a gift." Her eyes fell on the *Cygnet* but she said nothing.

Silence descended on the room. They sat staring into the flames, lost in separate thoughts.

CHAPTER 34

———◆◆◆———

As John's eyes adjusted to the feeble light, he became aware of a figure sitting in the shadows beneath the slit window. His breath caught in his throat, and the hairs on his arms stood straight out. The figure struck a match on the floor, and its steady flame rose to meet a candlewick.

Slowly, from out of the darkness, a woman materialized. She was old and shrunken, and John knew he was in the company of a witch. The crone smiled hesitantly and extended a bony finger toward her visitor.

John shrank back. He knew that his mind was playing tricks on him, that the scribe was manipulating his thoughts again. He wanted to run, but his feet were mired, refusing to move. When the apparition spoke, her voice was like dry grass. "It's been so long," she whispered. "I was beginning to feel that you didn't love me any-more. I've been waiting for you, John. I'm so pleased you're here. I have somethin' I'd like to show you. Somethin' grand…somethin' ye'll like a lot."

The woman rose stiffly and started toward him. Her long silver hair hung in matted ropes, partially obscuring the hollow eyes that watched him warily. A filthy dress hung like a shroud from her bones.

She stopped directly in front of MacIntyre, raised the candle, and peered briefly into his face, then turned abruptly and floated through the door. She moved quickly across the ramparts and began the long descent.

John was afraid, but felt compelled to follow. He hurried after her.

She scurried down the broken stones, as though she'd made the journey a hundred times. John simply couldn't keep up. He watched helplessly as, far below, she crossed the courtyard and disappeared.

When at last he reached solid ground, John didn't have to wait long. Another match flared, and he saw her standing in the shad-ows against the wall, waiting for him. As soon as he spotted her, the woman again turned away and appeared to melt into the stones. John followed her through a break in the wall and emerged inside the great hall. Being careful not to stumble over the large stones that littered the floor, he followed the light into a narrow passage-way, aware that he was on a downward path, descending deeper and deeper into the fortress.

A few minutes later, the light glowed brighter. John rounded a corner and entered a barrel-vaulted chamber. The woman stood with her back to him, facing a solid wall of stone.

"We're in the Crown Room," she whispered. "That's what Graham called it. It does look a bit like a crown, don't you think? This is the entrance."

He recognized something familiar in the woman's voice, but for the life of him, he couldn't place it.

As he moved closer, the crone reached out her hand and pressed one of the cornerstones. Immediately, the stone swung open. She reached inside, and a moment later, a strange grating sound reached John's ears. The sound seemed to be coming from far away. As he watched, fascinated, a portion of the wall swung open, and the woman stepped through. John followed after her into the darkness. The old woman descended a flight of steep steps, and they entered a tunnel where the air was so heavy that the candle flame struggled for breath and cast little light.

They reached an intersection, and the woman turned right. At the next junction, she continued going straight. John began counting his steps, wishing that he'd thought of it earlier, and when he reached fifty-four, his guide stopped and opened a small wooden door. John followed her through.

Inside, the air was better, and the flame strengthened. He stood in a small chapel, watching closely as the woman scurried to the altar and took hold of a stone crucifix. He tried to make out what she was doing, but before he could, the wall behind the altar moved. The woman beckoned to him and stepped through the widening gap.

Barely controlling his fear, he shook his head in an attempt to clear away the dream. Beads of perspiration flew from his brow, but otherwise, nothing changed. Trembling, he followed.

She removed a torch from an iron wall bracket and used her candle to set the pitch afire, then moved to the center of the chamber. As she raised the flame high above her head, John stared, transfixed. Behind the woman stood a huge stone coffin. Its surface had been intricately carved.

The rest of the chamber materialized in a slow reveal. Piled in one corner was a stack of canvas sacks, maybe fifty in all, some of which had burst open, spilling silver coins onto the floor. Lining the walls were long benches that held large wooden chests. Some were heaped with gold plates and jeweled goblets. John watched, stunned, as the old woman raised the lids of the chests and cast her light over the contents. Every chest she opened was stuffed with treasure.

John had many questions to ask, but he saw that the woman's eyes were now closed, and she was murmuring to herself as if in prayer. Without a word, he gently removed the torch from her hand and began to explore the rest of the room.

Hieroglyphics covered the walls as if the vault was an Egyptian burial chamber. The grand sarcophagus, though, was decorated with crests and rosettes, which were Scottish rather than Egyptian.

As he silently surveyed a treasure that had been buried for hundreds of years, John felt the hairs rise on the back of his neck. A strange chill fingered his scalp. "I'm in Campbell's tomb," he whispered, returning his attention to the woman.

She was studying him, as if gauging his reaction. "I had to bring you here," she whispered. "I had to show it to you. I just couldn't keep the secret to myself anymore. Ye see, I might not be here much longer, and there's such terrible things happening in the vale. I know this is the way Graham would want it." She glided slowly toward him and raised a trembling hand to touch his cheek. Her dark eyes were suddenly more alive.

"We've been waiting for a man like you, John, but you need to keep the treasure safe. Not a single piece can be removed from this place, ever, because that will surely bring death to the filcher. I should know, because I took a piece or two myself, and within the hour, death appeared. I don't understand why it didn't take me, though. You see, the trove belongs to the Keep, and the Keep's a right jealous beast."

John nodded.

The woman turned to face the sarcophagus. "In there is where the curse waits. It must not ever be opened, no matter the temptation. You must promise me, John. Please, will ye promise me?"

Her story told, she crumpled to the floor, unconscious.

John hurried to her side and knelt to examine her. He reached for her wrist, searching for a pulse, and was relieved to find one. He pushed her filthy hair away from her face so he could get a better look at her, and suddenly, he knew.

Although her locks had turned silver, and her physical condition rendered her nearly unrecognizable, he was gazing into the face of Moira MacLeod.

He touched her brow. It felt terribly clammy, and her breathing was shallow and ragged. John laid the torch across the corner of the coffin and lifted her up from the cold floor.

"Oh God," he breathed. "She's like a bird." He hoisted her over his shoulder, reached for the torch, and turned to leave the room.

Then he realized that the wall had closed behind them.

He crossed to the place they'd entered the tomb and pushed. *Nothing.* He placed Moira gently on the floor and returned his attention to the wall. He pushed again. *Nothing.* His chest tightened as he fought the rising panic.

Thinking he might have become disoriented, he scoured the other walls. *Nothing!* There was no way out. He returned to Moira's limp form, wondering what to do. He knelt down beside her and peered into her face.

Her jade green eyes were wide-open, gazing back at him. "It's all right, John," she whispered. "Don't be afraid. Look there in that corner. Look for the shield. Push it." Her eyes closed again.

Holding the torch above his head, John carefully searched the corner she'd indicated. He found it easily. High on the wall was a stone that had been carved into the vague shape of a shield. He pressed it firmly and was surprised when it gave way. Inside he found an iron lever. He grasped it tightly and pulled it toward him. Without a sound, the wall swung open. He gathered Moira up from the floor and hurried out of the chamber just before the slab closed behind him.

He hurried along the dark passageway, hoping it was the same way they'd come. With his added burden, it took fifty-seven paces to reach the first intersection. He continued straight until the next one and turned left, praying that he'd remembered correctly. Moments later, he reached the steps. By the time he reached the top, he was gasping. He leaned against the cold stone, waiting for his heart to recover.

Damn it, he thought. Before him was another solid wall. He'd forgotten all about it. He'd have to rouse Moira. As he tried to ease her from his shoulder, his trembling legs gave out, and he sank to his knees. Suddenly, the stone beneath him shifted a little, and almost immediately, the wall shuddered. The entire middle section started to move, rotating slowly on its axis.

"Amazing," he whispered. "Sure is a lot easier getting out of this place than getting in." Murmuring his thanks, he passed through the wall into the Crown Room and breathed a grateful sigh. He'd found the way out.

It took over an hour to reach the car, and by the time he did, he was done in. Moira moaned softly as he strapped her into the seat.

✖ ✖ ✖

The Jaguar pulled to a stop at Ainsley House, and John climbed slowly out. Valerie was waiting at the front door, her patience completely exhausted, ready to let him feel her anger.

"Well, I found her," he said wearily. He walked around the car to the passenger's side. "I'm sorry I skipped out on you guys, but I thought it was our only chance. I figured that if she saw two of us, she'd never show herself. Turns out I was right, for once."

St. Giles hurried from the house pulling a sweater over his head, crossed to the car, and without saying a word, helped carry the unconscious woman inside. They conveyed her into the living room and laid her on the couch.

Valerie quietly studied the paint-smeared face. "No," she murmured, "it can't be."

"I'm afraid it is," sighed John, as he collapsed into a nearby chair.

St. Giles returned from the bar and proffered a good-sized glass of amber liquid. John gratefully accepted and gulped it down.

"We need to call the doctor," said Valerie, matter-of-factly. "She's in a bad way."

At the sound of Valerie's voice, Moira opened her eyes. She searched anxiously until they came to rest on John.

Valerie hurried from the room and, a second later, returned with a warm washcloth. She knelt beside the girl and began to wipe the grime from her face. "Andrew," she ordered, "go to the kitchen and heat some soup, and get me another brandy."

St. Giles obediently poured the brandy and handed the glass to Valerie, who dribbled a few drops between the girl's lips. Moira coughed as the fire reached her throat, but swallowed and managed to sip a little more.

By the time Andrew returned with the hot soup, a hint of color had returned to Moira's cheeks. She offered no resistance as Valerie fed her. When Moira had consumed all the soup, Valerie turned to the men.

"Will you guys get her upstairs? I'll pour her a bath."

The men lifted the girl from the couch and carried her up the steps. Valerie ushered the men out of the bathroom and closed the door.

A half hour later, she rejoined the men in the living room to inform them that Moira was sleeping comfortably in the guest room, and that she'd locked the door just in case. She sank into a chair by the fire and focused her attention on her husband. "So what happened?"

She sat silently as John recounted the details of his visit to the Keep. By the time he'd finished the story and answered the questions, they were all exhausted. They mumbled their goodnights and stumbled off to bed.

The next morning, Valerie awakened early. She gingerly opened the door to the guest room and was relieved to find Moira still fast asleep. The girl looked so small, so helpless, that Valerie's heart went out to her, and she knew she wouldn't be able to cling to the terrible resentment she'd been feeling.

Downstairs in the living room, she found Andrew snoring softly on the couch, so she went to the kitchen to begin preparing breakfast, knowing her husband was going to be famished.

✿ ✿ ✿

The next two days were spent coaxing Moira back to the land of the living. Although she was looking a bit better, she still refused to speak. The only time a light appeared in her eyes was when John entered the room to sit beside her bed.

They had decided against calling the doctor. Moira was quickly regaining her strength, and they all agreed that there was a real risk of Wadsworth discovering her. They needed to talk to her before that happened.

By the third day, she was up and around, and that afternoon, she sat quietly in the living room. As Valerie read, Moira stared out across the loch, gently rocking herself, her secrets locked safely away.

St. Giles had moved in with the MacIntyres, wanting to be close by in case the girl decided to speak. They'd agreed to talk freely. They openly discussed Graham Nesbit and Moira's family, hoping that the girl would eventually participate. However, they avoided any mention of Graham's death.

That evening as they sat before a roaring fire, St. Giles turned to John. "Do you think you could find it again?"

"The tomb? Not a chance, Andrew. It's a labyrinth in there. First you'd need a map; then you'd have to know how to open all the walls."

"You know, for years, stories have circulated about that trove," said Andrew. "But contrary to the popular speculation, I think it's actually the lost treasure of King Charles."

Across the room, Moira glanced up.

"What's that?" John asked.

"Well, I believe the trove dates back to the early sixteen-hundreds. The Campbells were the most powerful clan in the country at that time, and the Keep was their stronghold. They conducted their brutal, bloody raids with absolute impunity, bullying every clan in western Scotland. They had always been rich and greatly feared, but the theft of the King's treasure was the act that ensured their invincibility."

Andrew sat back and crossed his long legs. "Through my research, I've come to the conclusion that the lost treasure of King Charles the First is not on the bottom of the Firth of Forth as so many of my colleagues believe."

Moira was paying rapt attention.

"Well you see," said Andrew, "in the sixteen-thirties, Charles ascended to the throne. Although he had been born here in Scotland, he'd lived in England since he was three. Anyway, the people here insisted that since he was indeed Scottish, he should be crowned on his native soil. He agreed to the request and made the journey north with a caravan of over fifty wagons and an army of troops."

Andrew took a swallow of brandy and continued. "The wagon train stretched for over two miles, and the wagons were filled with silver and gold as well as the Scottish crown jewels, which had been stolen by the English in twelve-ninety-six and taken to Westminster Abbey along with the Stone of Destiny, our coronation stone. The Campbells knew they wouldn't have the stone back, but they'd have a chance at the jewels."

John glanced across the room and noticed that Moira was paying very close attention to Andrew's story.

"Anyway, Charles refused to use any eating utensils or plates or cups that weren't made of solid gold, so he brought them all with him from England. He even required that his retinue be served on nothing less than silver. Well, needless to say, it was quite a load."

"Toward the end of his visit, the Idiot King, as he was aptly called, decided to cross the perilous Firth of Forth, no matter that he'd been warned about the folly of his plan. He loaded his treasure, including the half a ton of gold and silver, onto a little ship named, ironically, *The Blessing* and sent his fortune out into the Firth, heading for Leith, where his own galleon was waiting to take him back to the safety of England. Needless to say, a good old Scottish storm came up and swamped *The Blessing.* Apparently, the treasure went right to the bottom, lost forever."

Moira sat staring off into space.

"But for some reason, Charles, at the last minute, decided not to cross on *The Blessing,* so His Royal Highness was spared. The Scots, of course, proclaimed the sinking an act of God.

"Now, here's the good part. According to one account I uncovered, several days before the deadly crossing, the King's caravan was attacked by a band of Scottish warriors, and several of the wagons were taken. The King himself never spoke about the incident. He'd been robbed of the Crown Jewels, for God's sake, and the humiliation of his vaunted English troops being routed by a few crazy Scots was more than the King could admit to. There is no doubt in my mind that the Campbells were the culprits.

"So, when Charles returned to England, he rounded up sixteen alleged witches and had them executed for causing the mishap, kingly man that he was.

"Not long after all this, young Charles was beheaded in the Tower of London, so the whole matter soon faded into the annals of history."

Andrew took another sip of his drink and continued. "Meanwhile, the disposition of the missing treasure wagons remained a mystery, although shortly thereafter, the wealth of the Campbells had somehow grown ten-fold."

He glanced across the room at Moira. She was far away.

"For years I have believed that King Charles's treasure, and several pieces of the Scottish Crown Jewels, were hidden in the Campbell stronghold. As a matter of fact, I did my thesis on it at university."

"That has to be the treasure I saw," said John. "Aside from the jewel chests, there were stacks and stacks of gold and silver plates."

St. Giles nodded his head. "I knew it," he whispered.

CHAPTER 35

T he next day, Moira looked even better, but she remained
silent.

John tried speaking with her alone, but got no response.

Later that afternoon, he came up with an idea. He and Valerie
left the house and drove into the village, leaving the girl in Andrew's
charge. Just outside the village, Valerie dropped her husband at
Graham's house before continuing on into town. John ducked under
the yellow police tape and hurried to the rear of the cottage. He was
about to break a window, but decided to try the door first. Much to
his surprise, he found it unlocked.

Valerie pulled up in front of the chemist shop and ignored
the rude stares from people on the street as she walked inside. A
few minutes later, she returned to her car and drove off without

acknowledging anyone. As she approached Graham's house, she slowed, searching for her husband. He appeared from behind the hedge and hurried to the car, tossed the guitar case into the back seat, and climbed in.

Back at Ainsley House, they found Moira right where they'd left her.

St. Giles glanced up from his laptop and rose to greet them as they entered the room. "Fix you a drink, John?" he asked.

"Yes thanks. Scotch, please."

"Valerie?"

"Eh, no thanks Andrew, I've got something to do first. Moira," she said softly, "come dear, it's time for your bath."

The girl rose obediently, took Valerie's hand, and followed her through the door.

"So when do we involve the police?" John asked when they were comfortably settled before the fire. "Assuming we get nowhere with Moira…"

"Oh, I don't know. Obviously, we can't hide her here indefinitely. And if she's ever discovered, they'll have a field day. Obstruction of justice would be the charge." St. Giles chuckled to himself. "Anyway, I think we need to do our best to find the tomb. You never know…we might be lucky. You might remember something—"

John cut him off. "Why of course. How stupid of me. In the excitement, I forgot all about it. There's another chamber. It's under the church. There are papers there, old papers…and maps. Maybe there's some clue about the tomb. Drummond showed me the papers, but he wouldn't let me look too closely. We need to check it out."

"Of course we do, and as soon as possible. Like right now!"

Andrew's excitement was interrupted by the return of the women. Valerie entered first, leading Moira by the hand. The transformation was incredible. Gone was the silver hair. Instead, her tresses were once again raven black.

"Moira," said John, smiling broadly, "you look fantastic. You're just like your old self." He reached for Valerie and put his arm around her shoulders. "And you, my girl...you've worked magic. As a matter of fact, you are magic. You know, I always thought that stuff about hair turning white overnight was just an old wives' tale."

"Oh no," Valerie replied. "It's absolutely true. When someone undergoes terrible shock, it can happen."

"She must have witnessed something horrific," John murmured. Suddenly remembering, he left the room and returned a moment later carrying the guitar. Moira studied the instrument for a moment, reached to take it from him, and wordlessly nodded her thanks.

✯ ✯ ✯

That night, John parked the Jaguar under a huge elm and, with St. Giles right behind him, hurried through the dark graveyard toward the Campbell monument. A chill wind rustled its annoyance in the treetops, causing the first of the autumn leaves to spiral to the ground.

The carved rosette turned easily in John's hand, and the panel slid open. He descended the steep steps and waited for St. Giles to join him. The stone slid shut, blotting out what little light there had been.

John switched on his flashlight and sent its beam ahead of them down the shaft. They moved deeper into the ground, and a few minutes later entered the main chamber.

"Amazing," whispered the lawyer. "It's truly amazing."

John made his way to the table where he'd seen the papers, but the table was bare. "Damn," he whispered, "Drummond's taken them."

"Why are we whispering?" Andrew asked.

"I don't know," replied John, still whispering. "But it feels right."

They opened the two wooden chests that were lying on the floor. Inside, they found a couple of broken daggers and some tarnished coins, but no papers.

John stepped into a small antechamber and directed his light into every corner. He became aware of a sickly sweet odor coming from a small recess in the far wall, and although he had a bad feeling, he was curious. He crossed the room with St. Giles right behind him.

Propped against the wall, like a broken scarecrow, was the body of a man. Obviously, it had been there for days as much of the flesh had been ripped away. The rats had made quite a meal of it.

Andrew bent down to study what was left of the face. "Do you know him?"

John nodded grimly. "It's Alistair Frazier. He's a friend of Moira's. Let's get out of here."

Andrew readily agreed.

"So now what do we do?" John asked, as they drove back toward the house. "We've got to tell somebody about this."

"I don't know if that's really such a good idea. We have no idea what the hell's going on here, and until we do, I say we volunteer nothing. Ever since you told me about the call from Moira that got you caught out in the storm, I've been wondering if we're looking at this thing the right way."

"What do you mean?"

"What if Nesbit's death was a mistake?" St. Giles asked. "What if the crimped fuel line was purely an accident, and it was never tampered with? Maybe you were supposed to reach the Keep that night, and Graham Nesbit was simply in the wrong place at the wrong time. Maybe, instead of being framed for murder, you were supposed to be the victim."

"Who'd want to kill me?"

"Who would want to kill Graham Nesbit?"

"Me, supposedly."

"Listen to me, John. We assumed that someone wanted you stranded in the middle of the loch, and it made sense to us, because it guaranteed you wouldn't have an alibi. But think about this: Why would Drummond give up so many of his secrets to a complete stranger? I don't believe he would have, unless you were supposed to die."

As he theorized, St. Giles became more and more agitated. "And I'm convinced that Moira had a role in this. She must know what's going on. Could it be that she was pressured into seducing you? And if so, what was the purpose? What did they need from you?"

John started to speak, but Andrew cut him off.

"I'll tell you one thing, whoever engineered this thing is one clever bastard, no matter what the truth is. The whole village believes that you caused Nesbit's death, so now they're talking about you and their stupid curse in the same breath." He rolled down his window and took a long breath of the cool night air before continuing. "And now on top of everything else, we just happen to stumble over another body. Great! Just bloody great."

As they entered the house, the men heard the sounds of music coming from the living room. They peeked in to see Moira playing her guitar by the fire. Valerie sat across from her, listening. As the men moved into view, the girl stopped playing and placed her instrument aside.

"Well, did you find anything?" Valerie asked as she rose from the couch to greet them.

"Eh, no Valerie," St. Giles replied, casting a glance toward Moira. "We didn't find what we were looking for. Someone got there before us."

"Oh, that's too bad."

"It's bad, all right," the barrister muttered. "I'm afraid there's more to this than meets the eye, and as my dear, departed uncle once told me, there's no such thing as coincidence. It's all too pat."

A movement in the corner of the room drew everyone's attention to Moira, who was sitting on the floor, calmly removing the rigging from the *Cygnet*. John moved to stop her, but St. Giles signaled for him to wait.

They watched, intrigued, as the girl deftly removed the bowsprit and set it aside. She carefully gathered up all the little lines, removed the jib, and began to unscrew the mast. When the task was completed, she reached a finger inside the mast and pulled out a tightly rolled oilskin. She opened the pouch, removed some papers, and laid them on the table. There were two faded newspaper articles and a single sheet of writing paper.

So eager were they to have a look at the pages that they didn't see the girl remove the last remaining paper from the pouch and slip it into her sweater. She stood in the doorway and watched for a moment, then turned away.

Valerie quickly scanned one of the newspaper articles as John read what appeared to be a formal letter.

Valerie whistled softly. "So this is what they've been talking about. I knew there was something weird about this place."

She started reading aloud. The article, from the *Glasgow Herald*, dated July 16, 1966, was entitled "The Curse of the Keep." It described a gruesome double murder that had taken place in Kilbride village. The men listened intently as Valerie read about an ex-actress named Lorraine Marni who'd been cut to pieces by her thirteen-year-old son, Rupert. After the killing, the boy had continued living in Ainsley House as if nothing had happened. It had taken days to discover the crime. The grim discovery was made by a local boy named Graham Nesbit, who'd been a friend of Rupert Marni.

Valerie stopped reading as her eyes filled with tears. After a long slow breath, she continued. "The police found the woman's dismembered body meticulously reassembled, dressed in fresh clothes, and placed on the couch beside the fireplace, with a romance novel lying open in her lap."

She couldn't go on. She handed John the page and he continued reading. "A man's body was found later that day, dashed on the rocks beneath Campbell Keep. Police sources revealed that the man, who'd been identified as the dead woman's lover, had been genitally mutilated some time before his fall."

St. Giles carefully unfolded the second article and began to read it to them. The piece was dated eight months later and described the boy's trial and sentencing.

In his statement to the court, Rupert Marni had shown no remorse whatsoever. He'd determined that since his mother had been planning to send him away from home to attend boarding school, she obviously didn't love him. The new man in her life hadn't liked him, and Lorraine had invariably sided with her lover, so young Rupert, who had been his mother's sole companion ever since his father had deserted them, had expressed no emotion. He'd felt completely justified in slaughtering them. According to the boy, strange voices in his head had told him just what to do.

"Well, this certainly explains the curse," murmured Andrew. "No wonder people steer clear of this house and Campbell Keep."

The last document was a typewritten letter from a Dr. Jacob Barnabus at the Perthshire Hospital for the Criminally Insane, addressed to Missus Helen Nesbit. The letter discussed Rupert Marni's admission to the asylum.

Apparently Missus Nesbit, Graham's mother, had been involved in the evaluation of the young murderer. The letter went on to say that there wasn't much hope for recovery or rehabilitation. The boy remained completely remorseless, so there was a strong likelihood that he would spend the rest of his days in the hospital.

"My God," said Valerie, "why did no one ever mention this to us?"

"I'm surprised Graham didn't tell you," said St. Giles. "I thought he was your friend."

"He was my friend, Andrew, and I realize now that he tried to warn me. I guess I should have listened."

St. Giles continued. "So, we come to find that there's a terrible connection between this house and the Keep. I know there are answers there. We need to get into the tomb, John. I believe it will lead us to our killer. I have a feeling he's been there, and Moira knows the way in."

John shook his head. "She won't do it. I know she won't. She'll never go inside that place again. The poor girl saw hell there, but speaking of hell, that gives me an idea. Maybe you and I should pay a visit to the asylum in Perth and try to see this Marni character. He probably has some idea about what's going on around here."

"I don't know, John. I can't imagine that he'd be of any use. After all, it was years ago, and even if he is still alive, the man's completely mad."

"You never know, and as you've always said, we can't overlook any possibility. I say we should at least try. It couldn't hurt."

✲ ✲ ✲

Early the next day, John and Andrew climbed into Andrew's BMW and headed for Perth.

An hour after the men's departure, Valerie answered the door and was less than happy to find Kenneth Drummond standing there, smiling at her. Although he stood two steps down, his dark eyes were nearly level with her own.

"Morning, Missus MacIntyre. Is your husband at home? I need a word with him."

Valerie heard a creak from the stairs behind her. She quickly stepped outside and drew the door closed, as Drummond did his best to see past her.

"No, he's not here, Mister...eh...Reverend Drummond, but I'll tell him you stopped by. He should be home soon."

"Well maybe I should just come in and wait for his return. I have something very important to discuss with him...something that I'm sure will be of great interest."

Valerie was surprised. It wasn't often that someone from the village volunteered to enter the house. "Em...no, I don't think that's a very good idea. Actually, I'm on my way out. I have an errand to run, but I'll certainly give him your message just as soon as I see him."

"Very well then. As you wish."

Drummond glowered and headed for his car.

✧ ✧ ✧

During the drive to Perth, Andrew and John once again reviewed all that had occurred since the MacIntyres had arrived in Kilbride.

"I can't think of anything else, Andrew," said John, "other than what I've already told you. I'm wrung out."

"There's got to be something. Who did you make the arrangements with for the lease of Ainsley House? Could you have been set up from the beginning, I wonder?"

John thought for a moment. "Maybe," he replied. "But I don't think so. Ainsley was one among several houses that the rental agency submitted to us. It was just what we were looking for. Although, I do remember that the rental agreement was very involved. We had to answer so many questions, Valerie wanted to pass on the place— but I was intrigued."

"Maybe they were looking for a specific profile," said St. Giles. "Maybe you and Valerie were chosen very carefully."

"Come on, Andrew. Do you think that's a real possibility?"

"I don't know, but it's my job to find out. Where did you get the keys for the place?"

"We picked them up at a house in Edinburgh. The guy was a bit strange. As a matter of fact, he was downright creepy. He lives in darkness, so I didn't even get a look at him. Apparently, he administers the trust that owns the house."

"I'll need his name and address," said Andrew. "I think I'll pay this man a little visit when we're done with the job at hand."

"You think he could be involved?"

"I have no idea, but I intend to find out." He exited the A9 motorway and headed for the old town of Perth. "He must have known the house's history, and the information was kept from you on purpose. That tells us something."

John stared out the window at the blur of fast-moving scenery. The rushing countryside couldn't keep pace with his thoughts.

CHAPTER 36

Valerie and Moira sat on the verandah, gazing out over the stillness of the loch, absorbing the peace and quiet of the morning. Although the air was cool, the sun wrapped them in its warmth. Moira sighed periodically, but still didn't speak.

From time to time, Valerie glanced at the girl, feeling terribly conflicted. She knew she had every reason to despise Moira. After all, she had lured John into a relationship, which had placed his life in peril. He was now standing trial for murder, and Graham was dead. She realized that her husband was far from blameless, but he *had* been the victim of manipulation. Try as she might, Valerie couldn't muster the loathing she'd expected to feel. Instead, she felt sorry for the girl who had herself been a victim, and was now trapped with the horrors for which she felt responsible.

Expecting no response, Valerie leaned forward in her chair, and spoke. "So, how long have you known Graham? He told me you were good friends."

"Oh, I've known him for years and years." Moira replied, as if her silence had never happened.

Valerie was so surprised that she actually jumped. She remained quiet, however, and allowed Moira to continue.

"Actually, he was my best friend, at least until I got involved with Drummond and his Covenanters. Graham took me under his wing after my father left. The summer he came back to the village from university, my dad was gone, and Graham's fiancée was gone too. I think it was our sadness that made us friends. He taught me lots of stuff, like fishing and gardening, and he told me things he'd never told anyone else, or so he said."

She turned and stared out across the loch towards the Keep. She took a long breath and slowly turned back

"I used to spend hours listening to his stories. He loved all the old legends about hidden treasures and great warriors. Oh aye, Graham Nesbit could tell a story like nobody. He could fairly take you away with him, he could."

As Moira talked, Valerie's eyes filled with tears. She'd loved his stories too.

"One day, when I was about nine or ten, we were out on his boat, fishing. We were about a mile from the Keep, which was as close as he'd ever get. I'd never been inside the place at that time, because I was afraid of it like everybody else. Well, Graham told me a story that day, a terrible sad tale about a beautiful princess who'd been locked away in the fortress's treasure vault by her evil husband, the chief of the Campbells."

Valerie smiled in spite of her sadness. It was just like Graham to make up an impossible story that was somehow completely believable.

"Well, I took the story to heart. I was just a wee girl, you see, and pretty gullible. I always believed the things he told me, although I don't think he realized that."

Valerie saw Moira becoming more and more animated as she spoke.

"Later on, he showed me a map. He said he was showing me because I was like family and he had to pass the information on to somebody. He said I was the only one he trusted. By that time, he'd forgotten all about the story of the princess, but I hadn't. I believed she was still locked in the tomb, and in my version, it was up to me to release her."

"So, it was Graham who told you about the tomb?" Things were beginning to make sense. Valerie felt her excitement growing. She had so much to tell John.

"Aye, he did. Truth is, he was a wee bit tipsy at the time he showed me the map. He said it had been kept secret by his family for many years. Ye see, over two hundred years ago, Graham's ancestors were hired to rebuild the Kirk after the English had tumbled it. The Nesbits were the best stonemasons in the shire. Under the floor, they discovered the Campbell war room, and hidden in the wall, they found the map."

"Amazing," Valerie whispered.

"On the other side of the map was a list that Graham said was an inventory of a great treasure. He told me that when Campbell died, he had the treasure buried with him, but no one can ever touch it because it's protected by his curse."

"So where's the map now? Do you know where it is?"

"Oh aye, I know. Actually, it was inside the *Cygnet*'s mast with the other papers I showed you, but I didn't want anybody to see it." She shrugged.

Valerie studied the *Cygnet*, wondering why Graham had left it to her. Was she supposed to uncover the secret? Had he left her any other clues? She tried to recall, but nothing came immediately to mind. It would have to wait. At the moment, she was focused on Moira's story.

"One day when Graham was at the pub, I went to his house, took out the map, and using tracing paper, I copied it. The next day, I pinched his motorboat and went to the Keep by myself. I wasn't afraid…not at all. That's because I was on a crusade, you see. I was on a mission to save the princess. I didn't have time to be afraid."

Valerie pictured her own boys, remembering a time when their imaginations were completely unfettered—when fantasy was their reality. She missed those days.

"It took me a while to get the first wall open," Moira was saying, her voice quavering with excitement, "but after that, it was easy. When I finally opened the vault, though, I was terribly disappointed. There was no princess—only the treasure and Campbell's coffin."

Valerie couldn't imagine the poor brave little girl, all alone in the tomb.

Moira climbed out of her chair and headed into the house, returning a moment later carrying a piece of paper. She sat down beside Valerie, placed the paper on the table, and carefully spread it open.

"This is it?" Valerie's eyes opened wide. "This is the treasure map? Why on earth are you showing it to me?"

"Because I think you should keep it, Valerie. I trust you, and Graham must have trusted you, too. After all, he left the *Cygnet* to you, didn't he?"

Valerie nodded slowly.

Moira pointed to a drawing in the corner of the paper. "Now, this shield is the Campbell crest, and it's the key to the whole thing. The map's completely useless to anyone who doesn't know its significance."

"This is fantastic," said Valerie. "I can't wait until John gets home."

"Oh, you can't tell John, or Mister St. Giles either. We can't take the chance. The tomb is evil. It must not be opened again. I only told you in case something happens to me."

Valerie reached out her hand. "All right; as you wish, but there's nothing for you to worry about. We won't let anything happen to you."

Moira rose slowly to her feet and padded away. A minute later, Valerie heard the sounds of the guitar.

✿ ✿ ✿

John and Andrew arrived at the asylum shortly after noon. The place was hidden away, well back from the main road, accessed through a security gate. A twenty-foot wall topped with iron spikes surrounded the entire property. St. Giles flashed his business card, assuring the elderly guard that he had an appointment with the director. After helping the old guy find his name on the list, Andrew was waved through.

"Reassuring to know that security's so tight," he smirked, as they drove slowly down the long, tree-lined driveway. "Although, they're probably not too worried about people breaking in."

Some of the patients strolled the manicured grounds in the company of their uniformed keepers. Others sat in wheelchairs, or on park benches, staring at the sky or the ground, or things only they could see.

The men parked the car, climbed the wide steps, and entered the hospital. The lobby of the enormous old building was richly paneled and featured a sweeping staircase. It was more like the foyer of a private college or a gentleman's club than that of an asylum.

John stood surveying the lobby as Andrew headed for the reception desk. He smiled down at the pretty young receptionist and asked to see Doctor Barnabus. He watched the surprise flicker across the woman's face.

"Did you have an appointment?" she asked politely.

"Well, not exactly," Andrew replied, using his most winning voice, "but he's a friend of a colleague of mine. I was assured the doctor would be pleased to hear what I came to discuss with him."

The receptionist's professional smile didn't fade a whit. "I see," she said evenly. "The only problem is that Doctor Barnabus is no longer with us. Actually, he died some years ago."

The young woman continued to smile and calmly reached under her desk.

A moment later, a door burst open on the far side of the lobby. A dumpy, middle-aged woman with untidy hair, an outdated brown-tweed suit, and sensible shoes made a beeline for the visitors. She reached the men and scowled up at them. "Can I help you, gentlemen? I'm not aware of your appointment."

"Oh, Miss Cuthbert," stammered the receptionist, "I don't know how this happened. Somehow they got in through the gate no bother."

The woman glanced at the girl, then returned her attention to the men.

"Follow me," she grumbled. "I'm a very busy woman, and haven't much time for unannounced visitors. What is it you want?"

The men trotted after Miss Cuthbert as she scurried across the vestibule and into her office. She sat at her desk, tapping on it impatiently with a pencil as St. Giles explained what they were looking for.

"I have absolutely no knowledge of anything that took place before my tenure," she said when Andrew was finished. "You see, most of our files were consumed in a fire years ago, so there are no records for many of our patients."

She rose to dismiss the men, and St. Giles offered his hand and a smile. "Thanks for allowing us to intrude on your valuable time," he said warmly, and headed for the door.

John was surprised that his companion was so easily put off. "Just a minute." He pointed to the large landscape painting behind the desk. "Is that a Blaine?" he asked, sounding impressed. "Sure is a beauty. Piece like that should be in a museum." He recognized the artist only because there was a Blaine hanging in the upstairs hall at Ainsley. It was just as dour and lifeless as this one.

"Actually, it *is* a Blaine," said Miss Cuthbert, sounding surprised. "It was left to me by my grandfather. It's not something I could afford on a government salary, you understand. He was quite the connoisseur, my grandfather, and I'm told he knew Averil Blaine personally."

"How very interesting," John replied, ignoring Andrew's impatience. He moved closer to the painting. "Just beautiful," he murmured. "You're a fortunate woman."

By now, Miss Cuthbert was beginning to thaw. She smiled up at John, paying no attention to Andrew, who was pacing at the door. "You know, I'm thinking, since you've made the effort, maybe there is something I could offer by way of assistance. There is one patient here who may be of help. His name's Delacorte. He was the director here before he lost his mind. It happened around the time of the fire. I could let you see him for a few minutes, but I warn you, he's pretty far gone. Half the time, he thinks I'm his mother."

At Ainsley House, Inspector Wadsworth and Sergeant Bailey arrived unannounced. Bailey waved a search warrant, brushed past Valerie into the house, and headed for the kitchen as Wadsworth began to climb the stairs toward the bedrooms. Valerie was panicked. Moira, she knew, was upstairs in the guestroom, asleep.

The jig was about to be up.

Valerie followed the big man upstairs, wondering how she could divert him from looking in the guest room, but realized that there wasn't much chance.

"I'd prefer if you'd wait downstairs for me, Missus MacIntyre," grumbled Wadsworth. "There's no reason for you to supervise my work. I'm not a thief. Anything I remove will be documented and returned to you when we no longer need it."

"Show me in the warrant where it says I can't be in my own bedroom while you paw through my things," said Valerie. "Otherwise, I'll be right here watching you."

Wadsworth turned away shaking his head, ambled to the dresser, and made an elaborate show of going through Valerie's underwear drawer.

"And what would you be looking for in there?"

"Oh, you never know." The policeman didn't look up from his task. "Seems to be a favorite hiding place, though. I never could understand why. So, it's always the first place I look."

When he finished with the drawers, Wadsworth moved into the bathroom and calmly ransacked the laundry hamper before starting on the medicine cabinet. Valerie watched him, dismayed, twisting her fingers into knots and trying to think of some distraction. She realized that his next stop would be the guestroom where Moira was stashed.

The cop completed his search of the master suite and moved down the hall. As he opened the guestroom door and stepped through, Valerie was right behind him. The bed was unmade, but Moira was nowhere to be seen. Valerie held her breath as Wadsworth looked in the closet. Moira's guitar sat against the wall, but apart from that, she saw absolutely no evidence of her ever having been there.

"I see you have a guest in the house," said the inspector, surveying the unmade bed. "And who might that be?"

"Well, if you must know, Inspector, Mister St. Giles has been staying here," she said, relieved that her voice didn't shake. "He finds it a little more friendly than the Thistle. I'm sure you understand."

"Oh, yes indeed. And where is the good gentleman at the moment? I'd like to have a word with him."

"He's not here," she replied coolly. "He and my husband are doing some investigating on their own. We think it important that someone is actually looking for the truth."

She looked Wadsworth right in the eye. "You see, Inspector, whether you like it or not, my husband did not commit the crime you seem to have him convicted of. He couldn't have. We know that for a fact. So, instead of wallowing in complacency, you should be worried. There's a murderer in this valley, and he's walking around free."

As she held his gaze, Wadsworth softened. "Well, if you must know, Missus MacIntyre, I am no longer sure that your husband was at the Keep that night. It does, however, remain my responsibility to investigate him. I hope you understand."

"It's Kenneth Drummond you should be investigating. I know he's involved. He's a dangerous man."

"As a matter of fact, Missus MacIntyre, there are some things about Reverend Drummond that trouble me," Wadsworth agreed. "Some of his activities do need explanation, but unlike your husband, there's nothing to link him to the victim. There's no motive."

Valerie looked away.

"Should you or your husband discover anything," he continued, "anything at all, you must contact me right away. I can be of more help than you know. And finding Miss MacLeod would certainly be of value to us all, don't you agree?"

Valerie didn't respond. Instead, she left the room and headed downstairs.

A half hour later, Wadsworth had completed his search of the house. He took with him, among other things, John's hairbrush and two pairs of his shoes. He also removed all the printed pages from John's study, but left the computer. Valerie protested vehemently, but to no avail.

Sergeant Bailey returned from his search of the boatshed clutching a plastic bag, which he handed to his superior.

As he was leaving, Wadsworth turned to Valerie. "By the way... how much do you know about Andrew St. Giles?"

"I know quite enough, thank you, Inspector. I'm sorry if he's doing his job too well. I hope he doesn't cause you any embarrassment."

Wadsworth tried to smile, but the result was more like a grimace. He squeezed out the door and lumbered off to join his partner, who was waiting in the police car.

As soon as the car was out of sight, Valerie started to search for Moira. She explored every corner of the house, but had no success. Moira was gone. Again she felt the rising panic, realizing that if the police came across the girl and discovered she'd been staying at the house, things would be even worse for her husband. She decided to drive into the village. If Moira was on her way there, she might be able to intercept her.

She drove carefully, searching both sides of the lane for any sign, praying that Moira hadn't already been picked up by the police. As she neared St. Agnes church, she slowed, and much to her surprise, spotted the girl in the cemetery, kneeling beside the freshest grave, which had been strewn with wildflowers.

She parked the car and walked slowly to the plot. As Valerie knelt down, Moira opened her eyes but said nothing. After a moment or two, Valerie rose to her feet, took the girl by the hand, and led her away.

"I knew he was gone, you know," said Moira when they were safely inside the car. "That's why it was okay to tell you the secret. You see, I was there when it happened." She began to tremble. "Poor Graham. He looked so sad down there on the rocks, so lonely. But in the end, I couldn't do it. I tried to jump, but I just couldn't find the courage. Oh, Graham. He came there to save me, you know."

Valerie stopped the car right in the middle of the road. Her heart was in her throat. She reached for Moira and held her in her arms as though she was one of her own kids. She didn't speak until Moira broke the silence.

"I saw these men arrive at the house this morning, and I thought I'd better disappear for a bit. It's something I've become quite good at lately. I went out the window onto the roof. From there, it was easy—I'm good at roofs. I left my things hidden in the bushes where nobody would find them. I'll show you when we get back."

✡ ✡ ✡

Inquisitive patients watched nervously as the two unfamiliar men entered their ward. Miss Cuthbert pointed out Delacorte and waited by the door as John crossed the room to a long table and took a seat across from the old man, his back to the window. He was surprised that Andrew didn't join him, choosing instead to remain at the door with Miss Cuthbert.

"You're blocking my light," the old man grumbled, without ever looking up from the intricate architectural drawings spread out in front of him.

"I'm sorry, Mister Delacorte, but I have something to discuss with you—something important."

"*Doctor* Delacorte, if you please," said the man as he continued to draw. "*Doctor* Delacorte is my title. I'm not a medical doctor, you understand, but a doctor nonetheless. PhD, Psychology, Glasgow, 'Thirty-six. Top of my class, oh yes."

"I'm terribly sorry, Doctor, but if you'll forgive the interruption, we'll allow you to get back to your work in just a minute. Unfortunately, we've got a situation that requires your attention."

"Very well, my boy…what is it?" The old man pushed his papers aside and gave John his reluctant attention. Andrew continued to watch from the doorway.

"We're here to ask about one of your inmates, eh…patients," John began. "We're hoping you have some information about the man. I'm afraid you're the only one who can help. You're our last chance."

John smiled to himself as he watched the ex-director puff up with self-importance. "The man's name is Marni—Rupert Marni," he continued. "He was admitted here as a teenager because he killed his mother and her lover. It was a particularly brutal crime." An odd expression crept into the old man's eyes as he reached for his memory. He gazed warily at his inquisitor.

John gazed right back. A moment passed.

"How do you know him?" asked Delacorte. "How do you know Rupert? Oh, I tried to tell them about him, but they wouldn't listen. It was him that set the fire, you know. All the records…all my precious files gone up in smoke."

John glanced at Andrew and shrugged, seeking advice. When the old man followed his gaze, Andrew stifled a yawn with his hand.

Delacorte shook his head sadly. "I warned them. Oh yes I did. He was no ordinary boy, Rupert Marni. And he's grown into a very evil man. It's going to take forever to get things back in order, you understand. What a mess."

"Doctor," said John, desperate to regain Delacorte's attention, "I need to know what happened to him. Where is he now?"

"Who? Where is who?"

"Marni," urged John. "Rupert Marni. I need to find him. It's important...very important."

"Well that's just it, don't you see?" The old man gazed at his drawings. "You'll never find him if he doesn't want to be found. He's an artist, you know. He learned to create perfect documents. Oh yes, he's quite the forger. By now, he could be anybody...anybody at all." He pointed at John with a trembling finger. "All I can tell you is, he escaped from here weeks ago, on the night of the fire. He's long gone, and you'll never find him. He's far too canny for that."

Delacorte looked away. His attention was suddenly diverted by something taking place behind John's head. John turned in his chair and saw a large, gray moth battering itself against the window.

"He's troubled, you know," the doctor said softly, "very, very troubled, but oh, so clever. For a time, he was my protégé, until he learned all I could teach him. Unfortunately, we couldn't make him well, even though we have some of the best doctors in Perthshire."

Without warning, the doctor reached out and grabbed John's hand.

John tried to pull away, but the old man was stronger than he looked. He searched John's eyes, his own filled with desperation. "If you do find him, kill him! I'm warning you. You must kill him."

He released John's hand, stood up and began to creep around the table. He reached the window, snagged the moth, and returned triumphantly to his seat, where he began pulling the wings from the helpless creature. "Rupert used to do this," he said calmly.

Realizing that the interview had come to an end, John rose to his feet. "Just one more thing before you get back to your work, Doctor. Could you describe him to us?"

"Who? Describe who?"

"Marni," John urged. "Rupert Marni. Is there anything unusual about him? Anything at all that would make him easy to recognize?"

Delacorte pondered the question. "As a matter of fact, there is," he whispered. "He has no soul. You'll find that out, should you ever meet him. He tries to disguise the fact, but sometimes he gets careless."

"So the fire happened six years ago?" St. Giles asked as they descended the stairs.

"That's right," replied Miss Cuthbert, "but I must say, that's the first time I heard that somebody escaped that night. Do you think he was telling the truth?"

"Well we wouldn't know, would we? You're the expert. You tell us."

"I wish I could," she replied grimly.

"It's got to be Drummond," said John, once they were back in the car and pointed toward home. "How long has he been in Kilbride?"

"Just over five years," said Andrew, "and he certainly fits the profile."

John nodded. "I think it's time we told the police about the body under the church, don't you?"

"You're probably right but I think it should be an anonymous tip."

"Makes sense," John agreed. "Let Wadsworth piece it together. It shouldn't take long for him to come up with Drummond. God, it sure will be a relief to get this off my back."

"I know it will, John." Andrew sounded distracted.

CHAPTER 37

The men found Moira and Valerie hard at work reassembling the *Cygnet*. Valerie jumped up as they entered the room, eager to hear about the trip to Perth.

They all adjourned to the kitchen, where she opened a can of soup. When the men were done with the story, Valerie turned to Moira. "Would you run upstairs please, and fetch me my blue sweater from the bedroom?"

"Of course."

As soon as Moira had left the room, Valerie faced the men.

"As you can see, we've had a bit of a breakthrough here, as well. Moira's been talking to me all day. She knows all about Graham. As a matter of fact, she was there when it happened. She also knows who else was there, but she hasn't told me that. She's still pretty fragile, and I didn't want to push her."

"Wow. What else did she tell you?" John's voice quivered. "Do you realize what this means? We have a witness. They've got no case. Oh thank you, God."

He grinned at Andrew. "Isn't that right? We're home free."

"If the girl is to be believed, John," said the lawyer. "Her testimony will certainly be disputed. After all, she's completely loony. She'll never—"

The sound from the doorway stopped him.

Moira stood there, gazing at him. "I know I'm a bit daft, Mister St. Giles, and that's a fact, but not all of me is. I just see things differently now, that's all. I'll grant you, there are things I don't remember, but I take comfort in that. It's probably for the best."

"Well, I don't think you're crazy at all," Valerie said firmly, "It's just that you've been through some terrible things." She glared at St. Giles. "Moira and I had a very good talk while you men were away, and I think it's time we spoke freely in front of one another. We're in this together, after all."

She poured the hot soup into four mugs. "I, for one, am confident the police will believe Moira. John will be cleared—you'll see." As she passed out the mugs, she kept right on talking. "So Marni has become Kenneth Drummond?" she asked no one in particular. "It's too bizarre."

"We're thinking about letting Wadsworth in on what we know," John said, after draining his mug. "What do you think?"

"Well, if Andrew thinks it's the right time, I'm not going to argue," Valerie replied. "Oh, that reminds me. He was here today, Wadsworth, with a search warrant. He took some stuff, your book among other things. I tried to stop him, but I couldn't. Said he was within his rights. Is that true, Andrew?"

"I'm afraid so, if he had a warrant."

Valerie looked apologetically toward John. He shrugged his shoulders.

"Oh well, he'll find nothing incriminating in it. Actually, I haven't thought much about my book recently. I've had other things on my mind. The important thing is, we're going to be able to convince the police that it was Drummond, not me, at the Keep that night. We've got a witness."

"How is it that Wadsworth didn't find Moira?" asked St. Giles.

"Because she's a very clever girl, that's why."

"You're wrong, you know," said Moira softly. "You've got it all wrong."

They'd almost forgotten she was there. "It wasn't Reverend Drummond that pushed Graham. He wasn't even there that night. It was Alistair Frazier that pushed him. I saw him do it. I couldn't make myself believe it for a while, but it was him, all right. I wonder where he's hiding."

There was silence in the room. The men knew full well where Alistair was hiding.

"Well there goes our Drummond theory," said Andrew. "It was a great while it lasted, but never mind—at least now we have a witness who can prove John's innocence."

"Well, Andrew, if you feel it's time for Wadsworth to know about Moira, I agree," said John.

"All right. I'll call him first thing in the morning."

"But you can't go to the police," said Moira matter-of-factly. "They're on Drummond's side. Constable Smiley used to be one of his Covenanters."

"But we have no choice, Moira," said Valerie. "They have to be told what you saw, or John could be found guilty. You understand that, don't you? And don't you worry—you'll be safe with us."

Moira nodded hesitantly, though her distress was clear.

By the time darkness fell, they were ready to call it a day. It had certainly been an eventful one. Andrew stood and announced that he was off to the Thistle. He explained that he wanted to catch Wadsworth bright and early in the morning. They said their goodnights, and the MacIntyres climbed wearily up the stairs.

Moira returned to the living room, sat down on the floor, and continued reassembling the *Cygnet*, humming softly to her self as she worked.

An hour later, John slipped back down the stairs and into his study. He hadn't felt the presence since the night in the Oban jail, and, hoping beyond hope that the scribe was done with him, he decided to have a go at writing again. He'd left off at a very exciting scene. He stretched out his fingers and reached for the keyboard.

"Who's there? I say."

At the sound of Campbell's voice, Eileen's heart leapt into her throat. She spun to face her husband, ready to answer, and watched breathlessly as he fell back onto his pillow, still asleep. He'd been dreaming. She slipped back out the door and shrugged to the guard. He smiled appreciatively as he watched her hurry away.

In a small room adjacent to the great hall, she handed the key to Lasker. He had been assured that a visit to Campbell's treasury would be well worth his while, but that access to the secret chamber would be provided to him only after he'd helped deliver Robert Douglas from his cell. It had taken a little more convincing than Eileen had anticipated, but when Lasker was reminded that most of the guards would be asleep at their posts, he agreed to go along. He knew that the Campbell treasure was enormous, and that a few choice pieces could be removed without ever being missed.

Eileen waited in the dark as Hamish and Lasker headed for the dungeons and Robert. She had arranged for Meg to be waiting below the Keep with a small boat and a good oarsman. She knew that no one would be expecting an escape, especially in the direction of the loch.

Hamish and Lasker reached the iron grid that separated the prison cells from the rest of the vaults, and Hamish hid in the shadows as Lasker summoned the solitary guard. When the man approached the bars to inspect the visitor, he was surprised to see an elegant gentleman smiling at him.

"I've been sent by your master," Lasker intoned. "He decided that since you've been unfortunate enough to have drawn guard duty on this night of celebration, you should be brought a flagon to pass the night more easily."

The guard warily appraised the well-dressed stranger, but since the man was alone, saw no cause for concern.

"Lord Campbell is in great spirits this evening and is feeling benevolent," said Lasker. "I'm newly appointed as his taster and have brought you something from the best cellar."

Lasker extended the leather pouch, but as the guard reached for his prize, Lasker pulled it back just out of reach and smiled wickedly as the watchman made his fatal mistake. The man stepped closer and reached through the bars for the flagon.

At that moment, Hamish leapt from the shadows, grabbed the man's arm, and yanked it all the way through, right to the shoulder. The guard's head hit the bars so hard that he was knocked senseless. Young Douglas calmly reached through the bars and sliced the man's throat. Lasker jumped back from the angry gush of blood as the guard slumped to the floor, making a soft gurgling sound. Hamish reached for the ring of keys and found the one that would unlock the gate.

They stepped over the body and began searching for the right cell. "Robert?" Hamish called softly. "Robert," he called out again.

"Hamish," whispered a voice. "Is that you?"

The men approached Douglas's cell, and Lasker removed the special key from his pocket and unlocked the door. Hamish rushed inside and knelt beside his brother.

Robert was in a very bad way. He was racked with fever, and Hamish could smell the stink of putrefaction from the rot in his arm.

He summoned Lasker to help, and together, they lifted the groaning man from the cold floor. Hamish supported his brother as Lasker led the way out of the dungeons.

They reached the anteroom undetected.

When she saw Robert, Eileen burst into tears. He was so far gone, he didn't recognize her. She took him in her arms and laid him gently on a nearby bench. Stinking fluid seeped through the filthy bandage, now black with rot. Eileen considered cleaning the wound, but decided that it would have to wait until later.

Lasker approached from the shadows. "The secret," he snarled. "I've delivered your ransom."

"The trove lies beyond the dungeon where the cells are," said Eileen. "It's hidden behind the altar on the south wall of Campbell's private chapel. Place the fingers of your left hand into the gash in the side of the crucifix, and push. That will open a panel in the wall, inside of which you'll find an iron bar. Pull it toward you. It will release the slab.

"There is one thing, though, that I must warn you about, Mister Lasker. Don't go near the coffin that lies inside the tomb. Were you to turn the black rose, Campbell's curse would be released. It would destroy us all."

She remembered the day she'd learned the secret of the tomb. Campbell had been drunk and feeling expansive the afternoon he'd led her into the depths of the Keep, in order to impress her with his treasure. He was completely unaware that Eileen paid very close attention as he opened solid walls, until eventually they entered the tomb. She'd recoiled from the huge stone coffin that dominated the chamber, but her husband merely laughed at her.

"I see you've been told of my curse," he chuckled dryly, "but there's no reason for you to fear. My scourge is a right selective bastard—very particular in the delivery of its poison. So, m'Lady, when this cold *stone box becomes my place of rest, you must never touch the black rose that sits there in the center of my crest. You won't live to enjoy what you might discover. In truth, there is no curse, but anyone who would disturb my sleep will pay a dear price."*

John took a breath, waiting for the next words to come, grateful that he felt no pain in his fingers. He reached for his glass, but the damn thing was empty again. Irritated, he pushed back from his desk and headed for the living room bar. He'd already had more than enough to drink, but it had been a long night, and he'd lost count. He poured a stiff one, took a long gulp, and headed back to the security of his study.

He sat back down at his desk to reread the line where he'd left off, but the line had vanished. As he scanned the screen, the flush drained from his cheeks.

In the few minutes he'd been gone, the chapter had been finished for him. Holding his breath, he raced through words he hadn't written. Clearly, the scribe had returned and no longer required the earthly constraints of John's hands.

The only other explanation was that he'd completely lost his mind.

Eileen and Hamish lifted the unconscious Robert from the bench and hauled him from the room. They moved quietly toward the battlements, reached the top of the stairway, and started down. Suddenly, a guard emerged from the shadows and raised his pike to bar their way.

"Halt," he cried, "Who goes there?"

Hamish thrust his brother toward Eileen and drew his sword. The guard called out for help, and almost immediately, they heard the shouts from men rushing in their direction. Hamish felled the first man and turned to face five others, who were now advancing on him.

Eileen watched, horrified, as the boy was quickly surrounded and hacked to pieces.

"Damn you, Campbell," she cried. Suspicious even of his friends, her husband had posted a sentry at the secret path.

The guards grabbed Eileen roughly and tore Robert from her arms.

A few minutes later, Campbell arrived breathless into the great hall. He glared for a moment into the defiant eyes of his wife and glanced at the dying man on the floor.

"Take her to the tower and lock her in," he barked. "Throw this filth from the battlements. I'm going back to bed."

He turned and strode from the room.

Lasker found the little chapel, just as Eileen had described it. He slid his bony fingers into the slash in Jesus' side, and pushed firmly. A panel slid open in the wall, and he smiled as he grasped the lever. He stood watching as a piece of wall swung open. He took a trembling breath and stepped through into the vault.

As the light spilled into the chamber, Lasker began to giggle. He could see that as powerful as Campbell was in this life, he was determined to be even more so in the next. So overwhelmed was the chancellor that he failed to notice the slab closing silently behind him. The sound of it locking into place snapped him out of his trance, but by the time he reached the wall, it was too late—he was sealed in. In a rising panic, he began to kick and shove and scrape at the thick stones, but to no avail.

On the highest battlement of Campbell Keep, Eileen MacLeod stood quietly as Robert was lifted high in the air and flung over the wall. Mercifully, he had never regained consciousness, so he was completely unaware of his death. Eileen wept softly, but made no struggle as the guards led her toward the small wooden door.

She followed along obediently, her head bowed in acceptance. When they reached the door, the guard on her left released her arm and reached to his belt for the key. Eileen immediately relaxed her body and felt her other guard do the same. Suddenly, she screamed like a banshee, startling the man who was holding her. He froze for just a moment, but it was long enough. With unexpected strength, Eileen tore herself free, and before the guards could stop her, she reached the parapet. She clambered up onto the wall, crossed her breast, and leapt off. She knew that Robert was waiting below.

Horrified, John shut down his computer and hauled his aching body upstairs to collapse on the bed. Valerie mumbled something in her sleep, but he never heard it. His mind was in shambles. Whatever was happening, once exhilarating, now terrified him. His state of mind was more frightening than the bloody events of Campbell Keep. Clearly, the scribe wasn't done with him. He lay sweating in the darkness, convinced that Ninian Lasker was not only real, he was the dark presence guiding his hand.

As if he'd been invited, the image of Lasker began to materialize in John's mind, as real as the surrounding darkness. This time John knew he was not asleep. He watched the scene unfold before his eyes.

The chancellor was still imprisoned in Campbell's tomb, scratching and clawing at the stone walls, tearing his bony fingers to shreds. Mesmerized, John watched as the man's panic advanced into maniacal fury. Ninian ran screaming through the chamber, hauling ropes of gems from the chests and hurling them against the walls. When he reached exhaustion, he collapsed to the floor and buried his head in his bloody hands, ready to accept the finality.

As the torches sputtered in the dwindling air, Lasker looked up through his fingers and spied the sarcophagus. His eyes glittering, he rose unsteadily to his feet and stumbled to the center of the chamber. He draped his gaunt body over the end of the coffin and reached for the black rose centered in the Campbell crest.

John watched, both fascinated and repulsed as the coffin lid slid open and Ninian Lasker met with a gruesome death. He prayed that Lasker's bloody demise signaled the end of the possession—that his descent into madness was over.

CHAPTER 38

———◆◆◆———

At ten o'clock, Wadsworth, Bailey, and Constable Smiley were at the door, accompanied by Andrew St. Giles. Wadsworth looked none too happy.

Valerie showed the men into the living room, where the inspector carefully deposited his bulk into a comfortable armchair and sat tapping his stout fingers together, impatient for Moira's arrival. Bailey perched nervously on the arm of the couch, and Smiley stood by the door, more or less at attention, staring straight ahead, like he'd rather not be noticed.

"Tell me, Inspector," Valerie began, "while we're waiting. I have to ask. Do you know about the murder that took place in this room, twenty-five years ago?"

Wadsworth glanced at Bailey. The sergeant shrugged. "No," said the big man, "I can't say that I do."

"Well," Valerie continued, "I, for one, think it's time you knew. Ainsley House was the scene of a brutal murder. Actually, there were two killings, committed by the same person, but only one took place here. I don't know what bearing it has exactly, but I would have thought it might be of some interest to a criminologist of your stature."

Wadsworth said nothing.

She turned to Smiley. "So why didn't you acquaint your friends with the history of the house, Constable? You didn't consider it important? Why don't you fill them in on the details, while I go find the others?"

As she rose to her feet, John and Moira entered the room. Smiley reached for the girl's arm, but she managed to avoid him and huddled closer to John.

"Moira," said the constable, sounding nervous, "where have you been? We've been searching everywhere for you."

She refused to look at him.

John led her to the sofa and sat down beside her. Valerie crossed the room to join them, and took Moira's hand. Andrew settled into a vacant chair, leaned back, and crossed his arms.

"Now, if I might offer a suggestion, Inspector Wadsworth," he began, "rather than subjecting Miss MacLeod to a barrage of questions, maybe it would be more constructive if you allowed her to tell you her story from the beginning, in her own words.

Wadsworth studied Moira for a second and slowly nodded his huge head.

Valerie squeezed the girl's hand. "Now, Moira," she said softly, "there's nothing to be afraid of. It's just like I told you: You've done nothing wrong, and the inspector here only wants to know what you recall about what happened at the Keep on the night of the storm. Just as you remember it."

There was no sound in the room except for the soft ticking of the clock.

"Would you like to hear the ending or the beginning first, Inspector?" Moira spoke in almost a whisper.

"The beginning will be fine...if you like," answered the policeman, almost kindly.

Moira took a breath and began her story. "It all started around the time Kenneth Drummond arrived in the village. Until then, it was really nice around here. At first we were all a bit shy, him being from the big city and everything, but it didn't take long for things to change. He started this club for the younger boys. He was magic with them. He'd sit them down and tell them tales, tales of adventure, about great warriors and pirate ships and sunken treasure, things like that. He told them about his time in the guards and explained that they were to be the heroes of the future. The boys were a right-willing audience, and that's a fact. Most of them had never been out of the vale, you see, so his stories had a great effect. He could tell a story like nobody. Nobody except Graham, that is."

"And then what happened?" Valerie prompted.

"Soon him and his precious Covenanters were taking long hikes into the hills, looking for God knows what. They'd stay away for days, sometimes. The boys always came home a bit strange, but none of them would say what they'd been up to. I did hear about them finding the pagan temple, though. Alistair told me. He couldn't help himself. He was feeling like such a big shot for being the one to discover it. The folks in the village showed no interest at all. As far as I know, not a one went out to have a look."

She glanced toward the window. "I wonder where Ali can be? I know what he did was terrible, but there's no doubt Drummond drove him to it.

"Anyway, I decided I wanted to join the Covenanters. You see, the boys were having all the fun. So, Ali spoke to Reverend

Drummond, and he agreed to meet me one night at the church to see if I was brave enough to be a member of his troop. Ye understand, I was the only girl that ever wanted in."

At this point, Moira stopped talking and sat studying the floor, biting her lip. When she resumed the story, her voice was shaking.

"He took me down into a cellar, through a hidden door in the pulpit, and led me into a room where he asked me to show myself to him. I was completely humiliated and scared to death, but I was determined to pass his test. He assured me the boys had had to go through initiation too."

Her eyes remained downcast. "After, he let me put my clothes back on. We sat on the floor, and he told me things—things intended to frighten me. It worked. He said the curse of the Keep was real, and that he was its messenger. He said terrible things could happen to anyone who didn't obey him. After that night, I was allowed on the outings, and I took part in all the rituals.

"After a few weeks, Drummond said he needed to go further. That's when the animal sacrifices started, and I wanted no part of it. I was horrified, but the boys seemed to like it fine. It's something about boys I'll never understand. They were afraid of upsetting him, you see. They believed totally in his power. And they spied for him, too. Oh aye. They watched everybody. That's how Drummond knew everybody's secrets."

Moira raised her eyes and looked out across the loch as if searching for something.

"He was never worried about me telling on him because he controlled me completely by that time. You see, he had me doing things that I was ashamed of whenever we went to the chamber."

Her face flushed, but she kept on. "I knew it was wrong, but I was so afraid of him, and I had nobody to tell. Who'd have believed me speaking against the minister? They all thought he was a hero. I wanted to go to Graham, but Drummond had me convinced that he and Graham were on the same side. He said it was Graham that showed him the chamber beneath the church."

A tear spilled onto her cheek, and she angrily brushed it away.

"Chamber?" blurted Wadsworth. "What chamber? Is this the same place that he, eh…took you to?"

John glared at the Inspector until the man regained control of himself. Valerie squeezed Moira's arm. "You're doing fine," she said softly, "just fine."

Moira took a shaky breath and continued her story. "I knew Alistair Frazier suspected what was going on. He caught me coming from the church one night, and he knew something was wrong. I lied to him, but he knew, so in exchange for his silence, I showed him the chamber. Soon after that, he began to change. He started to hate Drummond's gang and Drummond too. He disappeared for a while, spent a year or two in Glasgow and Oban, and then he came back, and for some reason, he got involved again. I think it's him that's been stealing from the chamber, but I'm not certain."

"So, why John?" Valerie coaxed. "Why was he so important?"

"Drummond said we needed him. He said that as a famous director, he was the kind of champion our cause required—that we'd get him to do a film about Scotland being an occupied country even though it has all Britain's wealth 'cause of the oil in the North Sea. He said John could bring attention to the injustice, and that what we were doing was for Scotland's own good. He was convinced that the people could be made to rise up and throw the English out, just like before. And he hated the English like nobody's business. The boys ate it up. I wasn't so sure, but it became my job to get to John, so that Drummond could have power over him. I was just supposed to tempt him, but things got out of hand. I always knew there was more going on than what Drummond was telling, but I found out too late."

She raised her eyes and looked at the MacIntyres. "I'm so sorry, John. I'm sorry Valerie," she whispered. "I'm not looking for an excuse, because I did do what he asked, but I was afraid of him. I tried to refuse him, but I just wasn't strong enough."

Valerie stole a glance at Wadsworth and Andrew. Their faces were expressionless.

"But then I found that I couldn't live with myself. I started to really like you, John. You're a nice man, and I knew that you and your wife were going to get hurt, so I decided I had to get away from the vale. That's why I ran away to London."

She briefly described her London experience, but omitted the parts she didn't want to think about. "I was very unhappy there, so I thought I'd go to Oban, because I was too afraid to come home to Kilbride. But it didn't matter where I went; the curse was following me, just like Drummond warned. It nearly destroyed me. I had no choice, so I returned to the Keep."

As she listened, tears welled up in Valerie's eyes. She wanted to take the pain away, but she knew she couldn't. No one could. Although she'd heard the story before, it affected her deeply every time she heard it.

"It didn't take Drummond long to find me. I should have known his spies were watching. I mean the ravens. They answer to him too, you know."

Skepticism clouded Wadsworth's broad face. The MacIntyres' were not so ready to scoff.

"Anyway, Drummond arrived at the fortress one morning with a couple of his hooligans. They found me sitting in the courtyard enjoying the sunshine. I tried to run, but the boys caught me before I could get inside. Drummond was very angry. He said I had to contact John and convince him to come to the Keep or something bad would happen to my mother."

Wadsworth watched the girl closely. Moira caught his eye and held his gaze for a long moment before shifting her attention to

John. "So I phoned you from Kilmartin. There was really no choice. I never knew Drummond intended to do you harm at the Keep that night. I swear. You must believe me, John."

She searched his face.

"I believe you," he nodded.

Almost immediately, Moira's expression softened, and her voice strengthened. "After I called you, I changed my mind. I knew I had to escape Drummond's power all by myself, and that there was only one way to do it."

She averted her eyes and studied the carpet. "So, I returned to the Keep and made myself ready. I climbed to the very top and got up on the parapet, ready to jump. That's when I saw the man in the shadows. He tried to reach for me."

Moira's eyes filled with tears, and she stopped talking as she remembered the awful events. The ticking of the mantle clock got louder and louder.

"But it wasn't you, John," Moira continued, her voice breaking. "It was Graham that had come for me, instead. Graham loved me, you know, and he came to save me." She shivered but kept on. "Then another figure appeared out of the darkness, but Graham never saw him. Oh God, it was awful. I tried to scream, but I couldn't. He charged Graham from behind and hurled him up onto the wall. He just kept pushing and pushing until finally Graham went over the side." Her voice was an angry whisper. "That's when I saw who pushed Graham...It was Alistair Frazier."

Moira was now shaking and wringing her hands. Her face was ashen.

Unable to watch any more of the pain, Valerie reached for her and pulled her into her arms. "She doesn't really remember what happened next," she said. "All she recalls is waking up the next morning on the floor of the tower room, thinking it must have been a dream. She'd been having so many bad dreams."

Abruptly, the girl pulled away from Valerie and faced Wadsworth. "I forced myself to look over the parapet. I had to know for sure. Until my dying day, I'll never forget Graham lying on the rocks staring back at me. It was no dream." She closed her eyes.

"Well, well," murmured Wadsworth, "that's quite a story, young lady. I'd say it changes everything."

John took a breath, preparing to speak. He glanced at Valerie and caught the almost-imperceptible shake of her head. He let the breath go.

"That's it then?" asked the policeman.

Moira nodded her head.

"Do you have anything to add, Mister MacIntyre?"

"Um, no, Inspector. You have everything that I remember in the statement I gave you earlier. I suggest that you check out the room under the church, though. It may shed some light on this whole affair."

"Yes indeed," replied Wadsworth. "I think that's a good idea. Why don't you join us?" With some effort, he rose from his chair. "So, it seems we still have a killer on the loose—maybe more than one. Please, be careful, all of you. We have no idea what'll happen next."

The inspector ambled from the room, left the house, and shoehorned himself into the back seat of the police car. Before closing the door, he called out to the constable, "Smiley, go back to the office and see if my faxes have arrived, then join us at the church."

A few minutes later, two cars pulled into the graveyard behind St. Agnes church, out of sight of the manse. Moira led the group to Campbell's monument and reached for one of its carved rosettes. John and Andrew managed to look as surprised as the policemen did when the panel swung open. As Moira started through, John stepped forward and put his hand on her shoulder. "I'm sure they can find what they're looking for," he said. "Why don't we wait up here? I'm sure there's nothing we can do down there."

"Well Sergeant, off you go," said Wadsworth, "Have a look, and take your torch."

Bailey peered down into the dark hole, then looked back at his superior. "Sir, I eh...why don't we both have a look? You never know what might be waiting down there."

"Don't be ridiculous, Bailey," said the inspector. "How do you think I'd ever get myself through that hole?"

Bailey considered the situation and began to lose color. "B...but Inspector," he groaned.

"Oh, I'll go with you," offered Moira, "I'm not afraid."

"You're not going down there," John said firmly, reaching for the girl's arm.

"Oh hell, I'll go with you," said St. Giles. "I'd be honored to be the official hand holder for one of Scotland Yard's finest."

Wadsworth glowered. "Get going Bailey. Now!"

Fifteen minutes later, a pale-faced Sergeant Bailey returned to the surface, shaking his head. "It's horrible, just horrible. There's a body down there, and it's been half eaten by the rats."

"Who is it?" asked Wadsworth. "Do you know who it is? Is it Drummond?"

Without a word, Moira turned and walked away from the group. Valerie hurried to join her.

"It's not Drummond," said the girl. "I know it's not him. It couldn't be him."

Valerie placed her arm around her, and accompanied her to the car.

"It's not Drummond," Bailey was saying. "It looks like a much younger man to me."

Just then, Constable Smiley arrived on the scene and hurried over to Wadsworth. He handed the inspector a sheaf of papers, and they moved a few steps away, talking quietly. Bailey walked slowly to the police car, climbed into the front seat, and picked up the phone.

No one noticed as St. Giles emerged from the ground and crossed to John, brushing himself off. "Andrew," whispered John, "where the hell have you been?"

As Andrew opened his mouth to answer, Wadsworth approached. Smiley was close behind him.

"Smiley here thinks he knows who it could be," said the inspector. "Says you knew him too, Mister MacIntyre."

"Yes. Andrew was just describing him to me. I did know him. Not well, though. He was a friend of Moira's. I don't know how she's going to take this, on top of everything else."

"Yes it's a terrible thing," said Wadsworth. "I think it's time we paid Drummond a visit, don't you?"

Bailey returned from the car and announced that the medical examiner was on his way from Oban. Together, the policemen crossed the churchyard and advanced toward the minister's house. John and Andrew made their way to the corner of the church so they could watch. Wadsworth rang the doorbell.

A moment later, Drummond's mousy little wife answered the door. As Wadsworth talked, the woman's gestures became more and more agitated. John couldn't hear what was being said, but it was obvious the woman was upset.

Missus Drummond stepped aside, allowing the officers to enter the manse, and followed them inside, wringing her tiny hands. The door closed.

"So Andrew," said John as they waited patiently for the policemen to appear, "I guess from the looks of things, they won't be detaining us much longer."

"That's true, although they might want to keep you around for a bit since you're a material witness. However, I'd say it's safe to phone home with some good news for a change."

"Great. We'll call as soon as we get back to the house."

"Oh and John, I'd still like to get a look at Campbell's tomb, preferably before Scotland Yard finds out about it. Isn't it interesting that Moira chose not to tell them about it? I wonder why. Although I'm glad she didn't, I must say. It's bound to come out, though. I wonder if she's ready to help us to—"

The return of the policemen ended their conversation. Behind the inspector, Bailey and Smiley carried a stack of books and a paper bag.

"He's not here," said Wadsworth. "His wife says he left a few days ago for a conference in Glasgow. Says he isn't expected back until the day after tomorrow. Seems a bit cowed, she does. She was reluctant to tell us anything."

"So Inspector Wadsworth, what's the status of my client here?" St. Giles inquired. "It seems to me your case against him has gone out the window. Is it safe to assume that you'll be dropping the charges?"

"Looks like we'll have to, damn it." He glanced at John, and his face broke into a grin. "I would have loved to have gotten a Yank, though. Awfully good for morale." He chuckled to himself and lumbered off toward his car.

✵ ✵ ✵

The search for Drummond proved to be unsuccessful. The Glasgow police were unable to find any minister's conference going on in the city, and the friend at whose house he was supposed to be staying informed them that he hadn't heard from the man in weeks. Kenneth Drummond had disappeared.

The next day, the police called on Missus Drummond for more questioning, but the visit was unproductive. She had no knowledge of her husband ever being in a mental hospital. She actually scoffed at the idea. "He's a brilliant man, and very powerful—very powerful indeed. You know, there are many who support his cause. There are still quite a few nationalists in Scotland. You'd be surprised."

"Oh yes, madam. Yes, I would be," Wadsworth agreed.

Missus Drummond would not be convinced that the man Wadsworth described could possibly be her husband. She did acknowledge that the minister was a bit domineering, and suffered from terrible headaches, but insisted she'd seen no evidence of violence. The terrible acts that Wadsworth described were beyond her belief. She refused to accept that her husband could have been involved in such horrors. She did say that on occasion he disappeared for hours, sometimes even days, but that his absences were essential for replenishing his soul.

Her description of the Covenanter outings was completely at odds with the accounts provided by MacIntyre and Moira. Missus Drummond claimed no knowledge of pagan rites or animal sacrifices.

By the time he'd finished questioning her, it was clear to Wadsworth that the woman had no idea who she was married to.

CHAPTER 39

———◆◆◆———

L ife at Ainsley House was more peaceful than it had been in
weeks. Moira had agreed to stay on, and Valerie continued
her work in the girl's healing process. John marveled at his
wife's kindness. Not surprisingly, the girl's needs took precedence
over Valerie's own.

Andrew had returned to Edinburgh for a few days. He had some
things he needed to attend to.

Wednesday brought with it a lovely, warm afternoon, perfect
for a nice boat ride, and John's suggestion was well received. Valerie
packed some sandwiches and cold drinks, while Moira helped John
slip *Bridie* into the water. Although her beauty remained undeniable, John's feelings for Moira had completely changed. He could

not explain why he'd so easily fallen victim and felt disgusted by his weakness.

An hour later, they reached the northwest end of the loch. John had made sure to steer well clear of Campbell Keep. They entered a quiet cove, where he cut the engines and dropped anchor. It was a spectacular day. Valerie stretched out on the stern bench and closed her eyes, enjoying the warmth of the sun.

John still had some unanswered questions and figured it was as good a time as any.

"Moira," he began, as he reached for a handful of peanuts, "why didn't you tell the police about Campbell's treasure room?"

The girl glanced at Valerie before answering. "Because it's a powerful place, the tomb," she said quietly. "It must never, ever be disturbed by outsiders, and the temptation would be too great. The police would have tried to force me to take them in, but I'll not go there again. I shouldn't have gone the last time, but I had nowhere else. I thought I'd be safe there. But as soon as I opened the vault, the evil started again, and I made a terrible mistake. I took one or two trinkets for myself. I didn't care, you see, because I intended to die anyway, but the curse is unpredictable. Don't you understand? That's when Graham died, and then Alistair. It was him they found under the church, wasn't it John?"

John sighed and nodded.

"The curse of the Campbells is real, you see. This is not the first time it's revealed itself."

"Well, let's pray it's the last," Valerie murmured.

"John," Moira said, brightening, "I just remembered something. My scooter. I need to get it so I can visit my mum. Will you help me?"

"Of course," he agreed, "I'll take you to get it as soon as we get back. Where is it?"

"It's at the Keep, but I left it well hidden. I know it's still there."

"I'll gladly go with you to get it," said John, sounding more enthusiastic than he felt. "I wouldn't feel good about you going there by yourself."

"Thank you, but all I need is for you to drop me at the path. There's no danger for me at the Keep. Drummond's not there. I'm sure of it."

Her interest piqued, Valerie sat up. "Really? How can you be so sure?" she asked.

"Oh he's definitely not there. For one thing, he knows it's a place the police might look for him. Aside from that, he's afraid of the fortress. He isn't afraid of much, Reverend Drummond—just the Keep and that man he talks to on the telephone."

"What man?" John asked, grabbing her arm and spinning her to face him. "Who are you talking about?"

"I don't know who he is. I just know it's somebody Drummond's frightened of, somebody who makes him very nervous. He always gets a headache when he gets off the phone. Can we go for my scooter now?"

"Of course we can," John answered distractedly. His mind was on the man Drummond answered to.

✿ ✿ ✿

Early the next morning, Wadsworth received a telephone call from a shaken Missus Drummond. She informed the inspector that her husband had called in the middle of the night, demanding to know what was going on with the investigation. When she'd told him that the police had been at the house looking for him, he'd had a fit. He'd actually threatened her. It had taken hours for her to muster the courage to call Wadsworth.

"He didn't sound like the man I know," she said. "I'm afraid of him."

"Where was he calling from?" asked the inspector.

"I have no idea. He wouldn't tell me."

"Missus Drummond," said the policeman, softly, "I want you to listen to me carefully, and do exactly as I say." He could hear the heavy breathing on the other end of the line.

"I want you to leave the house at once, and check into the Crown and Thistle for a few days. You'll feel better there. I'll come over to see you in a little while. I have some other questions for—"

He heard a click, and the line went dead. He slammed down the phone and yelled for Bailey.

"Get out to the minister's house now," he rumbled. "Fetch the woman back here, and on the way, call MacIntyre. Tell him to come here too, because I need to talk to him. He's still in danger. It was him that was supposed to die, not Nesbit—though I can't figure out why."

Bailey hurried to the police car. As he sped away, he reached for the telephone and called the MacIntyres' number. There was no answer.

"Damn," he muttered. He knew the inspector would not be pleased.

✿ ✿ ✿

As Moira was saying her goodbyes in the driveway of Ainsley House, promising to stop by in a few days after she's spent some time with her mother, the phone began ringing inside the house. John tried to ignore it, but after four rings, he couldn't stand it. He raced into the house and picked up the receiver just in time to hear the caller hang up.

✿ ✿ ✿

It was late in the day by the time John and Valerie returned home. They'd escaped the increasingly pervasive gloom of Ainsley right after Moira rode away on her scooter, and had spent the day driving aimlessly through the countryside, enjoying the changing leaves and trying to find some peace. It was nice to have a break, even if it was just for the day.

As they entered the house, the telephone started ringing. Valerie hurried to answer it, listened for a moment, and held the receiver out to her husband.

"It's for you. It's Sergeant Bailey."

John took the phone from her, and when he was done with the conversation, announced that he had to run into Kilbride to see Wadsworth. "I'm not sure what it's about, but the Inspector wants to see me right away. Maybe you should come with me. I don't like leaving you alone."

"I don't think so," she replied. "I'll be fine, and I'm exhausted. I want to have a hot bath. I'll see you when you get back."

"Okay. Just make sure all doors are locked. I'll use my key to get back in." He gave her a warm kiss and left the house.

Valerie locked the door behind him, and went about checking the others before heading upstairs. She wondered what Wadsworth was up to. "I can't wait for this to end," she whispered.

She went into the bathroom, started her bath, lit two candles, placed them on the windowsill, and began to undress.

The water splashing into the tub masked the sound of the front door slowly opening. A tall figure dressed in black stepped inside. He stood in the darkness and listened. Then he dropped the key back into his pocket and ascended the stairs.

In her dressing room, Valerie reached for a robe. At that moment, a form appeared from the shadows behind her. As she began to turn, sensing the presence, a hand was clamped over her face, and she was aware of a strange acrid odor. A second later, she crumbled to the floor.

✿ ✿ ✿

At the police station, an impatient Wadsworth looked up from his desk. "Where the hell have you been?" he barked. "We've been looking for you all day."

"Actually, Inspector, since I'm no longer a suspect, I don't know what business it is of yours where I've been."

"Is that so, Mister MacIntyre?" The policeman rose grandly from behind the desk. "Well we can soon alter that situation if you like. Your fingerprints were found all over the chamber beneath the cemetery. It seems you neglected to mention that you'd been down there. If you'd like me to, I can soon reinstate your status—this time, as a suspect in the death of young Alistair Frazier. Now I'll ask you again: Where the hell have you been?"

John studied the big man's face and decided that it was probably best to not antagonize him any further.

"Well if you must know, Inspector, Valerie and I took a drive up to Fort William. We just felt like getting away from all this for a little while."

"Thank you." The cop sat back down on his chair, which creaked loudly in response. "Now, I have something to discuss with you, and since you decided to keep your visit to the chamber a secret from us, it occurred to me that there may be some other details you've left out."

John was sure the man was going to ask him about Campbell's tomb. *How did he find out?*

"Have a seat there," said Wadsworth. He indicated the wooden chair in front of the desk, "Tell me if there's anything about Drummond you've forgotten to share with me. I had a long conversation with his wife, and she informs me that you and the minister spent a good deal of time in each other's company. She said that sometimes you two disappeared for hours at a time. Anyway, your pal called his wife last night, and now she's very distraught. She said her husband sounded crazy, and she's convinced the killing's not over."

The inspector drew a long breath.

"And just like before, you could be the intended victim, so if there's anything you haven't told me, this might be a good time. We need to find this man, and soon. In the meantime, either Smiley or Sergeant Bailey will be posted outside your house."

A chill slithered up John's spine. He decided to tell Wadsworth everything he knew. Well...almost everything. He spoke quickly, telling the inspector about the strange rituals and the animal sacrifices and his own participation. He went on to describe Drummond's raging xenophobia and his strange hold on the boys, who were prepared do whatever he asked.

"I'm convinced they would kill for him. He's taught them to hate, particularly you English. He despises all of you, and he preaches that you are a plague on Scotland, and his mission is to eradicate all of you from this soil. I know it sounds farfetched, but the man believes it, and he's been creating his own band of brigands to fulfill his ambition. They're very dangerous. These boys have a cause, and Drummond believes there are plenty of radicals in this country who would willingly join him, given the opportunity. You could have another IRA on your hands, if you're not careful."

Wadsworth slowly shook his head.

"I've seen the man at work," John said, leaning in closer. "He's a sick, fanatical bastard, and what makes him dangerous is that there's a speck of truth in his rhetoric. Some of what he says actually makes sense. If Drummond had the resources, I believe he could be a force to be reckoned with."

"Okay," said Wadsworth. "I believe you. Now, I'll need the names of his gang members."

John gave all the names he knew.

"And there's one more thing, Inspector. I'm pretty sure Drummond's not who he claims to be."

Wadsworth frowned. "Go on," he grumbled.

John described his visit to the asylum in Perth. "We think he actually might be Rupert Marni, the boy who butchered his mother in Ainsley House all those years ago. He's returned with a new identity, because there's something in this place that he wants very much."

"Oh yes. We're already looking into the possibility of Marni's return. And thanks for your forthrightness. I was hoping you'd inform us about your visit to Perth."

It was John's turn to frown.

"You're free to go," said Wadsworth, "but for the time being, I suggest you curtail your trips out of the area without first notifying me of your plans. I wouldn't be keeping any more secrets, if I were you. And be very careful, Mister MacIntyre—you and your wife."

John stood up and shook the policeman's hand.

"Keep your eyes open and your doors locked."

"I will," said John.

As he walked to his car, John noticed that the bakery was just closing and hurried over. He purchased a couple of Valerie's favorite muffins and a loaf of bread and was pleased to see that the reception was not quite as chilly as it had been. He returned to his car and headed home.

He parked the car in the garage and entered the house, surprised to find the door unlocked. He called out for Valerie, but there was no response. He could hear the water running upstairs and assumed she didn't hear him. In the living room, he turned on a light and crossed to the bar to pour himself a much-needed drink, then went to sit by the fireplace and was surprised to see that the fire wasn't lit. A warm fire had become a nightly ritual since the evenings had turned chilly.

After a few minutes, John set his glass on the coffee table and headed upstairs. He could still hear the water. Smiling to himself, he tapped on the bathroom door and called her name, but there was no response. He opened the door and was surprised to see that, instead of the shower running, the water was pouring into the tub. For some reason, Valerie had forgotten to put the stopper in the drain, and the water was escaping just as fast as it poured in. Two candles on the windowsill were almost burned down to nothing, and molten wax dripped steadily onto the floor. It wasn't like Valerie to be so careless.

The hair began to rise on the back of John's neck. "Oh God," he whispered. He raced from the room, flew down the stairs, and ran through the house, searching everywhere, but knowing he wouldn't find her. He sprinted to the garage, and a moment later, roared out of the driveway, making for the church.

The sun was gone, and the air was cold and damp by the time John reached St. Agnes Kirk. He ran to the front door and threw it open.

"Drummond," he yelled, "It's me you want. I'm here. Let her go." Except for the sound of his own voice echoing back at him, mocking him, there was silence. He glared back at the towering image of Abraham that watched him from the chancel window. In the fading light, the patriarch looked like Drummond himself.

"Drummond, you bastard," he muttered angrily, as he raced down the aisle. "Where are you?" He climbed the pulpit steps and switched on the reading lamp, but found no sign that they'd been there.

His chest began to tighten around his heart. Suddenly, he knew where they were.

He raced back to his car and drove off like a madman, leaving behind him a great rooster tail of gravel. A few minutes later, he pulled the Jaguar off the road at what was now a familiar spot.

The moor was dark and silent. A raw wind moved through the grass, bending the stalks to its will. MacIntyre barely noticed the biting air as he raced on. He fell to the ground a dozen times, but simply picked himself up and kept running. Dark clouds moved across the face of the moon, transforming the hills from silver to pitch black.

A half mile later, he stumbled again and fell headlong into a large nest of pheasants, flushing at least twenty birds that scattered, screeching, into the night. He lay still, gulping great mouthfuls of air and trying to gather himself. As soon as he could, he clambered back to his feet and continued on.

That's when he saw it, off in the distance: a glimmer of light. He stopped to watch it, got his bearings, and moved again. By the time he arrived at a large outcropping of rock, where the light was very close, he was sweating profusely in spite of the frigid air. He picked his way across the boulders to a place where he looked directly down on Drummond's temple. The light source was a huge fire burning in the center of the circle. He scanned the area but saw no sign of Drummond, or Valerie. He climbed down from the crag and entered the clearing.

As if on cue, a low rumble of thunder broke the silence, and a fork of lightning split the sky. John crossed the circle toward the altar, and as he did, the wind intensified, moaning among the stones like a wounded soul.

He passed the roaring fire, and that's when he saw her. She was laid out on the bloody altar like a sacrificial lamb. She wore only a shredded bathrobe and one slipper. There were no ropes, no bonds, and no sign of life.

Choking back tears, John stared down at his wife, not quite comprehending, not knowing what to do. His mind refused to find reason. He reached out his hand and gingerly stroked her face. She didn't respond.

He closed his eyes, waiting for his mind to engage, and somewhere, far away, a voice whispered his name. His eyes snapped open to find her gazing up at him.

"John," she croaked, "are you all right?"

"Oh God," he murmured. "Oh thank you, God." He reached for her, drew her into his arms, and held her tighter than he ever had. She felt so cold. "Are you hurt?" he asked.

"I don't think so. I don't remember what happened. I feel so tired."

As her trembling started to subside, John became slowly aware of something moving behind him. They were not alone, and he was not surprised.

He gently laid Valerie back down on the stone. She closed her eyes and lay still, recaptured by the drugs she'd been forced to swallow. Angry and ready, John turned to face the damn curse, in whatever form it had chosen to reveal itself. He peered into the darkness but saw nothing, although he had no doubt he was being watched.

He took a few steps forward, then hesitated. He was moving away from the fire into almost complete blackness. He heard a soft squeaking sound, like a screen door swinging on rusty hinges. It was coming from somewhere in front of him. He crept forward.

"Drummond," he called in a loud whisper. "Where the hell are you? I know you're here."

Another bolt of lightning ripped the sky, and in the momentary brilliance, John caught a glimpse of the horror.

"Oh God."

At that moment, the rain began to fall, and within seconds, he was completely drenched, but he barely noticed. He stood staring up into the darkness, his mind in an uproar.

Above him, spinning slowly in the wind like a cloth doll on a clothesline, was the body of Kenneth Drummond. The minister was hanging by a rope from his own vile cross, his dead eyes bulging from their sockets.

Choking, trying not to vomit, John raced back to the altar, hauled his senseless wife to her feet, folded her over his shoulder and fled into the night, desperate to distance him self from the nightmare.

✳ ✳ ✳

The next day, while investigating the scene, the police found Drummond's suicide note safe and dry in a plastic bag under the altar. The minister had prepared for his death well in advance. The typewritten letter, three pages in length, explained everything.

Apparently, the accidental death of Graham Nesbit had been the beginning of the end for Drummond. The Covenanters had proved unreliable, and his dream of a resurrected Scotland had been dashed on the rocks with Graham.

He explained that John was merely a pawn in his quest and expressed confidence that, as a professional, John would appreciate the final bit of drama. He confessed to killing Alistair Frazier and expressed the hope that God would forgive him for both his sins and his failures.

Oddly enough, he made no mention of his alter ego, Rupert Marni, or the terrible iniquities of his past.

✿ ✿ ✿

Miraculously, Valerie had not caught pneumonia, and by the next afternoon, she was feeling better. The drugs had almost departed her system, and a throbbing head was the only remaining evidence. The horror was over. She reminded herself that in a couple of days, they'd be on the plane.

✿ ✿ ✿

Andrew St. Giles pulled back the curtains, and the cold light of autumn seeped in through the grimy windows. Edinburgh had been a dreary place for the last couple of days, and it was good to see the sun so early in the morning. From the cluttered office, he gazed out over the rooftops of the city, considering the possibilities. He'd decided to stay away from his house, just in case someone came looking for Gordon Erskin and ran into Andrew St. Giles instead. Drummond's colossal screw-up had probably ruined everything, but maybe not. St. Giles had always been an optimist, even at the worst of times.

He retreated from the windows and crossed the room to his desk, sat down wearily, and let his thoughts flow. He'd quite enjoyed the trek across the moors watching Drummond stumbling under the weight of the unconscious woman. His pistol had provided all the persuasion he needed. Outwitting the minister had been no real feat. Hauling him up onto the cross had been a hell of a task, but the effect had been well worth the effort. He considered the suicide note a nice touch. It would surely put any lingering suspicions to rest. But there was still much to do.

The shrill ringing of the telephone startled him. It occurred to him that his nerves were a bit on edge. He lifted the receiver and smiled, surprised to hear Valerie's voice. She sounded surprised, too, as if she hadn't expected him to answer.

He listened carefully as she informed him about the grisly discovery of Kenneth Drummond. He began asking questions, but Valerie informed him that at the moment, she didn't have time to answer them. She suggested that he call back later so he could talk to John, who had all the details. Before hanging up, she invited him down to Kilbride for one last celebration before their trip home.

Andrew sat quietly considering Valerie's invitation. He decided to take the MacIntyres up on their offer. Maybe there was still time.

CHAPTER 40

The news about Drummond and Alistair Frazier shook the little community, but at the same time, there was a profound sense of relief. The sky remained gloomy for the MacIntyres' last couple of days in Kilbride. Moody clouds hung over the hills, and a shroud of mist lay across the stillness of the loch.

On Thursday morning, a fresh salmon and a steak pie magically appeared on the doorstep of Ainsley House—peace offerings from the village. Valerie was reminded of how wonderful the place had seemed when they first arrived.

That afternoon, she and John drove into the village. They had one or two things left to do, one of which required a stop at the police station.

The inspector was busy poring over some papers as they entered the little office. "Morning Missus MacIntyre, Mister MacIntyre," he rumbled.

"Morning Inspector," said John, "we're off, the day after tomorrow, so I've come to get my passport."

"Oh, certainly. I can't think of a legitimate reason to keep you here any longer."

Wadsworth smiled, and Valerie felt it was truly sincere. It was actually quite a nice smile.

"Everything's pretty well wrapped up. A couple of questions remain unanswered, but that happens sometimes. Not every case is as neatly wrapped up as one of your Hollywood films, eh, Mister MacIntyre?" He chuckled. "Anyway, the questions are probably of no real consequence, but missing pieces do frustrate me, no matter how trivial they are. I never get used to it."

He reached into his desk drawer, removed a small manila envelope, and handed it to John. Inside, John found their passports.

✿ ✿ ✿

An hour later, Moira hid her scooter behind a tree and crossed the road to Graham Nesbit's house. She was saddened to see the state of the garden, and resolved to do something about it when she'd sorted things out.

At the back door, she removed a key from under one of the flowerpots, unlocked the door, and headed straight for the living room. She removed the photograph of the two young boys from the bookshelf and slipped it into the canvas bag she'd brought with her.

She then rode to the manse, where she found Missus Drummond in the middle of packing up the house. The woman looked as though she'd actually shrunk. The news of her husband's suicide and admissions had left her completely devastated. After a brief exchange, she nodded her head and allowed Moira in. She crossed to an orderly desk and gathered one or two papers. Moira glanced at the papers, pocketed them, offered her thanks, and hurried out.

Next, she rode into the village and stopped at the post office to have a word with Jock Tavish. She showed him the papers she'd gotten from Missus Drummond and waited patiently as he collected a thick book from the shelf behind him.

When she had the information she needed, she crossed the street to the police station and was relieved to find Constable Smiley there by himself. Smiley was so easy. After getting what she needed from him, she headed to the bakery and bought a meat pie. She then climbed back onto her scooter, stuck the pie into her mouth, and raced away. She knew she had a long ride ahead of her, and prayed her little bike would deliver her there and back safely.

☆ ☆ ☆

It was almost dark when she arrived at the house in Edinburgh. There was, however, just enough light for her to see that the gardens were almost as badly kept as those at the Nesbit cottage. The old woman who answered the door was less than forthcoming. She announced that her employer was not at home and refused to offer any further information, but when Moira pulled the pictures out of her pocket and held them up for the woman to see, she became at once cooperative.

The graphic photographs of Drummond hanging from the tree did the trick. The woman readily admitted that the man in the pictures had visited the house on more than one occasion.

Moira held up one last photo. It was an old black and white of two sullen-looking boys standing on a narrow street. Behind them stood a large church whose roof was in the shape of a crown.

"Do you recognize anyone in this photo?" Moira asked, before the woman had a chance to gather her wits.

"Yes," she replied, nodding slowly. "I think I do."

"Is it Erskin?" Moira pressed.

"Yes it's him. It's amazing how little he's changed over the years."

"I must ask you again. Where is he? I assure you, it'll be better for everybody if you tell me."

The old woman hesitated, then sighed in defeat and gave Moira the information.

CHAPTER 41

It was almost eleven o'clock in the morning when Valerie answered the door to find Andrew St. Giles gazing up at her. She noted that he looked tired and a bit drawn, not his usual charming self, but didn't mention it.

"Andrew." She reached out her arms in welcome. "I'm so pleased to see you. Come in, come in. We weren't expecting you so soon."

The attorney halfheartedly returned the hug and entered the house. "Where's John? Is he here?"

"He'll be back any minute. He's at the post office leaving our forwarding address. We're off tomorrow, you know."

"Yes, I know," said Andrew. "I'll miss you both. But hopefully, we'll meet again under less harrowing circumstances."

"I certainly hope so. We're going to miss you too, Andrew."

A half hour later, *Bridie* sliced through the black water and entered Ainsley cove. John cut the engines, allowing the craft to drift in. He grabbed the bow rope and leapt onto the jetty, secured the boat, and hurried to the house, carrying the bag of groceries his wife had requested.

He was surprised to see that Andrew was already there, and greeted the visitor with a big hug. St. Giles visibly recoiled. "I must say, you people do take a bit of getting used to," he grimaced.

Valerie fixed lunch as the men sat on the verandah enjoying the fresh air and the scant warmth of the sun. Although it was officially too early in the day, they were both sipping whiskey, having agreed that they had good reason to celebrate.

A few minutes later, Valerie called them inside, and they sat down to lunch.

"So John," Andrew began, "I hate to be a pest, but I've got to try one last time before you leave here forever. Couldn't we have one shot at finding the tomb? You realize it would be a monumental discovery, a significant archeological find, and it would be a real coup for me—a gilded feather in my academic cap. It's worth a go, don't you think?"

John nodded reluctantly. He didn't hold out much hope, but he did feel indebted to the man.

"Okay, Andrew. After all you've done for us, I'd be glad to give it a shot. I don't know how much help I can be, though. Last time I was there, it was very dark, and I was too busy trying to keep up with Moira to be paying much attention, but I'll try. It'll be a good excuse for one last run in *Bridie* anyway."

John knew there was no chance of success, but felt compelled to go through the motions simply to placate Andrew. Actually finding his way to the tomb, he knew, was out of the question, which was fine with him. He was happy to concur with Moira's request. In the unlikely event of a curse being unleashed, he certainly wanted no part of it.

After lunch, as the men washed the dishes, Valerie descended the stairs wearing a warm sweater and a MacIntosh. She walked into the kitchen carrying a couple of windbreakers.

"It could be a bit chilly out there," she said. "I think you'll probably need these."

"Thank you, Mom." John dutifully donned the jacket.

"You're going with us?" Andrew asked, surprised. "I thought you hated the place. You don't really need to go, if—"

"Oh I do hate the place, Andrew, but I'll be okay. John's not allowed out of my sight until we're on the plane." She spun on her heel and strode from the room.

John shrugged. He could see there would be no arguing with her.

Heading for the living room, Valerie was surprised to find Moira standing in the front hall. She looked both windblown and exhausted. Her eyes looked like she hadn't slept.

"Well good morning, Moira. What are you doing here? Are you okay?"

"Fine. A bit weary, but fine. Actually, I came to tell John and Mister St. Giles that I've changed my mind, and I'm willing to take them to the tomb. I know they're going to try anyway, whatever I do, and they'll be safer with me there. Besides, after what Mister St. Giles has done for John, I feel I owe him."

When they returned to the kitchen and delivered the news, Andrew flushed with excitement, and his lips tightened into a thin line. He nodded his head in eager agreement as he listened to Moira explain that although she was prepared to take them to the chamber, she would not reveal how she opened the walls.

The loch was in medium chop, and *Bridie*'s hull slapped loudly as she skipped across the water. Valerie rose from her seat, slipped her arms around her husband's waist, and hugged him tightly.

A few minutes later, they slowed and pulled into the cove beneath the fortress. Again, the cove smelled bad, and Valerie was sure the ruin was displeased.

Since the little dinghy was only capable of carrying two people at a time, John paddled Valerie ashore before returning to collect Moira and then Andrew. Alone on the beach, Valerie's eyes were drawn to the jagged rocks on the far side of the cove. She tried not to think about Graham lying there dashed to pieces, but her mind refused to obey.

When Moira hopped out of the dingy and called out to her, she flinched.

As soon as both the men were safely ashore, Moira led the way to the secret steps. Fifteen minutes later, they reached the top. They entered the gates, followed Moira across the courtyard, and entered the dimness of the Keep.

Valerie shivered, feeling a sudden chill.

The men switched on their flashlights, and Moira did the same.

With Moira leading the way, they made their way deeper into the fortress until she reached a break in the wall and stepped through. The others followed her into a narrow passageway that angled steeply downward. The only sounds were those of cautious footsteps and heavy breathing. A few minutes later, they arrived in a chamber illuminated by myriad shafts of silver light.

"The Crown Room," Andrew whispered hoarsely. "I'll be damned. This is it."

"Turn your backs," Moira said, and waited until her companions complied. They listened to a dry, grating sound as stone rubbed against stone. When they were allowed to turn back, the wall in front of them stood wide open.

"Incredible," said the barrister. His eyes shone with excitement.

They stepped through the wall and descended a flight of steep steps, trying to keep up with Moira. It wasn't easy.

They found her waiting for them at the door of a small chapel and followed her inside. She crossed the little room and stopped before the altar.

As John waited, it all came rushing back. The last time he was in this place, he was nearly trapped inside. "Oh yes," he murmured, "I remember this."

"Lights!" Moira whispered.

The resulting darkness was even thicker than before. A moment later, the wall was open, and they switched their flashlights back on.

One by one, they stepped through the gap into the chamber.

St. Giles stood transfixed as the light beams danced around the room. As his own light came to rest on the sarcophagus, the wall closed silently behind them.

"Incredible. It's a bloody Pharaoh's tomb. Where did they learn this?" He crossed to the nearest bench and started opening chests. Every one was stuffed with treasure. As the others watched in amazement, the usually dignified barrister dashed from table to table, throwing open the heavy wooden lids, thrusting his hands inside and washing them in gems. Suddenly, John experienced déjà vu so vivid that he shuddered, remembering that he'd witnessed the scene before.

Feeling strangely unnerved, John made an effort to distract the attorney. "So, what will they do with all this, Andrew? It's a bloody fortune."

As if he'd just remembered he was not alone, St. Giles turned to face his companions, wearing a strange dispassionate expression, one that none of them had seen before.

"First things first, John," said the barrister. "In case you didn't notice, we're all trapped in here. The wall closed behind us. A very clever trap, I must say. Thank God you know the way out, my dear Moira."

He chuckled and faced the MacIntyres. "Unfortunately, you two won't be coming with us. However, I must say, I am truly grateful for all the help you've provided." His darting eyes came to rest on Valerie, and something about his expression caused her to shrink back.

"What are you talking about, Andrew?" John asked. "Are you trying to be funny?"

He put his arm around his wife and drew her closer.

Moira stood perfectly still, registering no surprise whatsoever.

"I like you, Valerie," Andrew continued. "As a matter of fact, I like you very much. But you must understand that I have no other choice. This has been my greatest wish...my life's work. I'm inside Campbell's tomb, for Christ's sake! It's a miracle. And to think Drummond almost ruined it."

He frowned, shaking his head, and a flash of anger crossed his face.

John released Valerie from his grasp and pulled her behind him. "It's you! You're the man Drummond was so afraid of. You're the one he answered to."

"Oh, he answered to me, alright—the stupid bastard."

Just out of his peripheral vision, Moira shrank deeper into the shadows.

"It was no suicide. You killed him, didn't you?"

"Congratulations, John," Andrew said, smirking. "It certainly took you long enough. Drummond would never commit suicide. He didn't have the stomach for it."

John knew he had to act. Rational thought had given way to base instinct, and he knew the time was now. As he sprang forward, St. Giles took a step back, plunged his hand into his pocket, and removed a small shiny object. John recognized immediately that it was a pistol and that it was pointed straight at his face.

"Oh no, Andrew. Oh please don't," Valerie implored, seemingly overcome by the events. She grabbed for the nearest table in an effort to prevent herself from falling. Unnoticed in the shadows behind Andrew, Moira continued to search for something to use as a weapon

"Why, Andrew?" John asked. "You're willing to kill us for this? For money?"

St. Giles eyed the riches that surrounded him. "Oh, yes. I am indeed."

"I must admit, you had us fooled," said John, as he inched closer to the lawyer.

Before he'd managed to close the distance, Andrew calmly raised his arm and aimed the pistol at Valerie.

"Don't be foolish, John," he said wearily. "You've been pretty lucky so far, but I wouldn't press it, if I were you. She can be the first to go if you like. It makes no difference to me. Hell, it's probably more pleasant than suffocation anyway. And Moira, you nitwit, come on out here where I can see you."

"Andrew," Valerie whispered, her voice trembling, "please, explain this to me. This can't be the man who's been through hell with us over these past weeks. What's happened to you?"

He watched Moira appear from the shadows empty handed and smiled. "Dear Valerie, how foolish you were. How easy to convince. But then again, it's always so simple to win over a desperate soul. You were in such need that day you came to the office in Edinburgh, you were willing to believe anything."

"But how did you find us? How did you know I'd find you?" she asked.

"Oh, that part was simple. You told Wadsworth who you were meeting with in Edinburgh. Smiley intercepted the information and passed it on to Drummond. Todd Lyons, the man you were meeting, is a longtime associate of my uncle. In our business, friends are happy to exchange favors, but that's quite another story. You realize, of course, that dotty old fool wasn't really my uncle. He did, however, accept my impeccable credentials and allowed me to join his little firm. That part was essential. You see, Euclid was Mummy's solicitor. He administered the trust, which I needed access to, and his one-man firm provided the perfect situation for working out the details of my eh…design. Now, why don't you all sit down…there, where I can see you, and I'll try to answer some of your questions before you die. Seems only fair, after all you've given me."

The MacIntyres and Moira sat down on the cold floor as St. Giles climbed onto the stone platform that supported the sarcophagus and calmly perused his captives as if they were nothing more than merchandise.

"Why do you have to kill us, Andrew?" asked John. "You already have what you want. We're leaving the country tomorrow, and we have no reason to tell anyone. I'm sure Moira will remain quiet. She doesn't want to draw any more attention to this place."

"Ah, but that's just it, you see. If you and Valerie left the country, I'd miss you terribly. On the other hand, if you're safely locked away here surrounded by all the wealth you could ever ask for, I'd be able to visit anytime I wanted to. No one else will come to visit you—I'm sure of that."

"So Rupert, can I ask you something?" Moira's voice was strangely calm.

The lawyer's eyes flashed angrily as he turned his attention to the girl.

"How does it feel to finally be inside the tomb?" she taunted. "Is it everything you expected?"

"Damn you. What did you call me? Don't you ever call me that. No one can call me that. Not ever. Rupert Marni is dead. He died in a terrible fire."

"My God," John and Valerie gasped in unison.

"But that is, in fact, who you are," Moira continued evenly. "Why don't you admit it? We certainly can't give you away, can we?"

The barrister took a long, slow breath. "No one ever came to visit me, you know. Not once in twenty years. The other guests had visitors, and I hated them for it. For a long time, I wondered why my mother didn't come. Then I remembered what had happened to her. It was a terrible shame. She was a very beautiful woman, you know. She was an actress; like you, Valerie."

He regarded Valerie with an expression that was almost benign and seemed to lose his train of thought.

"Please, Andrew." Valerie spoke softly, intimately. She was completely composed. "Why did Graham have to die? Please tell me. I need to know."

John marveled. Before his eyes, she'd become Valerie Todd, the actress. He saw Andrew respond to her, weigh the request, and make the decision to go along.

"Actually, he was never meant to die. But everything went wrong, don't you see? It was a comedy of errors, actually. I liked Graham Nesbit...very much. We've been pals since we were boys, you know. He's the one who introduced me to the power of the Keep in the first place. Oh yes. The power made me do some terrible things, and it made me enjoy doing them."

He leered at Moira.

She looked away.

St. Giles giggled and wiped the resultant spittle from his chin. He returned his attention to Valerie and resumed his monologue. "When Graham was killed, I thought the whole plan was ruined. I thought he was the only one who knew how to access the tomb. Then it occurred to me: If I could somehow arrange to become your counsel, I could be close by without arousing suspicion, and I would have an opportunity to search Graham's house. I knew the secret had to be hidden there somewhere."

He shrugged. "Then, out of the blue, Moira handed me the key. It never occurred to me that she knew until she brought you here, John. I couldn't believe the luck. The fates were with me once again, wouldn't you agree?"

He sat down on the step and began to spin the gun on the floor between his legs. "Well, I'm afraid it's getting to be that time," he sighed. "How would you like to play a little game of spin the pistol? Let's see who it points to first."

"There's just one more thing, Andrew," John said, desperate to keep him talking. "Your theatrics were so impressive. I have to know. Where did Drummond fit in all this?"

"Drummond was an idiot, but he was just the fool I needed—another Godsend, if you will." Obviously pleased with himself, Andrew's eyes glistened, and his face curled into a maniacal grin. "Shortly after I was released from the eh…hospital, I came down here for a look around. I went to visit the church, which was very gratifying. It gave me an opportunity to place flowers on my dear mother's grave. Did you know Mummy was buried there? Anyway, that's when I first met Drummond. I rhapsodized about his stupid little sanctuary and even made a donation to the preservation fund. It proved a worthwhile investment. The man turned out to be a veritable font of information.

"I learned from him that Graham was still in the village, still doing his silly archeological digs, which was most encouraging. So, I nurtured Drummond's friendship. Occasionally, he came to visit me in Edinburgh, and I must say he enjoyed the respite from the constant scrutiny of the village. We'd drink and talk, sometimes for hours. I was always very interested in what was going on in Kilbride, and he was intrigued by my interest in archeology. You see, he was a bit of a buff himself." St. Giles took a deep breath. "Over time, I came to learn just how demented the man was. He was a bloody fanatic, and I quickly realized the potential. I told him what I knew about the Campbell treasure and suggested it could be the answer to his prayers—that it would finance his plot to save Scotland. He ate it up. As I said, the man was an idiot."

He lowered his voice to almost a whisper. "For purposes of insurance, I introduced him to an Edinburgh he'd never seen. I took him places and showed him things, and I must say, for a man of the cloth, he was not good with temptation."

Suddenly Andrew's mood changed. He grabbed the gun, rose to his feet and began to pace. All the time, he kept the light trained on the MacIntyres. "It was all going so well. His little troop became my eyes and ears, so I knew every move Nesbit made. I was convinced that one day he'd come back to this place, and we'd be watching. I was willing to wait. But as the years passed, I became more and more impatient. Then came the inspiration. That's where you nice people come in.

"It occurred to me that maybe if unspeakable things started happening again, if I could rekindle the curse, Graham would be forced to open the chamber. Drummond told me that Graham had been inside before, with his father, right after the last eh...tragedy. You know, when my mother died. They're a damn superstitious lot, these Nesbits, and there's a ritual they're required to perform if the curse appears."

"Oh, it's more than superstition." John said. "There is a powerful force in this place, a force strong enough to create or destroy whatever it wants to. It's too bad you'll never get to experience it, though."

Andrew's interest was piqued. "What are you talking about?" he said. "Look around. There's more wealth here than any man could ever want. That's enough power."

"Oh, but there's so much more. What you see here isn't the half of it. There's more here than mere wealth. The power of the Campbells is here as well." He indicated the coffin. "You see, Campbell had himself entombed with the Scottish crown jewels. He still wears the ancient crown of the high kings. It's these sacred relics that hold the power; however, they must never be removed from here."

"Show me," Andrew hissed.

"I can't show you. I don't know how to open the coffin. Only Graham knew."

As he studied John's face, he turned the gun on Valerie. "Is that so? Now, why do I find that so difficult to believe?"

Without looking, he fired. The sound was deafening. The bullet ricocheted, screaming, around the vault, missing Valerie by inches.

"Next time, she might not be so lucky," Andrew said. "Now open the bloody thing."

John walked slowly to the sarcophagus and climbed onto the stone step.

"No, John—you can't." Moira scrambled to her feet, frantic. "You'll release the curse. It'll have us all."

"There's no choice," John said. "Don't be such a child. We're all going to die, anyway, so he might as well have the damn things."

Moira started to cry. "But, I promised. I swore it would never be opened. I should never have told you." She glared at St. Giles. "It's a terrible thing you're doing here, Rupert. It's much worse than anything you've done before. If you release the curse, the vale will be destroyed."

He turned the gun back to Valerie. "Do it, John!" he said thickly. "Or watch her die."

John took hold of the black rose and tried to turn it, but it wouldn't budge. As St. Giles' impatience mounted and his trembling finger tightened on the trigger, John strained against the ancient stone.

"John, please don't," said Moira. She was sobbing and wringing her hands.

"I can't," he said, "the thing won't move." His face reddened from the exertion.

"Here, let me try." St. Giles's patience had run out. Pointing the gun into John's face, he climbed up on the step and waved him away. He grasped the rose firmly and twisted.

Amazingly, the stone carving turned easily in his hand, and he whooped in triumph as the coffin's lid shuddered and began to move. He was so intent on what was happening, he didn't notice the look of satisfaction on John's face.

"Just like Excalibur," Andrew giggled.

John stepped down from the platform, and went to hold his wife. Moira covered her eyes

The coffin's heavy lid slid silently, as if on rails, and as the rift widened, Andrew's eyes did the same. Inside, he could see the faint glint of metal, and, impatient to reach for his crown, he leaned in to have a closer look.

Like a cracking whip, something long and black exploded from the darkness. The first spike caught him in the left eye, popping the orb like a ripe pustule. A second spike found his gaping mouth, and drove straight through the back of his head, while a third tore open his throat.

Valerie screamed and buried her face in John's chest. Moira pulled her hands from her face and watched impassively as a stream of blood drained from Andrew's body and spread steaming across the stone floor. The only sound was the strange gurgling noise coming from his throat, as if he was trying to finish his story.

But his story was over.

The cleverly crafted steel antlers had lain in wait for many years, and had performed their task flawlessly. Campbell would have been pleased.

CHAPTER 42

"So, how did you know he was Rupert Marni?" Valerie asked when they arrived back at the cove. "And when did you know?"

Until then, not a word had been spoken. The shock of what they'd witnessed had rendered them all speechless.

"Actually, I didn't know for certain until I called him by his real name, although I was fairly sure by the time we reached the first chamber. Do you remember, he called it the Crown Room? Well, only Graham and I called it that, and I knew I'd never told him."

"But obviously you had some idea before that," said Valerie.

"Oh aye, I had a pretty good inkling, but I wasn't completely sure. That's why I agreed to lead him to the tomb. I was praying he'd give himself away. You see, I've been waiting for him to show up for years. Graham told me all about the murders. He was convinced that Marni would return here someday. He was constantly on the lookout, and so was I. I thought at first that Drummond might be Marni. That's one of the reasons I was so afraid of him. I even considered that it might be you, John, but I ruled you out because of your age."

"Well thanks," John said, "I think."

As *Bridie* floated slowly toward Ainsley House, Moira told them the rest.

"I knew when Drummond died that something wasn't right. I didn't think he was capable of suicide, and there were some pieces missing. I remembered the man Drummond spoke to on the telephone all the time, the man he was so afraid of. I managed to get the phone bills from Missus Drummond, and had old Jock trace the number to a house in Edinburgh."

Valerie smiled, impressed with Moira's ingenuity.

"I also remembered that Graham kept an old photo of him and Marni that had been taken in Edinburgh when they were boys. I'd looked at it many times. It was a strange, moody kind of picture. Actually, I never understood why Graham kept it, but he said he needed to be reminded. He wouldn't say any more. Anyway, in the photo, the boys are standing in front of a very unusual old church. That's what started me thinking. It's the most famous church in all of Scotland, and the coincidence was just too powerful. You see, the church is St. Giles Cathedral."

"Unbelievable," John murmured.

"So I took the photo, along with a couple of pictures of Drummond hanging from the cross, that I'd coaxed from Smiley, and went to the address in Edinburgh. The owner of the house wasn't there, but an old woman I spoke with confirmed my suspicions. She recognized the boy with Graham in the photo. By the way, it was the house where you picked up the keys for Ainsley, John. Gordon Erskin and Andrew St. Giles are, or were, the same man."

"Why didn't we figure that out ourselves, John?" Valerie asked.

After hauling *Bridie* into the boathouse, John followed the women to the house and found them in the living room.

"So John," Moira said as John settled on the couch beside his wife, "you've got some explaining to do, yourself. How did you know that the coffin was a Campbell trap? Even I didn't know. Graham didn't either."

"You're right. I knew what was waiting for anybody who opened the thing, but how I knew, is something you wouldn't believe. You see, I'd seen it happen before. All I can say is, it was a revelation, a gift sent to me from a place I've never been. For a while, I thought I was possessed by a man named Ninian Lasker, but it couldn't have been him. I watched him die trying to open the coffin."

"What are you talking about? And who the devil is Ninian Lasker?" Valerie demanded.

"He's a guy in my book—a really bad guy who I thought was trying to take me over, but whoever's been writing through me wanted to save us, not kill us. Maybe it's Eileen MacLeod, telling her own story. I know this is nuts, but it's like I was commissioned to write the book."

"So, whoever it is told you the coffin contained the Crown Jewels?"

"No, I just made that up. I remembered St. Giles telling the story about King Charles's treasure being stolen by the Campbells, and I thought he might buy the idea that the jewels were in there."

"Good work, John," said Valerie. "You should have been an actor."

"I don't think so," he replied, "One drama queen is quite enough for any family."

She hit him.

"Ouch," he yelped, feigning real pain. "I'm gonna report this. I suppose it's time I talked to Wadsworth, anyway. He's gonna love this story."

"You can't do that, John," said Moira, her voice filled with urgency. "We can't call Wadsworth. Don't you see? What happened in the tomb has got to remain our secret. Remember, if any item is removed from the vault, the curse will be released along with it. This valley will be destroyed."

John studied the girl's face for a long beat. "But there is no curse. As we know, the whole thing's a myth."

"I'm afraid she's right, John," Valerie said. "The secret has to remain with us. Anything else can only bring misery to this place."

John appeared confused

"There's nothing to be gained by telling Wadsworth," she continued. "The killers are dead. Justice has been done. Besides, the police have already wrapped up their investigation, and they're satisfied. There's no reason to tell them anything about this. What they don't know won't hurt them."

"So, we're going to simply walk away from a king's ransom? That hardly seems smart."

Moira searched his eyes. "Do you really think the risk is worth it, John? You know what would happen if the tomb was opened and the treasure removed. It would be a curse on this place; the vale would never be the same. Besides, don't you have more than enough gifts in this life already? How much does a person need?"

John felt his cheeks flush. "Okay, you're right," he said. "So, I was fantasizing. I agree, this is for the best. Rupert Marni will simply have disappeared from the face of the earth. He'll never be found, and it couldn't be a more fitting grave."

Valerie put her arm around Moira's shoulder and reached for her husband's hand. "So, we have a pact, the three of us," she said softly, "our own covenant. It's one we must swear to keep for the rest of our lives. The secret must remain with us."

"I swear," said John.

"I swear," said Valerie.

"I swear," whispered Moira.

✡ ✡ ✡

The next morning, as Valerie gathered things to pack, she stopped what she was doing and gazed at the *Cygnet* standing so proudly in the corner of the room. She knew the beautiful craft would be well taken care of by Moira, but she would miss it. She couldn't understand why she didn't feel more elation. Instead, she felt an unexpected melancholy, a real sadness about leaving. "It makes no sense," she murmured, "I've been praying for this day."

John finished wiping down *Bridie*, making sure he left her just as they'd found her. He felt a bit glum as he pulled the old tarpaulin over the vessel, unable to explain the emotion. He closed the boatshed doors, locked them, and trudged slowly back toward the house.

He climbed the stairs and crossed the bedroom, sidestepping the piles of folded clothes. He found Valerie in the bathroom, sitting on the edge of the tub. She looked up as he entered the room and tried to smile, but without much success. John sat down beside her and put his arm around her waist.

"I've been feeling it too," he said, knowingly. "I'm not sure I can explain it. Must be the old trench syndrome."

Valerie waited.

"You know, like soldiers returning from the war. They're supposed to be happy, but they find it hard to adjust. They miss the intensity. Oh I don't know, but for some stupid reason, I'm going to miss this place."

"Me too, and I can't understand why. It's been the worst experience of my life."

John nodded. "I agree."

"Tell me something, John. Why us? Why were we chosen?"

"Well, I don't think we were chosen specifically. It was just the luck of the draw. It could have been anybody, as long as they had no knowledge of the place's history. Andrew—or should I say Rupert—needed help to resurrect the curse, and we were it."

He gripped his wife tighter.

"I don't know how to even begin to tell you, Val," he said softly. "I know I placed you in terrible danger, and I'm so sorry for all the pain I caused you. I can't tell you how wretched I feel."

Eventually, their eyes met in the mirror. Valerie laid her head on her husband's shoulder, and he reached to stroke her hair.

CHAPTER 43

———••·•——

The Crown and Thistle was in a strange mood. It was the MacIntyres' last night, and the entire village, it seemed, had gathered to enjoy a rousing send-off. The place was decorated with bright streamers and colorful balloons, but still it felt more like a wake.

Valerie and John were seated at a table with Moira and one or two others. The tabletop was laden with drinks, the farewell offerings of well-wishers. A few minutes later, Wadsworth entered the room with Bailey in tow. He spotted the MacIntyres at once, approached the table, and asked if he might join them. Valerie nodded politely and the inspector settled cautiously onto the chair beside her.

"Inspector Wadsworth!" John said, "I'm surprised to see you here. I thought you had things all wrapped up."

"Well, there were a couple of loose ends I wasn't happy about, but I didn't get anywhere. I suppose I'll just have to live with it, but as I told you, loose ends distress me terribly."

He saw Moira steal a glance at Valerie.

"I know you're off tomorrow," he continued, "but before you leave, I want to express how sorry I am for all the anxiety you were caused. I hope that you survive the experience none the worse for the wear. You might even find a use for all this one day. Might make a hell of a film, don't you think?" His broad face broke into a grin.

"I don't know, Inspector. Too many loose ends...I don't know if the audience would buy it."

The inspector extended his meaty hand. John took it and shook it warmly.

As the evening progressed, the atmosphere became more and more somber. Finally someone called for Moira MacLeod, and the crowd heartily agreed. She made her way to the stage.

The Bell of Argyll sang a couple of favorites and then played one or two new songs.

After two encores, Moira set her guitar aside and looked toward the MacIntyres.

"You know," she said, "before this evening ends and dear friends leave this place to journey near or far, there's someone I've got to thank, before they speed away across the sea in their bonny boat. I'd like to sing one last song for that person, someone who's showed me the true meaning of the word love."

Moira stepped from the stage and walked slowly toward the MacIntyre's table. Valerie hid behind her hand. She didn't know if she could stand to watch the girl sing to John again. The very thought transported her back to the night when it all began.

She was aware of a warm hand being placed on her arm, and parted her fingers to see Moira kneeling on the floor in front of her. The girl began to sing as tears ran down her cheeks:

Say ye're no awa tae bide awa,
Say ye're no awa tae leave us,
Oh ye're no awa tae bide awa,
Ye'll aye come back tae see us.

✿ ✿ ✿

At London's Heathrow Airport, the MacIntyres boarded American Airlines Flight Two, bound for California and home. After takeoff, they reclined their oversized leather chairs and ordered cocktails and a movie. They always watched the same movie. It had become a part of the sharing thing that, over the years, had given them so much in common, so much to talk about.

There was still so much to talk about.

About an hour into the film, a romantic comedy that lacked conviction, John looked across at his wife and smiled to see her fast asleep.

"Finally, she's letting me out of her sight," he muttered.

He stopped the movie, folded the video screen into his armrest, leaned back, stretched his legs, and closed his eyes. He slept.

He dreamed of a man with nutmeg skin, sitting in lotus position on a high mountain, bathed in the golden light of the setting sun. Although his lips moved, the man made no sound.

Epilogue

The lone traveler arrived at the gates of Campbell Keep in late autumn. A biting wind whipped at the coarse woolen robe that covered his long frame from neck to foot. The dusty garment was girded by a woven leather belt from which hung a slender curved scabbard and three matched daggers. On his back, he carried a longbow and a doeskin quiver bristling with arrows. The bow was easily six feet long.

Campbell's sentries were wary of the stranger. He had long black hair and the darkest skin they'd ever seen, and although he spoke in an odd tongue, somehow the guards understood him perfectly.

"My name is Figlio Nuvola." He removed the strange implement from his back. "I've journeyed far to find your chieftain."

The guards immediately raised their swords, prepared to defend their castle and themselves. The man chuckled softly and held the bow out for them to see.

"I've got something to show him that I think he might be very interested in seeing." He smiled gently, offering no threat.

At that moment, a flight of pigeons swooped down from the battlements speeding toward the nearby forest. Instantly, the dark-skinned man slipped an arrow from his quiver, notched it in place, and drew back the bowstring. He sighted for a split second and fired. The missile fled from the bow and plucked one of the fleeing birds from out of the sky. Moments later a second bird had fallen, then a third.

The guardsmen were dumbstruck. The smaller of them spun on his heel and raced away.

An hour later, Figlio Nuvola was comfortably seated at the huge wooden table in the great hall of the castle, surrounded by Campbells. The warriors were fascinated by both the man and his exotic weapons.

He slid his scimitar from its scabbard, plucked a single strand of hair from his head, and neatly severed it before their disbelieving eyes.

"And I can assure you," he said, "It's equally effective on English throats."

The Campbells laughed uproariously.

The traveler patiently answered the barrage of questions, explaining that he had come from far away. He described a land of shifting sands, where warriors with skin as dark as chestnuts rode huge hump-backed horses with feet the size of chamber pots, creatures that could run like the wind for days on end, without ever needing water.

The Scots listened enthralled as the stranger went on to describe places and peoples, the likes of which they couldn't even imagine.

A few minutes later, William of Alsh appeared, and a couple of men moved aside, allowing Alsh to prop himself on the edge of the table, but the stranger didn't acknowledge the newest arrival. He merely continued with the stories.

That night, Figlio Nuvola was the guest of honor at a great feast prepared for him. Lord Campbell had been intrigued by what he'd heard from Alsh and pleased to have some diversion from the gloom that had pervaded the fortress in the many months since the death of Lady Eileen.

The Earl of Argyll had come to rue his impetuousness. He regretted the decision that had brought about the death of the only woman he had ever really enjoyed.

It was nearing the time of the clan gathering again, and Argyll had busied himself with the preparations for the event and the training of his warriors. This year he was determined that the Campbells would taste absolute victory. He'd ensured maximum effort from his men by threatening to banish any warrior who failed.

Campbell was very much enjoying the evening. It hadn't taken the cagey old chieftain long to realize that the newcomer might be of great service to him.

He could help ensure the Campbells' reign as undisputed champions among the clans. And beyond the Highland Games, a soldier like him, training warriors and instructing them in the manufacture of the new weapons, could assure the clan's supremacy for years to come. A display of total invincibility was just what the Earl of Argyll needed in these restless times.

"So what is the purpose o' yer visit to our fair country?" asked Campbell, as he heaped food onto his plate.

"I'm a man of all the world, sire," Nuvola replied. "I've been a mercenary soldier in Europe and the East for many years, and I've come here to offer to you my services and my knowledge. I've been told that you are a man of both great wealth and boundless ambition. It's a combination that a humble tradesman like myself finds hard to resist." He chuckled to himself. "But, if you have no use for my talents," he continued, "because I assure you the price is high, I'll gladly go on my way. I'm sure there are others in this land who will see the value in what I have to offer."

The stranger quietly regarded his host. "If you should think to detain me here," he went on, as if reading Campbell's thoughts, "or to do me harm, I can promise you that after I kill you, twenty of your best will die before I leave this place."

Campbell snorted like a stuck boar and glowered at his visitor, shocked by the effrontery. It had been a long time since anyone had spoken to him in such a manner.

The visitor turned his attention to the food in front of him and calmly reached beneath his robe and emerged with a strange three-pronged instrument. He deftly filled the thing with food and inserted it into his mouth. Campbell stared for a moment and began to smile. In a minute, he was laughing heartily. It was the first time he'd ever seen such a thing. It made his eating knife and greasy fingers seem crude by comparison. The other guests marveled as the foreigner demonstrated the marvelous efficiency of the fork.

Nuvola grinned and reached under his robe again. He removed another of the strange implements and, with a great flourish, extended it toward the chief. William of Alsh, perceiving a threat, leapt immediately from his place, drawing his sword as he rose. Instantly the foreigner was on his feet, balanced as a cat, scimitar in hand.

In the blink of an eye, Alsh's heavy broadsword was flying through the air, and the tip of the scimitar was at his throat.

The stranger smiled benignly, re-sheathed his weapon, and sat down. The Earl of Argyll roared with laughter, as Alsh's face grew crimson as blood.

"Sit ye down, William," Argyll chuckled. "The man means us no harm."

Alsh begrudgingly moved to retrieve his sword and resumed his place beside his chieftain.

"The fork is but one of many gifts I've brought for you, sire," said the visitor. "When you've seen the wonder of them all, I'm sure you'll appreciate the value of the services I can offer you, and understand what a bargain they are."

The dark man proceeded to thoroughly enjoy the feast.

By the end of the meal, Campbell was totally inebriated. The stranger had supped very little wine, but seemed to be enjoying himself immensely.

"I'd like to see your bow at work," slurred the Earl. "I've heard it's a thing of beauty."

Nuvola merely nodded his head.

"I'd like to see it now," said Campbell.

The visitor shrugged his agreement.

Argyll beckoned to a servant, who hurried over to the table, listened to the command from his master, and rushed from the room. As they waited, Campbell continued to engage the stranger in conversation. Nuvola patiently answered each question, happy to indulge his newest patron.

"So you're more than a warrior, I take it. You're a well-traveled and learned man. Are you a teacher? What would you call yourself?"

The visitor thought for a moment. "I am many things, my Lord, but primarily, I am a scribe. God has given me a very special gift. I have the ability to read and write in the dialects of all the places I've traveled. I recount stories I've heard, and share the knowledge given me by the world's wisest men. That is my trade."

A few minutes later the servant returned, carrying the longbow and quiver at arm's length. He placed them gingerly on the table in front of Campbell and hurriedly withdrew. Nuvola reached for his weapon, effortlessly bent the supple wood and notched the bowstring, explaining to his host how it worked.

"Shoot something, damn ye," roared Argyll. "Ye can tell me how the thing works in the mornin'."

"Who would you like me to shoot," He glanced in Alsh's direction. Campbell again roared with laughter.

"Shoot old Groton there. He's been crippled ever since the last hunt, he's no good to me anymore."

Nuvola looked around the hall searching for the person Campbell was referring to.

"There in the far corner." The Earl pointed to a sorry-looking deer-hound curled up against the wall, exiled from the other dogs.

Without a moment's hesitation, the robed man stood and raised his weapon. Groton opened his eyes and looked right into those of Nuvola. The man released the arrow, which entered the skull right behind the dog's eye, and the animal's body sagged. The poor creature faded without a whimper, completely unaware that death had come.

Friday afternoon, the clans started arriving. Hundreds crossed the hills, descending from every direction until the vale was filled with the sounds of merriment and the skirl of the pipes. The MacLeods and the Douglases, however, were conspicuously absent. Campbell had decreed that no member of either clan would be allowed to live, should they be found anywhere close to the Shire of Argyll.

Campbell's strong men easily won the caber toss and the hammer throw. After a few days of instruction from Nuvola about the principles of leverage, the men were throwing further than anyone thought possible. Argyll was very pleased.

When it came to the sword fighting, Figlio Novula participated himself. The crowds marveled as the tall, slim man in the robe deftly dispatched the best of their warriors with the grace of his body and the speed of his weapon.

In the dirk events, no man could match his skill. The perfect balance of his daggers allowed them to fly to their targets as true as light.

All who saw the demonstration were impressed by the instruments of death, so lethal in the sure hands of the foreigner. They were, however, completely astounded by the performance of the man's longbow. Nuvola could fire five of his arrows in the time it took a crossbowman to dispatch one bolt.

The crowd cheered as, time after time, he sighted on birds flying overhead and dropped them unerringly from the sky. They didn't yet comprehend the potential for domination that the stranger had brought to Argyll. At the end of the day, the Campbells were the undisputed champions. They had prevailed in every contest.

In the days that followed, the clans returned to their homes, and Campbell spent almost all of his time in the company of Nuvola, being educated about the world outside of Scotland. He listened attentively, hour after hour, as Nuvola told of his experiences in the armies of France and Spain and in the deserts of North Africa, where he'd learned from the Bedouins the secrets of survival in the most hostile of lands, and where he'd been introduced to the subtleties of torture and the art of slow death.

Each day, Campbell received instruction in the use of the scimitar and the longbow, until he became quite skilled. Nuvola then began schooling the warriors and teaching them how to manufacture the new weapons.

William of Alsh remained distant and suspicious as his position at Campbell's right hand was steadily usurped. He continued to seethe as Campbell and Nuvola became increasingly inseparable, and began to consider his options. He realized the stranger would be hard to get rid of.

A week later, one of Argyll's huntsmen was ushered into the great hall, where Nuvola was teaching Campbell the rudiments of chess, using pieces he'd fashioned from stone. The hunter informed the chief of an enormous stag that had been sighted in the hills above Cruach Mohr. The animal had only been spotted once or twice, but the man assured his chief that it was, by far, the finest ever seen. Campbell was thrilled at the prospect and began immediately to make preparations for a hunt.

The weather was bleak on the morning Campbell and his band rode out from the Keep, but the Earl eagerly led the way through Glen Lonan and up into the misty hills, carrying on his back the new longbow that Nuvola himself had fashioned for him.

Three hours later, they entered the region where the stag had been seen and stopped to rest. Alsh, instead of accompanying the chief as was usually his place, was assigned to the lurchers with Donald of Falkirk. Sutherland was reassigned to manage the hounds with Colin of Troon. This was the lowliest assignment in the hunt; the men worked as beaters, running behind the deerhounds.

None of Argyll's lieutenants was pleased with the new arrangements, and Alsh did little to conceal his ire as he rode away from the small column with the lurchers following obediently along. He and Falkirk would search out a likely crag and wait there for the baying of the deerhounds, indicating that the stag was on the move.

Argyll and Nuvola remounted and rode on for another hour to the narrow end of the valley and secured their horses in a thick stand of trees. They stretched out on the ground and waited.

Campbell passed the time listening as Nuvola told him a wondrous tale of alchemists in Florence who had apparently discovered how to turn base metals into gold. This was a subject that very much interested the chief.

"But even more amazing, my Lord Campbell, are the secrets revealed to me by the holy men of the Hindu Kush. From them, I learned that the mind is not limited by the strictures we mortals have imposed. Oh no, in truth, our thoughts can travel through time and space and, like our souls, can live

forever. It is by far the most valuable piece of wisdom I acquired during my travels."

At this suggestion, Campbell's patience wore out. He lay back in the grass, closed his eyes, and chuckled at the sheer stupidity of such a notion.

Just then, the baying of the hounds far in the distance reached their ears. They rose from the sweet grass and moved into the cover of the trees to await the moment. They didn't have to wait long.

They watched as one of the lurchers crested a rocky crag, appearing for brief moments between the patches of fog, and began to move swiftly toward the valley. The men searched the hills for any sign of their prey but were unable to spot it. They could occasionally see the dog moving closer, but still they could not pick out the stag.

Suddenly, far above them, the curtain of mist parted and their quarry stepped through. The enormous stag stood, quiet as an apparition, surveying the scene. Campbell trembled with excitement.

The animal began to move, slowly, cautiously, sniffing the air as it drew nearer to the place where the men lay in hiding. It was as if it knew they were waiting. From its great size and the battle scars on its deep chest, it was apparent that the beast had survived many contests, and Argyll was gratified to know that Nuvola was behind him.

The creature sniffed the air again and continued to move steadily forward. Campbell readied his bow, waiting for the perfect moment.

When the stag was no more than thirty yards out, it stopped and raised its massive head to watch the dog closing quickly from the hillside, but instead of fleeing toward the men as expected, the stag stood its ground and allowed the lurcher to close the distance between them. The dog entered the glen at full speed and launched himself at the stag's throat. At the last moment, the animal simply dropped its head. It caught the unfortunate dog on its antlers and tossed it high into the air. The lurcher landed hard and lay twitching, moaning softly, its back broken.

The stag turned back in time to see the second dog racing in from the other direction. As the lurcher hurtled itself into the air, the stag neatly side stepped the charge, turned its head, and raked the dog's belly as it flew past, slicing it wide open, spilling its steaming guts onto the ground. The dog lay still, its life slowly seeping into the grass.

The stag returned his attention to the stand of trees and scented again. He snorted angrily, dropped his antlers, and began to advance.

Campbell, despite his impatience, managed to wait until the animal was no more than fifty feet away. Trembling, he rose from his hiding place and raised his weapon. The creature stopped in his tracks, lifted his head, and stared contemptuously at the man before him. Campbell's heart was in his throat, his palms wet with excitement.

Slowly, he pulled back his bowstring, sighted down the long, perfect shaft of the arrow, and prepared to fire.

Suddenly, the bow snapped in two, and the arrow fell useless at Campbell's feet. Fear rose thickly in his throat.

Smelling the man's fear, the stag snorted again.

"Nuvola!" screamed Campbell.

There was no answer.

"Nuvola!" he wailed.

Nothing!

The stag calmly lowered his heavy head and charged. Malcolm, Earl of Argyll and Chief of the Campbells, scrambled frantically in an effort to flee, but as he spun away, he tripped over a fallen branch and stumbled to his knees. He struggled back to his feet just in time to look directly into the eyes of the dispassionate beast as its antlers pierced his chest. Unhurriedly, the huge animal lifted the man into the air and drove him five yards further, before impaling him on the trunk of a giant beech tree.

The stag carefully dislodged its horns, took two steps backward, and thrust again. This time, the crown spikes found their mark, puncturing Campbell's lungs. For a moment or two, the great red stag studied his adver-

sary, as if making sure the job was done. He then turned and, with regal dignity, walked away.

Figlio Nuvola moved silently from his position in the trees and approached the fallen chief. He crouched down beside the dying man. "A most unfortunate circumstance, sire," he said softly. "It seems as though God had his own plan for you, although I will admit that I am gratified to have been chosen to be of help. Before you leave us, though, there is something you should know, something to ponder on your long, dark journey. As I told you, my name is Figlio Nuvola. It means 'Son of the Clouds.'

He waited for a moment, watching the information sink in. "Do you understand, you evil bastard? Lady Eileen was my sister, my only sister. It's taken me months to reach you."

He bent closer to Campbell. "May your black soul rot in hell," whispered James MacLeod to ears that could no longer hear him.

The dark-skinned man moved unhurriedly to his horse, gathered the reins, and leapt lightly into the saddle. He nodded cryptically to the dead chieftain and disappeared into the roiling mist.

It was over an hour before William of Alsh rode into the little glen, accompanied by Donald of Falkirk. They remained seated, expressionless, quietly surveying the scene. After a minute, Alsh climbed down and crossed to Campbell's body.

"I had a fear, m'lord, that your weapon would fail you this day," he muttered, "but you were in a mind where I knew you wouldn't hear me. So, I couldn't warn you."

He reached down and carefully removed the silver brooch from Campbell's jerkin, hefted the weight of it, and inhaled deeply. He looked to the sky, mumbled some words, and pinned the chieftain's mark onto his own chest. He climbed into his saddle and turned his horse for his home and castle, the mighty Campbell Keep.

As his horse walked slowly from the vale, Alsh was thoughtful. Although he was convinced that Figlio Nuvola was gone and would not be seen again, he knew there was much to be done if the Campbells were to continue to control western Scotland.

High above the glen, the lone horseman surveyed the mist unfurling beneath him, until Loch Awe stretched golden to the distant hills. When Alsh disappeared from sight, the rider gently spurred his horse and continued his ascent of Ben Cruachan.

The scribe looked up to the shifting clouds for which his clan was named, and gave voice to the thoughts that had consumed him for nearly a year.

"Eileen, my dear sweet sister, I know my soul can never atone for leaving you to the whims of the Campbells, but I make you this pledge: whether heaven or hell be my lot, I will not rest until your story be told."